D0484197

An Honorable Profession

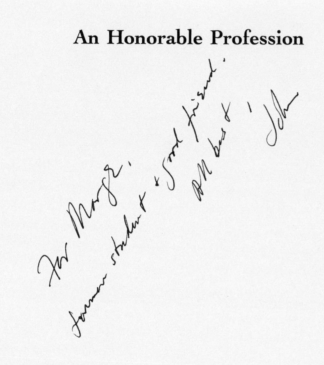

For Morgan,
former student & good friend.
All best & John

Other Books by John L'Heureux

Quick as Dandelions
Rubrics for a Revolution
Picnic in Babylon
One Eye and a Measuring Rod
No Place for Hiding
Tight White Collar
The Clang Birds
Family Affairs
Jessica Fayer
Desires
A Woman Run Mad
Comedians

John L'Heureux

AN HONORABLE
PROFESSION

VIKING

VIKING
Published by the Penguin Group
Viking Penguin, a division of Penguin Books USA Inc.,
375 Hudson Street, New York, New York 10014, U.S.A.
Penguin Books Ltd, 27 Wrights Lane, London W8 5TZ, England
Penguin Books Australia Ltd, Ringwood, Victoria, Australia
Penguin Books Canada Ltd, 2801 John Street,
Markham, Ontario, Canada L3R 1B4
Penguin Books (N.Z.) Ltd, 182-190 Wairau Road,
Auckland 10, New Zealand

Penguin Books Ltd, Registered Offices:
Harmondsworth, Middlesex, England

First published in 1991 by Viking Penguin,
a division of Penguin Books USA Inc.

1 3 5 7 9 10 8 6 4 2

Copyright © John L'Heureux, 1991
All rights reserved

LIBRARY OF CONGRESS CATALOGING IN PUBLICATION DATA
L'Heureux, John.
An honorable profession / John L'Heureux.
p. cm.
ISBN 0-670-82919-6
I. Title.
PS3562.H4H66   1991
813'.54—dc20   90-50196

Printed in the United States of America
Set in Meridien

Without limiting the rights under copyright reserved above, no
part of this publication may be reproduced, stored in or introduced into a retrieval system, or transmitted, in any form or by
any means (electronic, mechanical, photocopying, recording or
otherwise), without the prior written permission of both the
copyright owner and the above publisher of this book.

for my wife,
Joan Polston L'Heureux

Part I

1

FROM HIS CLASSROOM WINDOW Miles could see the football team scrimmaging down on the field. They were looking good today, or at least pretty good. Miles watched as the quarterback—it was Paul Ciampa—threw a long spiraling pass to a fat kid who missed the ball by yards and then fell all over himself trying to cover it. Tough luck, Fatso. Coach ran out on the field in his half-ass way, limping from the accident and from the booze. What a mess.

Miles shook his head and turned back to the classroom where the last two kids were serving their time in Detention: Polcari and some other little kid.

"Mr. Bannon? I think my time is up, sir? Can I go?"

"Sir?" Miles said, picking up the kid's tone. "*Sir?* You're a freshman, I take it." The kid blushed and nodded, stricken. "Sorry," Miles said. "It's all right to be a freshman, for a year anyway. And your name is . . . ?"

"Patrick?"

"No last name, Patrick?"

"Muldoon?"

"Muldoon? You're not sure?"

Muldoon grinned. He was a tiny little kid, and with his big nose and that wide grin, he looked like one of those mice in the cartoons.

"Well, Muldoon, I hope you'll mend your sorry ways." Miles ticked off Muldoon's name on the Detention list. That left only Richy Polcari, and then he could go and jog. Miles bounced up and down on the balls of his feet a couple times. Muldoon was taking forever just getting his books together.

"What the hell are you doing, Muldoon?" Miles said, and at once the books slithered from Muldoon's arms onto the desk and from there to the floor, where the boy began scrambling to pick them up. What a funny kid. What a funny-*looking* kid.

"How'd you manage to get Detention this early in the year, Muldoon? Are you a mess?"

"Yes, sir. The dog ate my homework"—Muldoon scooped up the last of the books—"and Mr. Douglas didn't believe me. But she did. Honest."

"Ah, the exacting Mr. Douglas, with his muse of fire."

"He didn't believe me."

"And what is the name of this excellent dog, Muldoon?"

"Doggina."

"Doggina?" Miles laughed out loud. "An Italian dog?"

"No, she's American, a beagle. My mother's Italian."

"Doggina. Well, you're marvelous, Muldoon. You are a many-splendored thing." Muldoon stood there, looking at him. "You can take off now," Miles said, "but if you ever get Detention again, Muldoon, I shall personally flog you to within an inch of your wretched life. Understand?"

Muldoon nodded and waved goodbye. Miles stared after him, fierce-looking, pleased.

Miles was proctoring Detention this week. Every teacher had a proctoring job—in the corridors, the toilets, the study hall, wherever kids could make trouble. Miles didn't really mind Detention, especially not at this time of year. It was still September, so the good kids hadn't yet begun to hate everything and the delinquents hadn't yet got caught. Besides, Detention gave him a chance to see kids on a nice easy basis. They were officially guilty of something, and that meant he could joke around with them or be tough with them or just ignore them while he corrected papers. Sometimes—when the kid was the last one there and one of Miles' favorites—he might even be personal and friendly. Actually this was a pretty good school, with a lot of nice kids and with very few tough discipline problems—if you didn't count Deirdre Forster, who was unlike anything Malburn High had ever seen. These were good kids and Miles felt lucky to have this job.

"Hey, Miles, how come he called you sir?"

Miles was still staring after the departed Muldoon, so clearly pleased that Richy Polcari took this as an invitation to chat.

"He called you sir, you know."

"Right."

"Do you want to be called sir? *I'll* call you sir, if you want."

"Richy . . ."

"It'd be kind of cool, if you want."

"You've got another half-hour, Richy. Study something, will you, please?"

Polcari was called Polecat by everybody, even by the teachers. Miles called him Richy, and so did a few of the women, but he gave Miles the creeps, frankly.

Miles turned to the window to check out the scrimmage and to put an end to Polcari. The classroom was on the second floor of the building, and the football field was at the bottom of the knoll, but even from this distance Miles could tell by the way the quarterback was running that it was Paul Ciampa. Paul was one of those kids who had everything. He was intelligent, he worked hard, he had 700s in the College Boards, he was captain of the football team. And he was polite, a really great kid. Quiet. Manly. Miles had passed him in the corridor just that morning and thought, If I'd had shoulders like that when I was in high school, I'd be Governor of Massachusetts today. He'd suppressed the thought immediately of course, because you didn't notice how kids were built . . . even if you couldn't help noticing.

Down on the field, things were at a standstill. Coach was walking back toward the school, lurching from side to side as he went. What a mess he was. The team stood in a sort of loose huddle, just staring after him. Then the student manager blew the whistle and they broke up into two teams for more scrimmage. The manager's name was Billy Mack and he was one of those spooky kids Miles could never figure out. Miles had taught him English last year, but Billy had never responded. He played dumb, refused to do assignments, worked just hard enough to pass. In class he would stare at Miles with a kind of contempt, as if Miles and the books he taught were a trap. Silent, humorless, basically hostile, he chose to attach himself to a football team he was not big enough to play on. He put up with their ribbing and looked after their equipment and accepted their condescension as the price of belonging. But at least out on the field he kept them all under control, something Coach was never able to do. Every team needed a kid like Billy Mack. And God knows Billy Mack needed that team.

Miles walked back to his desk and began looking over Monday's assignment. Edwin Arlington Robinson. That was always easy. And fun. The kids liked the fatalism and the gallows humor. They were teenagers, after all, and they knew they would never die.

But *he* would die, Miles knew. He had no trouble imagining his death. He'd seen his father rot away with cancer, and now his mother and the slow torture of her dying. Death was nothing. He didn't care about death. It was dying that terrified him—the infinite patience with which God squeezed the life out of you.

Miles shook the thought away and concentrated on tomorrow's work. He'd start class with a close reading of "Richard Cory" to show them how it's done. Or "Miniver Cheevy." Or both, if he had time. He'd talk about imagery. The voice of the author and the voice of the poem. Irony versus sarcasm; they never got *that* straight. Ask them to speculate on the reason for Richard Cory's suicide. Ask about appearances and what they conceal. Ask if we really know our friends or only think we know them. An easy preparation. He went on to "Miniver Cheevy," reading the poem slowly, moving his lips, ticking off the lines they'd want to talk about.

He took off his glasses and rubbed his eyes.

"What play are you going to do this year, Miles?"

Miles shrugged. In fact, because of the situation with his mother, he wasn't directing the play this year. He didn't want to talk about it, certainly not with Polcari.

"I'd like to try out this year. I don't know if I should, though. I don't know if I'd be good enough."

Miles put his glasses on and turned back to "Miniver Cheevy," determined to ignore him.

"How come you never became an actor, Miles? You could of, you know?"

"You could *have*. Not *of*."

"You could *have*. Why didn't you? I'd love to be an actor. I think you'd be great."

This is what pissed him off about Polcari: this smarm, this kiss-ass way of playing up to people.

"You still could be," Polcari said. "In the movies even. I mean, your looks . . ."

"What are you doing here anyhow, Polcari? How did you manage to get double hours of Detention?"

"I cut gym."

"That's all?"

"I cut it all week."

"And what else?"

"And most of last week."

"Jesus, Richy. Gym is part of the curriculum. You've got to do it, you know? You know that." Miles shook his head and went back to his book; he couldn't stand the creepy way Polcari was looking at him.

Polcari was a mess, and hopeless. He was tall and skinny, which was all right in itself, but he had all those loose feminine gestures, and that voice, and he went around practically begging to be friends. Any kid could see through that. They were scared and insecure; they protected themselves by calling everybody queer or fag, and mostly it didn't mean anything. But with Polcari, it did. The gossip was that he was a practicing homosexual and had been for years. Even his parents knew.

Polcari was quiet for a while and Miles pretended to concentrate on "Miniver Cheevy." He read it through again, but when he looked up at the end, Polcari was still staring at him in that puppy-dog way. It was a look of unabashed longing and Miles saw it for what it was. He felt a blush rising up his neck and then across his face and he felt simultaneously pleased and infuriated.

"Take off, Polecat," Miles said, slamming his book shut with a deliberate show of disgust. "You've suffered enough already today. And, Christ knows, so have I." He tried not to see the look on Polcari's face, but he saw it anyway.

Miles shoved his books into his backpack. He wanted to get out of here. He wanted fresh air. He wanted to run and keep on running until he was ready to collapse.

Miles pushed open the door to the faculty locker room and banged into Coach, who was on his way out. Coach stepped back against the wall, confused, and Miles closed the door behind them. The whole place reeked of booze. Coach looked at him woozily and then lifted his finger to his lips. "Shhh," he said. "I'm leaving a little early." His eyes weren't focusing.

"Jesus!" Miles looked around, but nobody else was there, and so he figured it was up to him. "Listen," he said. "Are you okay? Are you all right? Do you want me to drive you home?"

"I'm fine," Coach said. "I'm tip-top," and turned to go out. He tried to push the door open but it wouldn't give, so he pushed harder but it still wouldn't give, and then Miles said to him, "It opens in." Coach turned and looked at him and there were tears on his face. "Right," he said, and sat down hard on one of the benches.

Miles took charge. "Give me the keys to your office," he said, but Coach was bent in two, sobbing quietly, and Miles could see he'd get nowhere this way. He stepped out to the corridor and tried Coach's door. It was unlocked.

"Come on," Miles said, and he tapped Coach on the shoulder. "Come on. We'll go to your office and you can have a little snooze. A little lie-down. And then I'll drive you home. Okay? Come on." But Coach wasn't moving.

Miles tapped him on the shoulder again, and then shook him gently by the arm, and then shook him hard. Suddenly Coach came alive. "What?" he said. "What's the matter?"

"Take a snooze next door in your office and then I'll drive you home. Okay?" Coach just looked at him. "You can't drive like this. You don't want anybody to see you like this."

"Right," Coach said. "Right." He stood up and started toward the door. Immediately he stumbled against a bench and, trying to get his balance, he crashed into the wall. "Oh," he said, surprised, childlike.

Miles got one arm around Coach's waist and hoisted him up, but immediately Coach slumped against him and nearly knocked him over. He pushed Coach away and said, "Jesus. Come on. You've got to walk."

"Right," Coach said, and got himself together for a moment. His eyes focused and he draped his arm over Miles' shoulder and they started out of the room. By the time they reached the door, however, he lost interest and began to slump again.

But Miles had a good grip on him by now and there were only a few feet left to go, and he managed to half-carry and half-drag Coach to his office next door. He lowered the body onto the cot and then crouched beside it trying to get his breath. That Coach was one heavy mother. Miles left him there to sleep it off.

The faculty locker room and the boys' locker room were side by side, and so once he'd locked Coach's door, Miles took a peek into the boys' locker room to make sure he hadn't been seen—disposing of the body, so to speak. The place was empty. So the poor old bastard was saved once again. But, good God, he'd have to get his act together pretty soon.

Miles changed into a sweatshirt and running shorts and sat down on a bench to put on his sneaks—Nike Airs. The damned things had cost him seventy-three bucks. The boozey smell of the place was giving way to the smell of antiseptic filtering in from the boys' locker room on the other side of the wall. Miles hated that smell. He had always hated gym. He could just imagine what that poor schmuck Polcari went through twice a week. He shrugged and got out of the building, quick.

He did stretching exercises for a couple minutes and then took off down the main drive, away from the football field. The last thing he needed was some smart-ass linebacker whistling at him. And once you got kids in a group, they were capable of anything. When he jogged, Miles always stuck to the back roads as much as possible. He was too thin to be running around in gym shorts, he felt exposed, he just wasn't comfortable with bodies, his own or anybody else's. That's just how it was.

A car honked from behind and he edged over to the right, out of its way. "Miles!" they shouted, "Milo!" It was a bunch of kids in a junk convertible and they waved, shouting his name. He grinned and waved back and kept on jogging. Now that was nice. It was *really* nice. Kids were terrific sometimes. They liked him, the smart ones did, and even the others realized he liked them and wanted to help. He got on well with kids. When you thought about it, he was probably the most popular teacher in the school. Who'd believe it, he said to himself.

He had taught at Malburn High for eleven years and everybody called him Miles or Milo, faculty and students alike. He was popular, he was smart, he was funny. He said outrageous things that all the kids reported later at the dinner table. Parents never complained. Miles was a character, all right, but a wonderful influence on their kids. Even the English faculty, who disagreed about everything, agreed on Miles: he was a little bit eccentric, maybe, and always demanding, but God knows he did his job well. And certainly he loved the place. His wit had turned to irony lately, it was true, but that was because he had home troubles you didn't even want to think about: a father who had died a couple years back, a mother who'd been dying slowly ever since, and a girlfriend he couldn't marry until . . . well, until his mother finally did it. Died. Milo had it tough. Endicott, the principal, was less quick to find excuses for Miles, with that sharp tongue of his and all that leftish talk, but he was impressed by results and Miles certainly produced them: his students worked hard, they scored high on the College Boards, there were no complaints from parents. All this was very good. Still, in Endicott's opinion, Miles bore watching. Endicott had been a captain in the Army before he retired and became an educator.

Miles had been jogging for twenty minutes and so far he had not succeeded in taking off. On his best jogs there was always a moment when his conscious mind gave way to his body's fatigue, and after that he was aware only of the pounding of his heels against the pavement and the shock of each footfall as it carried to his knees and his hips and shoulders; his teeth felt loose in his head and eventually he became immune to the pain, or one with it, and his mind went blank—he just sort of took off into space, above it all— and he could go on and on like this forever. But today he just couldn't get there.

His mind kept going back to that feeling he'd had all week, that everything was about to break apart. He'd experienced this feeling before, when his father died. And before his mother's collapse. And when he was first getting involved with Margaret. He felt that any minute his whole life might just break in pieces, crumble into dirt, and then he would look up and see they were all staring at him because he was exposed at last for what he was. But what was that? He didn't want to know.

He ran faster. From Lowell he turned into Mitchell Park, with its neat jogging trails of packed sand, and here—suddenly, gratefully—he took off. His mind soared. He rose above himself. He was disappearing into warm darkness. He gazed at the path before him and he listened to the sound of his breathing, but he felt nothing and he wanted nothing and there was no fear anywhere in him. He pushed himself hard, mesmerized. He ceased to exist.

He had been running this way for some time, in a kind of trance, his mind blank, when suddenly he heard himself say, "Richy Polcari." And with the name came the image: those wet brown eyes, the smarmy, adoring look that turned to something else—a look of despair—as Miles called him Polecat.

Polcari filled him with revulsion. He did not want to be loved by somebody like this. And yet he saw himself embrace Polcari, pull that skinny, wretched body to his own, and clutch him tightly, saying, "It's all right. It's gonna be all right."

At once Miles came down hard. He stumbled and then stopped. He spat, trying to get that acid taste out of his mouth. He doubled over, gasping, and then he retched, but nothing came up. He retched again. He felt poisoned, dirty, and there was no way to get this stuff out of him.

He crouched low, one knee on the ground, and breathed deeply. Eventually the image of Polcari left him. He got up and walked for a while, and then he started jogging again, slowly. After a mile or so, he began to hum, deliberately, and then to sing "My Girl," falsetto, like The Temptations, and by the time he reached school, he'd begun to feel pretty good. It was just a crazy phase, a momentary fit, and it was gone now.

He'd have a shower, and then dinner with Margaret, and they'd make wild crazy love, and everything would be terrific again. Terrific, you betcha.

As Miles entered the school basement, Paul Ciampa was coming out. "Hey, Milo," he said, and gave him a high five.

"Looking good out there," Miles said.

"Well, we're still pretty slow."

They stood for a moment looking at each other, while Miles held the door open, and then he said, "Well, take it slow," and they sort of nodded at each other and turned away. But Miles recognized that moment: they could have talked, they wanted to talk, if only they'd had something to talk about.

"Terrific," he said, happy all over again, and as he walked down the corridor to the faculty locker room, he burst into song à la Merman, "Gotta sing, gotta dance, gotta da da DA da da da."

A bunch of kids came out of the locker room, slinging their book bags around, shoving one another. "Do it, Milo baby, do it!" somebody said.

Miles grinned at them, just one of the guys.

He knocked at the door to Coach's office, but there was no response. A couple more kids came out of the locker room. "He's gone, Milo," a kid said, cocking his thumb at Coach's door. "He's lonnnng gone." They laughed and kept going. Miles knocked harder and leaned close, but he could hear no sound at all. He'd try again after he showered and dressed.

There was a lot of laughter coming from the boys' locker room, the usual stuff. A short harsh shout and then the crashing sound of somebody slamming into a locker. "C'mon, you guys," somebody said—Billy Mack, no doubt—and then twice as much laughter. Billy was a lot more successful at controlling them out on the field; in the locker room he was always at their mercy.

Miles paused a moment, listening, and then he went into the faculty locker room and closed the door behind him. He took a peek into the shower section to make sure he was alone. He did some leg and back stretches to cool down and then said to hell with it and just sat on a bench for a few minutes with his head in his hands. His heart was racing—from the run and from the encounter with Paul Ciampa and from that despairing look on the face of Polcari. He didn't know what he ought to feel, but anyhow he felt pretty good.

After a while he became aware of something different around him. He listened and realized that next door in the locker room there was only silence. Not the silence of nobody there, but the hushed silence of movements that were deliberately quiet, of a raised voice and then a hush, the swishing noise of whispers. Drugs, he figured; they're smoking pot. He *should* go in there and stop it, but—God—walking in with all those guys, breaking up their fun, turning them in to the office? And they'd all probably be standing around bare-assed. No. He would deliberately not hear them. Some teachers actually used the student showers—Jeff Douglas, and Foley, and the vice-principal—but Miles would rather be tarred and feathered, thank you, than undress in front of kids. He began to get undressed now, singing. He'd let them know he was there, at least. Maybe they'd clear out and go smoke it somewhere else.

He was about to step into the shower when he heard the giggling; loud, silly, a bunch of guys gone high, childlike, harmless. "What the hell," he said. He turned the shower on full blast and stepped into the freezing water, then after a single penitential minute he turned the dial to Warm and began to soap up. He would spend ten minutes now thinking of Margaret and the great evening they were going to have.

Next door in the boys' shower room they had killed the pint of Jim Beam that Cosmo had brought to celebrate Hacker's birthday, and they'd each done a line of coke, and now they had finally convinced Billy Mack to do a line too. This was too funny. They pushed together in a group and watched, giggling.

They were the Roid Boys, the crowd that took steroids and had the great bods. Billy was just a set-up, just for fun.

Billy put the straw to his nose the way the others had, and snorted the white powder with such determination that he was still inhaling when there was nothing left on the mirror. Then he ran his finger across the glass, looked around at the others, and touched his finger to his tongue.

"Aw-*right!*" they said and clapped him on the back.

Everybody laughed, and Billy let out a high giggle, and they laughed some more.

"We're all ripped," Billy said.

"Balls, man," somebody said, "Old Billy's got balls," and so Hacker made a grab at Billy's crotch.

Billy pulled away from him and said, "Geez, Hacker."

But Hacker, who towered over him, said very seriously to the others, "I think we gotta take a look at Billy's balls. I think we gotta do a research project and get those pants off him and check out his katonks."

Within seconds, Hacker had Billy's arms pinned behind his back and they had his pants down at his ankles. "Get 'em *off*," Hacker said, and as Billy kicked and squirmed, Hacker said, "Get the shoes off. The tee-shirt too." It was so funny. They could barely hold on to him they were laughing so much.

"That's a mean dick for a little guy like you, Billy," Hacker said into his ear. "Jack it around, Cosmo, and see if it gets any bigger."

"You dirty guys," Billy said, "you motherfuckers."

"I'm not touching that thing," Cosmo said. "He's probably got AIDS or something. Let Tuna do it."

So Tuna flicked it with one finger.

"Come on, you guys. Bunch of fags."

"He's calling us fags but lookit this dick," and Tuna flicked it again, as it began to grow larger.

"Oooooh," somebody said. "Billy *likes* us."

And Tuna flicked it again as it became more erect.

There were five of them and they were laughing and pushing each other around and it was funny as hell. The harder Billy became, the more they laughed; it was so funny, this little skinny guy with this great big dick sticking up at them and they were taking turns flicking it with their finger and it was getting redder and hotter and they couldn't stop laughing and even Billy tried to laugh once because all week they'd been promising him they were gonna play Violation on Friday and he figured this was it. But then Hacker said, breaking through the laughter, "As master of ceremonies, *ladies* and gentlemen . . ." and they all collapsed at that and Billy almost got loose for a minute, but then they grabbed him again, ". . . as master of ceremonies, I think it's time we played—you guessed it—Vi-o-LA-tion."

They all let go of Billy then, and he crouched on the floor with his knees together, shielding himself. They just stood around him, uncertain themselves what to do next. There was a moment of tense silence and then Billy jumped up and tried to make a break for it. He wriggled between Hacker and Cosmo and nearly made it to the door when Tuna got him by the arm and yanked him back. They stood around him in a circle. They were laughing; it was a game again. Hacker got the broom from the empty locker where it had been standing all week, just waiting, and as Billy sunk to a crouch, Hacker prodded him in the ass with it. They looked from one to another. Billy looked up and said, "What?" Cosmo shook his head and said, "Shit, I don't know," and started to turn away. But then Hacker got the broom handle down between Billy's legs and was trying to push it in. Billy leaped up suddenly and charged at them, trying to break out of the circle, and then all the guys together, without even thinking, grabbed him and turned him over face down and tried to spread his legs so that Hacker could get it in. "Bend his knees. He's gotta bend his fucking knees," Hacker said. Billy was fighting with all his strength, and more. He was frenzied. He was half crazy. He wriggled and kicked and bit Cosmo's hand as they wrestled him to the cement floor and got him to kneel with his ass in the air so they could get it in.

"I can't get it *in*," Hacker was saying with a kind of panic in his voice, "you fucking guys, *hold* him. Hold him for Christ's sake. He doesn't have any fucking asshole. I gotta get this in." He pushed and the flesh gave way but still the handle wasn't going in.

Everybody was angry now. They wanted it over with. They were sick of holding this guy down. "Do it, for Chrissake," Tuna said. It wasn't funny anymore.

"I'm trying," Hacker said. "I'm trying. Hold him, will you?" And he gave a terrific jab with the handle and Billy let out a cry—not a shout and not a scream but something worse—and at that moment Hacker looked down and saw on the floor between Billy's legs some stuff that looked like blood or shit, and he thought he'd make just one more try to fuck him in the ass with the broom handle, because after all that's what they had planned to do, and it was supposed to be a joke, but suddenly all the fun was going out of it and he really would rather have just called it off.

Miles stepped out of the shower and heard the racket next door. There were shouts, and a struggle of some kind was going on, he was sure of that, and it didn't sound like horseplay. It went on and on. Miles picked up his towel and held it in front of him, listening. After a while there was silence for a minute and then suddenly an awful sound—a cry like a wounded animal's, he thought—and after that, silence again. He was listening, his head cocked, and there was no sound.

He was toweling off, thinking what a strange thing it is to recognize a sound like the shriek of a wounded animal when you've never heard the shriek of a wounded animal, and all of a sudden somebody ran by the door and took off down the corridor. And then somebody else ran by. He wrapped the towel around his waist and opened the door to the corridor. At that moment he saw Cosmo Damiani come out of the boys' locker room, running. Miles closed the door and waited. He heard two more of them go by. Then there was silence again.

He opened the door and, barefoot, dripping, he edged over to the boys' locker room and looked in. Nothing. It smelled of sweat and steam and antiseptic. He went all the way inside and looked into the L-shaped area and there on the floor was a body, naked, lying face down. He approached it slowly, as if it might suddenly attack him. As he got close he saw that one leg was pulled up toward the boy's chest, and he could see the torn scrotum and the circle of black blood slowly spreading on the concrete floor. He moved quickly to the body and bent over it and saw that it was Billy Mack. He put his hand on the boy's shoulder and whispered, "Billy. Billy?"

The boy lifted his head and turned upon him a look of such

hatred that for a second Miles stopped breathing. A pain ran through his chest and he thought he was having a heart attack, but then he said, "I'll get help, Billy. Just lie there and don't move." And at once he was out of the locker room and pounding at Coach's door.

Miles was still pounding at it, shouting "Coach, Coach," when the principal came down the corridor, with Cosmo beside him looking terrified.

The principal barely gave Miles a glance. He just said, "Get dressed and go to my office and stay there, Mr. Bannon. Do you hear me? Go to my office. Wait for me there." And then he followed Cosmo into the locker room as Miles stood in the corridor feeling very sick.

2

MARGARET CLEARY WORKED through lunch hour on Fridays so that she could leave the office at four o'clock. She was an assistant in Babcock & Collins, Accountants, and though she worked overtime whenever she was asked, on Fridays she was out of there at four o'clock, no matter what. Nobody minded, because she always got her work done, and other people's too. She was efficient and reliable. She was always pleasant. She was discreet. Responsible. Everybody had a good word for her. She made the office run as smoothly as it did, and if she wanted to leave early on Friday afternoons, it was nobody's business.

Still, they wondered. Her Friday escapades had been going on for an awfully long time, for more than a year. They hoped she was having a love affair. She deserved a little romance in her life—everybody knew about her rotten marriage—and she was attractive when she fixed herself up. But if she was discreet about company business, she was absolutely secretive about her private life, so nobody asked her why she left early on Friday afternoons.

Margaret left early to get ready for Miles. Friday was the one night he had free from his mother, so they always spent it together. She might cook or they might go out for dinner, and recently they'd

been making love—tentatively, not always successfully—but whatever they did, she found it nice just to be with this gentle, good,
loving man for an evening.

Besides, they went back a long way. They had grown up in the
same neighborhood and had gone to the same schools, though they
never really knew one another until a year and a half ago when
Miles moved back home to take care of his mother.

They had met in the supermarket. Miles seemed desperate to
talk, and he told her about his father's death and his mother's
collapse, her mind imprisoned in a body that was turning to stone.
She had ALS, he said, Lou Gehrig's disease. And he rushed on,
almost incoherent: her throat—she could barely talk—fed through
a tube—crippled—the muscles collapsing one by one. And her
mind, still sharp as a razor, trapped. She was trapped, alive, in a
dead body, he said. He did not have to add that he was trapped as
well.

He had said too much. Margaret could see he was embarrassed
at telling her all this and ashamed of the way he felt, so she tried
to reassure him. She understood, she said. She had had feelings
like that, and worse, much worse. She was divorced now. She knew
how he felt.

They were still standing at the vegetable counter in Star Market.
They were at an impasse. There was nothing more to say, but they
were too embarrassed to part without saying something, so Miles
said, "Come back with me and say hello; she'd like that," and
Margaret went.

The old woman was feisty, and funny in her way, and they had
liked each other from the start. Very quickly and without a word,
they recognized how each of them stood with Miles. Margaret was
a permanent part of their lives now, with Friday reserved for her
and Miles only.

This Friday, as always, she was ready when Miles came. She had
her dark hair combed back in a French twist and she wore her blue
knit suit that could be dressed up or down with jewelry, depending

on where they decided to go for dinner. She had Miles' good sports jacket and a clean shirt ready in her closet and, in case he didn't feel like going out, she had thawed two steaks that she could pop under the broiler. She was relaxed, perfumed, ready for anything.

She opened the door to him as he came up the walk.

"Miles," she said. "Come in, sweet thing."

He took her in his arms and held her. She could feel him trembling.

"Come in," she said. "Come on in." And then, "Miles, what's wrong? Is it your mother?"

"No, no," he said. "No. Everything's fine. It's just something that happened at school. It's nothing. I'll tell you later. How are *you*?" he said. Despite his wide smile, his boyish face looked haggard.

"What is it?" she said.

"I need a drink first," he said.

So she knew it couldn't be too serious, whatever it was.

He followed her to the kitchen and sat at the table while she made his drink. He took off his glasses and put his hands over his face, rubbing. "Ugliness, misery, and piss," he said. She placed a large scotch on the table before him.

"I'll just make this and then you can tell me," she said. She poured a shot of rye into a shaker, and then water, and then the little packet of whiskey sour mix. She shook it and dumped half of it into her glass. "There," she said. "Come on."

In the living room they sat on the couch. He took a long drink of his scotch and then he slouched way down and just stared up at the ceiling. She leaned against him, smoothing his hair back from his forehead.

"Don't," he said.

She sat beside him, silent, waiting until he was ready to talk. After a while he turned and looked at her. She wished for his sake she were not so plain.

"You know," Miles said, "you are the only altogether nice thing in my life."

"I know that," she said. "I work at it."

He kissed her lightly on the lips.

"Do you want to tell me what happened?"

"Not now," he said, "not yet. Let's just sit here for a while and then I'll have another drink and tell you about it." He took her hand and held it tight, and began at once to tell her everything: the crazy feeling he'd had all week as if he was losing it, as if his whole world was about to break apart, and then the Detention with Polcari and calling him Polecat and the look on his face, and then poor old drunken Coach, what a mess he was, and then jogging and getting sick—though he didn't tell her why—and finally, when he had built up to it enough, when he could face it, he told her what he had seen in the boys' locker room.

"You think they actually tried to rape him?"

"Or something."

"With a broom handle? That's so sick," she said. "That's crazy." A tremor started in the back of her neck and she could feel a nerve pulsing in her forehead. She reached for her drink.

"I know," he said. "You can't believe a thing like that could happen." He closed his eyes for a moment. "It had to be a game that went bad; that has to be it. They were drinking, I suppose, just horsing around, and they were probably playing castration or something, some sick game, and it got out of hand. It happens. Like those kids in New Jersey or Delaware who raped that retarded girl with a miniature baseball bat; a whole bunch of them watched and nobody even tried to stop it. Not one of them. It's as if their craziness feeds off each other."

Margaret closed her eyes, tight.

"Kids, boy, I don't know. Kids are a very strange breed, especially in a group, and athletes are the strangest of all. They knock the shit out of each other out there on the field, it's kill or be killed, but at the same time they do all this fanny patting and macho hugging and bare-ass roughhousing, and I've always been convinced there's something a little fishy about it. A little homoerotic play they only half understand, if they understand it at all. And it can get really ugly, like today. What do you think?" he said.

She hadn't been listening. "People do strange things," she said.

"Poor Billy Mack," he said.

Margaret reached for her glass. It was empty.

"I was useless, completely useless. I was paralyzed. I couldn't think what to do, or how to help. That look he gave me was pure hatred. I just kept banging on Coach's door, like a fool."

"You were coping. We all cope in different ways."

They sat in silence for a moment.

"I didn't go to the office. He told me to go to the office and wait for him, but I got dressed and got out of there."

"Yes," she said. "Who?"

"The principal. Endicott. The ambulance was just pulling in when I left." Miles took a sip from his scotch, looked at it, then took another. "The dumb shit. I know what he wanted, of course. He wanted to make sure I didn't breathe a word of this to anybody. When it comes out in the papers, he'll make sure it appears in some sanitized form. It was an accident, he'll say. It was nobody's fault. Billy Mack just slipped in the shower room and cut his balls off. It could happen to anybody."

"Miles," she said.

"Of course, then he'll have to establish that it was Billy's own fault that he slipped." He assumed a drill instructor's bark: " 'This school was in no way responsible. Malburn High has always made the safety of its students a primary goal of education. We put safety first at Malburn and we put education last.' "

Margaret laughed and kissed him on the cheek. "Sweet Miles," she said. "Let me get you another." Her own glass had been empty for some time.

They had another drink and then Miles changed his clothes for dinner, but just as they were leaving, the phone began to ring. "Maybe it's Tillie?" Margaret said, and moved to pick it up, but Miles said, "No, don't answer. It's that fool, Endicott." She answered anyway. She told Endicott that no, Miles was not here, and yes, he was expected for dinner, and yes, she would tell him to call the office, and no, it was no trouble, and goodbye, thank you, goodbye.

"Maybe you should give just a quick call home to make sure Eleanor is okay?" Margaret said.

"Not to worry," Miles said. "The dread Tillie has it all under control."

At Miles' house, things were not going well. Eleanor Bannon, Miles' mother, sat in her chair watching one of the three daily re-runs of "Benson," annoyed because she hadn't had her five o'clock feeding. She didn't care about the feeding—to tell the truth she didn't want it, now or ever—but it made her wild to think that Miles paid Tillie all that money and she didn't do a thing except sit out there in the kitchen looking at her wrestling magazines. *Wrestling* magazines. That told you everything about her you needed to know, Eleanor felt. In the old days she wouldn't have had a minute for a woman like Tillie. She'd have been nice to her if they were in the same church, of course, or in the PTA, or something like that, but she would never have invited her to her home even for a visit, and now here she was living in it and eating her food and, on Fridays, sleeping under her roof. It made her wild, just *wild*, to think about it. She tried to concentrate on her program, but her mind kept wandering off to Tillie, fat and comfy with her wrestling magazines and never sick a day in her life.

It occurred to Eleanor that any minute now she would have to go to the toilet. Well, she would *not* ask Tillie's help. Period. "Benson" ended and "Wheel of Fortune" came on, with the new man who replaced that dwarfy little one, Pat Something, and with Vanna, goofy as ever. The contestants didn't look very sharp tonight. Eleanor felt that twinge in her bladder and realized there was no more postponing it. She would have to get to the toilet, but she was damned if she would ring her little silver bell for the wrestling queen. She'd manage by herself. If only she could shift a little farther forward on the chair, she could get it rocking—it was a platform rocker—and sort of launch herself from it, and land with both hands on the aluminum walker. This was how she'd been doing it for some time now, and it almost always worked. She scrunched down and then leaned forward hard and indeed the chair began to rock very nicely. It would only be a minute now.

In the kitchen Tillie was studying *Wrestling World,* her favorite magazine. She liked the looks of a good beefy wrestler, all that flesh covering all that strength. She read these magazines because they were interesting—her Charlie, God rest his soul, had been a wrestler—but mostly she read them to keep herself from killing the old lady. This skinny little Miles had hired her to look after his mother, Lady Eleanor, which meant feeding her that nasty liquid dinner. You had to funnel it into a special plastic bag and then hang the bag from the top of a door so the fluid would run down a tube that hooked up to the tube sticking out of her stomach. You had to be careful to regulate the flow so that it took about forty minutes to get into her . . . and then an hour later you had to take her to the bathroom to let out the foul stuff that you had just put in. It was disgusting and nobody should be expected to do that for another person. She had to, of course, because Charlie had left her with nothing. On top of this, Miles expected her to keep the old lady company. But Eleanor didn't want company. What she wanted was a slave who would appear whenever she clapped her hands for you—though she couldn't even clap, she was in such bad shape with the ALS—and then disappear when she didn't need you anymore. What she wanted was to be the Lady of the Manor, and not to be old and sick and have a stranger in her house looking after her. Well, too bad about her. She *was* sick and she *was* old and Tillie was in her house, like it or not. And Tillie was not going to be anybody's slave. To hell with Eleanor. And to hell with her five o'clock feeding. She was going to read *Wrestling World* and to hell with everybody.

In the living room Eleanor was rocking back and forth, back and forth, trying to gauge the right moment for takeoff. The problem was that she had skootched a bit lower than she should have; now, though she could propel herself nicely out of the chair, she was at the wrong angle to land squarely on her feet within grabbing distance of the walker. She tried to shift her weight higher in the chair, but the damned thing just kept on rocking and she could see there was no going back now. "Jesus, Mary, and Joseph," she said—a sort of prayer—and leaning as far forward as she could, she just took off. She hit the walker squarely but with too much force, and she took it with her as she crashed to the floor. The noise was tremendous.

She lay there dazzled for a moment and then she tried to get up. Her little legs flailed a bit and she could see her pink booties moving back and forth at some distance, but she couldn't get them under her and she couldn't push herself up with her hands. She was like that bug in the Kafka story Miles always talked about. It was really quite funny when you thought about it. She began to laugh soundlessly. She wasn't hurt, or at least she didn't think so. She just couldn't move. She began to shake with laughter.

Then Tillie moved into her line of vision and Eleanor could see she was white with rage.

"*Now* what have you done?" Tillie said, and stood above her looking down.

"I'm sorry," Eleanor whispered in what was left of her voice, but it was too late because Tillie was already at the phone, calling for Miles. Eleanor continued to laugh.

They had dinner at L'Auberge, with some good wine and a little Armagnac afterwards. When they got back to Margaret's place, the phone was ringing. Margaret made a move to answer it, but Miles was feeling very much in charge by now and he got there first, answering at once in an overripe British accent: "Hallo? Hallo? Are you there?" He paused for two seconds and then said, incredulous,

"Miles? Sorry? No, there's no Miles here. There's never been a Miles here, you know. You've rung up the wrong number, cocky. Best to check a directory, I should think. Well, then, there you are." And he hung up.

Margaret was standing beside him, her hand at her mouth. "He'll know," she said. "Won't he know it was you?"

"Of course," Miles said, completely satisfied. "He'll be certain it's me, but he can't *prove* a thing. And there'll always be a tiny bit of doubt in his tiniest of minds. Or at least there should be."

Before she could answer him, the phone rang again.

"It's him," Miles said, whispering. "He thinks he really did get a wrong number."

"What should we do?" she said.

"Shhh," Miles said. He stood with his hand on the receiver until it stopped ringing; then he removed it and turned it on its side.

"Sweet Margaret," he said, kissing her hair, and then he led her into the bedroom.

They had been in bed for ten minutes now, with the lights off at Miles' request, and still nothing was working.

"Don't rush it," Margaret said. "We've got all night."

"I want to *do* it," Miles said, "but I just can't get this goddam thing to work." There was a terrible urgency in his voice.

"We don't have to *do* anything," she said. "We can just lie here and hold one another."

"No, wait a minute. I've got it, I've got it, I'm getting nice and hard."

"Okay, okay," she said, picking up his urgency.

"Here, now, I'm getting it."

"Push it," she said, "just push."

"You can't just push spaghetti."

They laughed, together, because it was so absurd. Then Miles rolled to the side, done laughing, but Margaret laughed again. "Spaghetti," she said. "You can't push spaghetti. What a funny man you are, Miles." She sighed. "That's funny."

"But it's exactly the problem, isn't it. I'm just spaghetti. I'm limp."

"Oh, come on," she said. "It doesn't mean anything. It's just because we've had so much to drink."

"Yeah, sure, but *you* don't have to perform."

"Neither do you, Miles. Not with me."

He was silent for a while and then he said, in a tone that had changed completely, cold now, and hard. "I begin to think this whole thing has been a mistake. A bright, glamorous, glittering mistake."

He was lying on his back, his hand over his eyes, but he could feel her whole body stiffen beside him.

"What?" she said. "What's been a mistake?"

"Us. You and me. As lovers."

She sat up in bed and looked at him. She got out of bed and threw on her dressing gown. It was white silk, lustrous in the dark, and much too expensive. She had bought it for these Friday nights with Miles.

"We can end it if you want, Miles. Right now. All right? Only don't be mad at me. Please."

Immediately Miles was out of bed too. "It's all right," he said. "It's not your fault."

"Oh Miles."

"It's all *right*. It's me. I'm full of booze and I just can't perform. I'm sorry." He took her hand in both of his.

"But we can end it if you want, Miles. I won't call you. I won't bother you at all. I . . . ."

He waited, but she had nothing more to say. "Let's go into the living room and talk about it," he said. "I'm going to have a drink, okay? I might as well. It can't do any more harm. Right? Do you want one too?"

"Yes," she said. "Let's. And we can talk."

They talked, and after a while Miles began to see his anger was not at her but at himself, disappointment and a special kind of doubt. He wanted to tell her. He leaned forward and traced with one finger the line of her breast. "I'm just not much of a man," he said, confessing. "I just can't make love like other men. That's it. That's what it comes down to."

"That's not true," she said. "You make love wonderfully. It's natural and gentle with you."

"Sure, when I *can*."

He caressed her slowly from her breast to her waist. He let his eyes follow his hands. He kept on this way for some time, until he felt his pulse racing and he had to catch his breath. It was very quiet in the room.

"This is how it used to be," she said. "Why can't you just let it be like this, without worrying about a performance. We don't ever have to go to bed again. We can just sit here forever in the living room, touching, and that's a kind of lovemaking. It's enough for me. Isn't it?"

He lay back against the couch and looked at her. "You're wonderful to me," he said. He continued to caress her breasts, quietly, carefully, even after he was hard and knew he could do it successfully this time. They half-sat, half-lay on the couch, their hands moving across each other's body until, sodden with desire, they stood and moved slowly into the bedroom.

3

MILES PARKED IN FRONT of the house so that Tillie would be able to pull out of the driveway unhindered. Anything to make life easier for Tillie, since God knows she was a handful. Tillie had to be coddled, especially when she was throwing a snit. Home Help was very hard to come by.

Miles got out of his battered old Pinto and was walking up the driveway to the back door—he always entered the house through the kitchen—when suddenly Tillie stood before him, quivering in her considerable bulk, her face the color of raw meat. She had her magazines rolled up under her arm. And she carried a shopping bag containing her nightgown, her robe, her slippers, and her "personals," as she called them.

"I quit," she said. "Mail the wages by *check*, please."

"What's happened?" Miles said. "What's the matter?"

"Not responsible for that woman. I am a health care, not a nanny. I quit." She fitted herself into the driver's seat of her little Volkswagen. "Do not send cash in the mail," she said. "Send a check." She backed out of the driveway with the no-nonsense dispatch she had brought to the care of his mother.

Miles stood in the driveway, staring after her.

"Ugliness, misery, and piss," he said. He was furious at Tillie, not only because she'd quit but especially because she'd ruined the best night of his life.

He and Margaret had just made love and they were lying in bed, his arms loosely about her, her head tucked into the hollow between his neck and shoulder. They fitted together perfectly, they were the perfect couple, he was at last perfectly a man. He didn't want to disturb this mood; he wanted it to go on forever, but he had drunk all that booze and now he had to pee. He leaned over her and whispered, "I'll be right back," and eased himself gently out of bed. Passing through the living room, he paused for a second by the telephone, and then put the receiver back on the cradle. Instantly the phone rang. It was Tillie.

"I've been calling for hours," she said. And in a low voice, she added, "I've had enough."

Unlike the others, Tillie had never threatened to leave. She had contented herself with shooting an evil glance at Eleanor or from time to time sticking out her chin at Miles. Her contempt for both of them was palpable. She didn't have to threaten. They knew that unless they were careful, she'd leave. Period. And they'd not been careful enough. So when she said, "I've had enough," she meant it. Tillie didn't fuck around, so to speak. She had always demanded her money in good old tax-free cash—eight hundred a month, in twenties—and if she was willing to take a check, it was a sure sign she was all done. Furthermore—the killer detail—she had taken her wrestling magazines and her famous "personals." That was it. Over and out. Sayonara, Tillie.

He'd have to hire somebody new, before Monday, or miss a day of school while he took care of his mother. Imagine breaking that news to Endicott.

And what, he wondered, would he find inside the house?

In the house the only sounds came from the living room, where Johnny Carson was forcing laughs out of Ed McMahon. Had Tillie taken off without even getting his mother into bed? He tiptoed into the room and sure enough, there was Eleanor, propped up in her rocker, smiling at him.

She was wrapped in her pink wooly blanket, bright-eyed and expectant, glad to see him home at last. But where was he going to find another Home Help? And with only two days' notice? Had she no idea what she was doing to him? His fury at Tillie changed into fury at his mother.

He lowered the volume on the television, and when he turned to face her he could see the eagerness drain from her eyes. Good. But then at once he went to her and, moving her aluminum walker out of the way, he knelt beside her and kissed her on the cheek.

"Are you all right, Mother?"

She nodded, wary. She knew how angry he was.

"Well, what happened with Tillie?"

She shook her head and whispered, "Nothing," but no sound came out. She gestured toward her little pad, and when Miles gave it to her, she wrote: "Nothing."

"Nothing? Did you fight with her?"

She laughed, a breathy sound, rasping. "How could I?" she wrote.

"Well, she quit," he said.

She only smiled.

"But why, Mother? Why would she quit?"

She bent over her pad, writing, and when she was done she laughed silently and looked up to see if he was laughing too. She had written: "Bitch."

He clenched his teeth hard so she would see how annoyed he was, and then he said, "I'm going to take a look upstairs."

He went upstairs whenever he felt about ready to kill her.

Upstairs were the two small bedrooms that had been his and Erin's until they'd left home—Erin when she married Joe Flaherty and began to have all those kids; Miles, when he went to college and grad school and then got his own apartment in Cambridge. He'd come back home a year and a half ago, just after his father's death, when it became clear that Eleanor needed somebody to take care of her. His sister Erin had pointed that out. "I've got my family in California," she said. "I've got my life out there. Anyway, you're the son."

He had moved into his old room, and almost at once Eleanor went to pieces. It was as if she'd been holding herself together by an act of the will, and now that she could collapse, she did. Her speech went first, and then her ability to swallow food, though she pretended to Miles she nibbled during the day and that's why she was never hungry at dinner. She had trouble walking. She dropped things all the time. She was very weak. Dr. Archer had long since diagnosed the problem as ALS and had promised a fairly painless death, though a slow one. This sudden deterioration took the doctor by surprise. She gave Eleanor a thorough examination. She called in a back-up physician. They consulted. Eleanor was hospitalized for severe malnutrition, a gastrostomy was performed, and she was fed by tube after that.

This was over a year ago, and since that time Miles had been his mother's nurse and companion except when he was teaching school or when he had his Friday night off.

Eleanor's own schedule was unvaried. Once a week she had the therapist, and every morning at nine the nurse's aide came to bathe her, dress her, and get her ready for the day. And then, at ten, the Home Help of the moment turned up; for several months there had been Edna Gutkin, mad as a hatter, and then Angie Slocum who wanted to write poetry, Bertha Jones who didn't want to do anything, Susu Waters and Pilar Sanchez who lasted only three days each, and now the dread Tillie, though even she was a thing of the past. These Home Helps had cost him first his salary, then his small savings, and finally he had taken a second mortgage on the house— the money from the large first mortgage had gone to Erin to help with the family—and now he was wondering if he could get a loan through the Credit Union at school. He *had* to get a new car. The orange Pinto was rusted out underneath and was falling apart bit by bit. It would never last the winter.

Miles stood at the window of his old room looking out at the

small backyard. The picnic table his father had built so many years
ago was warped and pitted from the winter snow and from all that
rain in spring. The fireplace looked bad, too. His father had built it
with brick but without mortar, just in case they ever wanted to
take it apart and move it somewhere else. It had stood there for
more than twenty years, half-covered now by the clump of birches
broken in the ice storms last March. A ruined garden, he thought
to himself. Like "Araby." All they needed was a bicycle pump coiled
beneath a tree. "I saw myself as a creature driven and derided by
vanity," he said aloud, and wondered how often James Joyce had
fed his mother through a tube in her stomach or helped her to the
toilet in the middle of the night or tried to deal with Home Helps
whose only interest was in wrestling magazines.

"Poor moi," he said aloud, impatient with himself, and then he
went down to his mother, taking two stairs at a time.

"Okay, you sweet old thing in your pink blanky," he said, "we're
free at last of the dread Tillie." He did Martin Luther King, Jr.:
"Free at last, free at last, thank God A'mighty, we're free at last."
He knelt by her side and gave her a hug.

"My good old mum. Did she give you dinner? That stuff?"

Eleanor nodded yes.

"And got you to the toilet okay? Are you all right?"

"I fell," she wrote.

"Are you okay? Are you hurt? Mother?"

Slowly, laboriously, she wrote down what had happened. Then
she added, "I felt like that bug," but she could see he didn't get it.

"But you're all right?"

She nodded, pleased, and wrote, "I got to the bathroom and
back, by myself."

"You're a trouper," he said. "You're a tigeretta. A student told
me today he has a dog named Doggina. And Margaret sends her
love. You're really all right?"

He helped her to her room and began the nightly ritual of getting
her into bed. He took her robe and lay it on a chair, waiting while

she shuffled back and forth and got herself into position to plop down on the side of the bed. Once she was sitting, he let her catch her breath, then he lifted her legs and eased them under the covers, getting her backrest at the proper angle so that she was half-sitting, half-lying. She caught her breath again as Miles hovered, useless for the moment, while she somehow edged her body over inch by inch until she was in the center of the bed. He put the box of tissues near her left hand and made sure the buzzer was near her right. He kissed her on the forehead. He smiled at her.

"I'll be in the next room," he said. "Okay? So don't worry about buzzing."

He settled on the living-room couch, his head in his hands, still breathing hard. At once he remembered his promise to call Margaret. His head ached, he didn't want to call anybody, he wanted to scream and then cease upon the midnight with no pain. But you just had to get through these things. You just had to do them.

"Ugliness, misery, and piss," he said.

He phoned from the kitchen, squinting against the bright overhead light. Margaret answered at once.

"What's the matter?" she asked. Her voice sounded very far away.

"I promised to call," he said. "About my mother."

"Oh."

"You asked me to call." He paused. "You wanted me to let you know if everything is all right."

"That's right, that's right," she said, and laughed softly. "Well, when am I going to see you again?"

"What?"

"Come on, now. Come on. When am I going to see you again?" She was being coy.

"Are you drunk?" he asked. "Margaret?"

There was silence for a moment.

"Margaret, what's the *matter* with you?"

"Nothing."

"Well, why are you talking like that?"

"Like what? What is the matter with *you*, Miles?" Her voice was suddenly very clear. "Well?"

"Tillie quit."

"I don't happen to like being told I'm drunk, Miles. I've been through that with one man and I'm not going through it with another."

"I'm sorry," he said. "It's just that you didn't sound like . . . yourself. And I'm semi-distraught. And that bitch Tillie has quit on me."

"I don't happen to like being called a drunk."

"I'm sorry. I didn't mean anything. Okay?"

"I don't like it."

"I'm sorry, Margaret. Really."

"Okay. So when am I going to see you, hmmm?" Her voice was far away again.

"Tomorrow," he said, shivering. "I'll call tomorrow."

"Yes," she said. "Sleepy, drowsy. Nighty-night." Her voice was blurry and she was repeating "Sleepy, drowsy," as she hung up the phone.

Miles put down the receiver and stood, dumb, with one hand over his mouth. He couldn't grasp it. Someone he knew and loved had just slipped into darkness. Had gone away. Had become some other person. Some thing. He would call her back right now.

He was reaching for the phone when it rang. He checked his watch. 1:00 a.m. Someone was phoning him at 1:00 a.m.

"Bannon? Miles Bannon?" It was the principal, of course.

"Yes?"

"This is Bill Endicott and I've been trying to get ahold of you all night long."

"Do you have any idea what *time* it is?" Miles said.

That slowed him down.

"Are you at all aware that I have a very sick mother who gets very little sleep at the best of times? Do you have any idea what it's like for her when the phone rings in the middle of the night? Do you?"

"I'm sorry about your mother."

"Yes, well. What do you want?" It was nice, even for a moment to feel you had the upper hand with this bastard. And to hell with the consequences. "Well?"

"That incident today, in the locker room. Did you see it? How come you were there?"

Miles explained briefly, angrily, that he had been showering, that he heard noise and then kids running, that he had gone to investigate and found Billy lying in his blood that way. "Of course I wasn't there," he said. "Of course I didn't see it. Are you out of your mind?"

"Well, I want you to forget about it. I want you to forget it ever happened."

Forget. Wouldn't that be nice, Miles thought.

"Miles? Do you understand?"

"You want me to forget," Miles said.

"They've treated him at the hospital and he's going to be just fine. It's a small tear in the testicles, they gave him stitches, and he's going to be fine. They were just horsing around, just kids, that's all it was, and it got a little out of hand. The parents are not pressing charges. I told them how the publicity would be bad for the boy. They could see that I was right. So they're not pressing charges. And the police are going to overlook it. I know the Chief. But it's the boy I'm thinking of. The boy wants to just forget about it. So it's better that this shouldn't get out. You know, to other parents, or to the kids, or to anybody. So. Do you understand?"

"You mean you and the police are going to cover it up."

"Jesus Christ, Miles, don't you ever listen? The boy doesn't want any publicity on this. And neither do his parents. It's our obligation as educators to protect the boy from public embarrassment. It's *their* wish. It's *their* right to decide this. I'm only doing what's best for the boy."

"And for you. For your job."

There was silence for a moment and then the principal said, in the hard voice Miles knew best, "Listen, Bannon. You come and see me Monday morning as soon as you get to school. And not a word about this incident to anybody. This will all go away if nobody says anything. Understand?"

Miles said nothing. He felt sick.

"I will hold you personally responsible if this gets out. I'll have your ass. Do you understand that? Are you there?"

Suddenly the room vibrated to a loud clanging sound, metallic to begin with and then amplified many times over. Pure irritant. It was Eleanor's night buzzer.

"What the hell is that?" the principal said. "Did you do that deliberately? Right in my ear?"

"You woke my mother," Miles said, and hung up.

The buzzer sounded again. Miles had asked the electrician to install something that could wake the soundest sleeper and this is what he got, a torture device.

"Coming, coming," he called, and in seconds was at his mother's bedside. "It's the nice lady who's full of pee," he said. "Come on, you sweet thing, I'll help just a little." He slipped his right arm beneath her shoulders to lift her up, and with his left arm he pulled her legs toward him until finally, exhausted from the effort, she was sitting on the side of the bed. She had to wear a short night-gown, since she could not manage the toilet with long ones, and now it was hiked up to her thighs. She plucked at it, but could not pull it lower. "It's all right, Mother, you're fine," he said, tugging it down for her, and then he slipped her bedjacket over her shoulders and positioned the walker. She sat on the bed moving her feet up and down. "Slippers," he said, "of course," and knelt to put them on. Her feet were icy and stiff-jointed, bloodless; the feet of a dead person.

Was she dying? He looked up at her and she was looking back, a strange expression on her face. Sometimes she looked right into him and knew what he was thinking. He could feel himself blush.

"All rightikins," he said, "that takes care of the footies." He positioned the walker for her once again. She looked at it. "What?" he said. "Are you all right? Are you okay? What should I do?" He could hear something in his voice—panic or desperation or maybe just tiredness—and she heard it too, and so she went into action at once. She leaned forward on the bed and put her two hands on the walker. She spread her feet a little and rocked back and forth on the bed and then made a lunge at the walker. She didn't quite make it. She fell back on the bed and started again, rocking slowly, concentrating. "Here, let me help you," Miles said, but she shook her head no, and made another attempt. This time she got it. She stood, testing for balance, and when she was sure she was steady, she gave him a big smile. "Not dead yet," she said, but no sound came out. He smiled back. The thing to concentrate on was just getting through this, even if he *did* want to scream. Get through it. Be kind. Period.

She shoved the walker forward a few inches at a time, while Miles moved slowly behind, ready to catch her if she should collapse. He began to sing through his nose, à la Willie Nelson, "On the road again, full of pee and on the road again, she's going someplace that she's often been before," until his mother stopped and bent over the walker, shaking with laughter, and he was glad because he was getting through it without making her feel bad. Finally they were there. He sat her on the toilet seat, and said, as always, "You take your time, and bang your walker when you're ready for me. Okay? Okay."

He went out to the kitchen and stood next to the phone. Should he call Margaret? Endicott? The Suicide Prevention Hotline? He sat down next to the phone and stared at it. How could you explain Margaret? She must have had a drink, or *five*, as soon as he'd left. Or maybe she wasn't drunk at all; maybe she'd been knocked crazy by that bastard husband of hers and the craziness only showed up an hour or two after sex. He smiled. The sex had been good, very good, after that awkward start. It was too bad he couldn't just enjoy it instead of treating it like an audition for a part he wasn't going to get. "I'm sorry, Mr. Bannon, but you're not the right type. We're looking for someone harder, longer, and with a little staying power. You're more the Silly Putty type. But we have your address and if something comes up for you, har har, we'll get in touch. Don't call us, we'll call you." He thought of Paul Ciampa; now *there* was a man. And then at once he thought of Billy Mack lying on the locker-room floor with the blood spreading beneath him. Poor Billy.

"How you doing in there?" he said through the bathroom door. The toilet seat banged down. "Are you decent?" He heard her rap out an answer with the walker. He pushed the door open and said, "It's just like Morse Code, isn't it: beep beep, bee bee ba-bee, beep beep." But she wasn't paying any attention to him. She was standing at her walker waving back at the toilet. She'd used the sink to pull herself upright and she'd lowered the seat, but she couldn't reach the handle that would flush the toilet. He looked at her gesturing wildly and at the fierce determination in her face and realized she wanted one thing before she died; she wanted to flush the damned toilet and she wanted to flush it now. She glared at him. He was about to explode into laughter—she was so determined, the whole business was so preposterous—when suddenly he saw through this broken old woman to the young woman she had been, proud and independent, capable of anything, and at once tears sprang to his eyes. "Oh Mother," he said, and put his arms around her, "Oh God." She began to shake silently and Miles held her. In a moment he pulled himself together. "Okay," he said, "I've got it. *Voilà!*" and, with an extravagant gesture, he flushed the toilet. "How's that?" he said, and gave her a little smooch on the cheek. "Okay?" he said, more to himself than to her. "Okay."

They began the trip back to her room. "On the road again, flush the john and on the road again." He sang to her, improvising, the sillier the better. He interrupted himself once to suggest it might be easier for her to use the johnny-chair, but she stopped and shook her head no, NO, and he knew she meant it, so he went on singing. "On the road again, headin' home, we're on the road again."

Finally, it was done. She was in bed, the tissues near her left hand, the buzzer near her right, her body propped at an angle that guaranteed she could never get really comfortable. She touched his hand and nodded. "Good night, Mother," he said and turned out the light as he left.

He went into the tiny den, his bedroom ever since he'd come back home to live. He got into his pajamas and stretched out on the daybed with his robe thrown over him; no sense mussing up the sheets. He glanced at his watch—1:32. So the business with the toilet had taken only twenty-five or thirty minutes, just about average. She'd need help in another two hours, and two hours after that, and two hours after that, providing everything went smoothly.

He began to speculate on which was worse: knowing someone you love is in excruciating pain or knowing that in the end the thing you feel most is the boredom.

Of course you feel love and anguish and pity. Of course you want to take away the pain, even take it on yourself. And of course you do what you have to do, and you try to do it gladly. But thinking about it is one thing, and doing it is another. And when you've done it over and over, preparing yourself for the shock of death, rehearsing the feeling of loss, of grief, of getting on with life, and still the dying goes on and on and on, you realize that the thing you feel is boredom. And shame and guilt. But boredom mainly. So which is worse? Knowing someone you love is in excruciating pain or . . .

He hadn't nearly finished his night thoughts when a ringing began. It took him a minute to realize it was not his mother, it was the telephone. He dashed to the kitchen, eager, hopeful. It was Margaret, surely. It had to be.

"Hello," he said, breathy, dragging out the sound the way she liked. And when there was only silence on the other end, he said, annoyed, "Yes?"

"Mr. Bannon? Is this Mr. Miles Bannon?"

"Yes?"

"The English teacher? At Malburn High?"

"Yes," he said. "What is it?"

A choking sound, like someone holding back tears. "I have to talk to you," a woman said, "about my son. He was one of your students."

"Are you crazy? Has the whole world gone crazy?" Miles spoke slowly, letting the words sink in. "It is the middle of the night. My mother is a very sick woman. And you phone me here, at home, to have a little parent-teacher conference? It's, it's . . ." but he could find no word that would accommodate his sense of outrage.

"I'm sorry," she said. "I'm Eileen Mack. Billy's mother."

"*I'm* sorry, Mrs. Mack. I had no idea it was you. I'm sorry."

"I'm sorry. I've said that though, haven't I. Well, I am. I'm sorry to be calling you this late. I'm sorry about your mother. I have to talk to you about Billy, Mr. Bannon. Now."

"Yes," he said. "Of course. Of course. Is he all right? Is he going to be all right?"

"You've got to talk with him, Mr. Bannon. That's why I'm calling. There's nobody else I can turn to. Our priest can't talk to him, and of course I can't. You're the only one he trusts."

Trusts? Billy Mack? He heard again the cry that Billy made as they were raping him with the broomstick. A wounded animal.

"Will you?" she asked. "Please? Will you talk with him?"

"Mrs. Mack," he began. "Surely you and Mr. Mack are the ones he needs at a time like this. Not a stranger like me. It's his mother and father he needs."

"Mr. Bannon, Billy hasn't talked to me in years, or anybody. And his father is a police officer."

"Oh."

"He's a *cop*. That's the whole thing. That's why I'm calling you.

His father, when he heard about it, he was furious. He said to him, he said, 'How come you? How come they did it to *you?*' And he made Billy lie on the bed and take off the bandage so he could look at the stitches, and when he saw them he got even madder and he said, 'Listen to me'—and he called him a terrible name, with the F word—'listen,' he said, 'there's gotta be a reason why they picked you, and *you* know what it is. So tell me. So tell me.' And he kept saying that over and over and after a while he said, 'It's because they think you're a fag, isn't it? That's why they did it to you.' And my Billy, he just kept laying there with his hands over his face, and when his father finally stopped and left him alone, Billy just cried and cried. I went outside the door and waited till he was done crying, and then I went in and told him never mind, it didn't mean anything, but Billy just gave me that look he's got and said to me, 'Get out of here and go back to *him.*' I did, and I went down to him in the kitchen where he was having coffee before work—he's on nights—and I said to him, 'How could you do that to your own son when he's just been practically murdered?' and he looked at me the way Billy does and said, 'You're the one to blame for turning him into a . . . queer' . . . and he used the F word again. I ran out of the house in just my housedress and I walked and walked and walked, praying. I prayed that God would tell me what to do for Billy. And then all of a sudden I knew I had to call. I knew you were the one who could talk to him." She sobbed once, and was silent and then she added, "He used to love his father."

"Mrs. Mack, I don't know what to say. I'm terribly sorry about Billy and what happened to him with those kids and now with his father, but the fact is that I just don't know the boy."

She tried to say something but she was crying and he couldn't make out the words.

"I tried. He was in my English class last year, but I just couldn't get through to him. He just didn't respond."

"No, Mr. Bannon, you've got it all wrong. He talked about you all the time. You're the one name I ever heard him mention. He'll talk to you, if you just give him a chance, if you just ask him to have a little talk with you."

"Yes, of course. But . . . yes, I'll try."

"On Monday, will you?"

"But surely he won't be back that soon. Won't he be needing care? I mean, shouldn't he be lying down?"

"The doctor said he could go back to school as soon as he was comfortable enough, and the principal—Mr. Endicott—he came to the house and he said Billy should wait a few days, and my husband told him he didn't care what he did." She began to cry again. "He'll be there on Monday, Mr. Bannon. I know him. And you'll talk to him, please. Please. You're the answer to my prayers. Just make him not feel so bad."

"Oh God," Miles said. "I'll try. All right?"

"He'll be so grateful," she said. "And I'm so grateful. He thinks the world of you, Mr. Bannon, he does," and she went on like this until Miles interrupted and said, "Get some rest, Mrs. Mack. You'll be more help to Billy if you get some rest." And then they both hung up.

Miles looked around the kitchen, a little dazed. What kind of father did the poor kid have? To make *him* feel responsible for some insane . . . thing. Didn't he understand how kids acted in a group, especially when they were at that age, and fueled by a little booze or grass or whatever they had, and by their runaway hormones? He was a cop. Surely he knew that you didn't have to be guilty of anything to be made a scapegoat; all you had to do was be around and look right for the part.

It was unthinkable, all of it, and he was going back to bed.

He lay there and lay there, wondering if he would ever get to sleep, and then the buzzer from hell went off, electrocution by ear, and he sprang up and ran into his mother's room.

"Here I am, you sweet thing," he said, jovial and full of energy, and he began the long process of getting her out of bed for another march on the bathroom. While he helped her with her slippers, he glanced at his watch—3:05. Not bad. Two more trips, minimum. Five at the worst. He'd get through the night easily enough. And weekends were always manageable. He was a lucky man.

He moved slowly behind her, singing because it made her feel he didn't hate doing it all, "On the road again, full of pee and on the road again, going someplace she has often been before, she can't wait so she's on the road again."

4

MARGARET TURNED IN HER SLEEP, sharply, and her body convulsed as if she were in pain. She brought her hand up to her face to protect it. She made a small whimpering sound.

She was having another dream. Roofer was alive again; they were married; everything was like it had always been.

"Come here," he said, and she approached him slowly. She should have run. She always knew she should run, but she never could. People didn't understand that. Roofer was naked, and though he touched himself, plucking at that big soft thing, he couldn't get an erection, so she knew what would happen, but still she couldn't run. She didn't.

"Come here, I said," and he grabbed her arm and pulled her toward him, loosening his grip a little so he could twist his fingers on her soft flesh and make it burn. He placed his other hand lightly on her breast and with his thumb and forefinger teased the small nipple until it grew erect. Then, his eyes on his hardening penis, he dug his thumbnail deep into the nipple, twisting it until she cried out. He slapped her and threw her on the bed and—thick and hard at last—plunged into her, driving, slashing, as if his penis were a knife and he were stabbing her. He kept on and on, a sweat broke out on him, sour, poisonous, and still he went on, punishing her, plunging in and in again, until at last she felt nothing and then he stopped, suspended, drew in a long shuddering breath, and as he came—his head thrown back, his chest convulsing—he whispered over and over again, "Roofie's a good boy; good boy, good good good good boy."

He collapsed against her and she woke.

5

MILES HAD FALLEN ASLEEP toward morning, a deep untroubled sleep, with no dreams, no cramps in the foot, no sudden convulsions of arms or legs. It was as if he had taken his mother on that endless trip to the bathroom for the very last time, and now nothing remained for him to do. No obligations. No worries. No disturbing sexual desires. Just a long untroubled sleep, for eternity.

He turned in the bed—there was a noise of some kind—and for a moment he tried to fight his way to consciousness, but it was a hopeless task, and he smiled in his sleep as he abandoned himself, luxuriously, to a world without feeling.

The alarm clock had been ringing for almost a minute before Margaret realized what the sound was. She threw back the covers and was in the bathroom brushing her teeth before she was even fully conscious. Saturday morning. She had to get over to Miles' place, pronto.

She had taken a Xanax the night before, but when that did nothing for her, she had had a glass of wine and a Nembutol and eventually she fell asleep. After the nightmare, she'd taken another

Xanax, not to make her sleep but just to relax her nerves, to help her get through another day.

It was morning at last and she swallowed a couple aspirins. They would take care of the hangover and serve as breakfast too, since she didn't have time to eat anything. She fussed with her hair for a few minutes, applied some blusher to her cheekbones, and ran a pale lipstick across her upper lip. She put on her new bra. She struggled into the damned pantyhose, a deep blue, rolling the waistband down so that it wouldn't cut into her waist. She would have liked to put on jeans, but she was dressing for Eleanor, and so she put on a white blouse and a blue denim jumper, a compromise. And low heels.

She glanced at herself in the mirror. She checked the time. She was running late, but she could still be at Miles' house by seven-thirty, and with luck she'd be able to get Eleanor up and bathed and in her chair while Miles was still asleep. He loved that. And she loved doing it for him. She owed him everything. He would marry her eventually and then she would rid her mind forever of all the horrors of her first marriage. Everything would be wonderful, or at least endurable. Miles was her salvation.

William Endicott, the principal of Malburn High, awoke early Saturday thinking of that skinny little shit, Miles Bannon. Bannon was the only one who might give him trouble. At the hospital yesterday he had ensured the silence of the Mack family, and he had taken care of Coach immediately afterward. And talked to the chief of police, of course. Today he would haul out the heavy artillery against the parents of those five kids. That should put an end to the incident. It was an exercise in containment. Damage control at a high level. He could handle it.

Endicott had been a captain in the army, a twenty-year career man who had served his country in Korea and in Nam before devoting his life to education. Between his two wars he had earned a quick M.A. in educational administration, with a thesis applying the principles of military life to the training of youth, and when he took his army pension at age forty-three, he was a hot item on the education market. He got a vice-principal's job immediately, and in a few years he moved up to principal; ten years later he was made principal of Malburn High.

He was sixty now, with a straight back and a strong mind and *two* successful careers under his belt, and he was damned if he'd have a scandal on his hands just because that little shit Bannon couldn't keep his mouth shut. He would have to deal with Bannon on Monday.

He reviewed the situation once again. The Mack kid would keep quiet, of course. The doctor was on the School Board; no problem there. The Mack father was the lunatic type, but he was also a cop, so he could be counted on to take care of the police. Besides, the police chief was an old buddy. He could be trusted. And as for Coach, well, good old Coach knew that if the incident got out, it was the end; he might as well bend way over and kiss his ass goodbye.

He anticipated no great difficulty with the five sets of parents; he had scared them shitless with his phone call last night. A follow-up visit this morning would keep them quiet forever.

The problem of containment was up to him, of course, no question about that. The superintendent was off in San Diego at a curriculum conference and he'd prefer *not* to know any facts, please, and his own vice-principal was incapable of anything except nodding in agreement or shaking his head—also in agreement. It was his problem and he was gonna contain it.

So the only loose cannon was that little shit Miles.

He paused for a moment. In fairness—and he tried always to be fair—Bannon was a smart man and a good teacher and, so far as you could tell, morally responsible. There was just something about him. In any case, he would neutralize Bannon first thing on Monday.

He showered, dressed, and ate his breakfast. He kissed Missy goodbye, but she turned away. "Your breath," she said. They had a rule about not talking until after breakfast and these were the first words between them this morning. She took a roll of Certs from the catch-all dish on the refrigerator and pressed one into his hand. "Give them hell, Captain," she said and, because it annoyed him, she gave the V for Victory sign.

Missy's sarcasm was the great burden of his life.

Coach hadn't slept all night. It was Saturday morning now and he had the shakes, but he was holding on, at least for the time being. Yesterday evening during the eleven o'clock news, Endicott had pummeled him awake and told him about the incident in the locker room.

Despite the fact that Billy Mack had told him nothing about what happened, Endicott had managed to piece together a vivid and bloody account of the incident, and he spared Coach none of it: he told him everything he learned from the attending physician and from the five boys who did it and from the evidence of his own eyes—since he had insisted on seeing the wound before and after the hundred twenty-seven stitches. He even included details about the booze and the cocaine, though to the parents he'd mentioned only the booze. Coach listened to the account in disbelief, and then in horror, and soon—while Endicott made him black coffee and repeated the story yet again—he came to accept it as another tragedy for which he alone was responsible.

It was the same way after the accident. They'd been coming home from a party one night after a lot of drinks. The pavement was wet and he was driving slowly but he sort of nodded off for a second, and when he came to, he realized that his foot was heavy on the accelerator and they were headed straight toward an abutment. Frantic, he pulled the wheel hard to the left, but it was too late. Carol's right side was crushed—her leg, her arm, all her ribs on that side were broken. Her right lung was punctured, her face badly disfigured. For three weeks she hung on, half-alive, and then she died. Coach was not injured at all, but mysteriously he developed a limp that seemed to get worse as time went on. In fact, it kept even pace with his drinking.

People understood, they said. Who could blame him? He'd snap out of it in time. Endicott had even covered for him, telling parents it was medication when they complained that Coach was drunk at games. But that was all over, as of right now.

"I'm to blame for everything," Coach said.

"It's true, you are to blame," Endicott said. "But it's not enough to just accept it and drink yourself to death. Look at what you're responsible for. Make no mistake, you are responsible and, if this gets out, *you're* out. That boy's gonna be marked for life, and it wouldn't have happened if you'd been doing your job."

"I know. I know."

"So do it." Endicott punched him in the arm, not too gently. "You *can* do it."

"You mean, stop drinking?"

Coach had not slept the rest of the night. He turned on the television, switching from station to station as each of them went black, and ended finally with Creature Features so abysmally stupid that even he, frantic, desperate, could not bear to watch any longer. He got out a fresh half gallon of Seagrams and put it on the coffee table and sat watching it until the sun came up, lighting the bottle from behind and turning it pale gold.

Saturday morning. He felt like he'd been sitting there for weeks. More than anything in the world he wanted a drink, and more than once he made a move toward the bottle, but always the thought of Billy Mack, torn and bleeding, came between him and the whiskey. In the end, he got up and made himself a pot of coffee instead. He hated coffee. But he drank it dutifully and then went to shave.

A day at a time. Others had done it. That fool Dietz, for one.

Billy Mack lay in bed waiting for his mother to wake up and start breakfast. He had cried himself to sleep after his father left for night duty. Sleep had surprised him, because he thought he would never sleep again, or be able to eat, or read a book, or do any of the things he had always done. He could see now that he was wrong; he would sleep and eat and read, but he knew he would never be able to laugh again. Never. Not after what they did to him. And what his own father had said about him.

He slipped a hand down between his legs. He was still badly swollen there, and it hurt him to walk—he had tried it last night—but he was going to walk to school Monday even if it killed him.

In a way, he understood his father. His father was afraid, that's all; he just wanted a son he could be proud of, a real man, not some sissy fag. He wanted to please his father and he couldn't, and so his father frightened him. But his mother drove him crazy. All last night she'd been after him to have a talk with Mr. Bannon, just please have a little talk with Mr. Bannon, Mr. Bannon called and says he wants to have a talk with you. But he wasn't talking to Bannon or to anybody.

Last year when he had Mr. Bannon for English, he liked him at first because he was different and said crazy things, and he even talked about him at home, but then he had that dream. It wasn't like any dream he could remember and in a way it changed his life. In the dream, they were on the school picnic, at a playground or a beach, and they walked out to the end of the wharf, just the two of them. It was late afternoon—the sun had gone down—and he could barely see the others back there on the shore. Everyone was very quiet. Mr. Bannon was smiling at him the way he did, and he asked, "Why are you smiling at me like that?" and Mr. Bannon said, "You know why, don't you?" and he said, "No, no, I don't," and, terrified, he ran from the wharf back onto shore. Nobody would talk to him, and they all moved away in little groups, whispering together, glancing back at him. And out on the wharf, Mr. Bannon was still smiling at him, looking.

After the dream, he didn't like Mr. Bannon anymore. He knew

it wasn't Mr. Bannon's fault that he'd had the dream, but the dream was like a warning. It scared him in a way nothing in his life had ever scared him. Because, what if it were true, and he had been born a queer, and that's why the guys had done this to him? And what if Mr. Bannon knew it?

Richy Polcari was up early and out. He had made coffee for his parents, watered the houseplants, and tidied up the living room so as not to shock the cleaning lady who came late Saturday mornings. Richy had a natural sense of order that compensated for the chaos of his parents' lives. His two older brothers, one twenty-seven and the other twenty-nine, both attorneys now, had pretty much raised him by themselves, since their parents were so clearly unequipped to do so. When they'd left for college, however, Richy was on his own.

His parents were academics, his father an economist at MIT and his mother a professor of human biology at Boston University. His birth had been an accident, of course, and his father simply didn't know what to make of him. His mother did. She knew he was gay almost from the start, and whenever she thought of him, it was of "poor Richy." When he was twelve, she gave him a firm talk on sexually transmitted diseases and, though she would have liked to do more for him, what could anyone do? You can't change nature. You had to acknowledge and respect it. Richy was intelligent and attractive, he was outgoing, he was comfortable with being gay. They would just have to hope for the best. Sex would always be a problem, of course, but perhaps Richy would meet some nice young man and they would be good to one another; it was not impossible. In any case, she had done what she could.

This morning Richy was on his way to the Boston Public Library because he did not want to deal with the cleaning lady while he was trying to decipher Vergil's hexameters. He had to put in at least two hours to get ahead in next week's work so that he'd be free to spend Saturday night and Sunday with Robert.

Robert had picked him up in the men's room at the Boston Public Library last summer—Richy, in his suit and tie, had looked a safe twenty-one—and now they saw each other at least once a week at Robert's place. In Richy, Robert saw himself at seventeen, and he was determined to help. He gave frequent instructions on how to survive when you're simultaneously in and out of the closet. He was an expert on that, having led a very active gay life in D.C. and San Francisco while holding political jobs that required him to at least look straight. He knew that Richy listened and shrugged and went on being queenish, but he also knew that Richy was very smart and eventually would settle down and make the compromises necessary for survival in the real world. Robert himself was employed as a personal aide to a state senator and had taken an unwise risk in picking up Richy in the first place. Moreover Richy was a minor, and for that reason Robert was careful not to be seen in public with him, let alone in the Combat Zone where Richy liked to go exploring. Richy could be maddening with that non-stop chatter, but Robert liked his gawkiness and his sincerity and his ability to improvise at sex games. Besides, he had a schlong that just wouldn't quit.

Richy was seventeen and Robert was the first person who had ever accepted him as what he was—except for his mother, who didn't count. He knew that Robert was right, that he should just lie low, play it cool, try to pass unnoticed in the straight crowd. But he couldn't help himself. He wanted them to like him. He wanted to be popular. He wanted to be like Paul Ciampa or even like Cosmo or Billy Mack.

As he locked the door and started for the subway, he found himself, by habit, saying his prayer for school days: "Please, God, just don't let them make fun of me today." Which, this morning, made him laugh. It was Saturday and he didn't have to pray and he didn't have to worry. He could walk the way he wanted, he could wave his hands when he talked, he could let his voice sound as fruity as he liked. Deliberately, he tossed his hair back like a girl.

He could be Judy Garland if he felt like it. He began to skip down the yellow brick road.

When Miles woke on Saturday, he knew something was wrong. There was too much sun in the room, there had been sounds of movement in the house for quite a while, he heard someone laugh. He sprang from his bed and was at the door in seconds.

"Margaret?"

"We're in here," she called.

So, he had overslept. Miles tiptoed into the living room, and there was Margaret, standing behind his mother, carefully combing out her hair for her. "Sleepy-drowsy," she said. "Eleanor's had her bath and her breakfast and *we're* getting on with life." She blew him a kiss.

"The blue momoo," Miles said to his mother. "How're you, sweetie pie?"

Eleanor had the blue blanket around her this morning and she was bent over her writing board in fierce concentration. Miles knew what that meant. Whenever Margaret came over, Eleanor always took care to write out instructions for when she would be hospitalized: "No extraordinary means, no life preservers, no machines to keep me alive." She'd been a devout Catholic all her life, and she would never dream of committing suicide, but she wanted to make sure they didn't attach her to one of those machines and keep her officially alive. She wanted out as soon as it was her turn to go.

"Momoo!"

She looked up and shook her pencil at him.

"Got it," he said, pointing to her writing board. "No veg for you, sweetie pie."

"Miles!" Margaret said.

"I'm outta here. I'm history," he said. "I'm gonna shower."

He took a long, warm shower and leaned against the tile wall, thinking. This is how it would be afterwards. They would marry, and he'd have a full night's sleep now and then, and in the morning Margaret would be there, looking terrific, and no grim tasks to perform. He would definitely marry her when this was over. It was what she wanted. And he owed it to her. And, of course, he wanted it too.

He felt a little shudder run through him as he thought of all those years ahead of them, all those times he would have to perform. He reached down and touched himself. At once he began to get hard. He soaped his body all over, and then he stood with his face turned up and let the water wash the soap away. He closed his eyes and let his hands work slowly down his chest to his stomach, and then lower, exploring his body the way Margaret liked to. He was perfectly erect. Like a steel rod, he told himself, and he pressed down to make it even harder.

All his life he'd been embarrassed by his body, by nudity of any kind; it was forbidden, it was frightening. But look at this. Just *look* at this. This was terrific. Forget about forbidden; it was exciting.

He could fuck them all with this thing. Margaret. Diane Waring. Every girl in the senior class. He thought of jacking off, but no, he'd save this for Margaret.

He began to feel better. He began to feel wonderful. It was a beautiful September day, he had a full, rich life, and—who knows?—he might get really good at performing. He might even get famous for it. Old Miles Bannon, the sex machine. The pneumatic drill. Stud City.

Well, why not?

6

THEY HAD BEEN WATCHING Saturday football for some time—or rather, Margaret had been watching while Miles slept on the living-room couch—when suddenly Margaret called out, and he woke to see his mother slumped in her chair, her mouth open, her head tilted to the side.

"I can't get a pulse," Margaret said.

Miles froze on the couch, looking. So this is it, he thought, this is death. And for a second—for less than a second—his heart beat faster and something opened inside his mind and he was about to think, At last, but he refused to give the thought entry. "Oh no," he said.

"I can't get anything," Margaret said.

"Let me try," Miles said, and at once he was on his knees, beside her, his fingers on her wrist and then on her neck. "She's breathing," he said, "I've got a pulse. Feel." And he touched Margaret's fingers to the spot on Eleanor's neck where, faintly, a pulse continued to beat.

"I'll call the ambulance," Miles said. "I'll call the doctor."

The ambulance would be there at once. Dr. Archer's answering service promised to do what they could to reach her. Again Miles felt his mother's pulse; it was the same.

"Stay with her for a second," Miles said. He dashed to his room and changed from his jeans and sweatshirt to his new wool pants, with a jacket and tie. Hospital workers were all snobs, he knew, and they'd give his mother better care if he looked like somebody. That's just how it was.

The ambulance pulled up, and in minutes they had Eleanor on a stretcher and, with lights flashing, were racing down the through-way and into the narrow streets of Cambridge until they slowed nearly to a crawl as they reached downtown Boston. Then it was one delay after another as they fought traffic and road repairs and construction machinery and crowds of pedestrians who feared and respected nothing, not even an ambulance. Finally, on the periphery of the Combat Zone, they reached New England Medical and his mother was rushed into Emergency.

Miles paced for a while and then he sat, waiting. Margaret had followed in her car and now she joined him in Emergency and they waited together, silent.

No one came and no one left. A black woman held her small child in her arms, crooning to him, and every so often he would whimper. In a corner of the room, turned away from the others, an elderly man who looked like a derelict sat hugging his chest. He rocked back and forth in his chair, and when he paused for a minute and lifted one arm from his side, Miles saw a huge splotch of blood on his shirt, as if he'd been stabbed in the chest. There were others: two little boys, albino twins, with a teenage girl who looked to be their babysitter; an elderly woman who sat bent nearly in two; a pregnant woman with a stained washcloth she kept press-ing to the side of her head. No one spoke. No one complained. It was a scene from Kafka, Miles thought.

"It's going to be all right," Margaret said after a while, and she put her hand lightly on his knee.

He was thinking about that tiny moment of relief when he had thought Eleanor was dead. He hated himself for that. His eyes stung, and he turned to Margaret quickly, so she would see his tears, if there were any.

"I loved her," he said.

"I know. I know," Margaret said.

An hour passed.

While he was growing up, Miles had never gotten along with his mother. She had preferred Erin in everything; it was as if Miles had committed some unforgivable act in being born male. But in this past year and a half, now that his mother was dying, they seemed to have reached an understanding. She often gave him a look that was not forgiveness, really; it was a look that said there was nothing to forgive. And sometimes she seemed to want forgiveness for herself. It was an odd mixture of love and resentment they shared, and they both knew it.

Miles went to the glass booth and stood there. The nurse was studying a long sheet of names and times and cryptic abbreviations. After a while, she reached the end of the page, flipped to the next one, and looked up at him.

"Is there any news on my mother?" he asked. "They brought her in about an hour ago?"

"We'll let you know," she said, and smiled, returning at once to her sheets of figures.

"She's an elderly woman? Eleanor Bannon, her name is?"

"We'll let you know," she said, and she did not look up.

"They'll let us know," Miles said to Margaret, and made one of his faces. She smiled and took his hand.

Another hour passed.

"I'll get you some coffee," Margaret said. "Would you like coffee?"

"We should get lunch, actually," Miles said. "But it seems awfully callous, doesn't it." He looked at the glass booth where a new nurse had come on duty. "I'll give it another try," he said, but this nurse was even less approachable than the first. She had dyed red hair and tiny eyes, and she looked like she had just smelled something foul.

"If we had new information," she said, "we would have given it to you." She gave him a firm look.

Margaret left and brought back coffee and a sandwich, but Miles could not bring himself to eat it there, so they went outside and shared the sandwich, eating surreptitiously, as they walked up and down in front of the hospital. Then they went inside, to wait. The twin boys had disappeared.

After another hour, Miles approached the glass booth and asked apologetically if there were any information yet. It was the nurse with the dyed red hair, and she squinted hard at Miles.

"Name?"

He gave his mother's name and address, the doctor's name, the reason for her being in Emergency, and then his own name.

"She's not here," the nurse said, checking her charts. "She was brought up to Intensive Care a good hour ago. You'll have to en-quire at the front desk."

"But is she all right?"

"We're *very* busy here, sir." She squinted at him as the corners of her mouth turned up in a small smile. "Front desk," she said.

Miles and Margaret had been waiting outside Intensive Care for only a few minutes when Dr. Archer approached them. She shook hands with them, briskly, and said, "I'm sorry."

"Yes," Miles said.

"Of course," Margaret said.

"It's always strange with ALS," Dr. Archer said. "These things happen and we don't really know what they are. Strain on the heart, sometimes. Sometimes a kind of stroke, some cerebral ac-cident that we can't explain. Sometimes, it's almost as if they can't endure the immobility any longer and they just *let* themselves go."

"They want to die?" Miles said.

"No, not that. Not positive volition; just non-resistance. It is, as

I say, a strange phenomenon. And with your mother, I just don't know. She's not up to a CAT scan yet, or an encephalogram; she's much too weak. And I wouldn't advise an arteriogram at all, because in her condition it could actually precipitate a stroke. So there are certain things we can't rule out and there are others she's not well enough to allow us to test for."

"But she *is* dying," Miles said, as if he wanted confirmation.

Dr. Archer looked at him sharply.

"She doesn't want any extraordinary means taken, is all," Miles said. "She doesn't want to be kept alive by machines."

"She was always very clear about that," Margaret said.

Dr. Archer gestured toward the door to Intensive Care. "You can stay a minute or two," she said. "One visitor at a time. She's the third bed over."

Miles was struck first by the near-darkness of the room and then by the pervasive noise. He could make no sense of the glistening metal, the plastic bags with fluid, the dark forms moving in the distance. There were, perhaps, no more than twelve beds, but in the dim light they seemed to stretch out beyond his field of vision, and in each of them lay someone in pain. Men and women side by side, a child, another child, a near-skeleton, and all of them exposed in their agony, indecent. Some had needles in their arms. Some had tubes in their noses and mouths, with other tubes collecting wastes in bottles underneath the beds. There were moans of pain, muffled crying, the hard rasp of labored breathing, and, beneath these sounds, the constant low hum of machines that performed the work of living for bodies that had nearly given up.

Confused, frightened, Miles at first could not find his mother's bed. And then he saw her. She was propped up at a sharp angle, and a young nurse bent above her, a tube in her hand. The tube ran from a metal case on the floor, with a bottle and a motor attached. Miles watched as the nurse eased the tube into his mother's mouth, and pushed it gently, and then flicked a switch behind her. At once the machine came to life, with a choking sound, and the nurse moved the tube gently inside his mother's mouth, and then her throat, pushing it slowly downward. He could hear it sucking up phlegm, a gargling sound, terrible. His mother's body convulsed and the nurse pulled away, but kept the tube moving in her throat until that gargling sound died away and there was only the hum of the machine itself. The nurse winced, and drew the tube out slowly. With care, she wiped his mother's mouth, then looked at her. Slowly, she shook her head.

Miles moved toward the bed and looked at his mother. She was gray. Her head was thrown back and her mouth was open; she drew breath in short harsh gasps. So it was nearly over. For her sake, he was relieved.

The nurse became aware of Miles and, looking up at him, she whispered, "You're not supposed to be in here. Who let you in?" She raised her voice. "You are not supposed to be in here."

Miles nodded, and left the room quickly.

They were waiting again.

They had been waiting for hours in the lounge outside Intensive Care, and now, hungry at last, they decided to go get something to eat.

It was nearly eight, just beginning to get dark, and there was almost nobody in the street and very little traffic. But as they walked, silent, they passed a derelict and then some kids looking to score drugs. They saw two women who might be prostitutes. The women interested Miles because they looked like any other women, except that these seemed to be available. One of them stared him straight in the eyes as she passed. They saw another derelict. A long blue Cadillac pulled up to the curb in front of them, and they watched as a man in a black suit got out and somebody inside, whom they could not see, handed him a small TWA travel bag. He took it and, tucking it under his arm, crossed the sidewalk and disappeared beneath a marquee that said *Girls Girls Girls.* At once there was loud music and the lights on the marquee lit up, blinking *Girls Girls Girls,* off and on.

"God, what an area," Margaret said. "Combat Zone for sure,"

and she put her arm through his, stopping him. "Let's turn back, Miles. Please."

They turned back and Miles said nothing, because he would have been glad to keep on. Only a few people were around and the streets were nearly silent, but he could feel the place was just about to come alive. He wanted to see more. Anything could happen here. It was exhilarating.

For a moment, for the smallest part of a moment, he had completely forgotten his mother was dying.

They walked back toward the hospital, and passed it, and then they found a McDonald's. They ate quickly, talking very little, and when they had finished their cheeseburgers, Miles got them coffee, and Margaret said, "Take one of these." It was a tiny pink pill, the size of a pea. "It's only Xanax," she said. "It will help you relax."

"No," Miles said. "I don't like pills." And later, "Do you take those often?"

"No," she said.

"Did you take one last night? After I left?"

Margaret only looked at him.

"Well, you must have taken something. I thought maybe you'd had another drink or . . . well, you were so different when I phoned. It was like you were another person."

"What are you talking about? Why are you doing this, Miles?"

He felt he had done something wrong, and so he said, almost an apology: "When I called you last night? You asked me to call and say how Mother was? Because of Tillie?"

She looked at him with incomprehension.

"You don't remember. Do you."

"Oh yes," she said, in a light, high voice. "I may have had another drink. I was tired, and I wanted to be fresh for your mother this morning." She was looking beyond him. She might have been making smalltalk at a cocktail party. "It's not important, really. These things happen. Right?" She smiled in his direction.

Something about her frightened him and so he smiled back. He placed his hand on hers and smiled again. I don't know who she is, he thought. I don't know anything.

"We need some rest," he said. "Why don't you go home right now. Don't go back to the hospital. It's killing. It's too depressing. I'll phone you if anything happens. I'll wait a couple hours, then get a cab. You go on home, Margaret."

She walked with him back to the hospital and waited with him outside Intensive Care. There was nothing to say. There was nothing to do. They waited.

His mother remained the same, the nurse said. Why didn't they just go home? Get a little rest.

But it was not until eleven o'clock that Miles persuaded Margaret to leave the hospital. He would follow later. She kissed him goodbye, finally, and left.

Miles waited fifteen minutes, and then ten, and then he asked about his mother. She remained the same, the nurse said.

He paced the length of the corridor, and then again, and finally he took the elevator to the lobby. In the elevator, he made a pact with himself. If there were a cab at the door, he would take it straight home to Malburn. That was the deal. Straight home. He found himself hoping there would be no cab.

The elevator doors opened very slowly, and as he stepped out into the lobby, Miles could see the cab—its roof light on, the driver waiting—parked square in front of the entrance.

He went down the stairs, shook his head, no, at the cab driver, and set off walking to the Combat Zone.

It was another world. He could look around now and take it all in, but he was afraid to look around very much. What if someone saw him? There was only one reason to be in this part of town. He tried to walk casually, as if he were just out for a stroll.

He was on the same street he had walked earlier with Margaret, but it was a different place now. The derelicts were gone, there were more people—men—in the street, and the prostitutes looked different. These were pros, he could tell. They had on more makeup, their hair was deliberately wild, they wore short skirts of satin or leather, and they seemed to be on an invisible leash to some man who stood leaning against a wall or a doorpost or who sat slumped in a Cadillac or a Lincoln Town Car or a Mercedes. It was like Hollywood's version of a red light district, except these women were not attractive and the men did not look menacing.

There was traffic now, cars with men mostly, gawking or whistling, and some cars with tinted windows, and some that just moved quietly through the streets. And on the sidewalk there were young men, alone or in small nervous groups, eyeing the prostitutes or the posters slapped onto the brick walls, or stopping to look into one of the bars where there was loud music and smoke and men drinking and sometimes a yell or a laugh.

He came to the end of the street and looked right and then left. A police car tore by, its siren shrieking, and in the distance another siren made a whining sound, but nobody seemed to notice or care. They all seemed to belong in this place. Miles was the only one who looked around, guilty, but there was no place for hiding here. Everything was up front and brightly lit. *Pussy Galore*, a sign said, *Naked*, spelled out in lights. *On Stage, Live.* Miles slowed his pace. Flanking the entrance were life-sized photos, framed and under glass. A woman of at least forty, nude, with impossibly large breasts, crossed her legs and arched her back in a simulation of sexual frenzy. She was sitting on a little stool, and even with her back arched and her shoulders squared, her immense breasts billowed up and out and down, hanging nearly to her waist. Her name appeared in huge letters beneath the photo: Ineeda Mann. On the wall opposite there was a light-skinned black woman, Ginger Fox. She was young, no more than twenty surely, and she stood in profile, bending from the waist, so that her breasts—normal-sized, Miles noticed with relief—swung out in points. Her hands burrowed between her legs. Miles stopped for a second to get a better look, and at once a large black hand gripped his arm, and he heard, "You want some black pussy?'' For a second he could not get his breath, and then he turned and looked up into the face of the largest black man he had ever seen.

"Thank you, no," Miles said, but as the man kept looking at him, he smiled formally, and said, as if he were addressing a salesman at his door, "Not interested, thank you."

"Boys?" the man asked. "Young? Nice fresh meat?"

"Good Lord, no!" Miles said, trying to free his arm from the man's grip. "No!"

"What're you, then? You some kind of crazy cop, dressed up like that? You from Omaha? What're you?"

"I'm . . . I just . . .'' But the words would not come. "I'm in the wrong place," Miles said. "I shouldn't be here."

The man looked hard at Miles, and then he grinned, and the grin turned into a soft laugh. "First time," he said. "That's okay, man," and he released Miles' arm. "You-all come back and see us, now. Y'hear?"

Miles turned away from him and started back toward the hospital. Everything was different now, and real. It was filthy. Disgusting. He must have been insane to come here. With prostitutes and pimps. And dressed like this. He was wearing a tweed jacket, like a schoolteacher. And a shirt and tie! He must have been crazy.

He walked quickly, not looking around because he was sure everybody would be looking back at him. Laughing. But laughter was the least of it. Imagine if somebody had recognized him! He began to walk faster. It struck him finally that it was taking longer than it should to get back to the hospital, and so he paused for just a moment and looked up and down the street. At once he saw that he must have taken a wrong turn. He'd never been here before.

He retraced his steps to the corner, looked left, then right. Yes, down the street to his left was the marquee for Ineeda Mann, and beneath it, leaning against her photo, was the huge black man who had stopped him earlier.

"Hi, sweets," someone said behind him, a girlish voice, and then there were giggles as two young men came through an open door and brushed past him. "Love your tweeds," one of them said. They were convulsed by this and went off down the street, laughing, slapping at one another.

Miles was sick, he wanted to be out of here, but automatically he turned to see where they had come from, and found himself looking into a dark, smoky room. Hard rock was playing and for a second he caught the sound of glasses clinking and then a loud male laugh. He moved away from the door, and looked at the sign above it: "The Tom Cat Lounge," it said, and there was a picture of a black cat with its tail erect. So, this was it. A gay bar.

Miles moved away quickly, panic-stricken, and walked straight to the end of the street. He turned right, and walked some more, and there ahead of him, at last, he saw the hospital, and a cab to take him back to Malburn.

So, there was a merciful God after all. He had not been caught. He had not been seen.

In this, however, he was mistaken.

Miles had moved quickly from the open door of the Tom Cat Lounge, but not before Richy Polcari, who was standing by the jukebox bopping to the rhythm, turned away from the bar and saw in the doorway a guy who looked to him like Milo, only older and not so handsome. He reached for his drink, and when he took another look, the guy was gone.

Richy turned back to the bar, frowning so that he'd look a little older, squaring his shoulders to make his suit hang better. Milo, he thought, imagine that. Miles Bannon, in a gay bar.

And in the voice of the Church lady, Richy said, "Now, wouldn't that be special."

7

ON MONDAY, Miles went to school as usual. His mother was still in Intensive Care and might die at any minute; nonetheless, he had to go to school, he had to teach. He gave himself many reasons why: it was Monday; it was the start of the school year; he was at a crucial moment in poetry; he had prepared no lesson plan for a substitute teacher, and in any case substitutes were either dumb or incompetent. Besides, he owed it to Diane Waring who chaired the English Department. And to that sonofabitch Endicott. He would just have to teach.

In fact, Miles went to school as much out of desperation as out of duty because two nights earlier, on Saturday night, while his mother lay near death in Intensive Care, he had been tiptoeing around the Combat Zone in search of trouble. What if she had died at that moment? He was overcome with guilt.

All through Sunday, until well after midnight, he had waited in the corridor outside Intensive Care, Margaret at his side. He skipped lunch. He skipped dinner. It's better that she die, they told each other. She's been through too much already. But she had not died on Saturday and she did not die on Sunday and they kept waiting dutifully outside the door. At one in the morning, they left the hospital.

And now it was Monday and Miles was still wracked with guilt and his mother was still the same. He called the hospital before he left for school, and he would call after each class, but he had decided not to mention her to anyone in the teachers' room. Who wanted pity?

He pulled into the parking lot, in the section reserved for faculty, and deliberately chose the slot next to Kathy Dillard's new Buick. They sometimes kidded Kathy about substituting cars for a love life, but in fact Kathy had more intimate relations with more people than anybody else in school. They just weren't sexual relations. Kathy was everybody's confidante and cars were her consolation, or so Miles supposed. Anyhow, his battered Pinto was a standing joke, and his peeling orange paint made a nice comment on the glistening silver of her new LeSabre. The contrast was laughable.

Miles himself didn't feel much like laughing. He took a deep breath, and just for a moment he lowered his head to the steering wheel and tried to imagine this was all over. No more hospital. No more craziness. No more obligations. He couldn't imagine it.

He sat back from the steering wheel and tried instead to prepare a face to meet the others. It was the same group every day—Kathy, Jim, Coogan, Miles—the early starters. Kathy was always the first one there and she always brought pastry from Dunkin Donuts. In the old days Miles had made the coffee, but Jim Dietz did it now, or Diane Waring if Dietz was late. Dietz needed lots of coffee, since he drank it in place of alcohol. And then there was Coogan, needy, enthusiastic, a mess. Often there were others—four or five, depending on the day—who just sat around and drank coffee and let Dietz tell jokes while they got used to the idea of another school day. It was a good group.

"Show time," Miles said aloud and got out of the car. As he slammed the door, a hubcap on the back left tire fell off. Miles looked at it, looked around to make sure nobody was watching, and then he jumped up and down on it. It was good to get the poison out. When the hubcap was nice and flat, he tossed it into the back seat of the car and slammed the door. At once the front left hubcap fell off. He burst into laughter. Sometimes that was all you could do.

Jim Dietz was one of the few teachers who hadn't given up cigarettes, but he managed to fill the lounge with smoke all by himself. Nobody complained; the ones who had quit smoking could enjoy it vicariously and the others liked Jim enough to put up with it.

As Miles opened the door he met only expectant silence and a cloud of smoke, and then Jim's voice broke through with his punchline, wet-mouthed, Hungarian: "You mean it was the rooster, darling?" Everybody laughed, and Mike Coogan beat on the table until, as usual, he spilled his coffee.

"God, that's funny," Coogan said. "Have you heard that one, Miles? The Zsa Zsa one? Tell it again, Jim."

Everybody turned to Miles. "How's your mother, Miles?" somebody said, and somebody else said, "Have some coffee. There are major donuts over there, Miles. Jellies." Diane Waring shifted her chair a little so Miles could join them.

The women's-room door banged open and Kathy Dillard stood there. "The custodian forgot to put toilet paper in there *again*. Can you believe it?"

"Listen to this joke, Kathy," Coogan said. "You missed it. You too, Miles. You'll love it. Tell it, Jim."

"There is no toilet paper *again*," Kathy said. "God!"

Kevin Foley came storming in the door. "You know what kills me?" he said. "You know what?"

"What?" Miles said, the straight man.

"What kills me is the copy machine. It's broken again. Already. How can it be broken on a Monday morning?"

"It's not broken," Kathy said. "You've just got to know how to use it."

"Well, how do *you* use it? *I* can't use it. I can't make it work, and I need it more than anyone." Foley taught American history and gave a daily quiz, multiple choice. "Show me how, Kathy, if you're so smart."

"God!" Kathy said.

"It's easy, Foley. You just open the front part, count to five, and close it again," Miles said. "Then it works."

"That's impossible," Foley said. "Mark my words, it won't work," but he went away anyhow to give it a try.

"I'll do it for you," Diane Waring said, following after him. Diane taught English, but she could handle any machine ever invented.

"Tell it, Dietz," Coogan said, "the Zsa Zsa Gabor one. Come on."

"Give it a rest, Coogan," Dietz said. "Holy fucking Christ."

There was silence for a moment. Dietz was prone to wild shifts in mood, and it was never wise to push him.

"So what's up?" Miles said to Coogan. Nobody had mentioned Billy Mack. Did they know? "What's the gossip?"

Coogan was saying nothing. His feelings were hurt and he was not going to talk.

"None?" Miles looked around the table. "No gossip at all?"

"Zilch," Kathy said. "This is Malburn, you know."

"What about the team? Did we win Saturday?"

"Well, there *is* gossip," Dietz said. "Scandalous, too." Slowly he lit another cigarette. "Coach showed up sober for the game."

For a moment nobody said anything, and then Kathy broke the silence. "God, Dietz, that's really low." Suddenly everybody got interested in coffee, and Kathy said, "I'm gonna have another raisin danish. Anybody want a pastry?"

"Well, we won a game for once," Dietz said. "In fact, we won by six points. Thanks to Ciampa."

Miles said nothing. Evidently they didn't know about Billy Mack. The incident, as Endicott called it.

"Good for Coach," Kathy said. "He's a great guy."

"Right."

"Right."

"He's a mess, really," Miles said, and immediately wished he hadn't. Why should he join Dietz in being ugly? Dietz thought he had the right to show contempt for everybody's alcohol problem because he himself had had one and licked it. What an asshole. Only somebody as gross as Dietz would make a joke about Coach. But of course Dietz would sell his soul for a joke. Which was appropriate, Miles said to himself, since that's all it was worth. What a case *he* was. Unhappy, frustrated, surviving on coffee and nerves. A mess.

The Mafia came in, poured themselves coffee, and left. They were Nina Marchese, Tina Castiglione, and Frank Ferrugia—Nina, Tina, and Frank. It was like a bad joke. Nina and Tina were student counselors and Frank Ferrugia, the one certifiable idiot among them, was assistant superintendent. All three wore dark suits and they always traveled together, hence their nickname, the Mafia or, sometimes, the Kneecappers. Dietz stood up and toasted them, "Gentlemen!" when they came in, and again, when they left, he said, "Gentlemen." They nodded both times.

"And we wonder why the kids are screwed up," Kathy said.

Dietz found his good mood restored by the Mafia, and he lowered his head and shook his jowls so that he looked like Ferrugia. "Who do I shoot?" he said.

Everybody laughed except Coogan, so Miles leaned over and punched him lightly on the arm, but Coogan was having none of it. He was giving it a rest.

"Come on, Coogs," Miles said, but Coogs was still holding out, and just then Diane Waring came back into the room.

She gathered up her books, stood for a moment laughing si-lently—which made Miles say, "What? What?"—and then she said, "Kevin just told me this, and I shouldn't repeat it, but I've just got to. It's a Deirdre story."

"Deirdre!" Miles said. "Terrific!"

Deirdre Forster was seventeen years old and, although she had skipped two grades, she was still in high school because her parents had wasted a lot of time in negotiation with other schools. She had been thrown out of Northfield and Andover and Beaver Country Day before her parents realized their folly and sent her to Malburn High, which cost them no tuition and where the tolerance level for Deirdre seemed quite a lot higher. The problem was that Deirdre had a gift for language, and she said anything to anybody, in words that were often exquisitely right. More than a few of the faculty were terrified of her.

"Poor Kevin," Diane said. "You know how Deirdre gets just before the bell rings—she goes around greeting all her friends and cheering up the lavatories and redecorating her locker, until the spirit moves her to come to class. Well, on Friday, she came twenty minutes late to Kevin's class—they'd already finished the daily quiz—and the usual thing happened: Kevin asked for her pass, she didn't have one, he told her to go get one, she told him that if he wanted one he should go get it himself, and it ended up with Kevin telling her to go to the office immediately. Usually she just says, 'I won't go, and you can't make me,' but this time she stood up and waved her hand airily and said, 'Nothing would please me more than to go to the office . . . and tell them what a complete asshole *you* are.' And off she went." Diane laughed and so did Miles. "Poor Kevin," she said.

"Poor Deirdre," Dietz said, and that made everyone laugh, though nobody was sure why.

"I've got to go," Diane said. "Bye, Miles."

"What? I'm not here?" Dietz said. "I'm invisible? A hundred forty pounds of quivering malice and I'm invisible?"

"Bye," Miles said, smiling.

"I didn't mean . . ." Diane began, her face flushing. Then she shook her head in that way she had, muttered, "You guys," and left the room.

They all laughed.

"She's hot for you, Miles. She's after your body, what little there is of it."

"You're sick, Dietz."

"He's right, for once," Kathy said. "Diane is mad for you, Miles. Really. She's sort of pretty too, don't you think? That gorgeous red hair? If she'd just *do* something with it, take it out of that damned bun." Kathy fluffed her own short hair. "What's it like, Miles, being pursued by all these women?"

"Come on." Miles shook his head, just like Diane, and everybody laughed—even Coogan—as if they had proved something.

"Tell that joke now, Dietz," Coogan said, "quick, before the bell rings."

At once the warning bell rang—ten minutes to homeroom—and everybody cleared away the coffee cups, picked up their book bags and papers, and in a moment Miles was the only one left.

So. Diane Waring was hot for his body. His ridiculous body. He'd have to tell Margaret.

And nobody knew about Billy Mack's rape or his hysterical mother or the stitches holding his krogies together. Poor Billy. Endicott had managed it somehow, swept it all under the carpet, and had sobered up Coach into the bargain. How had he pulled it off?

Miles chugged the rest of his coffee and was just getting up to go when Jeff Douglas, his face white with anger, threw the door open and looked wildly around the room.

"It's just me," Miles said. "I'm it. I'm the whole audience. And I'm about to leave."

"That bitch," Jeff said, "that miserable, tight-ass, mean-faced cunt of a bitch."

"Cunt of a bitch," Miles said, repeating the words slowly, analytically. "Well, that localizes the problem. Is it our esteemed Endicott you're invoking?"

"Diane," Jeff said. "*Your* friend, Diane. Do you know what she's done now? Do you know what she just said to me?" He waited for an answer. "I'll tell you what she said. She said, 'I'd advise you for your own good to look for a job elsewhere. I don't see how I can recommend that your contract be renewed.' Can you believe that? And do you know why? Do you know what her reason is for not renewing me—even though I'm the best English teacher in this motherfucking place? I'll tell you why. Because she has 'grave doubts' about my professional judgment. Grave doubts. *Her* grave doubts. Who the hell is *she* supposed to be, Madeleine Hunter?"

"Who's Madeleine Hunter?"

"*I* happen to have written a novel, for Christ's sake, and I've got a publisher who's very interested in it. I went to fucking Harvard. I'm the most successful teacher *in* this hellhole. And she has grave doubts about my professional judgment? It makes me laugh. Ha!"

"Diane left here just a minute ago. She said all that in a minute?"

"What're you saying, Milo? I'm lying?"

"I'm just marveling at how fast she must have talked."

"What she said, as a matter of fact, in that tight-ass voice of hers, was 'Please see me after school, Jeff, *after* you've read my note.' The bitch. The note was just a copy of last spring's evaluation."

"So, in fact, she didn't say anything except that you should see her after school."

"She's out to screw me and I'll tell you why. Because I'm the real thing and she's just a fake. She can't stand having somebody around who's really in touch with the kids and who knows what they need and what they want. I know how to *talk* to those kids. That's what she can't stand—having a *real* professional around who makes her look bad."

"This is too complicated for me," Miles said, and slung his book bag over his shoulder. "I'm jes a simple ol' high school teacher. Besides, I've gotta make a phone call."

"Sure, *you*'ve got tenure. You've got everybody's sympathy because of your mother, *and* you've got fucking tenure besides. You don't give a shit about anybody else."

Miles turned away from him and started to the door.

"Don't you dare turn away from me."

Miles paused.

"You ignorant little Irish queer."

Miles stopped then, and rounded on him. "Jeffrey, you are an immature, self-important, self-deluded Harvard . . . novelist. Which is to say that you are irrelevant to me and to my life. But when you call me an ignorant little Irish queer, it makes me want to crush you, like a gnat. And I'll do it, if I have to, if you make me. So stay out of my life. Got that?"

Jeff stared at him, astonished.

"You disgust me," Miles said, and closed the door quietly behind him. He went to the office to phone about his mother.

The bell rang for homeroom.

Endicott was concluding his little blackmail talk to Hacker, Tuna, Cosmo, and the two others, and he was feeling satisfied. They were on the run, they had the proper hangdog expressions, and there was no suppressed laughter that would surface as soon as he turned his back. They knew this incident had landed them all in deep kaka.

He had been right to get to the parents first and to come down hard on them. And he had been smart to handle Billy Mack's parents the way he did; that redneck father could now be counted on to keep the matter quiet. But it was only after he had phoned Miles in the middle of the night, and Miles had been such an uncooperative little shit, that he had thought of this double-bind: use Miles and these five kids against each other and guarantee silence forever.

"I'm not going to make any kind of threat to you boys; I'm not even going to raise my voice. I just want to point out—quietly but clearly, so you'll remember my words—that what you're guilty of is a felony, a crime punishable by a lengthy term in . . . jail. It means that you'll have a record, that jobs you'll want—in the post office, the police department, any federal agency—are closed to you forever. It means your parents will never be able to hold up their heads in this community again."

He paused and the boys shuffled their feet; he had, of course, kept them standing.

"You understand that, I see. Now let me be clear on this most important point: what you're guilty of is provable in a court of law. It wouldn't be your word against Billy Mack's. There was a witness."

Cosmo stood with his head lowered and the others shot glances back and forth at each other.

"Mr. Bannon is that witness—Cosmo Damiani can verify that for you if you have even a moment's doubt—and Mr. Bannon is fully prepared to testify in court. So you see, you're not just accused. You've already, in a sense, been found guilty." He paused, three beats. "However, I have no intention of ruining your future lives because of this one great mistake. Nor, frankly, is it in the interest of Malburn High to have this unfortunate incident appear in the newspapers. So I have spoken to Mr. Bannon about this and I have secured his silence. And now I want to be very clear with you."

He stood up.

"I am prepared to forget this incident ever occurred . . . unless, of course, it somehow gets out and becomes public. If it becomes public, gentlemen, then—we had a saying in the army—then your ass is grass. I won't lift a finger to keep you out of jail." He paused. "If, on the other hand, it remains buried, forgotten, then I too will forget about it."

He sat down. "Am I clear?"

All five of them nodded solemnly.

"There will, of course, be an appropriate punishment for each of you. I will look into that matter later in the year. For the time being, this incident has never occurred. You may go."

They filed out, not even daring to look at one another.

Miles was on his way to the office to phone the hospital and check on his mother. He was still shaking from his encounter with Jeff Douglas, and as he passed the five boys, he blushed and lowered his eyes, as if—absurdly—he were the guilty one.

Billy Mack was coming out of the first-floor men's room when he heard someone call his name. He looked around, but the corridor was empty. "Billy," he heard again. He walked to the stairwell, and there, halfway down the stairs to the basement, he saw Coach beckoning to him.

"I've got a pass," Billy said, and held it up—a little red plastic square that showed a student had permission to be in the halls during class time. But he could see that Coach didn't care whether or not he had a pass. For once Coach didn't look drunk. He was gray. He looked dead.

"I've got to talk to you, Billy."

Billy shook his head, no.

"Please." His voice broke. "Please, Billy."

Billy looked around, hesitated, and then he went down the stairs and stood next to Coach. "What?" he said, and his voice was hard.

"Billy, I'm so sorry," Coach said. Tears started from his eyes and he threw his arms around the boy, clutching him to his chest. "I'm sorry. I'm sorry."

For a second Billy began to surrender to the tears and the embrace, but only for a second. He pushed against Coach's chest, whispering, "Let go of me. Let go of me." Coach understood finally and released him. And Billy, half blind with fury and contempt, leaned into him and said, "You bunch of faggots. You fuckers. You rotten fuckers!"

Billy began to tremble and he tried not to cry, but suddenly everything went black and, where Coach should have been, there was only a shimmering gray outline of a man. Billy blinked, but his vision would not return. He felt a hard vein pulsing in his head and he couldn't think. He wanted only to plunge a knife into that shimmering gray outline till it ran red with blood. He turned to go up the stairs, but he could not see and his legs would not support him. He leaned against the banister and sank to his knees on the basement stairs. Slowly he curled up in a ball, silent, as Coach stood above him with his hand outstretched, afraid to touch him, afraid to offer help.

At this moment Miles was coming down the stairs from the second floor. He was feeling high-spirited because he had just conducted a lively discussion of "Miniver Cheevy" and it had gone very well. He was reciting the poem to himself as he descended the stairs.

Had he turned his head a few inches to the right, he would have seen Billy Mack crouched on the stairs below him and Coach leaning over the boy, afraid to help and afraid to leave him. But Miles was still caught up in his class discussion and, staring straight ahead, full of bounce, he said aloud,

> He wept that he was ever born,
> And he had reasons.

He went to the main office to phone the hospital.

It was now the period before lunch and Miles was prefecting study hall. Most of the kids were hitting the books, or pretending to, and Miles was more amused than annoyed by Mark Russo and Michelle Stein who held hands across the aisle while they studied, so it was a nice time to take a breather and correct a few mini-essays. He called them mini-essays to flatter the kids into writing them. In fact they were paragraphs, and damned short ones, too.

He had taught two good classes on Edwin Arlington Robinson this morning, and they had left him feeling nice and high, but his third-period class in composition had brought him back down to earth. Comp was always a problem. He began to plow through the stack of papers, paragraph by paragraph. Comp was *definitely* a problem.

Now, a half hour into study hall, Miles pushed aside his papers and looked around at the kids, a cross-section of Malburn High: a couple of goof-offs, a loser here and there, the president of the Senior Class, half the girls' basketball team, two of the ten blacks in the school, one of the Puerto Ricans, a few guys from track, Jeannie Adams who wanted to be a fashion model and certainly had the looks for it, and a whole lot of semi-anonymous, hard-working, good-looking kids. They were a really nice crowd.

Then, from the back of the room, in the last seat in the row near the windows, he saw Billy Mack staring at him. No emotion on his face. Just that intense look the kid had so often fixed on him last year in English class. Flustered, he smiled at Billy and nodded, but Billy just looked back at him, expressionless.

Miles returned to correcting his paragraphs, though he had trouble concentrating until he hit Lombardi's—a lulu on using AIDS for population control—and then finally the study hall was over. Everybody began talking at once, and slamming desktops, and charging for the corridors. Mark Russo and Michelle Stein, still holding hands, were making their way slowly out of the room, silent, staring into each other's eyes. From the corridor came the crash of metal on metal as the locker doors were slammed, and slammed again, kicked open, slapped shut, punched and counterpunched, in the continual effort to ring as much noise from them as possible.

Miles had long since learned to live with the locker noise and he used these few minutes of shouting and slamming and frantic movement to finish corrections on one of his little paragraphs. "Terrific," he said aloud, piled up his papers, and shoved them in his backpack. He stood up and looked around the empty room and only then did he notice Billy Mack standing at the door.

"Billy," he said. "Hi."

Billy left the door and came to stand in front of him, his eyes lowered. He opened his mouth to speak, but nothing came out. He had the look of a condemned man.

"How're you doing, Billy?" Miles said, and put his hand on Billy's shoulder. "You all right? Are you okay?"

Billy flinched and Miles withdrew his hand.

"I don't know what to say, Billy, except I'm really sorry about what happened."

"My mother said you wanted to talk to me."

"Sure," Miles said, swallowing. "If you want to talk? Sure."

Billy shrugged and looked down.

Miles could see he was in agony. He wanted to put his arms around the kid and tell him it was all right, he should just cry, just let it out. But, for all his history of imprudence, Miles knew that you never—underlined—*never* hugged a kid.

"Look, Billy, you don't have to talk with me. Why don't you talk to one of the counselors? That's what they're for. And maybe you'd feel more comfortable with one of them than with me. Okay?"

Billy took a step toward him and, fighting back tears, he said, "Last year in class, did you . . . ?" But the tears started, and he raised his hands to his eyes. At that moment, of course, the door swung open, banging the wall, and that idiot Polcari came charging into the room. He looked scared, but his face cleared and he smiled as soon as he saw Miles.

"Hey, Milo. How're you doing?"

"Not now, Polcari. Would you mind staying outside?"

Polcari looked over at Billy and then back at Miles. He went white. "Hey," he said, and pointed to Billy. "Is he all right?"

"He's fine, Polcari. And I'm fine. And you'll be fine if you just get your miserable behind out of this room."

"My lunch," Polcari said, moving toward his desk, his attention fixed on Billy the whole time. He got his lunch, held the paper bag toward Miles, and said, "See?"

Billy walked quickly from the room.

"Geez, Milo," Polcari said. "He was *crying*."

"Get out of here, Richy. For Christ's sake, just get out!" Miles grabbed his backpack and took off for the principal's office.

Once again Endicott stood at the window overlooking the front entrance to the school, his hands braced on the window ledge, ignoring the person behind him. It was a posture he was famous for; it meant he was furious. Right now he was furious at Miles.

During the daily announcements he had had Miles paged, and then during each of the morning classes he himself had said over the intercom that Mr. Bannon should report to the principal's office, and finally, during study hall, he sent a boy with a note summoning Bannon to his office at once. Now, during the first of the two lunch periods, Bannon had the gall to show up without an apology, an excuse, or any sign that he realized he was in deep kaka.

The principal turned and faced him.

"I'm glad you finally found the time to come and see me," he said, his voice rich with sarcasm.

"I'm a teacher—I was in class. And then in study hall."

"I summoned you. How did you know it wasn't an emergency? Or something about your mother?"

"Because I phoned the hospital between each period. I knew my mother was all right."

This was too much. "You mean you were out in that office"— he pointed to the reception area, beyond his door—"using the phone to call your mother, and you chose to ignore my repeated . . ." He cut himself off. About-face! No point in expending ammunition on the wrong target.

"It's about the Mack incident," he said, his voice calm. "The boy is back in school. He's had a few stitches, but he's fine. He's doing very well. I've spoken to his parents, as you know, and to the parents of the boys involved—good boys, very promising. No sense injuring their futures by letting any of this get out. Everybody— everyone without exception—has agreed it's better for all concerned to just keep this incident quiet. No teasing of the boy, no punishment for the others, and so forth, et cetera. The less said about any of it, the better. And nothing in the papers. Do you see?"

Miles looked at him.

"You understand, Bannon?"

"It's your incident," Miles said. "I'm sure you're dealing with it as you see best."

That was good, but not the guarantee he'd hoped for. "I'm thinking of *you* as well, Bannon. If you see what I mean."

Miles gave a half-smile. He didn't see.

"It would be hard, it would be . . . difficult . . . if you had to explain how it was that you witnessed the incident."

"I didn't witness it. I heard the noise and I found Billy Mack lying there."

"But you know how people are. They'll wonder how you happened to hear the noise and why you did nothing to interfere. The question will be, Why did you let this happen?" He paused. "Isn't that right?"

"You *know* how I heard the noise. Faculty lockers are right next to the boys' lockers, and you can very easily hear when they're roughhousing. And that's why I did nothing to interfere. I thought it was just teenage horseplay. You *know* that."

"*I* know that, of course. But you know how people are. Someone is bound to ask, If you thought it was just teenage horseplay, why were you snooping around in there after you thought they all left?"

"That's not how it was."

"But someone is bound to ask it. What were you doing, at five o'clock, in the boys' locker room?"

"Okay, let's stop all this crap," Miles said. "What is it you want from me? You want me to promise I won't talk about this in class? I won't. You want me to promise I won't put it in the newspaper? I won't. If the best thing for Billy Mack is to keep this thing quiet and let those five rapists off scot free, then go ahead and do it."

"Very good. Very good. Then you see my point."

"But *don't* try to blackmail me into silence in this sleazy way. I'm clean as a razor. You don't have a prayer."

"Blackmail is scarcely a word I'd ever use, Miles. I was merely trying to point out to you what people would think."

"They'd think I was hanging around locker rooms to watch teenage boys undressing? That's what they'd think?"

"Now, now. Why do you take everything to extremes?"

"I know the families of these kids a lot better than you do, Endicott, and I can assure you *they* don't think that way."

"Let's get back to the issue, Miles. I was urging you not to mention the incident to anyone because that is what the boy wants, and what the family of the boy wants, and because, as you yourself see, that's the best thing for the boy."

Miles moved in close and jabbed Endicott's lapel with his index finger. "Don't *ever* try to blackmail me like that again," he said, and walked out of the office.

Endicott watched him go and then, a little unnerved, he turned to look out the window. Miles Bannon was a talented teacher, maybe, and he had a lot of home troubles, certainly, but the U.S. Army would see him in a different light. Besides the insubordination, they'd see there was something peculiar about him, something soft and a little bit feminine. He was emotional. He was one of those artsy bachelors addicted to movie gestures, like that ridiculous jabbing with his finger. He was very possibly a closet queer.

But, to be fair, he was good at his job. The kids learned something. The parents were crazy about him. He was very, very articulate. Nonetheless, Miles Bannon would bear watching. And if he ever got anything on him, anything that would stick, old Miles could just bend way over and kiss his ass goodbye.

Upstairs, in the corridor outside Dietz's homeroom, the horseplay was just beginning. It had started simply enough. Polcari was going through the doorway where a bunch of the Roid Boys were standing and Hacker turned suddenly and bumped into him, hard, and Polcari had said, "Hey!" a high, girlish, complaining sound that made them laugh. "Hey!" Hacker said, and then Tuna said, "Oh you!" and slapped Polcari's chest with a limp, open hand. "Meanie," Hacker said, and he too slapped Polcari. They laughed loudly, and everybody around them laughed, and so they did it again. "Hey!" one said, and "Mean thing!" the other one said, more girlish and more exaggerated this time, and then the horseplay began in earnest.

It was safe enough, because homeroom hadn't yet begun and besides, they had seen Dietz step into the bookroom for a quick cigarette. They had at least ten minutes for a good time with the Polecat.

"Mean thing!" Hacker slapped Polcari harder.

"Hey!" Tuna slapped Polcari harder still.

"Meanie!"

"Hey!"

Polcari pulled away, but they followed, slapping at him till he made a break for it, running down the aisle between the desks to the door at the front of the room. But there he was confronted by two other Roids just waiting for him.

"Oh, he's so fresh!" one of them said, and punched him on the arm.

"Fresh thing!" the other said, and punched him harder.

Polcari stood for a moment, looking from door to door while they punched him, and then he ran across the front of the room and down the aisle to the center.

Swiftly, silently, with no need to plan, Hacker and Tuna peeled off and took the far corners of the room. Now there was no exit. They began slowly to close in on him. Nobody was laughing, and the four began to shout to each other in order to get through this.

"He's looking dangerous," Hacker said.

"He'll scratch our eyes out."

"Here, kitty, kitty. Here, kitty."

"Here, pussy, pussy."

This made them howl with laughter. "Here pussy, pussy," they were all shouting, and then the bell rang for the start of study hall.

The other kids began to drift into the room, so two of the Roids just stopped and wandered out to the corridor to get their books, but Hacker and Tuna closed in on Polcari. Hacker grabbed him around the chest and pulled his arms behind him and held them there while Tuna, not knowing what to do, just looked on. But then he was inspired, and he opened the desk nearest him and pulled out a felt pen. "Pussy, pussy," he said. "Nice little pussy polecat," and while Hacker held Polcari's arms behind his back, Tuna drew long blue whiskers on Polcari's face, crooked ones because Polcari kept fighting him, twisting his head away.

"Dietz's coming," somebody shouted, and Hacker and Tuna let

go of Polcari and made a dive for their seats. Kids started slamming lockers and others tossed their books around—onto their desks or onto the floor—and a few were opening desktops and banging them down just to add to the noise a little. Pretty soon everybody was seated and still there was no sign of Dietz.

It was Cosmo Damiani who had shouted, "Dietz's coming." He hadn't been able to think of any other way to make them stop, and he couldn't endure it, and he couldn't go away.

Dietz came out of the bookroom then, and seeing Miles coming up the stairs, gave him a thumbs-up sign. He looked around the corridor and saw that for once there were no kids still loitering; just Cosmo Damiani, who was bent over on one knee rummaging through his locker. "Get a move on, Cosmo," Dietz said, and moseyed into his study hall.

When Miles reached the top of the stairs, he paused for a second and thought of saying something nice to Cosmo, but he had just phoned the hospital again and could think only of his mother, who was the same—not really alive and not really dead—and he couldn't think of anything to say. Besides, Cosmo looked as if he was burrowing into the damned locker, so why bother him? Miles went down the corridor to his last class, in American Lit.

In study hall Dietz flipped through a pile of papers and then glanced around to see who was absent and then he strolled to the window and looked out.

Polcari sat motionless, staring at his hands. He felt wet and cold and his shirt was sticking to him, but he had lived through it, it was almost over. There were giggles, of course, and kids kept sneaking looks at him, until finally Dietz turned from the window and noticed what was going on.

"For God's sake, Polecat," he said, "go and wash those whiskers off your face. You look like a clown."

Polcari got up and left the room, and it was over.

It was two o'clock and Diane Waring had been waiting a full half hour for Jeff Douglas to show up for his appointment. As English chairperson, it was her job to write quarterly reports on new teachers and, at the end of three years, to recommend tenure or dismissal. A final decision depended on others—the principal, the superintendent, the School Board—but the process began with her.

This was the one part of the job she really hated: sitting down with a teacher to tell him yet again that he was doing unsatisfactory work. Actually, in Jeff's case, the work was more than satisfactory; it was Jeff himself who was the problem. He was completely lacking in professional judgment.

Already this year—and they were barely five weeks into it—Jeff had told Cosmo Damiani that he was so full of shit his eyes were turning brown; he had asked Michelle Stein not to sit near the window because the light came right through her head and caused a glare; he had called Mark Russo a dago—Mark Russo, no less, whose father was a member of the Family and could have Jeff terminated in less time than it took to apologize. These things were reported at home, and the parents called in, or sometimes they came in, and always it was Diane who had to deal with them. Jeff had no sense, no professional judgment, and she had been unable to get him to realize this and do something about it.

Their interviews always followed the same worn track. She would explain the problem, give examples, and insist he at least watch what he said. He would claim he was a writer and therefore an exception, or the others were jealous, or there was no place for first-rate teaching in today's schools. And they would end where they began, with his insistence that he was above mere rules.

"I'm the best teacher you've got," he always said.

"You're a very good teacher," she would say.

"I'm the best."

"No, as a matter of fact, you're not. There's Miles, and there's Ellen, and Pat, and Susan, and there's a number of people who have equal success in the classroom. And, in addition, they have good professional judgment. They know—and you should know—there are things a teacher simply does not say. Or do."

"I'm unconventional. I get right to the kids and they respond to me. That's why the others are jealous."

"Jeff. You're very bright. You're very good with *some* of the kids, but . . ."

"I happen to have written a novel! I happen to have a publisher who is very interested in it!"

"But you cannot make jokes about one student in front of the others, and you cannot insult them. These students are people, they have *feelings,* and you cannot ridicule . . ."

And at this point Jeff would walk out or fall silent or cross his arms in front of his chest to block her out, this stupid, tight-assed, jealous woman.

That was the invariable track their interviews followed, but this one would be different. She had rehearsed what she would say to him when he arrived. *If* he arrived. She would be brisk and professional. She would be firm. She would lay out the facts for the last time—he was to shape up or else—and then she would call an end to the session. None of his pouting, this time. No claims to superiority. No novels and interested publishers. This time, as Endicott liked to say, his ass was grass.

The minutes ticked by and Jeff failed to appear. She had papers to correct, classes to plan, book orders to fill out, but she could concentrate on nothing. Where in hell was he? Gossiping about her somewhere, probably. Down in the men's room, telling them all she was tight-assed and mean. She stood up and ran a hand from her waist down over her buttocks. She tried to relax. Tight-assed, indeed. What infuriated her most was his freedom to say anything he liked about her and about his tenure case, whereas she was obliged to confidentiality. She could not even defend herself. It was maddening.

Finally the two-thirty bell went off, the end of the school day, and immediately there was the slamming of desktops, lockers being kicked and shaken and banged, shouts up and down the corridors, whistling, cursing. It sounded more like a jailbreak than the end of the school day. And still no sign of Jeff Douglas.

She waited until the corridors cleared a little and then went down to the main office. She would check for messages and pick up the Xeroxed sheets for her department meeting, and she would put Douglas out of her mind until she actually had to deal with him. Fuck him, she thought.

Endicott came out of his office as Diane entered the reception area. There was a divider with a nice wide countertop that separated the secretaries' desks from the waiting area, and Endicott leaned across it eagerly for a little chat with Diane.

"Everything going well?" he asked. "I don't get to see enough of you these days."

"I'm fine," she said. "Just getting my Xeroxes," and she scooped them off the counter and cradled them in her arms. "And—I suppose you should know—Jeff Douglas failed, again, to show up for his tenure conference."

But Endicott had other things on his mind. "No school gossip I should know? Just to protect my flanks?"

"So far as I know," she said, "your flanks are perfectly safe."

They laughed together, and the secretaries laughed, and then someone said, "Official merriment! Now that's a first at Malburn!"

Diane turned and there beside her was Jeff Douglas. She was determined to remain pleasant, just in case he had a legitimate excuse, and so she smiled. "You stood me up," she said.

"What do you mean by that?"

"We had an appointment at one-thirty this afternoon in my office. Remember?"

"One-thirty is my free period."

"That's why I asked you to meet with me *then*."

"Yeah. Well, I had something else to do."

"You might have had the courtesy to let me know."

"Why? Were you going somewhere?"

Diane looked at him, and then looked at Endicott, who winked at her as he disappeared into his office. She said to Jeff, "I want to see you in my office, please. Now." She turned smartly and started down the corridor. She could hear Jeff saying something to one of the secretaries and then there was a small burst of laughter. Her eyes stung but she kept looking straight ahead.

Miles was waiting outside her office door.

"Diane," he said, "could I be excused from today's meeting? I've got to get to the hospital."

She fumbled for her key and finally got the door open. "Yes," she said. "Of course. Is it your mother?"

"She's dying," Miles said, "she's in the hospital. I haven't mentioned it to the others. So I'd prefer . . . ?"

"No, of course not. I won't mention it to anyone." Tears sprang to her eyes, because she wanted to murder Jeff Douglas, and because she felt bad for herself, and because nice people like Miles had to cope with the long slow deaths of their fathers and mothers, and because it was all so unfair. "Take care of *you*, Miles," she said, and placed her hand on his cheek. She gave him a tight smile, and went quickly into her office.

Miles, near tears himself, went back to his homeroom to get his books. He was so absorbed in his thoughts that he failed even to notice Jeff Douglas, who all this time had been standing at the end of the corridor, watching.

Miles had used his free period to sketch out lesson plans for the rest of the week, just in case a substitute took over for him, and as he slipped the plan book into the top drawer of his desk, he felt the weight of all the make-up classes he would have to give. Time now in the hospital. Time future making up for it.

He stood at his desk, about to cram his battered Strunk and White into his backpack, when he looked up and saw Billy Mack standing just inside the door. He thought of Diane as she fought back tears, and of his mother who was dying in the hospital, and now here was poor Billy looking dazed and lost, and he would have a hundred make-up classes when all this was over, and it was all too much. He had nothing left to give.

Nonetheless, he did what he had to do. He sat down and tossed Strunk and White onto his desk. Hooking his foot around a chair leg, he pulled the chair toward him, indicated it with an open hand, and said to Billy, "Come on. Sit down."

Billy approached the desk, shifted from foot to foot, and then sat down. "Well, what?" he said, belligerently.

It was the same hostility Miles had fought all last year, but now it struck him as just a pitiful kind of armor. He could reach over and push it away, and there, beneath it, would be the real Billy.

"You don't have to fight me, Billy. I'm on your side."

"What's that supposed to mean?"

"It means that if you want to talk, you can. If you don't want to, you can just sit here for a while, and that'll be okay too. Whatever you want."

"My mother said you wanted to talk with me."

"No, that's not how it was. She asked me if I would talk with you, and I said yes, of course, if you wanted to."

"She said *you* wanted to." And, under his breath, he said, "That bitch."

"Well, I do want to talk with you."

"So?"

So now he would have to improvise. Miles leaned back in his chair and rubbed his face with his hands.

"Look," he said, and leaned toward Billy. "What happened to you was really awful. I mean, the physical pain must have been terrible, just . . . terrible, but my guess is that the sense of being humiliated is even worse. Right?"

Billy's face was a frightening red.

"I know. I know. It was a game or a practical joke and it got out of hand. Right? They were just giving you a hard time because they like you and because you're just one of the team, right?"

Billy said nothing.

"These things happen. Crazy things. It happens when you get a bunch of guys together, teenagers, and they're all hopped up with hormones and everything, and if somebody has a drink or two . . . well, these things sometimes happen."

"But why me? How come they did it to me?"

"Oh, Billy, it could have been anybody. You just were there at the moment they went a little crazy. You were a little smaller than the others. You were the nearest target. Who knows why? It doesn't mean they don't like you."

"My father thinks so."

"I'm sure he doesn't think that. I'm sure he doesn't."

"My father thinks . . . Shit, never mind."

Miles looked at his hands and forced himself to say nothing. He'd been through this kind of conversation before, where the student claimed he didn't want to talk, when in fact that was the only thing he wanted. Some time passed.

"Did you—last year when I had you for English—did you think I was . . . ?"

Miles felt himself getting red.

"What?" Miles said, talking fast. "Did I think you were the butt of practical jokes? Did I think you were being teased by guys on the team? Did I think you were—I don't know what—*gay?* No. Of course not. There's nothing about you to make anybody think that, Billy. Of course not."

Billy kept staring at his feet, but after a while he raised his head and looked at Miles, with that same cold and unforgettable look of hatred, but Miles saw now that it was only a mask.

"You think you know me," Billy said, standing. "You don't know anything about me. *You* don't know. What do *you* know?" And he ran from the room.

Miles stood looking at the door long after Billy left. What should he have done? What *could* he have done? He asked these questions silently, the responsible teacher. And he answered them: he had done what he could, he had done what seemed best, he was a responsible teacher.

But he found his pulse racing and he was strangely excited, because he saw unmistakably, and for the first time in his life, that someone was in love with him.

8

MILES SAT IN HIS EMPTY HOMEROOM thinking of Billy Mack. It was exciting to be loved, and shocking; there was something exposed and raw . . . a capacity to hurt . . . he couldn't find the words. And the preposterousness of it. He laughed softly to himself. Billy Mack! Who'd believe it?

He crammed Strunk and White into his backpack and started down to the office to make one last call to the hospital. As he passed the conference room, he glanced in and saw Diane Waring and Jeff Douglas going at it head to head, already, with a department meeting to follow. That poor woman. He'd prefer Intensive Care, thank you.

In the main office, Endicott's secretary pursed her lips and looked busy while Miles made his call. He asked about his mother, listened for a while, and then he said, "Are you sure?" and listened some more. "Bannon, Eleanor Bannon?" After a while he said, "Thank you," and hung up.

He stood with his hand on the telephone, just staring ahead, until the secretary said, "Are you okay?"

"My mother's a little better," Miles said, wondering how that could possibly be.

"Oh good," she said.

"She's out of Intensive Care."

"Well, that's good news, isn't it?"

He bit his lower lip. "Yes," he said. "I suppose."

"Well, you certainly don't seem very glad about it."

Miles heard the annoyance in her voice and looked up. She was indignant. She expected him to be happy about this, of course. But how could he explain that his mother wanted to die? She *needed* to die. She couldn't draw a full breath. She couldn't clear her throat. She couldn't cough. It wasn't life; it was an endurance test, and it ought to end.

"I'm going for a jog," he said coldly, and watched the secretary as she pulled back in shock. Good, he thought, she needed a good shock. He was furious at the fatuousness of the woman—what did she know about dying?—and furious at his inability to explain or even to understand the situation himself.

How could you not wish death for his poor mother when she was in such agony? And how could you not feel guilty about that? Guilt. Guilt was his daily bread. For not having been there for his father's death. For not loving his mother more. For not loving Margaret as much as she deserved. For not giving his students more of himself. He knew about guilt.

It was a different kind of guilt he felt for going to the Combat Zone last night; no, two nights ago. Why did he do it? What was he looking for? He thought of Ginger Fox and that huge black man saying, "You want black pussy? Boys?" and he saw himself later standing outside the Tom Cat Lounge, terrified to be seen. Again his pulse began to race as he thought about going in there. Having a drink in a gay bar. Just looking around. Maybe chatting with somebody, if they wanted.

He changed into his jogging clothes. He would refuse to think of any of it. Not the guilt, not the curiosity, not that new hollow feeling in his groin.

He began to jog, slowly at first, and then he picked up a little speed. It was cooler this afternoon, football weather, and though he was running on exhaustion, he felt loose and strong and knew he could hold out for quite a while yet. Billy Mack was in love with him. Who could have guessed that? He himself felt nothing for Billy, except a little pity, a little sympathy, an odd, hollow feeling. Poor Billy.

He increased his pace. He listened to the jolt of his heels on the pavement. He put his guilt behind him, and Billy Mack with it, and finally his mind just floated free. It was good to be alive and running, running, running.

9

AFTER HIS JOG, Miles had stopped for a quick drink with Diane Waring. They'd had more than one, actually, and so when he got to the hospital and asked the receptionist for his mother's room number, he tried to hide the smell of the booze by talking away from the glass partition instead of through it. "Bannon," he said. "Eleanor Bannon."

"That name again?"

"Bannon!"

"Bannon?" the receptionist said. "No need to shout. Bannon, Eleanor? Yes, she's out of Intensive Care. Are you Mr. Bannon?"

"Can I have her room number, please?"

She smiled patiently. She had a naturally pleasant face, round, and a perfect little smile. "*Are* you Mr. Bannon?"

Miles nodded.

"Before you go up, Mr. Bannon, you've got to check with Social Services. There's a yellow sticky next to her name that says so."

Miles nodded again. She waited. "All right," he said.

"Eleanor Bannon. That's 680 West."

"Thank you," Miles said. "I'll check with Social Services immediately."

It was nearly five o'clock, and the traffic had been bitchy, and Miles just wanted to see his mother. He started toward the bank of elevators.

"Sir?" It was the receptionist. "Mr. Bannon?"

He kept on walking.

"Sir?" she called after him. "You've got to see them in Social Services before you go upstairs. Sir?"

Miles came back to her desk. "Why?"

"Because you've got to." She smiled, satisfied now. "Right through there," and she pointed to a double door.

A man about his own age was waiting to ask her something and he seemed amused by Miles' predicament. He wore a dark suit with a tiny red carnation in his lapel, and his amusement made Miles more annoyed than he was already.

"Shit," Miles said to himself, but loud enough for them to hear, and then he went through the double door into a corridor of offices.

He found that he had passed suddenly from the world of the hospital to the world that ran it. It had a different look, a different smell, even. He could have been in the corridors of some stockbroker, with all their computers clicking away and people in dark suits looking harried. Like E. F. Hutton or Merrill Lynch. He smiled to himself because of course he had never been in the corridors of Hutton or Lynch or anybody.

He looked around and saw a large sign, Social Services, with a red arrow pointing to a door that stood open. Inside, a young woman in a gray business suit and pink tie sat poring over computer printouts.

"Yes?" she said, not looking up.

"The woman at the information desk insisted I see you *before* I could be allowed to see my mother."

"Name?"

"Bannon."

"Ah, yes, Mr. Bannon." Suddenly she looked up, smiling, and startled him with how very attractive she was. "Thank you for coming in." She waved her hand toward a chair. "Please," she said, giving him her full attention. "We want to know what you plan to do about your mother."

"Do about her?"

"Yes, what are your plans?"

"I'm sorry? I don't understand."

"Your mother is not dying. She can't stay here."

Miles stared at her.

"If she were dying *now*, we could keep her here. But she has ALS, and that by itself puts her in no immediate danger of death, and so we cannot justify keeping her."

"I thought hospitals were for sick people."

"For people who are sick and get well. Or for people who get sick and die. But not for the chronically ill. ALS, as you know, is a terminal illness, but it carries with it no fixed term." She sighed. "I'm sorry, Mr. Bannon, I know this must seem hard to you, but you've got to understand this is a hospital, not a nursing home."

"She was in Intensive Care until this afternoon, she can't *breathe*, and you tell me she's not dying on schedule? So you can't keep her?"

"With ALS, she could go on for months. We are not equipped . . ."

"I'll have to speak to her doctor. I'm afraid I fail to grasp the niceties of your argument."

"Yes, speak to her doctor. But whatever he says, I have to advise you that your mother will have to leave here in a day or two, three days at most. So you'll have to make plans for a nursing home, or for Home Help if you can manage that, but in any case, you'll have to take care of it. That's not something we look after."

"Yes, I'll speak to her doctor. Indeed I will."

"Now, I understand that you're from California, so I can have someone refer you to a list of local nursing homes. You can inquire about costs, and waiting lists, and so forth. And since you're from out of town, if your doctor makes a particularly strong case for keeping your mother on, then she might get an extra day or two."

Miles stared at her. He needed another drink.

"Anything else?" she said.

"I'm not from California. My sister is. I'm from right here. From Malburn."

"That makes it all the easier, then, doesn't it," she said, finished with the matter, and went back to her study of the computer printouts.

"Who *are* you?" Miles said.

Without looking up, she gestured toward a brass nameplate on the corner of her desk. Mrs. Orbach, it said.

"Thank you, Mrs. Orbach. Thank you very much."

"Not at all," she said, immune to sarcasm. "We're here to help."

"Sorry," Miles said, defeated suddenly. "Thank you."

Miles got off the elevator and turned left, following the arrow for rooms 670 to 700. He rounded the corner and there, in a tiny sitting area with two chairs and a magazine rack, sat the guy in the dark suit and the carnation. He had a briefcase open across his knees and he held a sheaf of papers in his hands, but he was looking straight at Miles. He was a lawyer, surely, with thin dark-rimmed glasses and a fifty-dollar haircut. Miles pretended not to see him.

He went down the corridor to room 680, directly opposite the nurses' station. Before he could even put his hand to the knob, a nurse behind him said, "Not just now, please," and when he turned around, she said, "She's having a bath or something. Personal things. You can wait right down there." And so Miles was obliged to return to the waiting area.

The man was still there, carnation and all. "Lots of bureaucracy here," he said to Miles, closing his briefcase and shifting it off his lap.

Miles didn't want to talk about it. He waved his hand dismissively, as if he were brushing away a fly.

"Sorry," the man said.

Miles looked up and saw that stupid red carnation. Yes, this shit would know bureaucracy when he saw it. He represented bureaucracy.

A nurse leaned into the alcove and whispered, "You can see the senator now, sir."

"Thank you," the man said.

Miles looked up then to watch him go, but he was still sitting there, looking at Miles. "Sorry," he said again. His eyes behind the glasses were pale gray and his mouth was thin and wide and Miles could see he was handsome in that lawyerish sort of way. "Okay?" he said, still looking.

"Sure," Miles said, "sure." He could feel his neck and face continue to go red even after the man had left.

"Hello, sweet thing," Miles said, "how are you feeling? Are you all right?"

His mother smiled, her face clear and untroubled, as if she'd not been in Intensive Care for three days but just having a good sleep. Miles kissed her forehead, smoothing back her thin white hair, and looked into her eyes. One was half-closed, he saw now, and she kept them open only with an effort.

"How are your eyes?" he asked. "Giving you a little trouble? You *look* very good."

But she didn't look good. She looked more wasted than before, she had less muscular control, she could no longer write. They had given her an alphabet board with the letters across it in a rainbow, like a Ouija board, and a list of words down one side—hungry, bedpan, blanket, bathrobe, too cold, too hot, I hurt, I feel fine—to save her the trouble of spelling out things she could just point to instead. And they had rigged up the cord for summoning help so that it ran diagonally across her bed; no matter what her position, she could raise her hand a few inches and let it fall, hitting the cord and setting off the alarm at the nurses' station across the corridor.

Miles took in all these things and realized just how precarious her life had become. That smooth, untroubled face was not a sign of health; it was a death mask, the skin pulling tighter and tighter on the bones. And they wanted her out of the hospital?

"Are you in pain, sweetie?" he asked.

She shook her head.

"But a lot of discomfort, right? With your throat? Your breathing?"

She pointed at the alphabet board, and he propped it up before her, and after she studied it a while, she placed her finger under "I feel fine."

"Heifer dust," he said, using her word for it. "You're just being brave."

She laughed soundlessly.

"Tigeron," he said. "Tigeretta."

Her eyes closed and, with an effort, she opened them again. She was barely hanging on.

"I love you, Mother. You know that."

Moving her finger slowly back and forth across the alphabet board, she wrote, "I want to go." He nodded to her, and whispered, "I know, I know." She wrote, "Now."

He placed his hand on hers and was quiet for a while until, sensing someone behind him, he turned. Margaret stood there smiling at him.

"I didn't want to interrupt," she said. She had brought Eleanor a present, a pale blue nightgown with an inset of ivory lace across the breast. "It's short," she said, "easier to get in and out of. It's your color, I think." She kissed Eleanor, held the nightgown up for her to see, placed it carefully back in the box. She stood behind Miles, her hands on his shoulders.

She's the perfect daughter-in-law, Miles thought. Too perfect?

With effort, Eleanor raised one hand to her lips and blew Margaret a kiss. "Lovely," she wrote, and then, despite herself, she closed her eyes.

"You rest for a while, Mother," Miles said. "We'll just be outside. You rest."

He and Margaret went out to the corridor, where he kissed her lightly on the cheek and held her in his arms. The nurse was watching them and so he said, "We have to talk. Come down here with me, Margaret. There's a little alcove here for waiting, and we can talk." And when they were out of earshot, he said, "You won't believe this. There's this woman in Social Services and when I came in tonight, she said to me, 'Look, your mother isn't dying, so she'll have to go. Now what are you planning to do with her?' I swear to God, that's what she said. 'What are you planning to do with her?' As if she expected me to say, 'We're gonna make a rug out of her,' or something."

Margaret smiled. "Miles," she said. "A rug!"

"I've got to pee," he said.

"We'll talk to Dr. Archer," Margaret said. "She'll simply tell them down there that Eleanor can't be moved. And that's that."

"I'll be right back," he said. "I'm bursting."

He rounded the corner, looked back to wave at her, and bumped against a man waiting for the elevator. "Sorry," Miles said.

"Sure," the man said, and put a hand on Miles' upper arm as if to steady him.

Miles saw the man's red carnation and felt the warm hand against his arm and, shaken, continued on to the men's room.

So, this guy was queer, probably. That's what all the staring was about, all that eye contact. Miles stared at himself in the men's-room mirror. Did he look like somebody who could be picked up? No, he looked straight. He *was* straight, goddamn it.

He peed noisily into the center of the toilet bowl, a satisfying masculine sound, and then he washed his hands and went back to talk to Margaret. But his arm still burned where that creep had touched him.

They were sitting by his mother's bed, silent, when Dr. Archer appeared and waved them out into the corridor. She talked for a while about Eleanor's condition, the failing muscular control, the very little that could be done to make her comfortable. They would be suctioning her throat regularly, for instance, and though it was irritating and made her gag, the suctioning would relieve the pain of breathing.

"The pain of breathing," Miles said. "God!"

"She's very good," Dr. Archer said. "She's very brave. Unfortunately, she's also very strong, and the ALS is simply wearing her out before it kills her."

"But in Social Services," Miles began, "they say she's got to leave. They say . . ." He stopped because Dr. Archer was shaking her head, vehemently.

"Mrs. Orbach? Mrs. Orbach wants this hospital empty."

"She's a mess," Miles said.

"She's good with computers," Dr. Archer said, "but she knows nothing about patients and she does not determine hospital policy. You can forget about Mrs. Orbach."

"So," Miles said, relieved. "She *is* dying then."

Dr. Archer frowned. "Yes, well . . ." she said, and touched the thin gold chain at her throat.

It was only then, with that feminine gesture of hers, that Miles realized she was dressed for dinner, that real life was still continuing somewhere out there. She had on a black silk suit and a white silk blouse with no neckline; it just fell in folds, draped like something you saw in pictures of Greek statues, very chaste and very alluring. She was going out to dinner with someone, a lawyer perhaps or another doctor, someone good-looking and exciting and—what? Full of life. Full of sex. Someone who would take her away from all this death and dying, all these suffering people and their ineffectual families with their boring insistence on what they wanted, what they needed, and never mind about the one who was dying. Ugliness, misery, and piss. Small wonder she would put a thousand dollars worth of clothes on her back and take off for an evening in an expensive restaurant and then to a crazy musical where nobody died except the people who didn't matter, or if the hero died, it was a sanitary death that allowed him to go on singing, on key, through one last reprise of the musical's Big Song. Why not escape? Why not run naked through the streets, fucking everything and everybody, Margaret and Diane Waring and that guy with the red carnation? Why go on like this?

Miles remained silent, his mind racing, long after Dr. Archer had said goodbye and he and Margaret were again sitting in that little alcove, waiting.

"What are you thinking?" Margaret said.

"I need a drink," he said.

"But you've had one, haven't you? Well, haven't you? Come on, now. Tell."

Miles pulled a face.

"I could smell it when you kissed me."

"One," he said, "right after school. After jogging."

"Alone?"

"What is this, an interrogation?"

"I just asked. I thought it would give us something to talk about."

"I thought we *were* talking."

"No, you were just sitting there looking fierce, and I was waiting for you to realize that I was still here."

Miles took a deep breath. Why was everybody trying to suffocate him? And now Margaret. She always wanted to help, she always wanted to do the generous thing, but in the end it came down to this kind of . . . grasping. This possessiveness.

"Let's go get you a drink," Margaret said. "It will pick you up."

"God!" he said.

But later, after his first scotch and while the second was on its way, Miles relented a little and told Margaret that, yes, he'd had a drink, two drinks actually, with Diane Waring. She was in a bad way with that damned Jeffrey Douglas. He was going to sue for tenure. He was going to take her before the School Board and, if necessary, to civil court. Diane was a good administrator and very conscientious, but she was young and inexperienced, and that son-ofabitch Douglas could make a lot of trouble for her. He felt bad for Diane, he said.

"Why don't we invite her for dinner?" Margaret asked. "I could fix a nice roast or a leg of lamb."

"No," Miles said. "It's just a work relationship. I just listen and try to sympathize. I don't want dinner with her."

The waiter brought Miles his drink and they remained silent until he was out of earshot.

"Whatever you want," Margaret said, and gave him that melting look of hers. "No pressure."

Miles sipped his drink, thought for a moment, and then leaned across to Margaret, smiling. They clinked glasses, Miles with his scotch and Margaret with water, since she wasn't drinking alcohol anymore. "You're wonderful," he said.

The corridor was quiet now, and it had been quiet for some time. Around eight o'clock, or eight-thirty, there had been a brief flurry of comings and goings with the senator down the hall, as people brought flowers and gifts and conducted pressing business, but it was ten o'clock now and deathly quiet, and still Miles and Margaret sat beside Eleanor's bed, watching, waiting.

At eleven the night nurse suddenly appeared in the doorway. She was fat and cheerful, with a take-charge air about her, and she said to them, kindly but firmly, "Go on home, you folks. We'll call if anything happens." Miles merely shook his head, not paying any attention to her, but she placed a finger under his chin and turned his face up to hers. "Look at you," she said. "You're exhausted. You won't know what you're doing soon. Go home. Now."

"I'm a mess," Miles said.

"You got it," she said. "You're a mess. You're a cute mess, but you're a mess just the same. So go home." She threw Margaret a wink.

Miles drove to Malburn and stopped at Margaret's for a drink. He poured a scotch and drank it standing at the kitchen counter, talking, while she sat at the table listening to him.

"She'll be waked at Downey's," he said. "She did that herself, arranged it, when my father died. Picked the casket. Paid for it.

Everything. She was a remarkable woman, really. I wish we hadn't fought so much." He reached for the bottle of scotch. "And I've written the obituary. It's short, but nice, and she'd like it, because I cut two years off her age."

"She'd like that," Margaret said, and her voice sounded so strange that Miles, who was about to pour another scotch, looked hard at her and saw that she was nearly unconscious. She was sitting rigidly in the chair, as if she were holding herself upright by an act of the will.

"Sweetheart," he said, "I'm sorry. I'm so sorry. Here, let me help you to bed," and he led her from the kitchen, holding her up as if she were ill.

"I'm fine, I'm fine," she said. "Please, Miles," and there was an edge to her voice, as if she might cry or scream. And so he kissed her goodbye and left her to get to bed by herself while he drove home and got ready for another day of waiting.

It was midnight, Monday going on Tuesday. It had been the longest day of his life. It seemed years since he parked his beaten-up Pinto in the school lot and went inside for coffee and some chat with the gang in the teachers' room. Nobody except Endicott had mentioned Billy Mack all day. It was as if the incident—that distancing, clinical word—had never occurred. Except for Billy, of course. Poor Billy.

Miles got into bed and pulled up the sheets. It was hot tonight. It had been hot all day, but this was the first time he had noticed it. Life was going by and he wasn't even noticing. His life.

He remembered the days when he used to pray in bed. If he were to pray now, he would pray for one thing: to stop. Just to stop everything and rest. But he was too tired to pray and so he closed his eyes and in less than a minute was deep in sleep.

10

MARGARET LOCKED THE KITCHEN DOOR and stood looking through the little window until Miles drove away. Then she put away the scotch, rinsed Miles' glass, and turned off the kitchen light.

It was three days now since she'd had a drink. Or a pill. She stood in the darkened kitchen and shook her head. Why? What was this in service of?—as Miles would say. Why not get the bottle and have a drink and keep drinking until she went unconscious? What was the point of living at all?

She thought of Eleanor, gasping and gargling for a sliver of breath, that wretched tube pulling muck up from her lungs. And for what? For another day of this kind of pleasure?

In the dark, she moved to the cabinet where she kept the liquor—underneath the sink, with the Drano and the Ajax and the scouring pads. Funny. She was exhausted, she was half crazy, but she was fully aware of what she was doing and what the consequences would be. It was not a drink she was after. It was oblivion. She would pour a tumbler of the stuff and drink it straight down like some awful medicine that nonetheless would do the trick. And it would. She'd have a glass of water to relieve the burning and then she'd pour another tumbler. There was no stopping. It was the same with the pills. She might break them in half, and chase them with a tiny bit of wine, but in the end she'd take the pills until she went unconscious.

But then—she had not the least doubt about this—then she would lose Miles.

She turned away from the sink and the liquor and went into the bathroom. She took the Xanax out of the medicine cabinet, first the bottle of thirty she kept in easy reach and then the Empirin bottle on the top shelf in the back where she kept the fifty she had hoarded over the past year. She could flush them down the toilet and be done with them—she smiled at the easy thought—but instead she brought them to her bedroom and put them in the middle bureau drawer beneath her slips. And then she went to bed.

But in a minute she was out of bed and in the bathroom. The lights were on and she was staring in the mirror, her eyes wide with terror or with madness. "You fucking whore," she said, "you no-good cunt." She leaned hard against the sink, then pulled away and banged her pelvis hard against the porcelain. The shock ran up into her breasts and down into her vagina. She struck the sink again. And again. "You whore," she said, and grasped her night-gown at the neck, tearing at it with both hands, until the front ripped open and it fell to her feet. Her belly was crimson and already there were bruises coming up. She pinched her nipple hard, the left one, and then she twisted till the pain was unendurable. Then she did the right one. "Pig," she said. "Come here. Come here," and she crouched on the bathroom floor, masturbating with her fingers, with her fist, on and on until her hand was slick and bloody. Then she lay there for a long time, dead.

She arose finally and took a shower and put on a new nightgown and went to bed. She thought of phoning Miles, to ask if she could come over and lie down beside him, just *be* with him, but she knew this was the sure way to lose him. She would be patient. She would do the right thing. She lay in bed, wide awake, looking at the ceiling and saying aloud to the empty room, "He's my salvation. He's my life."

11

ON TUESDAY MORNING, Miles decided to take action. His mother might last a week or even two weeks or she might go at any minute. The least he could do was be there for her, and he would. He may have failed at everything, all his life, but he would do this one thing right.

And so, at seven-thirty, he called the school and told Endicott that he would be taking sick leave today and tomorrow, and possibly Thursday, because his mother was dying and he had to be with her. Endicott was polite, and said the necessary things, but Miles knew that after he hung up, Endicott would say to his poisonous secretary, "That Bannon character bears watching." Miles hated giving Endicott ammunition like this, but he had no choice.

Choice. When did anybody have a choice about anything, really? In college they'd spent all this time talking about free will and purely free will acts, but what act, what choice, was not determined by a million other things: who your parents were, how much money they had, whether they were educated or not, or loved one another, or loved *you* for that matter. And then the more immediate, personal things like your brain power, how tall or short you were, whether you were built like Paul Ciampa or like poor Polcari, or—speaking of Polcari—whether you inherited any funny genes that guaranteed you were gonna grow up queer. Or how you felt about your wonk.

Miles was in the shower and he touched his wonk, took a look at it, and realized that the whole history of his emotional life was in that wonk or, rather, in his attitude toward it: shyness, embarrassment, shame, terror, and lately—a couple times—a feeling of power and pride.

There is no free will, he said to himself. But then why was he wracked with guilt? "Fuck it," he said aloud, and began the boring business of masturbating, not even bothering to fantasize about Margaret, since he was short on time.

And then he was out of the shower, in his car, and at the hospital, for another day of waiting at his mother's bedside.

At ten he had coffee in the cafeteria. At noon he went out to McDonald's, the one on Tremont Street, not the one in the Combat Zone. Then it was two o'clock. Miles stood in the corridor while they suctioned his mother's throat. After an eternity it was four. At six Margaret came, and they sat by his mother's bed, and smiled at her, and sometimes held her hand, trying not to tire her, but reassuring her that they were there, that she was not alone. And then it was eight, and they had coffee—decaf—and went back upstairs to Eleanor's bedside, where they sat silent while she drifted in and out of sleep, the breath hissing and then clotting in her throat.

At eleven, the night nurse came on duty, and this time Miles gave her his full attention. She was fat, with thick black hair and the trace of a mustache on her upper lip. She had a deep, full voice that made her seem worldly and comfortable.

"Oh, good," Miles said, "I'm glad it's you."

"Ms. Sheehan, R.N." she said, "but you can call me Angie, and listen, your mother's doing fine, she's getting great care here, so I want you home in bed, honey. You're beginning to look your age. What is it, twenty-five? You need some rest." She winked at Margaret. "You too, hon, even though you look great. If I had your figure, I'd take right off for Hollywood, honest to God."

That was his day. He had sat with his mother and talked with Margaret and listened to Ms. Sheehan, R.N. Angie. He had done nothing, thought nothing, felt nothing but the desire—no, the need—to hang on until the end. A purely free act of the will, he realized.

Wednesday was the same, waiting, waiting, as if the day could not officially end until Angie arrived and told them to go on home and rest. All this time, of course, his mother lay in bed rasping out her breaths, laying her hand on the emergency cord to summon the nurse, pointing with her finger to "bedpan" or "blanket" or "I'm fine." She too was waiting.

On Thursday his mother was no longer able to open her eyes. "We could tape them open for a few minutes," the nurse said, "but there's no point, really. You understand."

Miles stood by her bed and talked softly to her. Her face was gray now, and the flesh was tight on the bones. She must be in agony. Her head was tipped back as if she were freeing her lungs for a single last gasp. "Mother," he said, reassuring her. She gave no sign of recognition.

When they came to suction her throat, Miles went outside and paced. At the end of the corridor, turning to come back, he saw two men step from the elevator—the senator's boys, with their suits and briefcases. "Robert," the short one said, whining, "Robert, you're not being reasonable." Miles took a second look because the one called Robert—not Rob or Bob, mind you, but Robert— was the guy who had touched him on the arm. And with or without his carnation, he was indeed *très gai*. Miles lowered his eyes and continued to pace and almost at once forgot about him.

His mother was dying now, no question. He sat beside her, holding her hand, until they came in to suction her once again. It took longer this time, and when they left the room, they were grim. They said nothing.

But by noon she was breathing easier. She looked less gray. Her vital signs were better. She was alive again.

In the early afternoon the nurse asked her if she would like to see for a while, and when Eleanor nodded yes, the nurse set about taping her eyelids open. Carefully she grasped the upper lid, tipping it up from the eye, and with a small piece of transparent tape she secured the lid and lashes to the flesh above. "There," she said, standing back to assess her work. Then she did the other eye. "Ten minutes only, though," she said. "More than that isn't good." So Eleanor was able to see her son again, for ten minutes.

Miles had looked away while the nurse taped his mother's eyelids, but now that she could see him once again, he talked frantically, telling her about school, about Diane Waring's trouble with Jeffrey Douglas, about the kids—Muldoon and Ciampa and the infamous Deirdre. He exaggerated, he invented stories, he turned them all into characters, trying to make them interesting for her. His mother nodded and smiled, but finally she lay her hand on the emergency cord to summon the nurse. Tears had begun to flood her eyes and, above the left one, the tape had come undone.

"But wasn't that nice?" the nurse said, as she removed the tape. "We'll do it again, later."

Eleanor, with her eyes closed, nodded yes.

Miles lowered his head to his hands and cried silently.

And eventually Thursday ended.

On Friday morning Miles sat by her bed, praying. Let her go, he said. Let her go now. Minutes went by, and then what seemed like hours, and he told her he was going downstairs for a sandwich or something. Her head nodded slightly and he took that for a sign she understood. "I'll be back after lunch," he said. "I'll be right here." And again he prayed, Let her go.

He had forgotten to wind his watch and so he was surprised to see that the clock at the nurses' station said ten past ten. He had been here a little more than two hours. It seemed like five. Twenty. His whole life, waiting.

For a moment he could not remember what day it was. This must be what eternity is like, he thought, this suspension in time.

He drifted to the elevators, but instead of going to the cafeteria he went to the little chapel. It was not a Catholic chapel, there was no tabernacle and no host, but out of old habit, he genuflected and knelt down.

He set his mind to prayer, but nothing would come. Over and over he said to himself, Let her go, Let her go now, and then for a long time there was nothing—no feeling, no thought, not even any empty words—just nothing. Still breathing in and out, he had somehow ceased to exist.

Time went by like this, with his mind dead. Finally, he came alive and found himself thinking once again that the most terrible thing about dying is not the suffering, or the pain you can do nothing about, or the love lost, or the hurt that can never be undone, or the cold cold hand around the heart; the most terrible thing is the boredom. The eternal, everlasting boredom.

To the silent altar, he said, "What about me? When do I live?"

He listened to his voice echo in the empty place and then he got up and left, without genuflecting, and returned to wait by his mother's bedside.

At twelve o'clock, with the sound of food carts in the hall, he went down to the cafeteria for lunch.

At one o'clock he stood outside his mother's room while they suctioned her throat, deeply now, because her breathing was almost completely blocked; afterward he sat and held her hand.

At two o'clock he told her he had to leave for a while. He was going to school, he said, just to check in. But he would come straight back. He would be here beside her again this evening.

At three o'clock—only an hour later but an entire world apart—he was standing in the school foyer, nervous suddenly, and very excited to be here. Had he been gone for only four days? The trophy cases looked clean and new. The posters for The Habit of Reading had been changed; they now featured U-2 in place of Sting. Pep rally flyers were everywhere. And he had forgotten the afternoon smell of the place—floor wax and hairspray and sneakers. The secretaries were arguing in the main office, and as he went down the corridor he could hear the Xerox machine clunking away, and he passed two kids roughhousing at their lockers—"Hey, you two, cut it out," he said, and kept walking—and he could hear the team yelling down on the field. Nobody was dying here. This was his home. This was where he worked and where he belonged.

He went up the stairs to his homeroom. He intended to make out lesson plans for the coming week and then tell Endicott he needed another few days of sick leave. Endicott couldn't complain, really, what with all the work planned out and with Miles' record of perfect attendance, but it was a pain in the ass to arrange for substitutes and, besides, most of them couldn't even control a class, let alone teach it. But his mother was dying; what else could he do?

At the top of the stairs, but off to the side in a little alcove, two kids were wrapped in each other's arms, deep in a kiss and oblivious to the sound of Miles' feet on the stairs. He cleared his throat loudly, and—still kissing—they turned to see who it was. "Milo!" the boy said, and quickly pulled away from the girl who, skilled in these matters, turned her head so she could hide behind her hair. To his astonishment Miles saw that the boy was Muldoon, with his big mouse nose and that smile and his now very red face. "Mr. Muldoon," he said evenly. "I'm glad to see you don't have Detention today." He went on down the corridor, pleased with how he'd handled it.

Miles' lesson plans for the next week took him longer than usual, because you could never plan on a substitute understanding what you had in mind. Usually Miles filled in the block for Monday with something like "text study of Sandburg ("Chicago," "Grass," "Cool

Tombs'') and Frost (everything in text),'' and then just drew an arrow across the next four days to indicate he'd give each poem as much time as it deserved. And in the Friday block he'd write "Comp," because writing was a lost art and he was trying to help them find it. But he made the lesson plans for this coming week a model of clarity and direction. He wrote out what to do and why, what he wanted to communicate in each lesson and how he planned to do it, and what exactly it would accomplish as part of the education of the high school junior. When he finished, he sat back and looked at the lesson plan with the hostile eye of Endicott; even *he* would be impressed.

Miles was putting his plan book in the top middle drawer when he heard a door slam out in the corridor and then somebody kicked a locker, hard. There was a short angry shout—Kevin Foley, he thought—followed by the unmistakable voice of Deirdre Forster. Miles went to the door and looked out.

Deirdre and Foley stood near the stairwell, glaring at one another. She seemed to have finished telling him off, but then she added: "You're a simpleminded, bug-eyed, petty little cocksucking idiot."

"Go to the office," Foley said, "I want you to go to the office immediately."

"I'm not going to the office," she said, "and you can't make me." At once she disappeared down the stairs, shouting "asshole" over and over, so that it continued to echo in the stairwell even after she had gone. "Aaaas-ho-ho-ho-ho-hole."

Miles ducked back into the classroom and, leaning against the bulletin board, he laughed out loud. "Simpleminded, petty," he said to the empty room. Where did she get these words? He couldn't wait to tell Margaret.

As he drove back to the hospital, however, he began to feel an exhaustion so complete that he thought he might pass out at the wheel of his car. He smiled at the thought and kept on driving. He didn't want to go back to the hospital. He didn't want to start that eternal vigil all over again. He wanted to be Deirdre and say, "I'm not going to the office and you can't make me." At that exact moment, as he was merging with the traffic on Storrow Drive, a woman cut him off and he put his head out the window and screamed "Asshole" after her. It was very satisfying. "Asshole," he said to each car he passed. "Ass-ho-ho-ho-holes." He positively sang it.

As he entered the hospital lobby, the Information lady waved him over. "Social Services?" he said, and she nodded, surprised, when he turned abruptly and marched through the double doors to the Social Services office.

"Ah, how nice," Mrs. Orbach said. "Now, I wonder if you've come to a decision about what you'll be doing with your mother?"

"She's going to die and we're going to bury her," Miles said.

"Yes, of course. But—and I think I've explained this before—we are a hospital and not a nursing home. A nursing home is equipped to handle patients who will die on no fixed schedule. But in a hospital, we are not. Our concern . . ."

He let her finish her speech, and when she had finished, she sat back to wait for his response.

He said to her, "I am a thirty-five-year-old schoolteacher, and I am not given to harsh or vulgar language. But if I were seventeen years old, with an eye for the truth and a tongue to express it, I would say this: 'You're a simpleminded, bug-eyed, petty little cock-sucking idiot.' " He looked blankly at her. "But since I'm not like that, I'll simply say, 'Have a nice day.' " And he left.

He was still feeling jubilant as the elevator stopped at the sixth floor, and when he saw Robert about to get on, he smiled and said to him, "We've got to stop meeting this way."

Margaret was waiting for him at his mother's room. They sat together by her bedside, and later they had dinner and waited some more, and finally, at eleven, Angie arrived for the night shift, and sent them on home.

It was Friday, the end of the week, and his mother was still alive and they were all still waiting.

. . .

On Saturday they waited.

On Sunday they waited. In the early afternoon the nurse taped Eleanor's eyelids open. Miles and Margaret talked with her, and Eleanor responded by pointing to letters on her board. Then the ten minutes were up, and they all returned to waiting.

"Nothing lasts forever," Margaret said to Miles, as she kissed him good night.

"No," he said.

"I love you, Miles," she said.

Monday was sweltering. It was the end of September; nonetheless the day was muggy and wet and there seemed to be no air at all. Miles sat by his mother's bed and tried to fight sleep.

He had lain awake much of the night, partly because of the heat and partly because he was thinking of his mother. When she dies, I'll be free to marry, he thought. And he also thought, if I marry, I won't be free at all.

For the rest of the night, he tossed around in bed, wondering: was this what life had brought him to? The bird escaped and at once flew out in search of a cage? But think of all Margaret had done for him! Think of all he owed her!

This morning, sleepy and a little cross, he sat by his mother's bed and concentrated on being good company, at least. "I'm here, Mother," Miles whispered. Her breathing was thick and slow, painful even to listen to, and she made no sign of recognition. He put his hand on hers, but took it away at once. The day was too hot for touching anybody.

Her breathing began to sound worse. Her fingers twitched and she frowned, trying to open her eyes, and after a moment she raised her hand just enough to let it fall on the emergency cord. The nurse came at once, took a look at her, and immediately sent Miles to the corridor. He stood outside and leaned against the wall, his eyes closed, trying not to hear the sounds as his mother's throat was suctioned.

"Is that better? A little?" Miles said, and sat down again by her bedside. He was very sleepy, and after a while his eyes closed involuntarily, and he decided to rest his head on the side of the bed. Just for a moment. When he awoke, his mother's breath was only a rattling sound and she was moving her hand blindly on the sheets, barely able to lift it and let it fall on the emergency cord. Miles touched the cord for her and at once the nurse came. His mother had to be suctioned again.

The day dragged on slowly, and the heat and humidity seemed to get worse. There were sirens, and from the window Miles saw an ambulance tear out from behind the hospital. Then came a fire engine, and another ambulance. Maybe this relentless heat had set fire to the whole city.

It was late afternoon now and a slice of sun lay across his mother's bed. The nurse had taped Eleanor's eyelids open and, in sympathy, Miles blinked into the light and smiled at her. "Momoo," he said. "You're a trouper. You're very brave." Now that she could see, Miles came alive and began to talk. "Do you want your board?" he said. "Do you think you could use it?"

He placed the alphabet board across her lap and sat back to take a look at her. "Don't use that thing if it's too hard for you, Mother. Really. We can just talk. I will, I mean."

With effort she got her hand onto the board. She leaned over it, studying the letters for a while, and then she shook her head and sat back. "It's okay," Miles said. "Not to worry." She made another try at it. After a long while she pushed a finger up to the N, stared at it for a moment, and then moved the finger to the O.

"No," Miles said, following her. "No what?"

She looked at the board, confused, and then found the M.

"No M," he said. "No Miles? No money?"

She tried to frown.

"No machines? No machines."

She sat back, exhausted, satisfied.

"No machines, I promise you, Mother. Okay?"

She nodded a little. And then he lowered his head and put his hand on hers, closing his eyes to fight back the tears. He felt her hand move slightly and he looked up, startled.

Her breathing had stopped; it had become a low, soft, gasping sound. Her face was white, and her eyes, taped open, stared straight ahead in panic. She moved her hand weakly, trying to lift it to the emergency cord, but she had no strength left and only her fingertips moved up and down, tapping on the alphabet board. She made a small moaning sound and her fingers fluttered for a moment and then stopped.

Miles stared at her fingers and at the cord a few inches above them and he felt the terrible heat in the room. The sunlight from the side window cut across her bed and lit her hands and the cord as if a spotlight had been turned on them. Miles stared, and did nothing. His mother had stopped gasping, and now a choking sound came from her, and still Miles stared at her hands and at the cord.

Outside the window a bird began to sing. Two nurses were laughing softly in the corridor, and Miles could hear the rumble of some kind of hospital cart. It had one wheel that wobbled, he could tell. It was so hot and there was no air in the room. How could anyone breathe?

A small shadow passed through the light on his mother's hands—a bird on the windowsill?—and then it was gone. If he could go for a swim, or for a long slow walk by the ocean, that would be really nice. Past the yellow eelgrass, over the rocks, looking for shells. They had done that when he was little, when it was hot and the sun was blinding, like this.

He looked up at his mother and saw that she was staring at him, her eyes bright with determination, as once again her fingers moved helplessly, an inch from the cord now. Staring at him, breathless, she lifted her hand slowly in the air—almost touching the cord, brushing the underside of it—and then her hand fell, useless, on the alphabet board. Her eyes clouded and seemed to lose the power of sight. There was silence. And then a different kind of silence. Her head sank back upon the pillows, and Miles lowered his face to his hands. The light continued to fall across the bed.

So he had done it. He was suspended in time now, truly, caught forever in this moment. He would never leave it; this would become the still point of his turning world.

Mechanically, he stood up and, averting his eyes from the bed where his mother lay, he started out of the room to tell the nurse. But then he stopped, because Margaret was standing at the door, pale and silent. How long had she been there? She took him in her arms. "It's all right," she whispered. "Everything is going to be all right."

Before Miles could respond, the nurse came in and said, "Time to get the tape off those eyes, darling, or you're gonna have an awful headache." She removed the tape and applied lotion carefully around the eyes. "Now I'll fix these pillows, and try to get you a little more comfortable." She placed the alphabet board on the metal night table and then she straightened the bedclothes and plumped the pillows. "Now there," she said, "isn't that a little better?"

And, while Miles watched, his mother nodded her head and gave the tiniest of smiles. Impossibly, she was breathing again.

On Tuesday, Miles lay in bed scarcely able to move. He had drunk himself unconscious the night before, starting at Margaret's house and finishing the job at his own.

They had been silent all through dinner, and silent at night too, even when Angie showed up to send them home. And at Margaret's house, they had quarreled.

She was leaning on him, constantly, he said. She was always putting pressure on him. Why couldn't she understand that marriage was out of the question until his mother died?

He had a hefty scotch.

She wanted nothing, she said. She only wanted to help. He needed help right now and so did his mother and she was glad to give it, with no strings attached. And no pressure. How could he accuse her of things like that?

Because, he said, because.

He had another scotch, and Margaret came and sat near him on the couch, but not too near, and after a while he began to talk sense. He was crazy, he said, with worry and with exhaustion and with . . . well, everything. He was a crazy, hopeless bastard.

Margaret was not drinking, but she poured him one last scotch. Drink up, she said. You've got to survive this, and you will.

And so he got drunk at Margaret's house, and once he was safely home, he drank himself unconscious. That was Monday night.

On Tuesday morning, he awoke scarcely able to move, but with a very, very clear mind.

He had let his mother die, he had no doubt about that. He had watched her try to pull the emergency cord, he had seen the look of panic and desperation on her face, and though he could have summoned help with a mere tap of his finger, he had done nothing. He had sat there, waiting for her breath to stop. And now he would have to live with it.

But she had not died, he told himself. She was alive. He had not killed her.

Still, he knew what he had done.

Miles drove into the city, but before going to the hospital, he walked over to Arch Street and the Franciscan church. They were famous for hearing confessions at any hour of the day—or at least they used to, when people still went to confession—and Miles thought he'd just take a look and see how things were.

It was cool inside, and clean, with the smell of candles and old incense and something unidentifiable . . . holiness, perhaps. It had been a long long time since he'd been in church. He closed the door, and the place seemed darker suddenly, and he felt a huge sadness settle on him. He had come very far from his old innocence, from belief. Still, he was standing here, and that was something.

A few old women were seated far over in the side aisles, near the confessional booths. Miles gave them a look—what did they want, these women; what were they sorry for?—and as he watched, sure enough, a young man pushed aside the green curtain and came out of the confessional and knelt down. Immediately one of the old women ducked in.

So he could go to confession if he wanted to. It had been how long? Fifteen years? Longer? He recited the formula and had it right, more or less. Anyhow, the last time he'd been to confession, they weren't much concerned about formulas. They were just glad you came. No, Miles decided, he wanted none of it. He would handle his guilt by himself, thank you.

As he turned to leave, he felt a hand on his shoulder. "Excuse me," a priest said, and pointed to the door that Miles was blocking. It was a confessional door, with the green curtained booths on either side of it. The priest opened the door and flipped on the light, and for the first time Miles saw inside the priest's booth. It was like an upright coffin, very narrow, with a wooden bench from side to side. The little confessional screens through which you whispered your sins were blocked by wooden shutters the priest could slide back and forth, isolating one penitent while he listened to another. Miles was still staring into the confessional as the priest settled himself inside, and he was not prepared to have the priest look up at him suddenly and say, "Okay," cocking his head toward the confessional on the right, and then closing the door and putting out the light.

Miles stepped inside the confessional—it was utterly black inside—and at once tripped against the kneeler. "Shit," he said softly, and felt around for where he thought the confessional screen ought to be. There was a racket as the priest pulled the wooden shutter aside, and then Miles could make out a vague profile through the thick mesh screen.

"Yes?" the priest said, and Miles caught the smell of wine; from mass, probably.

"Yes," Miles said, "Yes. Bless me, Father, for I have sinned. It's—God!—about a hundred and fifty years since my last confession and these are my sins." He stopped.

"Yes?"

Miles said nothing.

"I gather it's a long time since your last confession, and you'd like some help? Is that it, now?"

It was hopeless. He could say nothing.

"You're a good man, you know, coming to confession like this." Miles could hear something British in his voice, a peculiar sort of cadence as he talked. British? Here? "It's not easy coming face to face with yourself, seeing your worst failings for what they are, and then telling somebody else about it, asking for pardon. Only good people do that. So you're starting off with an advantage, aren't you." He paused. "You're still there, are you?"

"I let my mother die."

"I see. Do you want to tell me more than that?"

"She's in the hospital, and above all she didn't want any extraordinary means taken to keep her alive, and yesterday . . . I . . ." Miles choked up for a moment, but eventually he got the story out.

"And she's still alive," the priest said.

"But that's not the point."

"Oh, I get the point. Intention is everything."

"Yes, and I don't know what I intended, but I know what I did. Or, rather, what I didn't do."

"Yes. Tell me what you *fear* you might have intended."

Miles spoke for a long time, and when he finished, the priest said, yes, yes, these were human fears, and they sprang from human needs and human desires.

"You want forgiveness for being human," the priest said. "Our Lord himself cried out on the cross, 'My God, my God, why hast thou forsaken me?' That was a human cry, and it sprang from human needs and fears and desires. Do you see? Sometimes we simply have to accept our humanity for what it is, and throw ourselves on the blind and loving mercy of God. There's no forgiveness for being human. That's simply what we are. We have to accept it and get on with our lives. Do you understand? It's a question of faith. It's a question of hope." He waited. "Are you there?"

But Miles had left the confessional some time back. "You want forgiveness for being human," the priest had said, and Miles stood up in the darkness and pushed the curtain aside and left.

The words infuriated him because they sounded cheap and trendy, something you'd hear from a Maharishi on grass. "I give myself permission to let go of the guilt," is what he meant. Psychobabble. It was California talk and it was the last thing on earth he'd have expected from a priest. So much for the modern church. So much for a British accent. He'd been a fool to come here.

The rest of Tuesday passed him by in a daze. He was not forgiven. He could never be forgiven. He withdrew into himself in coldness and silence. Even Margaret was afraid to speak to him.

On Wednesday, his mother's breathing miraculously cleared. That rasping sound was gone, and so were the hideous gurglings and contractions of the suction machine. She breathed easily and well, and she seemed a different person.

The skin was still pulled tight across her skull, and the marks of death were on her, but serenity had replaced the look of agony and she lay calmly now, propped on her pillows.

"Can you hear me?" Miles whispered in her ear, urgent. "Can you understand? Mother?"

Her face remained clear, untroubled.

"Listen to me, Mother. Just make a sign that you hear me." And he lay his head beside hers on the pillow and pleaded for her understanding. "I didn't mean . . ." he said, ". . . I only wanted . . ." but her face remained serene and she made no sign. Miles labored on and on, more desperate and more exhausted.

In the afternoon, the nurse taped his mother's eyes open, and Miles leaned forward—this was his last chance—but she gave no sign of recognition. She only stared straight ahead as if all her thoughts were fixed elsewhere now. She stared, and she continued to stare. In ten minutes the nurse came and removed the tape, and Miles was left again in darkness.

And then it happened.

At five o'clock, with no warning and with no agitation whatsoever, she made a sighing sound and died.

"No," Miles said. "No!" It could not have happened this way, without even a glance of love or forgiveness, without some sign. And blind with despair, he saw how it must really have happened: at five o'clock, with no warning and with no agitation, she turned her blind eyes toward him and, reaching out, she touched his hand. A thin long breath escaped her, and she died.

But did it? Did it really happen this way?

12

It was just after midnight and the Tom Cat Lounge was at its busiest. The Stones had been blaring over the loudspeaker for the past hour, and the hard beat had gotten into everybody: some spontaneous dancing broke out here and there, drinks were moving at a good pace, and the whole room was pulsing with sex. It was hot, too. The weather hadn't let up, and the guys with good bodies wore their shirts open to the waist, and a few even had their top fly button undone as if this were Provincetown. You had to shout to be heard over the music.

Miles stood just inside the door, leaning against the mirrored side wall, where he figured he could view the action while remaining inconspicuous. He wore a green plaid shirt, and he held a beer in one hand. The other hand was tucked into the back pocket of his jeans, an attempt at jauntiness. He did not look drunk.

Everybody seemed to know everybody, or at least somebody, and there was a lot of touching going on: a hand on the nearest shoulder or massaging the hollow of a back or fingertips falling idly from shoulder to waist to the smooth curve of a buttock. It was all deliberately casual and all intended to arouse.

At midnight men had begun to drift out the door, in couples

mostly, but newcomers were arriving every minute: regulars who liked the after-midnight hour, conventioneers looking for a little wildlife, a few late workers from the State House, and one or two single prowlers, like Miles, out for a glance at what's going on, just curiosity, just a moment to see without being seen. And maybe they'd try something new. What the hell. Who would know? Who would care?

Miles was fascinated. He was also frightened and excited and more than a little drunk. But under it all he felt defiant, alive. Here he was in the forbidden city.

Moments earlier a tall, thin guy with a pinched face and a squint had come and stood next to him. He'd been staring at Miles for several minutes and now he stood only a foot away, looking him up and down. Miles pretended not to notice at first, but then he turned to the guy and said, "How you doing?" and the guy gasped and pulled away. "Trash!" he said to Miles. "Don't you be coming on to me, you pervert. I know *your* kind." And he moved down the line. Miles was shaken by this, but nobody else seemed to notice, and later Miles saw him doing the same thing to some other guy— it was just his little act, campy and crazy.

Miles shrugged. This was exactly why he'd come: for the recklessness and lunacy. And for the aura of forbidden sex.

On the loudspeaker, the Stones gave way to a heavy metal group Miles didn't recognize, but the guy in charge of music somehow left a momentary pause—fifty seconds, maybe less—between the two tapes, and in that pause the sounds of the bar were wildly, unnaturally amplified and exposed. Voices sounded sharp and desperate, and the shrieks of laughter sounded crazed, and Miles—for just one moment—thought of what had really happened that day, and said, "I don't *care* anymore," and clutched his beer tighter and leaned hard against the mirrored wall. And then the music came up again, this time even louder than the Stones. Miles cleared his mind—forced it to go blank—and tapped his foot to the insistent beat of the drum.

He smiled to himself to keep from laughing out loud. He was Miles Bannon, schoolteacher, responsible citizen, whose only sexual experience in his entire life was with Margaret Cleary, a battered wife and widow, and here he was standing against the wall in the Tom Cat Lounge watching a room full of gay men whose only intention—AIDS or no AIDS—was to get it on, now, hard and slow. It was impossible. It was downright funny. He *did* laugh out loud then and, to cover his embarrassment, lifted his beer bottle to his lips. He let the beer trickle down his throat, wiped his mouth with the back of his hand, and smiled to himself at his ridiculous performance. Could it fool anybody?

"We've got to stop meeting this way," someone said.

It was Robert.

"People will talk," Robert said. He was wearing a dark suit and tie, looking as if he'd come straight from work, and in his hand he held a small scotch and rocks. He was smiling.

Miles felt his neck go red, and felt the blush begin to spread over his face. He could think of nothing to say.

"I'm just here . . . I'm . . ."

"Of course," Robert said. "To have a drink. To see how the other half lives." There was no trace of irony in his voice. "Curiosity. Why not? Can I get you another beer? A scotch?"

"No! I've got to leave."

"Sure, I understand," Robert said, as Miles continued to stand there. "I liked seeing you at the hospital. You always seemed like a human being and, as you said—or maybe I said it—there's an awful lot of bureaucracy around that place. My name is Robert, by the way."

"I've really got to get going. I'm sorry."

"Sure, sure. And your name is?"

"I'm Bill."

"Bill. Good. Just in case I ever see you again, it would be nice to have a name."

"Right. Well, I'm off."

"Take care, Bill." Robert put his hand on Miles' arm, gripping it lightly. Miles turned and gave him a sharp look. Robert took his hand away at once. "Sorry," he said.

Miles looked around for a place to put his beer bottle, blundered into the mirror, panicked slightly, and by the time he got to the door, Robert was there holding it for him.

"I'm leaving too," Robert said. "It's too noisy in there. It's impossible to talk."

They were out on the street and Miles took a deep breath, as if he had escaped safely.

"Yes," Robert said. "I'm never really comfortable there, either. Do you want to walk a little? Get some air?"

"Why do you go there?" Miles said.

"It's harmless, Bill. It's just a bunch of guys. I usually don't go to bars at all, gay bars, but sometimes I just need a drink—like now, tonight—and at the Tom Cat there's the chance I'll see somebody I know, and we'll have a chat." Miles was listening carefully. "Or somebody I'd *like* to know, and we'll have a chat."

"I've got to go," Miles said.

Robert laughed out loud. "I knew I should have stopped while I was ahead of the game."

"What?" Miles said. "No."

"Why do *you* go there?"

"I've been drinking. I shouldn't have."

"You wanted some company, maybe. Maybe talk to somebody. Be a little crazy. Hmm?"

"I *am* crazy."

"You're very attractive, Bill, and my guess is that you're very nice. I don't think you've ever been to a gay bar in your life, and all I'm asking you for is a little walk. A little talk." He looked at his watch. "There's time. And I promise I won't press myself on you. Look, Ma, no hands." He backed away, his hands in the air. "What do you say?"

This, somehow, seemed wrong. Going to the Tom Cat Lounge

was just crazy, but this was serious business because he was using somebody. He wasn't attracted to Robert; he was just after the excitement of the forbidden. Robert's thin lips were turned up in a smile. He would have let his fingers trace the line of that smile if it were Margaret's. But with a man?

"Well?"

"My name's not Bill," Miles said.

"You don't have to tell me your name."

"It's not Bill. It's Miles."

"Let's take a little walk, Miles."

They took a right, and then a left where Miles hadn't seen a left, and then they went through a short dark alley, and in no time they were on Washington Street in front of Filene's. They walked in silence for a while, and then they talked, and then they were silent again.

"We can stroll down through Government Center," Robert said, "or we could stop at my place and have a drink. No strings. I live right here."

Miles had come out tonight with some vague notion of recklessness, of defiance. All his life, he'd been good and dutiful and frustrated, and now he'd had enough, he was breaking out. He, also, had a right to live.

They stood there on the street in front of Robert's apartment—Revere Street, but on the wrong side of Beacon Hill—while Miles, fearing and hopeful, tried to persuade himself not to go inside for a drink.

He had wanted sexual adventure, and here it was before him. Did he want it? Yes or no? On the very night of his mother's death?

His mother was dead: that was the fact he kept trying to obliterate from his mind and to which his mind, nonetheless, continually returned.

Miles stood beside the bed while the nurse closed his dead mother's eyes and then stepped outside to give instructions for removing the body. Alone with her for a moment, Miles bent down and, kissing her forehead, whispered, "I'm afraid."

Margaret arrived then, and they viewed the body together while the orderlies waited with their gurney. Margaret cried a little. They thanked the nurses. And, hand in hand, they left.

They felt lost without an endless series of obligations stretching before them. Funeral arrangements had been made, the obituary was written, and the hospital would take care of everything regarding the body. The funeral parlor had to be notified, and the church, but it was now only a matter of phone calls. No more hiring of Home Help people, no more Tillies, no more dashing from school, or work, to make sure Eleanor was being cared for. No more mixing that ghastly food formula. No more singing "On the road again." No more anguish over suffering you could do nothing to alleviate. And, to be frank, no more putting one's own life on perpetual hold.

They went to the Parker House for a slow, civilized meal. The food was delicious and the service perfect, but they found they were exhausted, with either nothing to say or too much, and they ate quickly and left.

At Margaret's house, they had a drink and Miles stretched out on the couch with his head in Margaret's lap. It was all done. They'd survived it and even acquitted themselves, so Margaret said, with a good bit of style. She decided to break her long abstinence and have a drink with him, to celebrate his goodness and to toast Eleanor for her courage and strength. They drank to that.

They had another, and after a while they stretched out together on the couch and were following the normal patterns that led to their making love. "Do you think we should, tonight?" Margaret asked. And Miles, hearing that long sigh that became his mother's final breath, said, "No. You're right, of course. Let's kiss good night and then I'll go."

Back home, he had another drink and thought of his mother's death. And then he thought of Monday: his mother, desperate, reaching out for the emergency cord. He watched her. He saw her watching him. He saw her look. And he did nothing.

He had another drink, he paced around the house, he had some coffee. He would go to bed. He would make his mind a blank and he would sleep.

Then, like a man possessed, without ever giving it a single rational thought, he knew what he was going to do, and he did it.

He put on jeans and loafers and a green plaid shirt. He got in his car and drove to Boston, with the rock station turned up high and the music pounding in his ears. He was parking his car in the usual place near the hospital, when he decided to hell with safety, to hell with concealment. He drove into the Combat Zone and found a place—too near a hydrant, true, but screw it—and parked the car just one block from the Tom Cat Lounge.

Now, here he was, standing in front of Robert's place on Revere Street, trying to pretend to himself that he might or might not go up and have a drink with him.

"I won't do anything you don't want me to do," Robert said. And because Miles was shaking so, he said, "I'll just hold you, all right? I'll just hold you loosely in my arms."

They were lying naked in Robert's big bed, with the sheets pulled up, and the lights dimmed. Miles did not seem able to control his shaking. It had begun with his hand when he placed it on Robert's hard thin chest, and then his whole arm had begun to shake, and soon his entire body was trembling violently.

"Are you sick?" Robert said, and Miles shook his head no.

"Are you frightened?" and Miles nodded yes.

"Is this all right?" Robert said. "I'll just hold you loosely in my arms like this. All right?"

"Hold me tight," Miles said. He spoke through clenched teeth because they were clattering so.

"I can do that," Robert said, "as tight as you like," and he pulled Miles close, running one hand across his back and down to his waist and then once more to his shoulder. He did it again, and this time he let his hand settle at Miles' waist.

"I'm sorry," Miles said, pulling away, "I feel like a fool."

"You feel good," Robert said, holding him. "You feel very good," and waited till he thought Miles was ready for further exploration. He was very slow. He was very patient. Sex seemed almost irrelevant to the movements of his body; his movements were so practiced, so intentional, they seemed like choreography. Finally, however, they had their effect. Miles came and then Robert came, and Miles was startled by the frenzy Robert brought to the act; for that moment, he became a different person, out of control, a little crazy.

Afterward, he held Miles very close again, saying nothing, kissing him softly on the neck, until after a long time he said, "May I?" He pulled away and slowly let one hand drift down Miles' body, touching him gently, carefully, circling in on Miles' crotch.

"Don't," Miles said.

"Well, look what's here," he said. "May I? Do you mind?"

And Miles said nothing because this, after all, was what he had agreed to. He lay back and let it happen.

Robert tossed the sheets aside, and slid lower in the bed. "I'm going to suck you dry," he said.

When Robert finished and had lit a cigarette, Miles said he had to go. At once. So Robert got up and dressed and walked him back to his car which, luckily, had not been towed, though there was a ticket on the windshield. "My treat," Robert said, and crammed the ticket into his pocket. He bent over to kiss Miles goodbye, but Miles turned his face away.

"Sorry," Miles said.

It was nearly four in the morning when he pulled into his driveway, and he was sick at what he'd done and dumb with exhaustion from the night, the week, the months of caring for his mother. He got out of his car and went into the house and let himself fall naked into bed.

Pulling into his driveway, Miles had failed to notice the car across the street where Margaret sat waiting. She had been waiting there since one that morning when she'd phoned—sleepless and wanting a drink—to ask if she could come and sleep with him, just be with him, just keep him company. But he had found some other company, she realized, somewhere else.

Part II

13

MILES SAT BACK and sipped his wine. He felt more relaxed than he'd been in years. A delicious coq au vin, a nifty Cabernet, a little discreet flirting across the table, and endless free time stretching ahead. This was the life.

He let his ankle brush her leg beneath the table, and instead of moving, she increased the pressure and smiled at him.

"This is going to end in bed, isn't it?" he said.

"I'd like that," she said.

He laughed, surprised at himself that he was looking forward to it. He felt that twinge in his groin.

"But you're supposed to be a big Catholic," he said.

"The Kennedys are big Catholics. I'm a little Catholic."

"But you go to mass every Sunday. Right?"

"And holy days of obligation."

"Yet you'd go to bed with me."

"Why not? I don't see what the two have to do with one another."

"The Church does. They call it mortal sin."

"Well, the Church and I disagree on that."

"But how can you be a Catholic?"

"I am one. Who can stop me?"

Miles laughed, a short burst of sound, and then he laughed a lot. "What?"

"I think you're wonderful, Diane. I think you're just incredible."

"Then let's do it," she said. "We can have dessert later." She started to get up from the table.

"Wait," he said. "Wait." His face went grim suddenly. "I have to tell you something," he said. "You may not want to then."

Diane waited, but after a while she could see he needed help. "You don't have to tell me anything. It's *you* I like."

"What do you mean?"

"This is a fling, Miles. It's a moment. It has no consequences and it's no more important than either of us wants to make it. You don't have to tell me anything."

"I've slept with a man," he said suddenly. "Gone to bed with him."

"Yes?" Not a trace of surprise.

"I thought you should know. I mean, I don't want you to think later that I've deceived you. Not that you'd ever find out. It was perfectly anonymous. And only that once."

"Did he have AIDS?"

"Good God, no! Well, of course I don't *know*, do I." He thought for a moment. "But we didn't do anything that could communicate AIDS. I mean, no exchange of bodily fluids, as they say on TV. At least I didn't get any of *his* . . ." He shook his head, blushing.

"You had a fling."

"That's right. It was just a fling. Once."

"So? That's fine with me."

"Well, it bothers me. A lot. I thought you should know *before*."

"Let me put on a new disk, Miles; some Chet Baker or something. How does 'Let's Get Lost' sound to you? It makes a nice background, and we can have dessert. Then, if you want, we can have some more wine and just sit and talk or whatever you want."

He watched as she moved across the room to the CD player.

Everything here was modern: brass, glass, Haitian cotton, a big leather Eames chair, and a lot of dull pastels. Her apartment took up the bottom floor of a two-story house, but once inside, you'd think you were in a Boston condo. He liked it. It was slick and modern. It was the very opposite of the closed, old, family feeling of Margaret's place.

Diane put the disk in the CD player and, with a casual, practiced motion, pulled the telephone jack from the wall. By the time the slow and smoky jazz began to seep into the room, Miles was in the kitchen scraping the dirty dishes.

"No, don't," she said. "Silly goose." She wiped his hands with a checkered dish towel and then tossed it away and stood close to him, looking into his eyes. "Lovely Miles," she said. "Good, good Miles."

She was smiling slightly and Miles traced the line of her lips with his finger, very slowly, very carefully. The image of Robert's smiling mouth flashed before his eyes, and Miles' expression changed for a second, but Diane said, "Sexy Miles," and he was back with her again. They kissed, passionless, but it was easy and natural, and in the end they went to bed without dessert.

Miles watched Diane take down her hair, that mass of red and gold cascading from the tight bun she kept it in, and he thought for a guilty moment of Margaret. She asked nothing, she put no pressure on him, she only waited. But she was always there in the background, always, a reminder and rebuke to him. He would call her tomorrow and ask her to dinner, but right now here was Diane, gloriously naked and fragile and not in the least a burden.

After they made love, they rested for a while. Miles was lying on his back and Diane lay beside him, her head supported in the crook of his neck. Her red-gold hair hung loose, spreading across her shoulders and spilling onto his chest. He had never seen hair like it, all copper and silk and the soft wet shimmer of gold. And when you looked at it under direct light—he lifted a long strand toward the lamp—it was many colors: soft brown and fawn and pale yellow and a dull subtle red.

"Why do you always keep this tied up in a bun?" Miles said. "This incredible hair."

"It keeps them guessing," she said, her voice dreamy. "It keeps my two lives separate."

He smiled and shifted a little higher in the bed, half sitting, and though he now rested uncomfortably against the headboard, he could see the long line of her body and its soft curves. It was the body of a young girl. Diane moved higher too, keeping her head in the hollow of his shoulder, but now her right breast shifted so that it rested against him, cool and firm. The halo around her nipple was a ripe pink, though the nipple itself was lighter, almost white. He touched it gently, rubbing, and it grew pink and hard. Diane sighed and stretched out her right leg. Her skin was pale without being white, and as she pulled her leg taut, he was surprised at the muscles in it and the rippling of her small belly. Her softness had surprised him, and as he watched, he saw the strength that lay beneath that softness. It excited him. He wanted to lay his hands on it, he ached to touch it with his tongue. He slid lower in the bed and began with the hollow in her throat, and then the slow rise of her breasts, exploring her body, and it was a long time before he was done.

Later that evening Margaret, who had been pacing for hours, put down her second glass of wine and picked up the telephone. She dialed Diane Waring's number, which she knew by heart now, and listened as the phone rang over and over and no one answered. She sat down and covered her face with her hands. She had given in again and called that bitch, and she was back where she started: knowing nothing except that she was alone and Miles was not.

She picked up her glass and sipped the wine slowly until it was gone. Then she leaned against the fireplace mantel and looked into the mirror at this aging woman. Thirty-seven. But she had black hair still, and a good figure, and a life, a *life* ahead of her if only she'd give up this stupid infatuation. Miles was not her salvation. Miles was not her life. Miles was the excuse she'd found for not living her own life. She knew this.

She began to pace again, avoiding the mirror, and after a while she poured herself another glass of wine, and sipped it slowly, and paced some more. She put her hand on the telephone, left it there a moment, and then walked away. She went to the kitchen and looked out into the dark backyard. She went to the bathroom and examined her face in the mirror. She paced some more.

And then she dialed Diane Waring's number and listened while the phone rang over and over and over, until the sound began to hypnotize her and she thought she could hear voices, laughter. She put down the phone.

Why did she care about him? It was over and done with. She should get on with her life. And yet she knew that in an hour, after another glass of wine, or two, or three, she would get into her car and drive to his house and wait outside until he came home.

She drained the glass of wine.

She detested herself.

Still later that evening Robert leaned back against the mirrored wall of the Tom Cat Lounge where he'd just spent a stupid hour dawdling over a scotch rocks. He was bored and he was disgusted. The same old music, the same old people, the same old mating dance. He'd come here in the hope of a lucky meeting with Miles Bannon. It was midnight; it was Wednesday; it could conceivably happen again. But there was no luck for him tonight and he tossed down the watery scotch and left.

When Robert first met Miles at the Tom Cat Lounge, the meeting was accidental only in a sense. He knew all of Richard's heartthrobs from his class pictures, and so when he saw Miles at the hospital, he had recognized him at once. Just for kicks he'd done his best to catch Miles' attention and then to hold it, and it had been fun.

The last thing he'd expected was to meet him cruising in a gay bar. But once he laid eyes on him, scared silly, leaning against that mirrored wall, Robert knew Miles was ripe for the plucking and he, fatherly and fit, would be the plucker of record. And it worked.

He'd seduced Miles without any effort at all. He'd done it for fun—to tell Richard and have a laugh and maybe invent a new game—but afterward, when he thought of Miles and the reluctant way he let himself be had, Robert felt ashamed and decided not to tell Richard after all. Let Miles stay in the closet if he wanted. What the hell. On the other hand, if Miles wanted to come out of the closet, he'd like to be around to welcome him. Nothing got to him like innocence and sweetness.

He walked home slowly, following the same meandering route he'd taken with Miles, and he remembered his first such walk: at fifteen, filled with terror and with eagerness and finally with relief to discover at last who he was and what he wanted. He had never regretted it. Not once.

Billy Mack lay in his bed thinking of Miles Bannon and wishing he could be like him. He would rather have been a cop like his father, or a sports star like Paul Ciampa, but these were impossible for him, he knew, and so he wished he could be like Miles. Miles always knew what to say and what to do. He was never caught off guard. And everybody liked him. Or at least nobody ever made fun of him. Which was surprising, because Miles wasn't athletic, and he could easily have been spotted for a fag, which he wasn't because of his girlfriend and all, but they *could* have given him a rough time if they wanted. Miles had a sort of dignity that made it impossible to mock him, no matter what he said or did.

Miles was nice, too. Practically the only person Billy talked to since it happened was Miles. He saw him every day in study hall. Miles would always walk to the back of the room for a while and then, when he passed his desk, he'd say, "How you doing?" or just "Bill," or smile and raise his eyebrows the way he did when he didn't know what to say. Billy just grunted, always, and looked away. And he saw him every afternoon when he ran on the back roads and through Mitchell Park. Billy would wait in the park until Miles ran by, and then he'd follow, keeping a couple hundred feet behind, sometimes losing sight of him altogether, but still it was better than nothing to be out running with somebody even if they didn't know you were there.

Billy heard his father's voice, and then he heard the door slam, and after a minute he heard the car start up. So he was off to work, still on night shift. And now his mother would come up the stairs, listen for a minute at his door, and then go to her bedroom where she'd pray all night that her only son wouldn't turn into a queer. She had told him she prayed for this every night. She asked him to pray, too. Well, she was off her nut. If he was gonna pray, he'd pray for a fucking bomb that would wipe Malburn off the face of the earth.

He rolled over then, and he did pray. He prayed, Never mind what she says, please let me not be a fag.

14

THE ALARM CLOCK HAD NEARLY RUN DOWN by the time Margaret fought her way from sleep to consciousness. She lay in bed a minute, stunned, and then she realized where she was and who she was and what she had to do. At once she was out of bed and into the shower, and a short while later she tossed down three aspirins. Fortified by these, she stood before her makeup mirror assessing the damages.

"A thing of beauty," she said, and leaned close to examine the dark splotches beneath her eyes. She could take care of those. And she could take care of the sick pallor of her skin. She'd use extra blusher today. But nothing could repair those fine lines at her eyes, around her mouth. Well, you did what you could, or what you had to—and she smiled to herself because she sounded so much like Miles.

Miles. Last night as she drank and phoned him, and then as she drank some more and phoned Diane Waring, over and over again, she could have killed him gladly, or killed for him, but this morning the cloud of insanity had lifted. She was only guessing about Diane, after all. She had no hard evidence, only intuition. This morning Miles didn't seem such a bastard after all. He was just another man.

He had wit and some charm and he was good-looking—and it was true he had been absolutely selfless taking care of Eleanor—but when it came to loving someone, he just didn't have it. He didn't know what love was. Devotion, yes. And generosity. And even sex, more or less. But love, no.

It was just over two weeks since his mother's death and they'd not been to bed once, nor had they come anywhere near the subject of marriage. He needed time, he said. He needed space. And she had the good sense not to push it.

They had dinner on weekends, and he called sometimes during the week, but something had changed between them and her rational mind told her it was over. He didn't need her anymore. Or want her. And very probably resented her. Men didn't like it when you knew their needs. Though, of course, the shrink disagreed with her on that.

Margaret had been seeing a psychiatrist regularly—different ones at different times—ever since that blessed night when Roofer, drunk and homicidal, jumped into his car and drove to the refuge for battered women determined to kill her, and killed himself instead. He'd run a red light just as a police car—lights flashing, siren blaring—came out of nowhere and hit him broadside, on the driver's side, doing a strong seventy. Incredibly, no one was hurt except Roofer, who was dead on arrival, another victim of drinking and driving. And Margaret, at last, was free. In a manner of speaking.

She had discovered how little free she was in the two years following Roofer's death, as she slowly put a life together, mastered a job, became a whole person again. She was her own new creation: loving, caring, forgiving, responsible; as much like God as she could be. But her several psychiatrists did not let her forget that beneath the surface of this new and healthy Margaret lurked the old one—angry, hurt, eager to find a persecutor. And beneath that, another Margaret, vengeful. Hers was a delicate balance, they said. And added, better not to drink.

They were right about this, she knew, because she had seen again and again how drinking broke down this woman she'd become and left her once again a frightened, cringing, battered woman looking for abuse. How could she—with her intelligence and competence and sense of what was right—how could she let this happen to herself? It had to stop. It would stop.

She finished her makeup and put on her yellow dress, a wool knit that emphasized her figure and drew attention from her face. Earrings, brown pumps, the matching handbag, and she was at the door. That was when the phone began to ring. She stood there for a while, just looking at it, and then she walked to it slowly, giving him one more chance to hang up. But he did not hang up, and she found herself saying, "Miles! How nice!" and, "Of course I'm free for dinner." So she had done it once again, put herself in that old trap, and she was very very glad.

15

JEFF DOUGLAS WAS HOLDING FORTH in the teachers' room when Miles
arrived, a little later than usual. "Miles!" Kathy Dillard said, and
Dietz and Coogan raised their coffee cups to him, and Diane—her
hair pulled back into a tight bun—nodded to him and smiled, but
Jeff Douglas went right on talking about what a pain in the ass it
was to deal with impossible parents.

"And then there's Mrs. Dodd. She keeps calling to ask when we
can have a conference about her Cynthia. I told her we can have
a conference on Parents' Night, and she says she can't wait that
long; she's got to talk to me now. So I said to her, 'Okay, go ahead,
talk.' That shut her up pretty quick. Her Cynthia. Give me a break."

"I taught Cynthia Dodd," Coogan said. "She's smart."

"She's screwed up," Jeff said. "And of course it's her mother's
fault."

Miles looked at Diane to see how she was taking this, but her
face showed no emotion at all. She was perfectly composed, the
cool administrator having coffee.

"Does she drink?" Dietz asked. "Usually, when a kid's screwed
up, you find a drinking problem somewhere in the family."

"The kid doesn't drink," Jeff said. "Maybe the mother does."

"It's usually there somewhere," Dietz said.

"The kid—Cynthia—is just an average kid. She's not a brain, but she's not an idiot either. B average, I'd say. But her mother wants her to get straight As, early admission to Harvard, et cetera, and Cynthia just can't hack it."

"Cynthia's smart. At least I thought so," Coogan said.

Miles winked at Diane, and she saw him, but she did not wink back.

"I had a talk with her," Jeff said. "I said to her, 'Look, what do you want out of life? What do you want? Not what does your mother want, but what do *you* want? And she said, 'I just wish my mother would stop bugging me about grades.' And I said to her, 'If you honestly feel that way, maybe what you should do is just go out and deliberately get Cs in all your courses.' She looked at me as if I were out of my mind, and I said, '*I'm* giving you a C in English,' and she damn near died. You should have seen her face." He laughed, rocking back in his chair, causing Coogan to spill his coffee. "I told her I was only kidding."

Diane got up and left the room.

"I don't think that went over too well, Jeffy," Dietz said. "You're not exactly helping the cause."

"What cause?" Coogan said.

Dietz shook his head in exasperation and lit another cigarette.

"His tenure," Kathy said. "His tenure cause, Coogan. Geez."

Kevin Foley stuck his head in the door and said, "Is Diane here? Where's Diane? That damned copy machine is broken again."

"She left," Kathy said. "Try her classroom." And to the room in general she said, "I just hope that damned custodian didn't forget the toilet paper again."

"So what's with the smile on you?" Jeff said to Miles. "You're looking a lot like the proverbial cat."

"What cat?" Coogan said. "Oh, I get it."

"The one that ate the canary," Miles said, just in case. "Maybe I did," he said to Jeff, "maybe I did." He got up and went out.

"The Princess Bride," Jeff said. "The Dowager Queen."

The Mafia came in—Nina, Tina, and Frank—and Jim Dietz lifted his cup to them in salute.

His two American Lit. classes had gone extremely well this morning—he'd finally made up the lost time—and Miles was feeling good about his teaching . . . until about ten minutes into third-period comp. That, as usual, managed to deflate him completely.

How on earth was anybody supposed to teach composition? Even after all these years, he hadn't figured it out. You were dealing with a largely illiterate generation. They didn't read books. They didn't even read newspapers. They had no model for excellence other than television, where even Tom Brokaw said "between you and I." And Tom Brokaw was the high point of television literacy. You couldn't count MacNeil/Lehrer because students regarded MacNeil/Lehrer as a kind of punishment. It was hopeless really. It was poor old Sisyphus all over again.

The kids seemed to think he made up the rules to mystify them and complicate their lives. Today, once again, they'd taken offense at his notion of the paragraph as a unit of thought, the logical development of an idea.

"We never had *this* stuff before," a kid said, miffed.

And another said, "We're never gonna use this stuff, Milo, so why do we have to study it?"

"I got friends who never use paragraphs," Lombardi said, "and they make a lot more money than teachers do."

"Sure," somebody said, "but your friends are all drug dealers, Lombardi." However, to show solidarity, he added, "Paragraphs suck."

Miles did his song and dance then about clear thinking and clear writing, about being able to write a letter of complaint to the IRS when they screw up your taxes, or write a coherent explanation to your boss about why you should have a raise, or—forget about actual writing—*explain* to your wife or husband why you can't afford a new car or why your mother-in-law shouldn't live with you or why you want a divorce. Clarity will cut down on family quarrels, it will help you get a job and keep it, it will eliminate some of the confusing crap from your life, "Lombardi . . . are you listening to me?"

"Yeah," Lombardi said, a little too belligerently. And then added, "Sorry, Milo."

"So let's get on with it," Miles said.

His concentration failed for a moment and he thought of Diane and Jeff Douglas in the teachers' room this morning, her passive reserve in the face of Jeff Douglas' idiocy. And he saw her naked, arching her back as he explored her body.

"Now where was I?" he said.

He couldn't remember, so he went to the blackboard where he had written a terrible paragraph, and began to take it apart. "Look at this ghastly piece of work," he said, and they looked, because it was both badly written and a little gross—the subject was why you shouldn't burp in public—and he proceeded to dismantle it, showing where logic and coherence failed. He had composed the paragraph himself, to spare kids the embarrassment of having their own work exposed in class.

He was working nicely from logic to coherence when Lombardi yawned loudly. "Sorry," Lombardi said, and then in that throaty, criminal voice of his: "We're supposed to be Basic, Milo. We're never gonna use this stuff."

"Basic" got to him. In the School Review documents, "Basic" was the term applied to students "who were still acquiring fundamental learning skills." In actuality, Basic meant uneducable; the idea behind calling these kids Basic was to keep expectations down—"realistic," the document said—and thus contrive to get them through school and out into the real world, where they would become auto mechanics and grocery clerks and good tax-paying citizens who would stay out of jail. The Basic kids had long since accepted the fact that nothing was expected of them, and so they expected nothing of themselves. It was this easy acceptance of their third-rate status that most bothered Miles.

"Basic bullcrap," he said. "If you *want* to be losers, then all you have to do is keep telling yourselves that's what you are." He was angry suddenly, and he defused his anger by lapsing into a rather good imitation of Lombardi's hit-man voice:

" 'I'm just shit, Mr. Bannon, so I shouldn't have to think.'

" 'Oh, and what kind of shit are you, Mr. Lombardi?'

" 'I'm Basic shit, Mr. Bannon.'

" 'No, you're pure bullshit, Mr. Lombardi.' "

Miles had their attention again and was able to get through the hour without any further interruptions. But he left the classroom wondering, did they really have any idea what he was talking about? And for how long could he keep trying to push this rock up the hill?

For one wild second he was assailed by the thought: they're right, this stuff is useless. We've come at last to a moment in history when logical, consecutive thought no longer matters. This is indeed the end time.

In the corridor between classes, though, he ran into Diane. She looked prim in her brown skirt and tan blouse, with her hair pulled severely back, and when she saw Miles, her look never changed. "Do you have a moment?" she said, and indicated the bookroom.

Diane closed the door and made sure they were alone, but before she could say anything, Miles said, "What is it? Is it Jeffrey?"

At once she smiled at him the way she had last night across the table, and said, "Are you free tonight?" and when Miles groaned and apologized and finally said no, he was not free tonight, she brushed his words away with a little wave of her hand and said, "Tomorrow night? Yes? Saturday too? Sunday?"

Miles leaned forward to kiss her but, with a look of annoyance, she pulled away.

"What?" he said.

"We're in school," she said. "Are you out of your mind?" Then that mesmerizing look again—desirability and availability combined. "Tomorrow night," she said.

Miles stepped into the corridor feeling just terrific.

"Terrific!" Miles said, barely loud enough to be heard. Lombardi heard him, though, and assumed that Miles was thanking him for his help in class just now.

"Milo, baby!" Lombardi said, and shot him a thumbs-up.

Miles returned the thumbs-up, and sighed, and said to himself, Of such is the kingdom of heaven.

Miles' high spirits continued into study hall. He didn't want to wreck his good mood by correcting compositions, so he read over the poems for tomorrow. Edna Millay. "What lips my lips have kissed, and where, and why/I have forgotten." Hot stuff. He would read it aloud, and they'd laugh nervously, but the truth was they'd love it. Millay was perfect for seventeen year olds. They were obsessed by sex, but they found love embarrassing and love poetry mushy and stupid, or so they said. But Millay was easy to read and all-stops-out, with just enough of the cynical to make her seem contemporary, and they ate it up. Moreover it gave Miles a chance to slip them the sonnet form without their protesting. Then he'd give them Frost: "Two roads diverged in a yellow wood." They'd love it.

He looked up, and sure enough there was Billy Mack staring at him. Billy pretended not to stare and Miles pretended not to notice. It was like their jogs through Mitchell Park. Did Billy really think he didn't know?

Instinctively, because it seemed the right thing to do and because at this moment he felt well disposed toward everybody in the world, Miles scribbled on a three-by-five note card: "Billy—Why don't you join me for a jog today? We can meet outside school or, if you prefer, at the entrance to Mitchell Park. I'll look for you.—Milo." He paced slowly around the room, dropped the note on Billy's desk, and kept on moving.

Suddenly there was the wail of a siren—an ambulance, Miles knew at once. And then another siren, this one different: a police car or a fire engine. Clearly, they were coming to the school. Within seconds everyone was up and at the windows and Miles was saying "Down. Sit down. It's not a fire."

Reluctantly, because they couldn't see the street from these windows, they began to trail back to their seats. "We miss everything," someone said. "We miss all the fun."

"Cheer up," Miles said, "maybe it's Endicott." Feeling wicked and satisfied, he returned to Robert Frost.

Billy was sitting on the stone wall at the entrance to Mitchell Park as Miles came jogging along. They fell into step without saying anything, as if they were both too winded to speak. After a while Miles looked over at Billy and said, "How you doing, Bill?" and Billy said, "Okay," and kept on jogging. But then he smiled. Miles had never noticed his smile and he was astonished at the transformation. All the anger and hostility and surliness fell away from the boy and he looked . . . good, like a choirboy or one of those boy saints you used to hear about in catechism classes. "I'm glad you came," Miles said, and they jogged on in silence.

It was football weather, perfect for jogging, with clear sharp air and no wind at all. The birches were just beginning to turn yellow and gold; some coppery maples, a red oak or two; and everywhere in the park there was a woody smell, earthy. It was great to be alive. No more dying, Miles said to himself, and at once he thought of those sirens during study hall.

"What's the story on those sirens, Bill? During study hall."

"False alarm," Billy said.

"A fire?"

"Suicide."

Miles stopped jogging. "Suicide! Who?"

"Cynthia Dodd. It was a false alarm."

"Is she okay?"

"She took her mother's tranquilizers, a little bottle only. They took her to the hospital."

"God. How awful. Does anybody know why? Do you?"

Billy shrugged. "Her mother was pissed off. She's done it before. The last time, she used a razor blade. On her wrists."

"God."

"She barely cut herself."

They started jogging again. That poor girl, Miles thought. And then he thought, this is curtains for Jeff Douglas, with his stupid advice: "Get all Cs to spite your mother. *I'm* gonna give you a C." Sayonara, Jeff.

"I didn't hear any of this," Miles said. "Where did you hear all this?"

"The kids. It gets around." And after a moment Billy added, in a hard voice, "Everything gets around."

Miles felt his face get red. Everything gets around. His fling with Diane? Or, dear God, his fling with Robert? Was Billy telling him something? He kept on jogging.

"Everything," Billy said again.

"Like?"

"Like me. They all know about me. They all know what happened to me."

"Bill. I'm sorry."

"Nobody ever says anything, but they all know."

"How does that make you feel?"

"I don't know. Like shit."

"Yes."

They passed the cutoff to Lookout Rock and were coming out of the park before either of them spoke again.

"It's not like when they did it to me. I was fighting then, and I didn't really know what was happening. But now, every time somebody looks at me, and I know they know about me, it's like it's happening to me all over again, only it's worse, because this time I can't even fight it."

"Yes."

"Yes? What do you mean?"

"I know. I understand."

"What do you know about it? You think you know so much. You don't know shit about me."

Billy sprinted ahead of Miles, and kept on sprinting, and soon he was out of sight and out of the woods.

Miles slowed to a walk, pondering, and then he said, "How can he endure it?" Still later he said, "How?"

He forced himself to get up to speed again. As he reached the school, the team was just coming off the field and Paul Ciampa waved and shouted hello. Relieved, happy again, Miles put Billy Mack out of his mind and stopped to have a chat with Paul and congratulate him on his winning team.

Paul Ciampa was a big, tough, smart, good-looking guy; manly and responsible. There was nobody like Ciampa. He was just the greatest kid.

16

MILES WAS FEELING VERY GOOD as he dressed for dinner and, as he glanced in the mirror, he thought he looked pretty good too. He was sleeping again, and that was a help. He'd begun to look healthy. Moreover he'd begun to feel healthy, thanks to jogging and regular hours and getting outside in the sun once in a while. There were other things, too. He'd put on some weight. He'd bought a new jacket and pants, a couple shirts, a tie. He wasn't constantly burdened with the thought of his mother dying. And he was in love. He *did* look pretty good.

He was seeing Margaret tonight for dinner. The thought gave him a hard lump somewhere between his throat and his stomach. In his heart, as a matter of fact. Since the funeral he'd seen her only three or four times—three actually—and each time under a kind of duress. She needed him. She wanted him. She never said it, but she made it plain enough with that melting look of hers, which had begun to exasperate him, and with that heroic way of never asking anything for herself. Sometimes, like now, when he thought of her, she loomed up as a giant figure of death, malign and devouring, waiting to consume him. That was ridiculous, of course. He was simply associating her with those awful days—months—when his mother was dying and Margaret seemed to be his one link to life. She reminded him of death. She reminded him of his worst failures. She'd been there through all of them.

And was that why he resented her now? Because no good deed goes unpunished? Why did he *have* these thoughts!

He just hoped, whatever else happened tonight, that he didn't have to go to bed with her.

He combed his thick sandy hair and glanced at himself sideways in the mirror. No sign of gray yet. A straight nose, an okay chin, and—though the idea was ridiculous—a sexy mouth; at least that's what Diane had said. And Margaret, too. And, unfortunately, so had Robert, though Miles wished he hadn't remembered that.

Well, he had only a few hours to get through with Margaret and then he'd have the entire weekend with Diane. Old Milo, the sex machine. He felt a light tug in his groin. Sex was great. Life was great. He could get through this evening easily.

Margaret stepped into the bath and lowered herself slowly into the hot, perfumed water. She made sure her hair was tucked into her shower cap, then she lay back, her head cradled against the little white bath pillow. She stretched out and let the water envelop her. Dinner with Miles, and who knows what might happen afterwards.

She tried to concentrate on that: dinner with Miles. She must exclude every other thought or desire. Never mind that she wanted him in bed for the night and for all the nights to come. Never mind that she wanted him to marry her and take away the terrors of loneliness. And the worse terrors of drink and pills and brutal sex. She wanted him, simply, to want her.

Margaret was thirty-seven years old, and she had barely survived a disastrous marriage as a battered wife, and she knew that in many ways her life was a textbook study in how not to live. Escaped from a sexual psychopath, she was pursuing a sexual adolescent. Miles wasn't ready to marry her or anybody else. He had spent all those formative years taking care of family, being responsible, being good. And now, sexually, he was fifteen and all excited about discovering sex. He was an innocent. That was why she needed him. But she knew it didn't have to be this way. If she could start from love rather than from need, she could do it right this time.

That, of course, was the stumbling block. She needed Miles. She didn't love him.

Still, he was all she had, and by God she was going to hold on to him. The secret was to practice the relaxed grasp. Never pull at him, or push, or force an issue. Never make demands. When he wanted a little freedom, give him a lot. Let him call. Let him invite. Don't check up on him. And never, ever, show a trace of jealousy. It was not easy to hold someone in a relaxed grasp, but it was the only way you could hold them at all. And in time—who could tell, as Miles would say—love might happen after all.

Miles came up the walk, expecting at any moment that Margaret would appear in the doorway, saying, "Miles, you sweet thing, come in, come in," and so he was surprised that he had to knock and wait. She opened the door, smiling, and said, "Come in, come in," but she had a cheese knife in one hand and a dishtowel in the other, and the embrace she gave him seemed rather more per-functory than loving. But he was relieved, in a way. He wouldn't have to fight her off.

They went into the kitchen and she asked Miles to make a drink, and make one for her too, while she finished drying these few dishes and put the Brie on a plate and got some crackers, the stoneground wheat ones he liked so much. The scotch was on the counter near the sink. The rye too. And the mix for her whiskey sour was in the cabinet above. How nice it was to see him and how handsome he looked. Was that a new jacket? And tie? Very attractive. Just perfect with his coloring.

She was so easy, pleasant, and relaxed that Miles began to feel a bit annoyed. She hadn't seen him in a long time, after all, and they had been accustomed to talking every day and seeing each other very, very often.

"What gives?" he asked, and handed her the whiskey sour.

She stopped talking then and turned to gaze into his eyes. "I'm *so* glad to see you, Miles." She kissed him lightly on the lips. "Dear Miles," she said.

He didn't like it. Had she gotten tired of him? Was there someone else?

Margaret was giving him her complete attention, or trying to.

"God, so much has happened," Miles said. "We're having Back to School Night next week, and the Halloween dance is coming up, and my classes have been going really well, I think. I think they're finally getting past their dislike of poetry. Where do they get that, anyhow? I've never been able to figure that out. Don't they hear nursery rhymes any more when they're kids?"

"No," Margaret said. "I suppose they watch television."

" 'Sesame Street.' Yes. But at least 'Sesame Street' has rhymes and songs and stuff. I don't get it. Somewhere, it gets bred out of them. Or the fear of it gets bred into them."

"But it's going well, you said."

Margaret leaned forward to hear more. He was looking handsome tonight. He'd put on some weight, and it was very becoming. Sweet Miles. He was always animated when he talked about teaching or about the kids. He had found something that filled his life and made it worth living. Lucky Miles. Good Miles. She wanted to touch him.

Miles had been going on about Millay and then Frost and the kids' response to them, but he stopped now and looked at her. "What?" he said.

"No, I'm just listening. I was thinking how alive you are when you talk about teaching. Go on."

"I am," he said, pleased.

"And it's very nice to see," she said. "Go on. You were talking about Frost."

" 'Two roads diverged in a yellow wood,' which reminds me: who do you think I went jogging with today? Whom. Guess."

Margaret smiled. She was thinking of Diane. Did she jog? Probably, that bitch.

"Billy Mack," he said. "It was between classes and I ran into Diane in the corridor—Diane Waring—and she asked me . . ." He paused, and Margaret could see a blush starting at his throat, and so, to cover his embarrassment, she reached for a cracker and began to spread Brie on it ". . . she said why didn't I ask him if he wanted to go jogging. Well, for one thing you don't go jogging with students, it just isn't done, and for another, I'd feel like a fool asking him. As if it were a date or something."

"I can see that," Margaret said. "Still, though."

"Anyhow, I ended up asking him. I was feeling very high during study hall because I had a decent comp class just before it, and I thought, well, the poor kid, and I dropped a note on his desk asking him . . ."

Margaret stopped listening. She was watching his lips move and noting the wonderful animation in his face and thinking how she did, quite simply, love this man. Need was not really an issue. She loved him.

". . . following me," he said. "I'm absolutely sure of it. And it's been going on for some time."

"What?" she said.

"Following me. I'm certain."

There was a fist at her heart suddenly.

"I don't know why. He wasn't really spying on me. Just following me, I guess. In Mitchell Park."

So he must be talking about Billy Mack and not about her. She began to breathe again.

"But this was our first and last jog, I can tell you that. He's too strange for me," Miles said. "God knows what goes on in that mind of his."

"Mad driven love," Margaret said.

. . .

Mad driven love, Margaret had said, speaking the exact words that were in his mind. They'd been like that in the old days, anticipating words before the other spoke them, thinking of the same line of a song neither had heard in years, intuiting each other's desires.

"You look lovely," he said. He reached over and touched her just above the knee. They were driving to Henri IV in his battered old Pinto and he was looking forward to a good meal with a good person to whom he owed a very great deal. "You look just beautiful." Margaret smiled and returned his touch, for a moment only.

What kind of louse was he anyhow, to turn away from a woman who'd done everything, everything, for him when he needed her most? She had cooked him dinners, taken care of his mother, kept him company when he couldn't go out, kept his mother company when he *had* to go out. And she'd spent those endless hours with him, waiting at the hospital. She was always there, and he'd never once had to ask. No wonder he'd agreed to marry her.

He must have loved her at the time, he supposed. But how did you ever know you were in love? Was he in love with Diane?

Diane. What an incredible woman. Two women, really. He was so excited by her, so infatuated, that he couldn't tell if he was in love. She made him feel completely at home in his skinny, awful body. She liked it, and convinced him to like it too, a little anyhow, because he could do interesting things with it in bed with her. It was hard to believe he'd had all those doubts about his own sexuality back in those difficult days. With Margaret.

A nice thought came to him: was it her own fault that he'd turned away from her? Margaret's?

But before he could think up an answer, he knew the truth. It was the Combat Zone, it was Robert that had come between them. He could not tell Margaret he had done that. Never. He would not. It would be exposing himself to . . . what? Whereas telling Diane had been fairly easy at the time. And now it meant nothing, of course; that phase of his life was behind him for good.

How wonderfully complicated he was, dating Margaret and thinking of Diane. A man with two lovers. Old Miles. Who'd believe it?

The restaurant was small, with small tables and small rickety chairs, but the food was excellent. It was more pricey than Miles could afford, but dining out was his one great pleasure and Margaret knew that he enjoyed spending beyond his means. They had had a simple pâté and a complicated salad—Henri IV refused to serve salad after the entrée—and now they were waiting for their rack of lamb.

Margaret thought of asking if he was in love with Diane, but then she reminded herself of the relaxed grasp—never make demands, never make inquiries—and she leaned back in her chair and casually asked him, "And how are things with Diane?"

"She's fine, I guess. Why do you ask?"

"She was having trouble with Jeff Douglas, I recall. About his tenure."

"Oh, that's fine. I mean, he's going to try to bring a lawsuit, apparently, but he's got to go through the School Board first, and I think they'll shoot him down. All Diane did was evaluate him as a teacher and then pass on her recommendation to the principal and the superintendent. He can't sue her. I'm not even sure he can sue them."

"So what will he do?"

"He's such a horse's ass. What he'll do is bitch and moan and drag down morale, and say things to his class about her, and generally try to make her life miserable. That's how he is. He's dangerous. For instance, today . . ." and he launched into the story of some girl, Cynthia Dodd, who had tried to commit suicide in the girls' bathroom. Margaret heard "her mother's sleeping pills" and "annoyed" and "razor blade," but she only stared at the white tablecloth, concentrating on a single crumb there, a flake from the breadcrust, golden against the smooth surface of the linen. She sat at the table and Miles continued to talk but Margaret was far away in time, back in that disastrous marriage of hers. Roofer had beaten her, and thrown her on the bed, and, in his way, made love to her. But she'd lain there like a dead body, and afterwards he rolled off her and said, "You want to be a dead body? I'll show you a dead body." He shifted over in the bed, placed his foot against her side, and, with one hard shove, landed her on the floor. She lay there, curled up, as he walked around the bed to her. He stood above her, looking. She did not look up. He prodded her stomach with his toe. "You dead?" He pulled back his foot and gave her a short hard kick in the stomach. "You dead?" He kicked her again. "Are you dead, I said! Are you?" She said yes. "I can't hear you? I said, are you dead?" And she said yes again. He kicked her in the ribs. "Yes," she shouted, and he said, "I'll give you dead, I'll show you dead, I'll kill you, you bitch, you fucking whore," and he kept on kicking her until he was exhausted. He rested then, and left. Margaret lay on the floor, battered, broken, and then she pulled herself into the bathroom and somehow, despite her broken ribs, lifted herself onto the toilet seat and reached up into the medicine chest and got the packet of razor blades. She sat there, blind with pain for a very long time, and then she took a blade and laid it hard against her wrist. Nothing happened. She rocked the blade back and forth against the white flesh. And then she turned it slightly to the side, and pressed. A tiny dot of red appeared on her skin and she held the blade where it was and looked at it. The blade, her wrist, the dot of blood. She was giving him her life. It was what he'd wanted from the start. There was almost no pain, just the warm thick blood on her wrist, and the feeling of release. But it was her blood, her life, and she stopped.

She stopped, and now, having dinner with Miles at Henri IV, she looked at the flake of breadcrust on the tablecloth, and she looked across at Miles, and she looked at the other tables where people were eating and talking as if none of them had ever attempted suicide or hated marriage or preferred death to living.

"Momentito," she said. She went to the women's room and locked the door and leaned against it, breathing deeply. This had happened before and she knew she could survive it. She sat on the toilet and hugged her mended ribs. It was just a matter of time. After a while she got up and stood at the sink. She shook a Xanax into her palm, paused for a moment, and then another, and finally scooped it back into the bottle. She glanced at herself in the mirror. She did not need Xanax. She did not need anything. She squared her shoulders. Not even Miles. She filled a paper cup with water and drank it.

She returned to the table just as the waiter was pouring wine for their dinner. She smiled at the waiter and she smiled at Miles. She had managed to get through a lot and she'd get through this, too.

"Mmm. Lovely," she said.

The lamb had been fine, and the conversation was good—he'd managed to talk all around Diane without ever actually mentioning her—and now they were sitting back over coffee and a little Armagnac and Miles was feeling expansive.

Margaret had forced herself to eat the bloody lamb, and she had managed to make adequate conversation—or at least draw Miles out—and she was so relieved to have the meal over with that she too was feeling expansive.

They looked at each other, frank and loving.

"Hello," he said.

"Hello," she said.

"You look very, very nice," he said.

"You *are* very, very nice," she said.

He squeezed her hand.

"I've missed you," she said.

He took his hand away. "I've been incredibly busy," he said. "Making up the time I lost when my mother . . ."

"I know," she said, "I know. It's just nice to see you again, that's all."

"Oh, I know," he said. "I mean . . ."

"I know," she said.

He sipped his Armagnac, looked into the amber liquid, and said, "Good."

"It's very good," she said, sipping hers. "It's been a wonderful dinner."

"And you aren't mad?"

"Why should I be mad? Of course I'm not mad. I said I missed you simply because it's a fact. It's nice to see you. It's nice to be with you. It's a compliment. That's all."

"But I'm such a shit. We had such a good dinner, and we were feeling so close and nice, and then I go and bristle when you're only saying it's nice to see me again. I'm a mess."

"You are a mess, but you're a cute mess."

"What was her name, the one who said that? The nurse?"

"Ms. Sheehan, R.N. But you can call me Angie."

"Angie, right. Those were good days, weren't they. I mean, they were hideous in most ways—poor Mother—but they were nice for us."

"Yes."

"And I've been very neglectful, haven't I. I've been awful to you. Not calling. But I mean to call. I just . . . well, I feel bad about it."

"Don't. You've got to be free. You've got to *feel* free."

"That's right. But even when I am free, I don't always *feel* free. I feel there are still all kinds of obligations on me, like when Mother was alive."

"Well, there aren't. You're free. Completely. You have no obligations to me or to anybody."

"No."

"You're your own man."

"Yes. But we were good together, weren't we."

Margaret smiled at him and nodded. She sipped her Armagnac. Miles sipped his, and then he held out his glass and they clinked them together. She smiled at him again.

"But we're still good together. Don't you think?" He let his ankle drift against her leg. "Hmmm?"

She didn't respond.

He lowered his head a little and looked up at her. "Hmmm?"

"I'm being very good," she said.

They looked at each other, teasing.

"Milo!" someone said. "Miles!" Miles turned and saw Coach being seated two tables away. He was with Kathy Dillard, nearly unrecognizable in a black dress that revealed a lot of shoulder and a very interesting cleavage. Her hair was brushed up and back and she looked a good ten years younger and a very good ten pounds lighter. Who'd believe it?

Miles stuck his hand up in a kind of greeting. Kathy smiled at him and Margaret, but Coach was on his feet at once and over to the table.

"Milo," he said, shaking his hand energetically. "Nice to see you. Good to see you." He turned to Margaret. "I'm the Coach at Miles' school. What a great guy, I'm telling you." Miles was trying to introduce Margaret, but Coach was just rolling on. "I'm a recovering alcoholic," he said to Margaret. "Can't touch that stuff. I love it, but it doesn't love me. You know what I mean? Miles was great to me when I was really down bad. Right, Miles? He was, believe me. I don't want to interrupt you folks. I just wanted to say hello. Nice to meet you, Margaret, a pleasure. You got a great guy here." He punched Miles on the arm and, reluctantly, went back to his table.

Miles nodded and smiled and, as Coach returned to his table, Miles waved again at Kathy. He turned back to Margaret, still smiling.

"Good God," he said.

"He's nice," Margaret said.

"But you'd think . . ."

"Afterwards," Margaret said. "Not here."

The romantic mood was completely dispelled by now, and so

Miles paid the bill and they left the restaurant and started walking slowly to his car.

"He's a fool," Miles said. "He's like Dietz."

"I thought he was very nice," Margaret said.

"*We're* nice," Miles said.

She slipped her arm through his, but Miles said, "Here. Like this," and he put his arm around her, kissed her on the forehead, and they walked in a comfortable silence to his car.

They were sitting on the sofa side by side, their shoulders touching, their heads within easy kissing distance.

Miles had a scotch on the coffee table in front of him and he was thinking about whether he should reach forward and take a slug or tip his head to the side and give Margaret a little kiss. There would be consequences, he knew. He was on his way to being drunk and a slug of scotch would only get him there sooner. And if he kissed Margaret, well, there was no telling where that might lead, though he could guess.

Margaret was fairly numb with wine and Armagnac. A little bit went a long way with her, and so she was done drinking for the evening. She sat shoulder to shoulder with Miles and she would have liked to turn her head and kiss him, but her relaxed grasp did not allow her to make the first move. Still, it wasn't clear that Miles was going to make one, so it was probably up to her. And it would be nice to go to bed with him again. A little kiss. A little peck. Would that be a threat to him?

He kissed her on the forehead. She murmured, and he put his arm around her shoulder. He held her close for a moment. He kissed her softly on the neck, then higher, then he nibbled at her ear. She made approving sounds.

He would like to go to bed with her. He loved her, even if he was not in love with her, and they had shared some of the most awful hours of his life. The only problem he could see, really, was that it might mean more to her than he intended. It might seem like a promise or a return to the old days. Could he do it so that it was just a fling? Like with Diane?

He kissed the hair above her ear and then he shifted his body a little so that she could rest her head comfortably against his shoulder.

She liked this snuggling. Was it foreplay? Did he intend to ask her to bed? She wanted it, yes, but she did not want to be the one to suggest it. Or seem to be the one to suggest it. The secret of the relaxed grasp.

Diane, he thought. A fling, he thought. He had learned from Diane, in one night, the art of giving pleasure. Well, that was absurd, of course. Rather, he had seen the possibilities of giving pleasure—the merest possibilities—and he was eager to explore them. He would spend tomorrow night with her, and all day Saturday, and Sunday. Diane. Luscious Diane. He felt himself getting hard.

Margaret saw that he was getting hard and she moved her head against his shoulder so that her mouth rested against his collarbone. She pressed her tongue against his shirt until she felt the flesh beneath it grow warm. She was taking the initiative; this was against her rules. Why was she doing this?

He did not want to take advantage of her. It was not fair to just fuck and say goodbye. He did not want to use her. On the other hand, she was an adult. She understood the nature of a fling. It would be nice. It would be fun.

She moved her hand across his chest and, slowly, slowly, down to his belt. She felt him move his hips a little, forward, upward. She let her hand fall to his lap. She could stop now. It was not too late. She should stop now.

He sighed and his chest heaved and then he moaned softly. It's just a fling, he thought. But did she understand that?

She pressed her hand against the bulge in his trousers, squeezed a little, traced the outline with her fingers.

Like a whore, she thought, I'm dragging him to bed. I want him. I need him. Like a whore.

"So long as you understand," he said.

"I understand," she said.

They went to bed, and they made love, and it was very satisfying.

Afterward, Miles drove home slowly, hurt and ashamed because he knew he had betrayed her. He poured himself a drink and went to bed.

Margaret knew that she had lost him now, forever. She poured herself a drink and drank it, and then another, and then another, and then another.

So, this was it. At last.

17

MILES HAD SPENT THE ENTIRE WEEKEND with Diane and he was weak
and dizzy when he arrived at school on Monday. What a woman!
What an incredible woman she was! She could screw all day and
night, get up early for Sunday mass, and then come back and screw
some more. She was filled with contradictions like this. She'd talk
about Jeff Douglas and how he was making her life miserable, but
she wouldn't say a word about his tenure case; that was confiden-
tial, she said, so don't ask. And they were perfectly compatible, too.
They talked about education, about teaching in high school and
how frustrating it could be, but how good you felt when you did
it right, and then, even before he sensed the talk had lasted long
enough, she would get up and put on a Chet Baker recording or
a Miles Davis, pour a little wine, and they might just sit there for
an hour, barely touching, or they might go for it at once; still,
wherever and however they began, they always ended in bed. Not
with blind passion, but with slow and easy lovemaking. He really
was discovering the art of giving pleasure. And there was no question that she had the most beautiful hair in the world.

Diane was in the teachers' room when Miles arrived this morning,
but as usual she was saying little, and as usual she had her hair

pulled back in that bun. She was wearing a gray wool windowpane skirt and a gray silk blouse. No lipstick. He could not believe this was the Diane with whom he'd spent the past three days. He wanted to shout, "Hey, everybody, if you only knew about *us!*" but instead he just said a general "Hi" and went to get some coffee.

They were all talking about Back to School Night, which was planned for Wednesday, and since he and Jeff Douglas were more or less alone at the coffee machine, Miles raised his eyebrows in a kind of hello to him. He felt so lucky himself, living this new charmed life, that suddenly he felt bad for Jeff.

"It was too bad about Cynthia Dodd," Miles said softly. "I'm glad she's okay."

But Jeff didn't seem to care who heard him. "She's back in school," he said. "She only missed a day. It's that asshole mother of hers that's the problem. Did you hear what happened? Do you know about it?" Miles shook his head, needlessly, since Jeff had already gone on. "Endicott phoned her right away, and she came up to school and saw the ambulance and everything, and she said, 'What's all the fuss about? That's all Cynthia wants—attention. She just does it for attention, you know.' And then she said, 'She doesn't need an ambulance. I could take her in my car.' To the hospital? Can you imagine? 'I could take her in my car.' "

"That's incredible," Miles said.

"Well, it's true. Literally. I wrote it down, verbatim, and I'm gonna use it in my next novel. I'm gonna expose this goddamn place for what it is. 'She just does it for attention, you know.' Jesus."

"God," Miles said.

The others fell silent then, and Miles said, "No pastry? Kathy, what gives?" He turned to look at her, short and plump as ever, and he remembered suddenly how she'd looked at the restaurant, in her black dress and with her hair done up. On a date with Coach, of all people. Who'd believe it? "Not even a doughnut? Not even a cookie?"

"The Mafia got here early today and cleaned us out," Kathy said.

"Too much partying?" Miles said. "At French restaurants?" He raised an eyebrow at her and smiled.

"I'm not a damned caterer, you know," she said, blushing.

Everybody turned to look at her.

"Sorry," Miles said. "Secrets everywhere. I'll bring the goodies tomorrow, Kathy. Okay? Okay?"

"Okay," she said. And gave him a firm look.

"So, is Cynthia Dodd all right, really?" Coogan asked.

"Do we have to talk about this?" Diane said.

"I didn't bring it up," Jeff said. "*Miles* did."

"Well, what I want to know," Dietz said, "is whether anybody's noticed that we've won the last three games. Three in a row."

"That Ciampa is such a great kid," Miles said.

"Did you know that Cosmo Damiani's off the team?" Coogan said. "He's got ulcers. How does a kid get ulcers?"

"Guilt," Miles said.

"What guilt?" Coogan said. "Why would he be guilty? Cosmo's a great kid. Everybody loves Cosmo."

"It isn't Ciampa and it isn't Cosmo. It's the Coach," Dietz said. "You mean you haven't noticed? Anybody?"

Kathy left the room without a word.

"He's dry," Miles said. "Is that what you mean?"

"Right!" Dietz said. "Coach is dry and the team is winning games again. He's just a goddamned great coach."

"He's in AA?" Jeff said.

Dietz looked pleased, but he said nothing.

"Well?"

"It's called Alcoholics *Anonymous*," Dietz said. "We don't say who's in or who's not in."

"So, what are you saying? We have to attend a meeting to find out? Frankly, I don't care that much," Jeff said.

Dietz's face got very red and for a moment everybody was afraid of what he might say or do. But he just laughed and said, "When they open a branch for Assholes Anonymous, Jeff, you'll be the first to know."

Jeff laughed, and then everybody else laughed, relieved, which made Jeff furious.

"Fuck you, Dietz," Jeff said, and made for the door.

"The novelist at work," Dietz said, "minting each phrase, making it eternally new. 'Fuck you, Dietz.' Very artful. Very imaginative."

"Alky!" Jeff said, and slammed the door behind him.

"Novelist!" Dietz said. His hand was trembling.

Coogan shook a cigarette out of Dietz's pack and handed it to him. "Try one," he said. "They're very relaxing." And then he said, "I think that's great about Coach. Do you think he'll stay in? I mean, presuming he *is* in."

"He's good," Dietz said, lighting up. "And even if he has a lapse, he has a place to go now. He'll be okay."

"So much for anonymity," Miles said. Dietz gave him a look and so did Diane. "Well, I'm out of here," he said. "I'm history."

"*I'm* history," Kevin Foley said, coming in the door. "*I* just made the copy machine work."

Everyone applauded and Miles slipped out the door, pausing just long enough to give Diane a long, solemn wink. She pretended not to notice, but later in the day she got him alone in the corridor and said, "Don't *ever* do anything like that again. I keep my private life and my public life absolutely separate. Do you understand?"

Miles said he did.

The teachers' room was getting to be a very touchy place indeed.

Miles used study hall to catch up on the work he'd let slide since last Thursday. He had two sets of comps from his Basic class and two sets of short essays from his American Lit. classes and he had to prepare something for Wednesday's Back to School Night with the parents. He was swamped. He looked up once or twice, noticed that Mark and Michelle were no longer holding hands, and went back to correcting the damned compositions. Billy Mack and his problems never crossed his mind.

The bell rang for lunch, but Miles kept on working, and when he finally finished all the Basic comps, he gathered up his papers and books and got ready to go down to the teachers' room.

He was about to shoulder his backpack when he noticed a little envelope sticking out. It was pale blue, that crinkly stuff you couldn't see through, and the note inside was unsigned. "Dear Miles, I'm sorry for what I said." That was all. It was from Billy Mack, of course.

I'm sorry for what I said? Miles had to think for some time before he recalled that on Thursday, after what seemed like a nice enough conversation, casual and friendly, Billy had turned ugly and said, "You don't know shit about me." Was that the problem? God, Billy was a case. Still—think of it—he certainly had his reasons. This afternoon he'd go out of his way to make the kid feel good.

Miles had been jogging for twenty minutes without one single minute of peace. It was like when his mother was dying, only worse. He was exhausted then, and half crazy with guilt because he resented having no life of his own, but at least he'd had Margaret to console him. Now his mind was just a nest of scorpions, and Margaret was one of them. Until he got that damned note from Billy, he'd been perfectly happy and peaceful remembering the weekend with Diane, hearing the music, recalling the new sexual pleasures he'd discovered. And then that note appeared in its absurd blue envelope, and right away he'd begun to think of Margaret and what a shit he was to just dump her like this, and he'd not had a minute's peace since. And now when he thought of Diane, it was her fierce look he recalled, and the sound of her voice as she said, "Don't *ever* do anything like that again. . . . Do you understand?"

He would phone her tonight—Margaret—and be friendly and nice. And eventually he would tell her he couldn't marry her. He'd fallen in love with another woman. And that would be the end of it. It seemed too easy. And, oh God, the guilt.

He stepped up his pace until he felt the jarring in his heels go straight up to his head. He didn't want to be out of breath when he met Billy at the entrance to the park, but if he ran faster, faster, he might get a little bit ahead of the guilt. He'd done it before.

But Billy was not sitting on the stone wall, nor did he join Miles as he continued on through Mitchell Park. Miles was relieved at first—he didn't want Billy to become a regular jogging partner—but after a while he was surprised to find he missed him.

Miles ate dinner standing at the sink—the six-piece special from Kentucky Fried—and then sat down at the kitchen table to correct the remaining compositions. Really, he'd be late handing back only one batch, the Basic ones, from Thursday. He always made a point of returning compositions the day after they were handed in. That way, what they'd written was still fresh in their minds and they could see the point of his corrections. If he waited even one extra day to return them, he might as well not bother, because by then they'd have moved on to other things. MTV was right; a teenager's natural attention span was twenty seconds or less.

He finished the compositions and transcribed the grades into his book and then leaned back and stretched. It was hopeless, of course, to try and teach them to write, but once again he'd done the best he could.

He poured himself a scotch and took it upstairs to his old bedroom. He put it on the night table and made a little backrest out of two pillows, punched them into position until they were just right, and then he stretched out on the bed luxuriously. The good life. He took a sip of his drink and then dialed Diane's number. He lay back and waited. The phone rang and rang but there was no answer. Off the hook, he figured. She's preparing class. Or preparing for Back to School Night. He thought for a minute of driving over there and surprising her, but that didn't seem like a good idea. A woman who didn't want a wink in the teachers' room would not take kindly to dropping over while she was preparing class.

He took another sip of his drink. "Very nice," he said aloud. It

was very nice scotch, it was very nice to have finished those compositions, it was very nice just to lie here and think of Diane. Even
though he was *not* a very nice man. If he were a nice man, he'd
phone Margaret and ask how she was doing.

He reached for the phone and began to dial Margaret's number,
but stopped, and dialed Diane's instead. Still no answer. He put the
phone down but kept his hand on it for a minute. He should call
Margaret. He owed it to her. He owed it to himself, to common
decency.

"God, what a shit I am," he said, and took a big slug of scotch
and went downstairs to prepare class. He'd phone her tomorrow.
Promise.

18

BETWEEN FIRST AND SECOND PERIODS, Miles ran into Billy Mack in the corridor. There were kids everywhere, and the usual slamming and banging of lockers, and so Miles didn't stop to talk. He just gave Billy a nod and kept on walking. But then he thought better of it, and turned back and said to him, "I missed you yesterday, Bill. I had to jog by myself."

He tried to say it softly so the others wouldn't hear him, but loud enough so that it would seem normal, but it didn't work. The kid at the next locker turned and looked at Billy and then at Miles and then, not even pretending to do anything but eavesdrop, he stood there waiting to hear what would happen next.

Billy muttered something, and Miles leaned forward and said "What?"—he'd heard only "asking"—but Billy shook his head, unwilling to repeat it.

"Take care," Miles said, eager to get away, and he turned abruptly and bumped into somebody very solid. It was Cosmo Damiani, looking huge and gray. Cosmo had been waiting for him.

"Sorry, Cosmo," Miles said, laughing. "I hope I didn't hurt you." But Cosmo didn't seem to get it. In fact, Cosmo looked completely out of it. He looked sick.

"Can I talk to you some time? After school?"

"Sure," Miles said. "I'll be in my homeroom."

"Today?"

"You got it," Miles said, and took in at a glance that Cosmo avoided looking at Billy and that Billy, who had been listening, suddenly got very interested in his books, and Miles realized that he himself was feeling very uncomfortable. He was more eager than ever to go teach the troubled poems of Robert Frost.

He put Billy and Cosmo and Margaret and Diane completely out of his mind and, impelled by all the things he was not thinking of, he taught a first-rate class. The kids liked Frost and they were beginning to like poetry and he could tell they already liked him. They let him stand up there and belt out "The Road Not Taken" and "Birches" and "Mending Wall." They listened. They got it.

And then, as the bell rang for the end of class, he realized what Billy Mack had said to him. "You didn't ask me." So? He had to be formally invited, by note, before he would go jogging? Miles had asked him in the first place only because he felt bad for him— and how could you *not* feel bad for him?—and he'd given him the note only because he didn't want to embarrass him by singling him out for a chat during study hall. He didn't like sending notes in the first place. And now this. Why did life have to be so complicated?

He was on his way to teach comp when he heard Lombardi call out, "How they hanging, Milo?" He smiled and pretended not to hear. But it was nice, in a way, to deal with good old Lombardi, whose greatest school problem right now was the nature of the paragraph and whose chief interest was in how they're hanging. Let's hear it for normality. Let's hear it for the simple things in life.

In study hall Miles strolled to the back of the room and leaned against the wall watching Mark and Michelle gaze into each other's eyes—the affair was evidently back on track—and Jennifer examining her face in her little traveling mirror, and the other kids studying or whispering or just waiting for it to end. The simple things in life, indeed.

After a while he walked by Billy's desk and dropped a note as he passed. "Jog?" it said.

Miles was already turning down Lincoln Road to Mitchell Park when he remembered his appointment with Cosmo Damiani. So here he was, pounding his mind into peaceful oblivion while poor Cosmo sat in his homeroom waiting for him. By this time, of course, it made as much sense to go forward as back, since he'd have missed Cosmo in any case.

Miles had never taught Cosmo and had spoken to him only two or three times as they passed in the corridor, and then just to say "Hi" or "Good game on Saturday," the way he would to any other athlete he didn't know. There was only one reason he could think of why Cosmo would want to speak to him now and that was the famous incident with Billy Mack. Cosmo had an ulcer. Cosmo was off the team. Who could guess what he wanted to talk about?

At the park entrance, Billy Mack jumped down from the stone wall where he'd been waiting, and fell into step with him.

"You're early," Billy said. "I thought you'd be later."

"I would have been, but I forgot an appointment."

"Oh," Billy said, and Miles could see he was smiling just a little. They jogged in silence for a while.

"So how're you doing, Bill?" Miles said. "All right?"

"Good," Billy said, and sounded as if he meant it.

Miles gave him a little punch on the arm and said, "Aw-right!" and Billy smiled that wonderful happy smile. They continued to jog in silence.

So this is love, Miles thought, when you're Billy Mack. Jogging with your former teacher, silent, hammering at the hard dirt trail. He glanced over at Billy and saw that he looked perfectly content. But he himself felt nothing. Nothing? A little bit of pity? Maybe even a little bit of contempt?

They came to the cutoff for Lookout Rock and Billy turned up the trail, away from the main path.

"I don't know, Bill. This is too steep for me."

"No," Billy said. "Come on."

They'd gone only a short distance up the steep path when Billy turned to the right, leaping over grass and shrubbery where there was no path at all, and then a new path appeared, narrower and ascending less steeply.

"I don't know," Miles said.

The brush got denser for a while, and then the path ran through a copse of fir trees, and suddenly it opened out a few feet and they could run side by side. It ended suddenly in a little rocky plateau, a rectangular open space no more than six feet wide. It was surrounded by high trees on three sides, and on the fourth it looked out over empty scrubland and, in the far distance, warehouses that looked abandoned.

They stopped jogging and looked out at the view. They could see nobody and nobody could see them.

"It's not exactly Lookout Rock, is it," Miles said. From Lookout Rock you could see all of Malburn and the towns to the north and south.

"It's my favorite place," Billy said. "It's private."

Miles stood on the little plateau and looked around at the brush pine and the ratty-looking bushes, and then out across the scrubland to the distant warehouses, and then at the empty air around them. He felt giddy. He felt like a fool. He threw his arms wide, included the entire scene in his embrace, and said—like Satan tempting Jesus in the desert—"All this will I give unto you, if you will fall down and worship me."

He turned to Billy and was horrified to see the look on the boy's face. It was a look he had seen before, though he could not remember where or when. And then it came to him. It was the look he had seen on Polcari's face, ages ago, just before he'd called him Polecat. It was a look of adoration.

He would not make the same mistake twice. He did not blush and look away and dismiss the kid forever. He looked back at him, gave a little half-smile, and put one arm around Billy's shoulder.

He gave him a little shake, said "Bill," and then took his arm away.

"Time to go," Miles said, and set off at a trot. Billy followed slowly behind him and they did not talk again until they were out of the woods.

"See you, Bill," Miles said.

Billy said nothing.

19

SEVERAL HUNDRED PARENTS were gathered in the auditorium where William Endicott, the principal, would give his opening address. Behind him, in a semicircle, sat the vice-principal, the dean of discipline, the guidance people, and the department chairpersons. In time, he would introduce each of these, but first he was going to charm and instruct the parents with a few of his ideas on education. This was the part of his job he liked best.

The auditorium was chatty, and then it got very noisy for a while, and finally it got quiet. Endicott stepped to the microphone. He welcomed the parents to this year's first Back to School Night and thanked them sincerely for coming. The purpose of this night, he explained, was not to provide conference time with teachers—they would have that on Parents' Night in January—but to introduce them to the students' schedules, to let them hear each teacher explain the aims of his or her class, and to acquaint them with this year's theme.

"Now," he said, ad-libbing, "I'll go through each of these points so there will be no misunderstandings." Then he returned to the safety of the printed page.

(1) A copy of each student's schedule was available at the information booth in the lobby.

(2) Parents would follow the student's day just as it appeared on the schedule: homeroom, first period, second period, et cetera. Each teacher would have seven minutes to teach a model class. Please note: where the schedule said study hall, they'd have coffee in the school cafeteria instead.

(3) This year's theme. He paused for effect. This year's theme was the most important issue facing America today: self-discipline. Almost all the major problems of our time—drugs, alcoholism, poverty, unemployment, crime in the streets, the trade deficit, racial disturbances, immorality in government, you name it—almost all those problems came down, in the final analysis, to a problem of self-discipline. A few years ago Nancy Reagan told America to "Just say no" and many Americans laughed. But we could see now that she was a woman ahead of her time.

At the back of the auditorium, Miles and Dietz and Coogan leaned against the wall and listened. They did not want to miss Endicott's address to the parents. For one thing, it would give Dietz gag lines that would last till Christmas.

Poor study habits go right back to the problem of self-discipline, Endicott said.

He had been reading from notes, but now he looked up and faced his audience, challenging them.

"You know," he said, "I was a captain in the United States Army and that took a lot of self-discipline. I fought for my country in Korea and I fought for my country in Vietnam, and *that* took a lot of self-discipline. But what takes the most discipline is being principal of Malburn High School. I do it because I've got self-discipline."

Miles loved this.

"When Hannibal crossed the Alps with a small army of men and a troop of elephants, they said it couldn't be done. But he did it. How? With self-discipline. They said the same thing to Julius Caesar and Napoleon Bonaparte and Douglas MacArthur, but they did it anyway. How? With self-discipline. Ask any Olympic athlete how he or she did it, and he'll tell you the same thing. Self-discipline. Ask that boy who hiked across America on crutches a few years ago, and he'll tell you the same thing. Self-discipline."

He leaned back from the podium for a minute and looked out, over their heads, inspired.

"No problem can be solved without self-discipline. And there's no problem that self-discipline can't solve."

Miles looked over at Dietz and whispered, "So much for AA." Dietz just shook his head.

"You people know that's true. You don't like to get up in the morning and go to work every day. But you do it, because you've got self-discipline. Sometimes your marriage doesn't seem to work, but you make it work, because it's important to you, and you've got self-discipline. And some of you didn't want to come here tonight, but you knew it was important for your kids, and so you came. Because you've got self-discipline. And yet you tolerate it when your kids tell you, 'I don't want to study,' or, 'I don't feel like studying.' Shouldn't *they* have self-discipline? How are they going to make it in this world? You've done everything for them up till now, but you can't keep on doing it the rest of their lives. Self-discipline is the answer. It's the answer to laziness and inefficiency and poor grades. It's also the answer to drugs and alcohol and the sexual perversions that are destroying our great land."

He stopped, saddened for a moment, and then he went into his wind-up.

"The Marines like to say they need a few good men. *We've* got a few good men. We've got a few good *women.* What we need at Malburn High is a ration of self-discipline. I've got it. You've got it. Make sure your children get it."

There was a lot of applause, during which Dietz and Coogan left. Miles waited, though, and was rewarded when Endicott introduced the department chairpersons. "And last but not least is Ms. Diane

Waring," he said, "Chairman of the English Department. Last because she is youngest. Not least because, more than anyone I know, Ms. Waring practices self-discipline to an impressive degree. She is the ideal teacher, supervisor, and professional."

Diane, dressed all in gray, rose from her chair and made a stiff little bow and then sat down. She did not smile. Self-discipline indeed.

During his homeroom period Miles introduced himself and explained how the homeroom system worked. Students had the same homeroom and homeroom teacher for the entire year. This allowed them to begin and end each day in a place that was permanent, with their own lockers just outside the door, with the same teacher always in charge. It also facilitated the making of announcements, distribution of notices, and, for more eager students, the beginning and ending of love affairs.

There was a little laughter at this. Years ago Miles had said to his homeroom that he urged them to study, think, or even sleep; that he could tolerate talking, knitting, whittling, combing hair, or putting on makeup; that he might even overlook discreet love-making so long as it did not distract the others, but the one thing he would not tolerate was eating. This, as he knew well, was repeated by each new class as if he had said it yesterday.

He went around the room then, getting the parents' names, mentally matching parents with students, complimenting, joking, putting them very much at ease. He opened the floor to questions and almost at once the bell rang for the start of first period. "Poor timing on my part," he said. "I need more self-discipline." The parents laughed and went away feeling good.

His two classes in American Literature went by quickly. He had Frost's "The Road Not Taken" on the board and he read through it—giving, he thought, a rather good performance—and then he gave as close a textual reading of it as five minutes allowed, and ended by reading the poem once more.

"I try to show them a poem or a story or a play," he said, "dismantle it so they can see how it's been put together, indicate that the artist's genius and not his control of mechanics is what produces the total effect, and then I show them the poem once again, whole, a kind of miracle. Just as I've done for you. More important, I try to show them how to do it. How to read this way, how to ask the questions, what questions need to be asked. I try to give them an approach that gets them inside any work of art, so that they needn't grow up a slave to book reviewers or film reviewers or Ten Best lists. I try to give them the ability to form an independent opinion that *means* something."

There was a smattering of applause after his first presentation. He tried to give a little more during his second, but apparently he gave too much or slanted it wrong, because during his talk he noticed some frowns and nervous shifting in chairs, and at the end there was no applause at all. "That was really fine," a man said. "Very impressive. But aren't you afraid you might turn them into little demagogues? Minor league pontificators?" Before Miles could answer, a woman asked if he didn't see any danger in exposing them to some of the books they read: "*Of Mice and Men?* The people in that book are immoral, all of them, and one of them has that glove?" "Glove?" Miles asked. "With Vaseline in it," she said. She couldn't approve of that. "The problem is," another man said, and he was a member of the School Board so he knew what he was talking about, "the problem is that nobody teaches them any moral fiber anymore. The drug problem and the alcohol problem, thank God, have not hit our school yet, but the moral fiber is being eroded, with too much talk *in the classroom* about love and sex and abortion and homosexual filth, and the solid values are being let go by the board. You cannot go telling students that homosexuality is just another lifestyle equal to marriage and not expect them to go experimenting and so forth. It all begins in the schools. I've heard things. I know what goes on."

Miles, stunned and speechless, merely stared at him. Who *was* this idiot? "Well," he said.

"I know a lot more than you think."

"I think we're just a little off the point," the first man said, with a knowing smile toward Miles. "The point is literary analysis and it seems to me that Mr. Bannon here is very good at what he does. I don't think we can hold him responsible for Steinbeck's glove or for the rumors that you've heard on the School Board. *My* fear is just that our kids are going to be sharper than us at that breakfast table, that's all. My son Greg is in this class . . ."

If he was Greg's father, he must be Thomas G. McGrath; that was all Miles could remember. Greg McGrath had a sharp mind, but he was quiet and never put up his hand or spoke outside of class, so Miles scarcely knew who he was. Thank God he had a father. He was still talking, and Miles was trying to listen, but his mind had gone out of control and he was praying, Please God, the bell. At last the bell rang.

As the parents began to file out of his classroom, Miles moved to the door to say goodbye, but he couldn't speak, and everyone seemed to be avoiding his eye, and he had nowhere to look, so he turned and walked slowly to his desk, his mind racing. What had that fool been talking about? Homosexual lifestyles. Filth. He had heard things. About him? The Combat Zone? Something he had said in class? It couldn't be class. If it were something he'd said in class, they'd have thrown him out years ago. It must be the Combat Zone. Anyone could have seen him in that bar; but of course that would mean they were there too, and gay themselves. On the other hand, who would be a more dedicated gay-basher than a gay School Board member? Look at Congress.

Miles pulled himself together then, because people were coming in for the next class and Thomas McGrath was standing by his desk with his hand extended.

"Thank you," Miles said. "Thank you very, very much."

McGrath gripped Miles' hand for a moment and looked him straight in the eyes. "Don't let that homosexual stuff get you down," he said. "You're good." He still held Miles' hand and he was still looking him in the eyes, and Miles began to redden. For a moment, the people entering the room became a blur of faces, and Miles couldn't focus on them and he couldn't think and he didn't know what was happening to him.

McGrath turned away and left the room, and already Miles could not remember what had been said, what he had done. He could remember only that look and the man's hand around his own and some warning about homosexuality. In public. In front of everyone.

"Back in a moment," he said to some woman sitting in the first row, and surprised himself with the steady, normal sound of his voice. He bolted from the room and down the corridor to the men's room. It was empty. He locked himself in a booth and leaned against the door.

For a long time he stood there, trembling. He had a terrible pain just behind his eyes. He hoped it was a stroke so he would never have to go back into that classroom. He tried to pray. He tried to make his mind go blank. Nothing worked.

The bell rang for class, and he heard talking at the men's-room door. He unzipped his pants and peed noisily into the center of the bowl. He would just forget that fool from the School Board. And McGrath, too. He would forget everything for the next hour and he would teach up a storm. He could do it. He'd done it before. He flushed the toilet and came out, humming.

"I'm sorry," he said, coming back into his classroom. "Now, let me give you my thoughts about this class. Students in this class like to call themselves Basic, or at least they pretend to like it because that takes away the sting. But there's no such thing as a basic kid; they're individual, each of them, with unique personalities and unique talents, and . . ." he went on smoothly to the end. He had asked to teach this class, he told them. He loved it. It was a challenge and a pleasure. There was a lot of applause when he finished.

"There's coffee downstairs in the cafeteria," Miles said. "I hope I'll see you there." He was tidying his desk and parents were filing out, when a woman leaned into the room and said, "Is this it? Is it?" He turned and looked at her. She was a tiny woman, blond and beautifully dressed, and as she came toward him, he could smell the drink on her breath. "I want that hoity-toity English teacher," she said, "the one who makes fun of my son."

"Oh God," Miles said.

"You're it, aren't you? You think because you've got a nice nose, you can make fun of my son's looks? What kind of man are you, anyway? He's a good boy. He's a smart boy. Why are you against him?"

"Who are you?" Miles asked. "I don't know who you are."

"What have you got against him? Why do you call him Mouse?"

"I don't know what to say," Miles said. "I don't know who your son is, or who you are, and I don't call anybody Mouse. Who *are* you?"

"I'm Angela Muldoon," she said, smiling, and at once it was all clear to Miles. Muldoon, of course. She had the same nose, the same funny little face, as that kid Muldoon, who looked like the mouse in those cartoons. Jeff Douglas must have seen the resemblance too, and named him Mouse.

"Mrs. Muldoon," he said, and took her hand.

"He's not a mouse," she said, and tears started. "Don't call him Mouse."

"Mrs. Muldoon, I'm not his teacher. There's been a mistake. Mr. Douglas is his teacher. Please understand . . ."

But she was crying in earnest now. "His nose," she said, as the tears continued, "and that girlfriend of his . . . grades and everything else . . . he was never like this."

"Mrs. Muldoon," he said, but it was hopeless. He sat her down and said he would be right back and ran to get the school nurse. By the time Miles returned with the nurse, Mrs. Muldoon had stopped crying but she had gone limp, and they could barely get her up. She was tiny, but in this semi-conscious state, she was very heavy. They supported her between them, half-dragging her, and together they got her to the nurse's office. He thanked the nurse and she thanked him, and by this time coffee was over and Miles had to go teach his final class in American Lit. He was relieved and angry and, in a funny way, jubilant, all at once.

On the way to class he ran into Diane. She gave him a stiff smile and said, "Later?" and he said, stiffly, "If you wish," and she said, "My place," and that was that. His class went very well.

Back to School Night was over at last. The final bell had rung and the parents had gone home and the school once again belonged to the students and teachers. Peace in our time.

Miles sat down at his desk to think. Had he, again, escaped free and clear? Or were things closing in around him and he didn't even know it? That clown on the School Board had said, "I know more than you think." And McGrath had said . . . what? Whatever it was, he seemed to assume that Miles was homosexual. Again Miles felt his face redden.

He closed his eyes and propped his head in his hands. What an incredible night it had been. With the Steinbeck stuff and homosexuality and poor Mrs. Muldoon drunk and disabled . . . another kick in the krogies for Jeff Douglas.

His head hurt. He should call Margaret. He would be spending the night with Diane, or at least the major part of it, and he didn't want Margaret to call and find him not at home. He owed her at least that much consideration. He owed her a lot more, in fact. And he'd pay up. He would. Somehow.

He rubbed his eyes, crooked his neck around from left to right, relieving the tension, and when he looked up, a man was standing there. He was a small, solid, angry-looking man who could only be Billy Mack's father.

"These floors are very creaky," Miles said. "You must be able to move without making a sound."

"That's right."

"How long have you been standing here?"

"A minute and a half."

"You're Billy Mack's father."

"That's right."

"I'm Miles Bannon."

"Right."

"But of course you know that."

"I know you, all right."

What kind of conversation was this? They had never met, and they were talking to each other like old enemies. Miles was determined to get it back to civility. He stood up and stuck out his hand. They shook. Miles pointed to a chair and they sat down.

"Well, I'm glad to meet you, Mr. Mack. Mr? Officer?"

"Jack."

"Jack Mack." Miles laughed quietly.

"That's right." He did not laugh at all.

"I'm Miles. Listen, I can't tell you how bad I feel about what happened to Billy. It was one of those insane jokes kids play that seems funny before the fact and tragic afterwards. You know what I mean? It was a joke. It meant nothing. Billy's a great kid and they all like him a lot."

"But they did that to him."

"It meant nothing."

"It meant a hell of a lot to him. It meant a hell of a lot to us. His mother's halfway to lunatic praying for him."

"I mean, it wasn't personal. It was just his turn to be the butt of a joke. It's some kind of sick initiation joke they play. I guess."

"How come you know so much about it?"

"I don't. I'm just guessing. Kids can be nice and decent and good, but put them together in a pack, and they can get pretty vicious. Sadistic even."

"I know about sadistic."

"Yes." Miles looked at him and, deliberately, waited for him to go next. There was a long silence.

"I want to help him, but he doesn't want any help from me."

"He does. I can assure you of that. It seems to me that, more than anything, he wants a father."

"He's got a father."

"Yes, of course. That's what I mean. More than anything, he wants your acceptance. Of him, I mean. As a son."

"His mother says he talks to you."

"Well, only a little. Jogging."

"Jogging?"

"We went jogging once. After that happened. He seemed to want to talk, so I asked him if he wanted to join me for a jog."

"This is all news to me."

"He hasn't mentioned it?"

"He doesn't talk. Period."

"He probably just needs time. Imagine how he must feel about . . ." Miles stopped, because he was thinking, Imagine how he must feel about what's been done to him, especially when he sees those same kids in school and knows they're looking at him and thinking about it and he's exposed to a shame so raw it's like being stripped of your flesh.

"About what happened? No. I can't imagine it. It would never have happened to me."

"There's not one of us that can't be broken in an instant."

They looked at one another.

"What can I do?" Miles said. "Can I do anything to help?"

"I just wanted to see you."

"I see."

"I just wanted to get a look at you."

Miles spread his hands and shrugged.

"Billy's not the same."

"He's a great kid," Miles said. "He's good."

They were silent for a moment, and then Officer Mack stood up, shook Miles' hand, and left without another word.

Poor Billy, Miles thought. Poor, poor, poor Billy Mack.

20

After Officer Mack left, Miles sat at his desk for a long while, thinking. He still couldn't sort out what had happened tonight; it was all too much, too confusing. Why was this happening? And why now? Just when Diane had entered his life and he could see some kind of future for himself. Diane sure as hell didn't think he was gay. She was waiting for him right now, in bed probably. Deliberately, he thought of her in bed—her breasts, her soft, responding body, sexy—and he waited to feel that tug in his groin. It didn't come. Never mind. It would be there when he needed it. And he resolved, for his own sake and for theirs together, to tell her nothing about what happened tonight.

Margaret looked at her watch, shook it, and then got out of bed and, very slowly and carefully, made her way to the kitchen to check the time. It was eight o'clock. At night, obviously, but what day was it? She had gone to work on Monday. Or was it Tuesday that she went to work? Or was today Tuesday?

She spilled some vodka into a tumbler and, standing by the sink, drank the stuff straight down. Then she filled the glass with water and drank that. She could not get rid of the taste in her mouth, like old wool, musty and thick. She had to find out what day it was. She went into the living room and switched on the television where some family comedy was playing, a fat wife and children. Was that Roseanne Somebody? Or was it another fat wife? She looked for the *T.V. Guide*, but couldn't find it, and then she couldn't remember why she wanted it. She turned the television off.

What was Miles up to? Tricky old pricky old Miles. She dialed his number but of course there was no answer. He was never home anymore. He never called. It was over and she knew it. But if it really was over, all over, done with, she would have nothing at all. And she couldn't live with that.

She would write him a letter, short but devastating, and she would make him feel the way she felt. But first she would have a little drink and then phone him again. She felt sick. Perhaps she should rest for a minute, just lie down here on the living-room couch until this sick feeling passed. She could compose the letter while she rested. She lay down.

Margaret had been drinking on and off for nearly a week.

When Miles left her bed late Thursday night—a new Miles, with confidence in himself and his sexual skills—they kissed and said goodbye and Margaret knew that she had lost him, forever. She sat at the kitchen table, and drank until she felt that reassuring click in her brain. She was safe now, for a while. The little trapdoor that shut out the worst of the terrors had at last slammed shut. No more panic drinking. Just maintenance now: smooth, calm, and comforting, glass after glass. Her mind was sharp and clear, and her feelings were wrapped in a thick woolen comforter, and she thought how easily she could hurt him as he had hurt her. She wrote a letter. She catalogued his cruelties to her, his neglect, his near-contempt, and at the end she went to the heart of things: "You have not spared even your mother. She struggled to pull that cord that would save her life, and you only sat and watched. You let her die. I saw you." She sat back, trembling, exhausted. She would put the letter in his door tomorrow. But right now she would have another drink. Nothing mattered anymore except this easy slow descent into stupor and death.

She slept all day Friday, and though the phone rang several times as people from the office called, she slept straight through. On Saturday morning, she read the letter and then destroyed it. She had some coffee and a little juice. She tried to eat a muffin. Later she drove past Miles' house and saw his car was not there. Nor was it there in the afternoon or in the evening. At night she wrote another letter, less detailed this time, less personal. She left out the injuries he'd done to her and concentrated on his failings as a man, a son. And she concluded, "You watched your mother die and did not lift a finger to help her. I know you and your kind. I hate you." The rest of the night she drank.

On Sunday she destroyed the letter. And she drank.

On Monday she went to work, sick and very pale, but after an hour she had to leave, she said, to pick up a prescription. She bought two half-gallons of vodka that she put in the trunk of her car, and a pint for her purse. In the parking lot, she unscrewed the cap and drank straight from the bottle. She did not even look around to see if anyone was watching. This was who she had become. She wiped her mouth with the back of her hand and returned to the office. Early that afternoon Mr. Collins himself drove her home. He had his secretary follow in a company car, and he had her make sure Margaret was settled comfortably in bed, and then they returned to work. Margaret, drunk but canny, got up and went out to her car and lugged the two half-gallons of vodka into the house. She did not want to be caught in life without protection.

On Tuesday morning she called in sick. She was better, she said, but she needed the day to rest. They put her call through to Mr. Collins and he suggested she get some professional help. She was seeing a doctor, she said defensively, a very good one. And she'd be at work tomorrow. She drank nothing all day. She had a lot of coffee, and she picked at some toast, and that night she drove past Miles' house and saw that he was home. His car was in the driveway and the lights were on. She drove back to her own place and stayed by the phone all evening. No call came. She dialed Diane Waring. There was no answer. She dialed Miles but the line was busy. Perhaps at that moment she and Miles were calling each other. She put the phone down and waited, looking at it, leaning over it, ready. It did not ring. At eleven, she had a drink. And then at eleven-thirty. At midnight, she took a drink in one long swallow, and then she got in her car and drove to his house and parked a little down the street. All the lights were out except his bedroom light, and finally that went out, and then she drove home. She went to bed but couldn't sleep, and so she took a Xanax and chased it with some vodka, and then she dozed for a while, and had another drink, and dozed some more. At dawn she slept.

It was eight-thirty now, on Wednesday evening, and Margaret was not sure what day it was, but she was going to lie down on the living-room couch for a little rest, just until this sick feeling passed, and then she would have a drink and phone Miles. While she rested, she could compose a letter to him, short and devastating. She stretched out on the couch and closed her eyes, waiting for sleep. She needed a pillow or she'd have a crick in her neck afterward. She fell asleep at once.

Propped up in bed with pillows at his back, Miles was in a confessional mood. They had just made love and were having a glass of wine and he was feeling trusting and expansive. He could tell Diane. Diane would understand. Diane would know how to respond.

She stretched out in bed just then, and drew one leg up over his. "What?" she said, her bedroom voice. "What are you thinking?"

"A ghastly thing happened tonight," he said. "Awful."

She'd been expecting love play, he knew, but he had made up his mind to tell her, and now he had to go through with it. He tried to speak and couldn't. He put his hands up to his face.

"Miles," she said, pained suddenly.

"I can't say it," he said. "God!"

Leaning over him, she took his hands away. He was astonished to see tears in her eyes. "Tell me," she said.

Slowly, he told her about the School Board member who had heard things and was upset at all the homosexual filth.

"That's Jared Whiting," she said. "Was he fat and balding? In a brown suit? That's him. He's a complete ass. He went from room to room saying the same thing to every single English teacher. He said the same thing to me. I sent him to Endicott."

"But why homosexuality? Why me?"

"He's a John Bircher or a Born Again or something like that. He's a complete ass."

"I thought it was about my fling in the Combat Zone."

"It wasn't about you."

"I wish I could believe that."

"It's true. Believe me. He doesn't know anything about you. Or care. He's just against sin."

"So it's only a coincidence?"

"He's just against anybody having a good time," she said.

"But then there was Greg McGrath's father." Now he told her about Thomas McGrath and how he gripped his hand and told him not to let that homosexual stuff get him down. "He just assumed I was gay," Miles said. "He said it in public, in front of all those people."

"But why would he assume anything like that? On what grounds? And even if he did, why would he mention it? It doesn't add up, Miles."

"Nonetheless, he said it."

"What exactly did he say? The exact words."

"He looked me straight in the eye and said, 'Don't let that homosexual stuff get you down.' His exact words."

"And this was *after* Whiting, not before?"

"After Whiting."

"Well, it's perfectly clear. He was telling you not to let Jared

Whiting get to you, that's all. With all that talk about homosexual filth."

"Oh."

She kissed his forehead. "You see?"

"I don't know, though."

"He was being supportive. He was being a friend. If he was thinking anything, he was thinking you're *not* gay and you shouldn't let that ass get to you."

"Do you think so?" He could see how it all fit. It made sense. But then why had he felt so accused? Was this a guilty conscience run mad? He looked at her, hard. "Do you think?"

"It's perfectly clear," she said. She relaxed. She would not have to tell him that she knew McGrath, he was a friend, they had had a fling. She kissed Miles on one eyelid, then on the other.

Miles closed his eyes. She was right, he knew.

He had thought that this was it, that all the follies and stupidities of the past year, of his entire past life, had caught up with him at last, and he was about to be exposed for what he was and what he had done, all his sins laid bare. It was the end of everything, he'd thought. Disgrace. Dismissal. But it hadn't happened. It had passed him by, and he had not been touched by it. It was a kind of miracle. A chance at a new life.

He opened his eyes and looked at her.

"You're a mess," she said, and lay her head against his chest.

He felt a tear fall on his chest and trickle slowly into the hollow of his neck. He had made her cry.

"Why?" he said, whispering.

"You're so good," she said.

He held her tight until her crying stopped.

Margaret woke with a painful crick in her neck. She had fallen asleep on the living-room couch, and as she rubbed her neck and shoulder, she looked around her for the letter. She was sure she had written it just before she lay down. "You let your mother die. I saw you. I know you." It was very short and very hard, and it did the job better than the long letters she had written before. She wanted him to know how cruel he was, to feel it. She wanted to kill him slowly. She wanted to hold him in her arms.

She stood at the sink and poured some vodka into a tumbler. She gulped it down, and waited as the burning in her stomach turned into that hot flush racing through all her veins. It was like poison, it was like fire. She stood there until she was sure the vodka would stay down, and then she went to the phone and dialed Miles' number. No answer. There was no answer at Diane's place either. And it was almost midnight.

Why did she care? Why did she bother? She looked again for the letter. She would tear it up. She was on her knees, feeling underneath the couch, when all at once she knew what she would do. She sat up and smiled. It was completely out of her control now. Her will was gone. Her mind was gone.

She took the keys and got into the car and drove to his house. She let herself in, as she had on all those Saturday mornings when Eleanor was dying and Miles was sleeping late. She put on the lights. She went to Eleanor's room, and afterwards to the den where Miles had slept when the Home Helps used his bedroom, and then to the kitchen. In the kitchen, she poured herself a drink and sat and remembered the good times. Miles asleep on the couch while she and Eleanor watched the football games. Miles coming up the walk from school, flushed from jogging, excited to see her. Miles in bed, his quirky smile, his earnest, determined lovemaking. That had changed, too. She shuffled through the bills on the kitchen table. She read the notes attached to the refrigerator door, reminders to himself: Make copies of Sexton and Plath, Ask Billy to jog?, Back to School Night!

She poured another drink and took it upstairs with her. She looked into the little bedroom that had been Miles' sister's. She went into the bathroom and opened the medicine chest. Aspirins, razor, razor blades, shaving cream, the stuff he had always had. No new things. No women's cosmetics. No trace of Diane.

She went into his bedroom and saw that he had not made his

bed. She threw back the covers, examining the sheets for stains, but they were clean, unmarked. She searched carefully through his bureau drawers, pushing aside his underwear, his socks, two shirts still in their plastic wrappers, running shorts, an old jock strap. There was a pile of photos under his handkerchiefs. She shuffled through them quickly; they were old ones; she had seen them all. She went to his closet, flicked aside his shirts, his jackets, his pants, his winter coats, all this stuff that said he was alive, in love with someone else. She was searching for a nightgown, a negligée, some proof of his betrayal. But she found nothing new, nothing suspicious. Still, it had to be here. She got a chair and stood on it, poking through the pile of notebooks and clotheshangers and old sweaters on the top shelf. She got down on the floor and looked inside his shoes. She turned his pair of boots upside down. She went through his jacket pockets. Nothing. In desperation, she pulled everything out of the trunk at the foot of his bed—a winter blanket, some flannel sheets, a cashmere shawl that had been his mother's—and then she threw everything back inside, a messy heap, and closed it. She sat on the trunk to rest. She emptied her glass. Why was she here? What was she doing? She looked around the room and suddenly caught sight of herself in the bureau mirror. Her face was blotchy and gray. She looked old. She looked crazy. She could not endure it a second longer. She pulled her dark hair down over her face and let herself scream. Afterwards, she cried, her face in her hands.

She stayed there, sitting on the trunk, until at last she was calm again. Then, avoiding the mirror, she took off all her clothes, slowly, and got into his bed. She lay on her stomach. She pressed her face into his pillow and smelled his after-shave, his clean skin, his hair. She was on top. They were making love. She touched her tongue to his lips, just a tiny touch, until his lips burned and he opened his mouth to her. But she took her tongue away and touched his eyelids instead, a burn on this one and on this, and then she went back to his lips. She writhed on top of him. She arched her back and ground her hips against his. She sat up and twisted her body, thrusting, so she could feel him move inside her. She kept on and on until the trembling began and would not stop, running up from him and into her, and back into him, and then again, and again, and more, and finally she collapsed, unable to go on. She lay there, exhausted, wet, and the sheets were wet.

Miles laughed and squirmed around in the bed and said, "What else? Tell me what else."

Diane was not a good mimic, but she assumed a voice of sincerity and desperation as she did Mrs. Higgins.

" 'I know my Francis is a slow starter, and I know he's not doing very well right now. But Miss Waring, believe me,' and here she reached out and put her hand over mine and looked me straight in the eye, 'believe me, Miss Waring: artistically, he's inclined.' "

"Oh, no," Miles said. "You're making this up."

" 'Artistically, he's inclined.' I swear it."

"Do it again."

The sheet was at her waist and her hair fell around her shoulders and her breasts were bare and full, but she nonetheless attempted to imitate Mrs. Higgins, fifty and frustrated, leaning forward to say with conviction, " 'Believe me, Miss Waring: artistically, he's inclined.' "

"What else?" he said. "Tell me more. Tell me everything."

This was turning into a perfect evening.

Margaret got out of his bed and got dressed and then stood there looking around. She was very calm now. She just wanted this over with.

She went down the stairs and out the front door to her car. As she started the motor, she looked over at his house and saw that she had left all the lights on. She had left the door unlocked. And her glass upstairs in his bedroom. She shrugged, and drove away.

At home, she ran a hot bath and emptied a small bottle of perfume in it. She smiled. The perfume was Obsession. She got a glass of vodka and settled into the tub. She lay there drinking while the water cooled. Then she put on her nightgown and her heavy satin dressing gown and sat at the kitchen table to write him one last letter.

"You let your mother die," she began, and for the first time in a very long while, she wondered if that were true.

But of course it was true. She had watched while his mother reached helplessly for the cord. She had watched as he sat there and did nothing. She had watched as his mother fell back against the pillows, dead.

But his mother hadn't died. The nurse had come and his mother had started breathing again.

But Miles knew, and she knew, what he had intended.

She threw away the letter and went into the bathroom and got the Xanax she had saved. There were twenty left, and fifty more hidden in the Empirin bottle. She filled a glass with vodka and washed them down, five at a time. They seemed to lump together in her chest.

She sat again at the kitchen table. It was hard to think what to say to him. She was very tired, very muddled. Now that she had taken the pills, now that it was almost ended, she felt no desire to hurt him. He had done his best, she supposed. He was, by his own reckoning, a good man. Good Miles. Poor Miles.

She took the pen and wrote her last note to him. "I know you," it said. And then, very slowly and with the greatest effort, she got up from the table and felt her way along the wall to her bedroom. She collapsed face down on the bed.

Miles brought his car to a slow stop and sat there looking at his house. Every light was on. If this was a burglary, it was the most public burglary in the history of Malburn. He got out of the car and walked cautiously to the side door. "Hello," he called, but there was no answer. He went from room to room. Nothing was missing. Nothing seemed to have been disturbed. He climbed the stairs to his bedroom and at once spotted the drinking glass on his bureau, the closet door ajar, the bed a mess. He ran his hand over the sheet, half expecting to find it warm, but it felt damp. He opened his top bureau drawer and then the others, one by one. His photos were scattered around and his clothes were all jumbled together, but nothing was missing so far as he could tell. He went downstairs and discovered the front door unlocked. It had to be Margaret.

Suddenly all the fun of the evening was gone. Gone too was the enormous relief he'd felt at finding his life was not ended but just beginning. Everything was poisoned once again. By guilt. By his neglect of Margaret. Poor Margaret. She must be half crazy.

Well, he would call her tomorrow. He would make a date and explain that he had fallen in love with someone new and he would beg her understanding and forgiveness. But right now, what could he do?

He went to bed.

In a moment, though, he was on the phone, calling her. He must apologize at once. He could not let her go to sleep feeling the way she must. He would beg her to forgive him. He would drive over there now, at once, if she would let him.

He let the phone ring and ring and ring. She was asleep. She must have taken a hefty sleeping pill. He hung up the phone. He would call her in the morning.

The phone rang and rang and Margaret slept on. In her dream, a fire alarm was ringing and she did not know why. "But why?" she said. "I only want to sleep." She saw then that she had set the house on fire, and they were trapped in it, she and Miles, and he was ringing the alarm. "No one will come," she said. "It's fine. We'll sleep like this, the two of us." But Miles was gone now, he had left the house, and she was alone in it, and the alarm continued ringing. If only the alarm would stop, she could sleep, and everything would be all right. But it would not stop—it went on and on—and she came conscious, finally, and got out of bed. At once she fell to the floor. She tried to stand, but fell again. The floor kept giving out beneath her, and so on hands and knees she crawled from the bedroom to the living room, still half-asleep. And then, all at once, the ringing stopped. She woke. Her hand was on the phone. She was cold and her face was wet and she understood that it was going to be very hard to live after this. Nonetheless, she made an enormous effort and dialed 911. She heard herself—or was it still the dream?—as she gave her name and address, and told them alcohol and pills, and then she lay on the floor, peaceful, because she knew she had done the right thing.

21

MILES SLEPT LATE, and when he called Margaret's number, there was no answer. She'd left for work, no doubt. He was frankly relieved, because he was very happy this morning, very up, and he didn't feel like taking a nose-dive into Margaret's depression or whatever it was. He'd deal with that later. Sometime. Right now he wanted to revel in the moment: he was in love with Diane, and he could see she was falling in love with him, and all the nightmares were over. No more vigils at a deathbed, no more insecurities about sex, and, by God, no more guilt. Period. He wasn't going to allow it. If a guilty thought came to him, he would dismiss it like a temptation to sin. "Behind me, Satan," he would say. He was going to live in the moment. For the moment.

Driving to school, he noticed how all the leaves had turned. It would be an early winter, probably a long one. But right now everything was at a peak, flame red, blood red, gold. And he was a part of it, alive and in love, and wasn't it terrific?

As he was about to enter the teachers' room, Diane came out. Miles stood just where he was, so that she had to brush up against him, and as she did, he stepped back from her and said, "Please," in an indignant voice. Diane smiled, despite herself, and tipped her head toward the end of the corridor. He followed her, and they went through the door to the stairwell. They were completely alone.

"Am I in trouble?" Miles said, smiling in that way she liked. "Was I bad?"

"Talking like this, here, is very indiscreet, Miles, so I want to be quick. All right?"

"Yes, ma'am."

"I can't have a misunderstanding about this."

"No, ma'am."

"This *is* just a fling. I like you a lot, and I like being with you, but we have no claims on each other, neither of us."

"Yes, ma'am. No, ma'am."

"Miles."

"It's a fling," he said. "It's a fling. I know that. We've always agreed on that, right from the start."

"You say it now. But what about afterwards?"

"No claims. No regrets."

"And that's okay?"

"I *love* a fling."

She looked down the stairs, and up. She leaned toward him, and Miles could see she was thinking of giving him a little kiss, but then she thought better of it.

"Do it," he said. "Give in to it."

"You'll be my undoing yet," she said.

"I certainly hope so." He made his eyebrows go up and down like Groucho Marx.

"We're prefecting tomorrow," she said, "at the Halloween Hop. You could come over afterward, if you want."

"I want," he said, "I will." And as she turned to leave, he said, "But it's only a fling."

He was at his classroom door just as the bell rang for the start of homeroom period. He dropped his backpack onto his desk and stood facing the class, his arms spread wide.

" 'Life is a banquet,' " he said, " 'and half the suckers out there are starving to death.' Thus far the Gospel according to Auntie Mame."

He proceeded to explain that when he was their age, a musical opened on Broadway called *Mame,* full of wonderful songs, and some good dances, and lines like "Life is a banquet," and so forth. "It's a pagan idea," he said, "but a good one on a fall morning like today when you've got your whole life ahead of you and you haven't yet screwed it up completely." He stood on his chair and, from there, he stepped onto his desk. "Live, live, live," he said, proclaiming it, and even he marveled at the fact that he could do these things and not feel like an utter fool. He laughed at himself and shook his head in disbelief and everyone applauded. A very nice way to begin the school day.

He was savoring every wonderful thing about his life today, and as he left his Basics class for study hall, he remembered how these corridors had looked, empty, on that day in September when his mother was dying and he'd come in to fill up a week of his plan book. Even then he'd seen that this was his life, this wonderful place where nobody was dying.

Today, as usual, the corridors were filled with students pushing and shoving or beating up their lockers, though most of them were just on duty and hanging out. They gossiped and complained. A lot of the boys used the time to comb their hair. The girls never combed their hair in the corridor; hair, makeup, anything personal was confined to the bathroom; the corridor was for visiting and for passing on the news. A couple boys were exchanging money and football cards marked with the point spread for the weekend games. Some of them, boys and girls both, were probably exchanging money and dope. It happened even here. But mostly they talked and touched: a high five, a punch on the arm, sometimes a wrestling match right in the middle of the corridor. The more interesting touching—and it was quite common—was the movie kiss or the clinch, where a couple seemed locked in each other's arms forever, and this could mean they were formally engaged to be engaged or simply that they liked one another and weren't keeping it a secret. The corridors were alive with raging hormones.

Today Miles found it wonderful, all of it. Muldoon and his blond girlfriend were on duty, lost to the rest of the corridor as they gazed into each other's eyes. No kissing, just this gaze. Muldoon was a good six inches shorter than the girl, and he had to look up to look into her eyes, but he was throwing himself into this with all he had. Miles paused and was surprised to see that she had quite literally decorated the inside of her locker. Freshman girls sometimes did this, but Miles had never seen a locker done up quite so thoroughly. She had wallpapered and carpeted the thing—light blue paper with little pink flowers on the sides, and a deep pink carpet on the floor—and she had hung small framed pictures of movie heartthrobs down the back: Rob Lowe or Tom Cruise or Tom Hanks, Miles couldn't tell the difference, since they all looked the same to him. On the shelf above, she had her makeup bag and her hairspray and a lot of other things that weren't books. Inside the door was a full-length mirror. Here was a girl who was ready and eager for homemaking. But even this seemed wonderful, and Miles laughed to himself as he rounded the corner and took off up the stairs.

In the corridor outside study hall there was the usual chaos. A bunch of football players were horsing around with some cheerleaders, and two idiots were throwing a football over the heads of the crowd, missing them by inches, and Deirdre Forster was singing a song by Whitney Houston, all stops out. The noise was getting to Miles, but still, he told himself, it was a place bursting with life and you had to admire that. Just then the football sailed past him and landed short, hitting Deirdre in the back of the head. She turned around and saw who had thrown it and yelled "Motherfucker" so that the sound bounced off the walls and Miles was obliged to say something to her. "Hey," he said, "how about a little dignity here." The guys laughed, and Deirdre turned away and made a face, and so Miles had to get serious. "Do you want Detention?" he said.

"Do you want to go down to the office?" He wished he hadn't said it, knowing how she'd respond, but it was too late now, so he put his hand on her arm and said, "Did you hear me, Deirdre?" She turned to face him. "He hit me with the goddam football," she said, "while I was singing." "Well, watch your language," Miles said. "Yeah, watch your fucking mouth," someone said, and everybody laughed. Miles shook his head and continued on down the corridor. "Sorry," Deirdre said, calling after him. "Sorry, Milo." A good kid, really.

Miles was about to go into study hall when he saw Cosmo Damiani standing in front of his locker. There were kids on either side of him, hanging out and talking, but even in the middle of a lot of activity, Cosmo seemed to be all alone.

So many times now Miles had meant to say something to Cosmo, to cheer him up or just to greet him, but it never seemed exactly the right moment. He would do it now. He *should* do it now, to apologize for missing their appointment yesterday when he went jogging with Billy Mack. But of course Billy Mack was what Cosmo wanted to see him about. What else could it be? Cosmo had been one of the guys in the locker room that day, and Cosmo knew that he knew. He wondered about Cosmo. He was a big, rough, bullish kid, but he must have another side to him, sensitive, or at least responsive. After the incident, he was the one who ran and got Endicott; that was something in his favor. He had an ulcer. He had dropped out of football. God knows what the kid had been through.

Miles approached him from the side. Cosmo's face was partly shielded by the locker door, but Miles could see that he was staring at something in the locker, a mirror probably. But he wasn't combing his hair or wetting his contact lenses or anything else Miles could see. He was just staring at something. Miles moved around the other side, prepared to say, "You're getting awfully vain, Cosmo," or, "Looking good," or something like that, but as he leaned toward Cosmo, he glanced into the locker to see what he was looking at, and saw that there was no mirror there. There was nothing at all there. Cosmo was staring, blank and fixed, at the back of his empty locker.

Miles opened his mouth to say something, anything, and then realized that Cosmo had not seen him because Cosmo was not really there either. He was in that locker somewhere, dead to this world.

Miles backed away, saying nothing, and went to his study hall. He had marveled enough for one day.

His jog that afternoon was an act of the will. The kids in his third American Lit. class seemed deliberately obtuse, their quiz papers convinced him that nobody listened to a word he said, and, besides, he was tired. Screwing all night was a great way to relax, but eventually you had to get some sleep, too. He would have liked a nap but, dutifully, he hit the pavement and in a while he began to feel pretty good.

Billy Mack was sitting on the wall outside Mitchell Park and gave him a big smile as he approached. Miles raised one hand in greeting and kept on jogging. Billy fell into step beside him.

It was a sunny day, but fall had begun to set in, and it was chilly in the park. Miles was glad he'd worn his sweatshirt. He glanced over at Billy in his flimsy teeshirt, and said, "Aren't you cold, Bill?" Billy smiled and shook his head, and Miles was again struck by how completely the boy was transformed when he smiled. Or rather, without that smile, he didn't even exist. The smile somehow called him into being. "Tough guy," Miles said, and punched him on the arm. Billy smiled once again.

They'd been jogging for some time when Billy said to him, "How old are you, Milo?"

"What?" Miles said, laughing.

"How old are you?"

"I'm thirty-five," he said, and gave Billy a look. "I'll be thirty-six in December."

They continued jogging.

"Why?" Miles asked.

". . . my father."

"What's that?"

"I said, you could be my father."

Miles kept looking straight ahead.

"You're old enough, I mean."

"Thanks a lot," Miles said, caustic. "What a pal you are. Listen, I may be old, but I can beat you any day. Come on." And he took off at a sprint.

He didn't want to be anybody's father, least of all Billy Mack's. But, God, the poor kid.

Billy passed him in less than a minute and kept on down the path. He was sitting with his back against a tree when Miles came into view, breathing hard. "You're getting old, Milo," he said. "I don't know."

They were at the cutoff for Lookout Rock.

"You want to take the hill?"

"Not on your life," Miles said.

"We could go to my lookout instead. It's easier."

"I'm too old," Miles said, and seeing Billy's disappointment, he said, "Next time. Maybe."

"If you want to," Billy said.

"Come on. You'll catch pneumonia." Miles gave him a hand and yanked him up onto his feet. They jogged in silence the rest of the way back to school.

Miles had phoned Margaret twice, with no answer, and he had promised himself he would call again just as soon as he finished this batch of papers. He had four to go. Then he would pour himself a scotch and phone her. But he was tired from his jog, and cranky because the papers weren't what they should be, so he got up and poured a drink anyhow. He took a good slug of scotch and listened while it trickled down and around and finally hit his stomach with that nice burning sensation. Actually, the scotch would help him get through the remaining four papers, and given the change in his mood, it would help the kids who wrote those papers too.

He finished up quickly. And then, as he'd promised himself, he went to the phone and dialed Margaret's number. He let the phone ring seven times, then eight, but there was no answer. This was very peculiar. He was standing with the phone in his hand when he became aware that someone was ringing the doorbell. Margaret? It could be. He put on a welcoming look, and with his glass still in his hand, he opened the front door. "Welcome!" he said. "Welcome." And his voice trailed off, because it was not Margaret but Jim Dietz. Skinny and shaking, he stood there with a pained look on his face.

"Dietz," Miles said.

"Can I come in?" Dietz said. "It's about Margaret."

22

MARGARET LAY IN BED with her eyes closed, looking at the darkness.
She had been in the hospital for almost a week and she would be
going home tomorrow. Home or hospital, it was all the same to
her, since nothing mattered in either case. On that first day, when
they brought her back to life, she had been distracted by the realization that, no matter how sick she felt, at least she was again
among the living. But when she got a good look at the land of the
living, she realized once more that nothing mattered.

That first morning, they had pumped her stomach and given her
shots of B-12 and tried to remedy her dehydration with an intra-
venous solution of sugar and water. They had done what they could
to make her comfortable. She slept for a long while, and was awak-
ened by a psychiatric nurse who asked her lots of questions, and
then she slept again. The next time she woke, a skinny little man
with the shakes stood at her bedside. He'd brought her a single red
rose and a get-well card. He was all concern.

He explained that he was Jim, a recovering alcoholic, and that
he worked with the hospital's volunteer staff for alcohol and drug
abuse problems, and that they had met once, back in his drinking

days, at a play Miles put on at Malburn High. *You Can't Take It With You,* Jim said. It was a very funny play.

"Who *are* you?" she said.

"My name is Jim Dietz," he said. "I'm a recovering . . ."

"Go away," she said.

He assured her that he understood, that it was fine, that this was all part of recovery, that he'd been through it too. He knew. He cared.

"Go away," she said, "please!"

He went away.

For the rest of the day Margaret lay in bed looking at the blackness, wishing she had never called 911. Her head felt swollen and mushy, and her skin hurt to the touch. Her throat was raw from the tube they had used to pump her stomach. Every joint in her body ached. But there was no ache for Miles. Indeed, she had not thought of Miles until that fool Dietz mentioned him. Perhaps suicide was the cure after all.

As the days went on, the one thing that interested her was her disinterest in Miles. She refused to see him, even when he sent in notes and then flowers, even when he sat all night in the waiting room on Halloween and again on All Souls Day. She saw Dietz and the group in Alcoholics Anonymous, and she saw people from the office—Mr. Collins, it turned out, was himself in AA—but she refused to see Miles. Her refusal was not an expression of anger or an accusation of betrayal so much as the simple desire, now that she'd gotten him out of her life, to keep him out for good.

Now, however, as she lay in bed looking deep into the darkness, she knew that it didn't matter whether she saw him or not. He was dead to her, and if he wanted so badly to see her, let him. An act of kindness to the dead. Why not? She would let him drive her home from the hospital.

This was not depression. She had been depressed for years, and she knew the shape and smell and taste of it. This was something different. It did not lead to suicide; it lay beyond suicide. Nothing mattered, not food or drink or even work, not even the kindness of other people, not even the love of Miles . . . if he loved her. Not even the love of God . . . if there was a God.

She lay in bed contemplating nothing. She was having a long, hard, cold look into nothing.

23

"It was a fling, Miles, and it's all over," Diane said, and she meant it. But Miles, like so many others in the past, refused to understand. They always began a fling with their eyes wide open and with a perfect attitude: enthusiasm, wackiness, the desire for a little fun with a good person, and then a kiss goodbye, and no regrets, no recriminations. They agreed to this. They wanted it, they said. It's what every man was looking for. But once they were into the fling and were having a good time, they wanted to make it permanent. They had never agreed to just a fling, they said. They weren't the flinging type. How could she betray them like this? And then came the letters and the phone calls and the bitter looks across the room, when she wanted only to move on and keep them all as friends. And now it was Miles. In school, moreover, which she found maddening.

"It was a fling, Miles, and it's over now," she told him, but he said she couldn't do that, he wouldn't let her, he was in love with her, and she loved him too, he was sure. "No," she said. "It's over." She hadn't known about the girlfriend or she would never have initiated the fling in the first place. It was just that, while his mother was dying, he looked so beaten up and brave that her heart went out to him. She'd felt bad. She wanted to help. She hadn't known about this other woman, but now that she knew, her fling with Miles was done with. Period. "It's over, Miles," she said. "And do not, do *not* bring this up in school again." She went to the women's room to get away from him.

She washed her face, put on fresh eyeliner, and then lay down on the daybed to think. In future she would draw up a written pre-fling agreement, to be signed by both parties, setting forth the limits of the relationship, tentative termination dates, and requisite post-fling attitudes. She would have it signed in the presence of a witness, preferably an attorney, and then perhaps she could enjoy a fling that was just a fling. She wondered, for a solemn moment, if she should just give up men altogether. Try chastity. Friendship, even. She would take that to prayer next Sunday at mass.

Endicott was standing at the window with his back to her. He was squaring those shoulders, she knew, for her benefit, but they were in school and she was damned if she'd notice.

"I want to update my report on Jeff Douglas," Diane said. "He is apparently calling a student Mouse. In class. And the unfortunate thing is that the boy *looks* like a mouse. He's being held up to public ridicule, his mother is hysterical about it, and she's complained to me, to the superintendent, and—so I'm told—to you. This is a perfect example of his complete lack of professional judgment."

Endicott was looking at her absently. He was thinking of that fool on the School Board, Jared Whiting, and all that talk about homosexual filth. Had the Billy Mack incident begun to leak?

"I've checked into this," Diane said, "and Jeff continues to call the boy Mouse. I've spoken to him about it. I've put it in his tenure report, as I told him I was obliged to do. And I told him I would speak to you. I've waited a full week since filing my report with you, and it's two weeks since this came to our attention. It's time that *you* do something about it."

"I thought it was your friend Miles who called him Mouse."

"No. It's Jeff Douglas."

"His mother was in here drunk on Back to School Night. It was Miles she saw, not Jeff. The nurse told me."

"She mistook Miles for Jeff. But it's Jeff who calls him Mouse."

Endicott lowered his eyes, pondering. Diane waited.

"Her name is Muldoon," he said, "but she's Italian. You almost never see an Italian with a drink problem. Not a woman."

"And she has a dog named Doggina! What difference does *that* make? It doesn't matter if she's Italian or Irish, drunk or sober, legitimate or illegitimate. She has a legitimate grievance. Her son is singled out for ridicule each day, because of his looks, and you cannot let this continue." She turned to leave the office, but thought better of it. She turned back. "I'd like to know what you're going to do," she said.

"Diane," he said, coming around from behind his desk. "You know me. You know I'll do what's right. I'll speak to him. He'll stop."

"Fine," she said, and started toward the door.

"Diane," he said. "How can you be so cold to me? You're a feeling woman. You're a good woman. I've never hurt you. Now, have I? So how can you be like this?"

"It was one night," she said. "It wasn't even a fling."

"And what about Bannon? Is he a fling? Is that your professional judgment in the matter?"

He put his hand on her arm, and as she tried to pull away, he tightened his grip. He was hurting her, but she only stared down at his hand until, embarrassed, he removed it from her arm. She left, without waiting for his apology. She had no idea how angry he was that he'd mentioned Miles Bannon. Somebody would have to pay for that now. Probably Bannon himself.

Diane was thinking hard thoughts as she waited for Jeff Douglas to appear at her office door. She knew he would.

The bell had just rung for the end of school when Jeff showed up. He knocked and came in without waiting for a response.

"I've seen Endicott," he said.

"Come in, please, and sit down," she said.

"Cut the sarcasm," he said. "I want to talk to you, for once, without all the bullshit."

She closed her eyes, slowly, and opened them.

"Look, what's the matter with you? What do you want?"

"I want you to conduct yourself professionally. I want you to respect your students as people. I want . . ."

"No, what do you really want?"

Diane looked at him.

"Power? Is that what you want? Are you bucking for Endicott's job?"

She laughed.

"What is it with you?"

"I want you to do your job and I want you to do it professionally."

"No, there's something else here."

"You cannot call a student Mouse. Did you ever stop to think how that student *feels?*"

He stared at her, bluntly. "You're not getting any, is that it?"

"I think this meeting is over."

"With that faggot, Bannon? I can imagine."

"Please leave my office at once." She stood up.

"Look, cards on the table. I've been thinking about you, trying to understand what makes you tick. I said to myself, if she were a character in my novel, what would she want? And right away it came to me: maybe I should fuck her." He watched for her response. "Is that what all this is about? You want me to fuck you? That's okay. That's okay." He smiled at her, charming, ingratiating. "You want it, you got it."

There was a knock at the door.

"Come in!" She stood up and opened the door.

Miles started into the room, but stopped when he saw who was there.

"Come *in*," she said, making her voice low and warm.

Jeff looked at Miles, and then he looked back to Diane, and sneered. "Good luck," he said to her, and left.

"What's all this?" Miles said, tipping his head toward the door.

"The same old thing," Diane said. "I've got to dash, Miles. I've got a dentist appointment."

And almost at once Miles found himself alone in her office. He walked across to the window and then back to the door. He looked around the room.

"I'm a mess," he said.

For dinner Diane had veal lasagna by Lean Cuisine, not because she was dieting, but because she could take it from the freezer and shove it in the microwave and, by the time she finished her bath, dinner was ready, or what passed for dinner. Food didn't really interest her. Nor did wine, though she was curled up now on the couch in the living room with a glass of Chardonnay in her hand. What interested her tonight was the perverse nature of men.

She was thinking particularly of William Endicott. Their one-night fling had taken place almost two years ago, on the evening of the school Christmas Party. Everybody had been half drunk or altogether drunk, and a lot of new liaisons were clearly in the making, when suddenly, around eleven o'clock, the guests all seemed to disappear at once, leaving Endicott to clean up the mess. Diane, sober and severe, stayed behind to help. That was when it happened. He had broken down and wept. His wife had left him, he said. On Christmas Eve, he said. Oh Diane, he said. And she had consoled him, that one night.

His wife, good old Missy, left him regularly and came back just as regularly, though he failed to mention that. They liked it this way. They enjoyed the break and they enjoyed getting back together again. It was a military marriage. Everyone knew this, of course, except Diane.

She was curled up on the couch now, a glass of wine in her hand, the image of academic repose. But she was thinking she had been a fool, that her Christmas fling had been a major indiscretion, that Endicott might even be tempted to use this, some day, if he turned against her. Men were capable of anything.

The doorbell rang and it was Miles. It was all over, it had been a fling, but she let him in nonetheless. And, because she was weak and worried and alone, she went to bed with him.

He came up smiling. It was her genius to let men think they had discovered the art of giving pleasure.

24

It was the third week in November and the whole world had gone cold. Miles jogged along the grassy path beside the asphalt road, but the ground was frozen so hard that the pounding of his heels was a hammerblow to the brain. His head ached. His body ached. His teeth and all his joints ached.

Everything was so bleak that for the past nine days he'd given up running. He was short of breath, and he was certainly short of patience, and almost every night he had these awful dreams about his mother. By morning, he had forgotten the dreams, but he remembered his mother clearly, and when he did, his chest ached.

Today, feeling sluggish and cold and ugly, he decided to give himself a jolt with some physical exercise and maybe with an act of charity as well. So he'd dropped Billy Mack a note—''Jog? What the hell, let's do it!''—and now here he was, like an idiot, running in the cold and freezing his ass off.

The truth was that Miles invited Billy jogging because he felt bad for Cosmo. In the teachers' room that morning he heard Coogan say that Cosmo was out sick, under a doctor's care. He needed rest, the doctor said. The others had nodded and said nothing. But at once Miles raced through the list of possibilities. Depression? Despair? Because of what he'd done to Billy Mack? Was he losing it? Coming apart? It made sense. Miles recalled him staring into that empty locker. But wasn't there anybody to talk to the kid about guilt? That's one of the nice things the Church used to do: put guilt into perspective. You had to live with guilt, it was part of life. It just had to be domesticated, that's all. Left alone to grow wild, it could kill you. And so, unable to do anything for Cosmo, he invited Billy to go jogging with him.

He listened to the sound his heels made as they struck the ground. Death blows, every one of them, he thought, and wondered why.

He supposed it was because everything in his life was ugliness, misery, and piss—beginning with school. The kids in class had suddenly turned dull, refusing to laugh at his jokes, refusing to get interested in the short story. They had just learned how to read poetry, and they felt he was unfair and unreasonable to expect them to give it up and learn something new. They didn't want to read fiction; it wasn't like poetry at all. And their writing, which had risen from bad to passable, appeared to have leveled off there, neither bad nor good. They were bored. He was uninspired. He was a mess.

It wasn't only the students who had turned cold on him. Endicott had too, even colder than usual. And the secretaries. And often now, when he came into the teachers' room, there was a break in the conversation and then they started in on something new. Kathy was the same as always, of course, but he was a little strange with her since that night at Henri IV when he'd seen her with Coach, as if being in on her secret life put a distance between them. Dietz was giving him the cold shoulder because of Margaret, as if he were to blame for her drinking.

That was the real problem. Margaret. And Diane. Margaret spent her free time at AA meetings and made it clear she didn't want to see him. Diane went farther and refused outright to have anything to do with him. It was shitsville.

He began to sing "God Rest Ye Merry, Gentlemen," in tribute to the cold, but gave up after the first verse.

Margaret was the mystery. He would never admit it to her, and certainly not to Dietz, but after that first night when he'd sat up in the waiting room, he drove to her house and let himself in. He had no idea why, or what he was looking for, but he went through all the rooms, peeking into drawers, lifting up books and magazines to see what was underneath, even getting up on a chair to investigate the top shelf in her closet. He'd gone through her medicine chest. The place was a shambles, and his search convinced him that she led a very messy life, but not a secret one. When he was done looking, he poured himself a drink and sat down at the kitchen table. There, in front of him, he found a note that said simply, "I know you." He read it and felt his face grow red. It was in her handwriting. He read it again. It was not addressed to anyone, but he knew it was intended for him. He could see her, late at night, drunk, bent over this little piece of paper, searching for the three words that would pierce through his hardness and hypocrisy and destroy him. "I know you." They said it all: she had given everything, her help, her time, her love; she had lavished hours of attention on his mother, for him, always for him; she had stayed with him through those endless weeks of dying; she had refused him nothing; he had never had to ask for anything. What had he given in return? He'd used her and he'd left her. "I know you." How could he ever have thought he wanted to be known? Nonetheless, he went back to the hospital and waited to see her. She would not see him. He lurched off to see Diane and then he came back and waited some more. Then suddenly, for no reason he could see, she sent out word that he could drive her home. Because it didn't matter anymore, she said.

It didn't matter. Not to her, perhaps, but he had his betrayal to deal with, and he needed to know how to feel. At first he was relieved that she was done with him because now he was free to pursue Diane. He was a little hurt, of course, because who wanted to be told they didn't matter any longer? Still, the important thing was that he was free. On the other hand, he felt they should still be friends. Margaret didn't want that. It was better simply not to see him, she said. He needed her, though, couldn't she see that? You just didn't cut people off completely. They had had a good relationship and he couldn't just allow it to be trashed. She smiled. No, she said, of course not.

Miles thought of her note and blushed.

Then, when everything seemed about to fall into place—a nice friendship with Margaret, a nice love affair with Diane—Dietz, the Great Communicator, told Diane about Margaret and Diane refused to see him again. "It's all over, Miles, it was just a fling," she said. "I mean it." And she did. She wouldn't talk to him on the phone and she stood at the door, refusing to let him in, whenever he went to her house. So it came as a surprise when she let him in that night, a week ago. Persistence was the answer. He'd get her back. She didn't know how persistent he could be. She didn't know him at all. He began again to whistle "God Rest Ye Merry, Gentlemen," despite the awful cold.

Billy was running in place, trying to keep warm, when Miles entered Mitchell Park.

"Women," Miles said to Billy. "They'll be the death of me." He was pleased with how that sounded. He was breathing heavily, and his legs hurt, but he rather liked the idea of himself as a young middle-aged man, out for a run, trying to forget the problems he was having with all his women. He felt middle-aged but fatherly.

What Billy needed, Miles knew, was a father or an older brother, somebody who could listen to how he felt about what had happened to him, somebody who could reassure him he was still a man, a good one, and that a perfectly normal sex life lay ahead of him. And maybe a buddy he could talk dirty with. And then a girl who would love him. Miles couldn't help smiling; he himself had had none of these. His father had been more shy about sex than

Miles himself. And talking dirty had always been out of the question; whom would he talk dirty *to?* And Margaret was the first girl who'd ever loved him. And now she didn't.

"Women," he said. "I don't know, Bill."

They ran in silence for a long time. Miles had a little pain in his chest that he tried to rub away, but it kept needling him, and so he slowed down. Billy slowed down with him.

"My mother," Billy said. "She's always after me."

"Right," Miles said, and pressed his fist against his chest.

"She wants me to pray. She keeps telling me to pray . . . about things."

"Mothers," Miles said.

They kept on jogging, neither saying a word. Miles was listening to the even thud of his heels against the frozen ground, pounding, pounding, sending a needle of pain up through his legs and spine and into his brain. Mothers, Billy had said, or maybe it was Miles himself, and the thudding of his heels picked up the sound, and the one word, Mother, echoed hollow in his skull, over, over, Mother, Mother, and suddenly he remembered his dream. It was not a dream at all.

He was back in her hospital room and it was again—and always—that moment when he would let her die. Her white face was a death mask as she stared in panic at the emergency cord she could not reach. Her fingers moved, but she could not lift her hand, and then she did lift her hand and almost touched the cord, but not quite. She couldn't reach it. She was a single breath away from dying. He would be free. He could marry, or not marry, or run away from all of this and start his life again, as a man this time, not just as a dutiful son tied with this silver cord to a dying woman. A bird began to sing somewhere, and there were nurses laughing in the corridor, and life was perfectly normal except that it was hot and muggy and there was no air in the room. He couldn't get a breath. If he could go for a swim, or for a run, if he could just get a breath. But of course he *was* running and all this would be over in just a second. He looked up and saw that she was staring at him, and he knew she knew.

"No!" It was a high, piercing cry, and he gripped his chest, and pitched straight forward on the ground.

He lay there, silent, and Billy, who had run on ahead, stopped, and looked back at him. No one made a sound, there was no wind, even the ordinary forest noises ceased. But the cry Miles had made went on and on, echoing in the trees.

"Miles," Billy said, whispering, "no." He pushed aside his panic then and ran back and bent over the body. Miles was lying face down, unconscious, with one arm folded beneath his chest and the other flung out at his side. Billy kneeled and felt his wrist for a pulse, but he could get nothing. He placed his hand on Miles' neck. It was warm and wet and Billy thought he felt something, but he wasn't sure. Don't move the body, he said to himself, but he couldn't leave Miles like this, unconscious, with his face in the dirt. Carefully, he pushed the body away from him until Miles rolled over and lay face up. His head lolled, and he remained unconscious, but he seemed to be breathing. Billy unzipped Miles' windbreaker and placed his hand on his chest. He could feel his bones, his ribcage, and he could feel his heart beating. He bent close over the body and said, "Miles? Milo? What should I do?" But Miles remained unconscious and there was nothing to do except to run for help. Billy stripped off his jacket and laid it across Miles' chest. He stood up, prepared to run, and then he made a short, soft, whimpering sound and knelt down again at Miles' side. He bent close to his ear and whispered, "I love you." And then he sat back on his heels, and placed his hand on Miles' chest, and said again, "I love you, Miles." He stood up, ready to run, when suddenly Miles moved his arm and made a moaning sound. Billy bent over him and saw his eyelids flutter and then Miles opened his eyes and looked around, confused. "Don't move," Billy said. "Just lie there, and I'll get help." At once Miles sat up and said, "What . . ." but he stopped as he felt that stab at his heart again. They stayed there,

Miles half-sitting, Billy crouching beside him, until Miles said the pain had stopped and he was freezing his ass off, and so they were going to get up now, and walk back to school, slowly, and everything was gonna be just fine.

Everything was fine. At school, Billy ran to get the nurse while Miles waited with Coach and Paul Ciampa who were just coming in from the field. Later Coach drove Miles to the hospital. They gave him an EKG, and when that showed nothing, they gave him a stress test, and then a variety of stress tests, and told him finally that he should get more sleep and lay off the rich foods and go easy on the scotch. He was fine, they said. He had the heart of a man thirty-five. But he *was* thirty-five, Miles said. Exactly, they said.

Miles went home and had a drink and then he phoned Diane. No answer. He phoned Margaret and told her he'd had a heart attack—"Well, not really, but everybody thought it was at first"— and she came over and made him a drink and got his bed ready for him. He waited downstairs. He was embarrassed to be up there with her now, after she'd ransacked the place, but she was unaware of his embarrassment and seemed to have none of her own. How did you explain women? She sat with him and asked questions and for a while she seemed her old, lively, interested self. He felt good. He could see now what he had seen in her once before. She was attractive and vital. She was witty. She was fun to be with. What a shame he was not in love with her.

After Margaret left, Miles went upstairs to bed. He was very tired. The pseudo-heart attack had been bad enough, but the EKG and the five hundred stress tests had finished him off. The tension those people managed to pack into the simple act of wiring your chest. All that forced calm! They kept that reserved smile on their faces while secretly they were sending you the message that this little test, kiddo, could mark the beginning of the end of your short life. He'd never get to sleep.

He was asleep almost at once. He dreamed he was at his mother's bedside, waiting, but he turned away from her and left her room and went into the room next door. But the room he entered was her room, and so was the next, and the next. He stopped finally, and she beckoned to him from her bed, smiling. "It's always this room," she said. "There isn't any other room."

He approached her bed and they took their places, she with her head lowered on her chest, he with his eyes closed, his hand resting on hers. They waited like this. Then he felt her hand move a little. He looked up. She was trying to reach the emergency cord. He watched her fingers move against the blanket. He saw the panic in her eyes. He knew she was drowning. He wanted to go for a swim, to take a walk. He wanted to catch his breath and begin living. Light was pouring into the room from outside but they were shut in here and they would never get out.

She looked at him, and he looked back, and he saw that she knew him. He was suspended in time, caught in this moment. This was the still point of his life.

But light from the window continued to fall across the bed. "I love you," someone said. "It's fine. It will all be fine."

He shifted in his sleep, trying to find a more comfortable position, and apparently he found it, because the dream stopped, with only the memory of a voice that was not Margaret's and not Billy Mack's and not his mother's. The voice said . . . but he could not remember what it said, and it didn't matter anyway, because words never accomplished much in any case. As he knew well from his teaching. He must give more thought to his teaching. He had to get it back on track, get the excitement going. It was hard work, of course, but he loved it. And work could be its own reward. Work could be a man's salvation.

He fell into a deep, dreamless sleep, and when he woke, he was surprised to find himself thinking of his mother, how very funny she had been, how brave, how generous. He'd hurt her so often—unforgivably, he supposed—but always she'd forgiven him, as if nothing mattered more than the fact that she loved him. Is that what love is: taking it on the chin, and saying, That's all right, hit me again? What a ghastly idea.

He swung his legs out of bed and sat there for a moment, arrested by a new and wonderful thought about his mother. He thought, without a single pang of guilt, what good work she had made of her dying.

25

MARGARET WAS WORKING LATE at Babcock & Collins even though it was Friday. Cheerful, energetic, thorough, and generous with her time, she was her old self again, only a month after her collapse. She looked better, actually, with her new haircut; short and fluffy, it made her look much younger. Only the dark circles beneath her eyes hinted at what she'd been through. At first, when she came back, some of the others in the office had been uncomfortable and embarrassed around her; after all, she'd drunk herself into a collapse and she'd tried to commit suicide. But Margaret herself didn't seem to realize she was supposed to be embarrassed, and before a week was up everybody else had slipped back into behaving normally too.

Tonight she was putting some new accounts on computer. This was just busywork she could easily have left to one of the new clerks, but she liked working late and she liked the idea of getting things done when nobody was around. It was economical, somehow. She was just finishing up when Mr. Collins came through the office on his way home.

"Doing well?" he said, pausing at her door.

Margaret smiled and shrugged a little. She knew he meant AA. "I'm still new," she said. "I'm working at it."

"Is your group a good one? Have you got a sponsor yet?"

"Not officially," she said. Dietz would die if she didn't ask him to be her sponsor—she knew that—but she didn't think she could stand it. All that clubbiness. All that preaching.

"You've got to get a good group, one that's right for you," he said. "They're all different, you know. Each one has its own pitch. Tone, I mean. Sometimes you fall into a crowd that's just using AA as a substitute for a drinking party. It's kind of a profession for some of them. That's not the group you want. I mean, from what I know of you."

"I'm giving it time," she said.

"Good," he said. "That's good."

She smiled.

"Do you want to come have a drink with me, Margaret? We could talk." He was a married man, she knew. "Coffee? Tonic water?"

"I'm just finishing up here and then I've got a meeting, actually. Some other time?"

"Some other time," he said.

He left, but in a moment he was back. "I meant only a drink, you understand. I'm a married man. No offense."

"Of course," she said. "Some other time would be fine. I'm grateful."

He gave her a wave and left.

"My name is Margaret and I'm an alcoholic. It's been a month and a day since my last drink."

Dietz led the scattered applause.

"I began drinking fifteen years ago when I was in a painful marriage. It was an escape for me. It dulled my sense of what was happening, and though I knew the drink wasn't helping the situation, I told myself that it was getting me through it. Afterwards, when the marriage was over—he died—I began to drink socially. I had a cocktail before dinner, a glass of wine with, some brandy afterwards. It all seemed pretty harmless. But somewhere along the line, I began to use alcohol as a reward and a punishment. A reward for hard work or for being patient with fools or for not making demands on someone I was in love with. A punishment for not working hard or for not being patient with fools or for making demands on someone I was in love with."

Dietz shifted violently in his chair and looked around at the others, to make sure they were getting this.

"Eventually, drinking seemed the easiest way to commit suicide, which of course is what I'd been working toward all along. I'm back among the living now, and I hope to stay here, with the help of my higher power and of you people in AA. Thank you."

Margaret returned to her seat, utterly composed, with no sign of anxiety or stress. She had dropped from her speech everything that mattered to her, everything that was real. She had made herself a cliché for them. And she was a cliché, she felt. Just another drunk, trying to hold it all together.

"Terrific," Dietz said to her. "I'm proud of you." He took her hand in his, and she let him.

Margaret sat in front of the television looking at Johnny Carson. He touched his eye, wiping away tears of laughter brought on by his joke about Tommy Newsome. Ed McMahon tried but he just couldn't stop laughing. Tommy was standing there like a goof, enjoying the joke with his boss and the boss's sidekick. The band, for the most part, was politely amused.

So this was life. At its fullest, perhaps. Margaret watched this performance with the detachment she brought to everything she did, only now, at home, she didn't have to wear her other face— of interest, enthusiasm, liveliness, involvement. This was the real Margaret and she knew herself.

She did her work at Babcock & Collins and made other people

feel good about having her there, she went to AA meetings and performed for the kind and generous people who cared about her staying sober, she had coffee with Dietz, she had coffee with Coach, she had coffee with her entire AA group. And she went to Miles when he called her and she asked him questions and she listened to the answers. He didn't matter to her, so why not do it for him? She had made, so far as anyone could see, a perfect recovery. She functioned well, she took the necessary practical steps to get through life one day at a time, she was happy. She had even gone to mass once, looking for a higher power, but she didn't find him there.

Her higher power, she decided, was the tenuous but real grasp she had on the one thing left to her: her dignity.

It was her sense of dignity that made her public performance so believable, that kept her functioning so well. Beneath that dignity lay nothing except despair, the deep and dark perception of nothing, nothing at all.

26

MILES HAD BEEN GOING TO MASS every morning for the past week. He had no clear idea why. It was silly, really. It was just that he felt so different now about his mother's death, and his part in it, that it seemed right to celebrate the way that she would, by taking this new feeling of pleasure to mass. God knows, he had little enough pleasure in his life these days. Diane was still holding out; she wanted nothing to do with him and he was beginning to believe she meant it. How could she just have a fling like that and then abandon him? It was never just a fling. *He* had never intended a fling. How could she turn on him this way? And Margaret was impossible, too. He made it a point to call Margaret at least twice a week, and she always pretended to be glad to hear from him, but she wasn't really. She was being kind. Which he found particularly annoying, because in calling her, he wasn't being kind. He was calling because he was frustrated at not being able to see Diane. And nobody had taken his heart attack seriously. He himself hadn't either, to tell the truth. He had gone jogging a couple days later, though he'd taken the precaution of dropping Billy a note asking him to jog along with him, just in case he should drop dead again in the middle of Mitchell Park.

They'd jogged every day last week, he and Billy, and now it was Monday and they were jogging again. Billy was a different kid these days, sane and talkative, with none of those angry silences that drove Miles into panic. It was a nice change and Miles enjoyed being with him. Right now Billy was talking about what he'd like to do after graduation. He might be a cop, like his father, or maybe an engineer. He had an uncle who was an engineer. Or maybe he'd be a teacher, like Miles.

"Sounds good," Miles said, half listening to Billy and half to the sound of his own heart, pumping strong and steady. "Whatever satisfies you, Bill. Life is so damned short that it makes no sense to do something you don't want to do, just for the money or to please somebody else or because it's what society expects of you. You've gotta do what answers to your own needs. You know? You've finally just gotta be who you are."

Billy didn't say anything for a while, and then he said, "I will. I am."

Miles pretended to give him a punch on the arm.

It was one of those late autumn days, sunny and warm, that sometimes follow a cold spell in New England, and they'd worn sweatshirts and jogging shorts even though it was the first week in December. The day was so mild that the running seemed very easy, and when they got to the cutoff for Lookout Rock and Billy jumped the bushes that shielded the entrance to his own trail, Miles thought, Why not, and ran along behind him.

They came out on the little rock plateau and, breathing heavy, they stomped around until they caught their breath. All the leaves had fallen, but the fir trees still formed an impenetrable barrier behind and around them. And in front of them lay the ugliest landscape Miles had ever seen. He laughed and said, "Paradise," stretching out his arms to embrace it. Billy laughed too, and looked at him.

They stood there, side by side, looking out on the scrubland and the distant warehouses. Miles was thinking how lucky he was to be alive and in love—never mind that Diane insisted it was over—

and, besides, his teaching seemed to be back on track again, and, Christ Almighty, for the moment life was just *good*.

He was smiling to himself, barely aware that Billy's hand was on his shoulder. "What?" Miles said, and stood there paralyzed as he felt Billy's arm tighten around his waist and felt Billy's head press against his chest. The boy pulled himself tight against Miles, hugging him hard, their two bodies pressed together. Miles stood with his hands out from his sides and said, "Bill. Billy. Come on now." But Billy clung to him, breathing sharply, saying something into his chest. Miles put his arms around the boy's shoulders for a second, gave him a couple pats to show it was all over, and tried to pull away. But Billy would not let go. Miles got his hands between them, and tried to push him off, saying, "Bill, Bill, you don't want this. This isn't it at all." But the boy was trapped in this frenzy, and Miles realized suddenly what was happening, and pushed him hard, and said, "No!" Billy stumbled back from him, his eyes snapped open, and he looked at Miles with an empty look, and then he fell in a crouch, his hands between his legs trying to stop the orgasm that was shaking him to death. Miles stepped back and looked away and said, "Oh, God," and then moved to the boy and put his hand on his shoulder and said, "Billy, it's all right. It's nothing. It doesn't matter." But Billy gave a short, sharp, strangled cry, and then he ran. Miles sat down, his head in his hands, saying, "Oh, God," over and over again.

Miles walked back to the school, slowly, despite the fact that suddenly the day had turned cold. He showered and drove home and went directly to bed, sick and feverish.

By the time he reached home, Billy's throat was raw and his lungs felt hollow from his last, long run. He was shaking all over and he could not stop shaking. He went upstairs to his room, took off his clothes, and crouched on the rug by his bed, hugging his knees to his chest. He knew what he would do, but he had to wait until the shaking stopped so he could write his note first.

After a long while, he got up and put on his robe and went

downstairs to the hall closet. His father kept his gun there, on a shelf behind the Sears' Emergency Road Kit. He put the gun in his bathrobe pocket and went to the breakfront in the dining room where, under the turkey platter, his father kept his ammunition. "Billy?" His mother called from the kitchen. "Yup," he said. "Did you have a nice run?" she said, but he had already started back up the stairs. He loaded the gun and put it on the desk near his elbow.

He got out the blue stationery—only four sheets left—and wrote: "Dear Miles, I'm sorry." He stopped and looked at that for a while, and looked at the gun, then crumpled up the stationery and threw it in the wastebasket. It was a white plastic wastebasket with blue flowers, his mother's, and he was ashamed that he liked it. He took another sheet of stationery and wrote: "Dear Miles," and stopped. For just a second, the thought came to him that maybe he didn't have to kill himself, or maybe he didn't have to do it right away, but the thought couldn't stick, because he knew the truth now, and Miles knew, and it was too late to do anything except end it. He had gone beyond shame. He had gone to a place you didn't come back from, where everybody knew about you, and what they knew was true. He crumpled the paper and took the third sheet. "Dear Miles, You are the only one," but he scribbled out the stupid words. This was not a time for explanations. "Dear Miles," he wrote on the last sheet. "I'm sorry."

He lowered his head to the desk and closed his eyes. He couldn't find the words, and there was no more paper, and it didn't matter anyway, because even Miles wouldn't like him now. He raised his head and looked at the gun. He picked it up and fitted the barrel into his ear. He had done this often before. He knew just how to angle the shot; at least this was one thing he wouldn't fuck up. He should hide his clothes. The stuff had hardened on the jockstrap, and they'd know what had happened. And he should shower. Or at least get into the tub, with his robe off, so that they wouldn't have too much trouble cleaning up. But it was too late for any of this.

The gun was at his ear, and he was waiting, and he pulled the trigger. He angled the shot perfectly. There was a loud popping sound, nothing like he expected, and he caught sight of the white wastebasket with the blue flowers as he fell to the floor, dead.

At seven o'clock that evening, Endicott telephoned Miles to say there was bad news and he should know it at once. Billy Mack had killed himself with his father's revolver. There was nothing more to say.

Part III

Part III

27

IT WAS ENDICOTT CALLING.

"Billy Mack has killed himself."

Miles sat up in bed, the phone in his hand, and said, "Oh, no!"

"With his father's revolver," Endicott said.

"What can I do? Can I do something?"

"Just make damned sure you say nothing, Miles. About anything. Think of the boy's family. Think of the boy. There's nothing more to be said."

Miles got out of bed and knelt down and tried to pray. But he could only think, Make it not be true, make it not be true. That desperate kid. And suddenly, too late, Miles loved him.

Why hadn't he just held him in his arms? Why had he pushed him away? Billy hadn't *known* what he was doing. He was just saying, Help me. Love me. He was just saying, Let me love you.

Miles slid to the floor, bent double, and pressed his fists into his belly.

Billy Mack was dead, with his father's gun in his hand. Now that Miles had heard the words, he could see that of course Billy had committed suicide, he could see that in a way it had always been inevitable. Billy would kill himself one day, or kill twenty others.

And, Miles knew, he was to blame. He had been to blame right from the start, over a year ago, when he saw that Billy had lost interest in class and didn't try hard enough to win him back. He was busy winning other people back—brighter, better looking, more fun to teach. And he was to blame this year, after the incident, when Billy came to him and said his mother sent him to have a talk. He should have packed him off to the student counselor at once. Or listened to him more than half-heartedly. Or been honest, and said, I can't help you, work it out with your father. Or been brutal, and said, My mother's dying, I'm in sexual knots, I'm so afraid I'm queer that I'm gonna hit a gay bar at my first opportunity just to find out, so don't you—whatever you do—don't *you* get messed up with *me*. Because it's me first. And I'm not a suicide.

And he was to blame more subtly, more perniciously, these last two weeks. "Women will be the death of me, Bill," he'd said, proud of his pitiful accomplishments in bed, trying to convince Billy that he was popular and attractive to women. And how did this make Billy feel, really? He had used the boy, he had played with him the way he'd play with a puppy, getting back the sounds he needed to hear. And had congratulated himself on his kindness meanwhile. He was being a good teacher, a friend, he'd told himself, when really he was the boy's worst enemy. He had been amused, and flattered, and silly with pride that Billy Mack was in love with him.

There was no room for prayer here. Miles got up and went to the bathroom and stood under the shower, trying to cry. He let the water run hot, and then hotter, and when he thought he couldn't endure it anymore, he crouched on the floor of the tub and let the water beat his back raw. And then he knelt there, saying, "Bill, I'm sorry." Still, the tears wouldn't come.

He dried off from the shower and got dressed to go out. "Think of the family," Miles said aloud, "think of the boy," and he heard in his voice the hollow echo of that Franciscan priest at Arch Street, urging him to accept his own humanity when he confessed he had just let his mother die. But he didn't have time for his own humanity right now; he had to think of the Macks.

As he pulled up in front of their house, he saw that all the lights were on and there were people talking together on the porch. Two patrol cars were pulled up at the curb. Miles drove past them, made a U-turn at the end of the block, and parked his car across the street from the house. For a long time the figures on the porch did not move. They didn't seem even to be talking. But eventually they all came down and stood by the cars. Nobody wanted to go. Then, suddenly, the radio in one of the patrol cars crackled with static, and there was an urgent voice in the air, shouting, and the four cops got into the cars and drove off. Billy Mack's father and mother watched them go, and then they turned and went back to the house. Jack Mack put his arm around his wife's waist, and she leaned against him as they walked together up the path and went inside.

Miles sat in his car, thinking. Then he got out and went up on the porch and looked through the front window. The living room was tiny, with two overstuffed chairs and a sofa and a huge television set in the corner. The television was on and Miles could hear canned laughter and see the silvery flicker of the screen. How could they bear it? He went back down the path and around to the side entrance. Through the glass in the door, Miles could see them sitting at the kitchen table. Jack Mack held a cigarette he wasn't smoking and a glass of beer he wasn't drinking. He was staring at his wife, who held her hands pressed against her heart. Nobody moved. Nobody said anything.

Miles tapped softly on the glass. Almost at once Mrs. Mack was at the door, her husband behind her, telling Miles to come in, come in. "Oh, thank you, thank you, thank you," she was saying, and her husband was saying, "Let me get you a beer. You want a drink? Or a beer?" Miles didn't want anything, but Jack Mack brought him a beer and a glass—"I use a glass," Jack said, and shrugged—and then they stood there in the brightly lit kitchen looking at one another.

"I'm so sorry," Miles said.

They nodded, and Jack Mack put his hand on his wife's shoulder.

"I wish I could say something," Miles said.

"There's nothing to say."

"Still. He was a wonderful boy. Man."

Mrs. Mack began to cry softly. "Eileen," her husband said. And to Miles he said, "They were close, and it's a big shock."

Then, instead of leaving, Miles sat down at the kitchen table and they sat down with him. They waited for whatever he would say.

"He's *your* son," Miles began, "and so whatever I say about him is a kind of impertinence, because I'm an outsider, and I knew him only as a teacher, and I didn't know him very well, until . . . well, until what happened this year. And then I got to know him better, and I saw what a wonderful kid he was, and the important thing I saw was that he loved you so very much. Both of you."

"I know," Eileen said. "I always knew that."

"They were close," Jack said.

"No, both of you, Jack." Miles used the name tentatively. "He idolized you. I think what he wanted most was to be just like you."

"I couldn't get in touch. I couldn't get through."

"You yelled at him," Eileen said, just a fact.

"I had to yell at him. You have to raise your kids, right? And sometimes I yell. I just couldn't get through."

"He was a good boy," Eileen said. "He prayed. And I prayed, but I guess I didn't pray enough."

"Prayer," Jack said, and lifted his glass of beer.

Miles shot him a sympathetic look and said, "This has to be awfully hard on you two. It's wonderful that you're pulling together."

Jack sat back and looked at the table. The cigarette had gone out by itself; a long ash lay in a saucer. Jack crumbled it with his little finger.

"He left you a note," Jack said.

Miles' heart stopped for a second and he said, "No."

"It said, 'Dear Miles. I'm sorry.' " He looked at Miles. "That's it."

Miles closed his eyes.

"He loved you. He trusted you," Eileen said.

"I guess he did," Jack said.

There was silence in the room, and it went on and on, until it seemed pointless to even try to say anything. Jack got up and went to the refrigerator. He came back with two beers, and put one down beside Miles' glass, even though Miles hadn't touched the first one.

"I've seen this before, you know," Jack said. "You never think it's going to happen to you. You're a cop, and you raise them right, and you let them know it's all shit out there, but they never listen. I've seen it. Kids killed in hit-and-runs, kids driving drunk, kids trying out a new drug and taking too much. They end up with their guts on the highway or they rot away in a hospital with an eggplant for a brain. I've seen it over and over. But it's never going to happen to you, you think. Because you're a cop."

"Yes," Miles said.

"It does—shit—it happens to you. The grief counselors from the hospital come at you, and the school counselors, and Father Ortega from down the church, and they tell you it wasn't your fault, these things happen. And the whole time you know they're thinking that it hasn't happened to them, so why did it happen to you? You know? Where did you go wrong? You didn't love him right, or treat him right, or didn't give him the proper values. 'The home situation,' they say, as if that's supposed to explain everything. It does, too, at least to them. It explains that you went wrong, you fucked up, you didn't raise him right."

He paused for a moment, and when he started in again, his voice had changed and he looked angry.

"But let me tell you, mister, with your Harvard education and your books and your poetry, that raising a kid isn't easy. We're just ordinary people. We like a beer and some television, and I like to get drunk with some of the guys now and then, and Eileen does her church stuff, and we don't *talk* about a lot of things. That's true. We don't talk a lot. But we did our best to raise that boy right. So when you all come in here and tell us it's not our fault, we did what we could, and then turn around and go out and say, 'It's the home situation,' you should know that we're gonna go on living with it for the rest of our lives. For us, it's not just a case, or another statistic that we get the police report on, and then forget about. It's our lives we're talking about. It's our boy. And we've got to live with it. So don't, just *don't* give me any home situation shit. I don't want to hear it. We failed with him. And he killed himself. He's dead. Isn't that enough? Isn't that bad enough? Isn't it?''

Miles looked down at his hands and Eileen sobbed quietly and after a while Jack took out his handkerchief and blew his nose.

"So, that's how it is," Jack said. "Look, do you want another beer? Some scotch?"

Miles shook his head.

"Some coffee?" Eileen said. "I'm going to make some coffee. We'll need some tonight anyway, so I'll just be a minute and make some."

Miles waited until he thought it was safe to speak, and then he said, in a low voice. "Billy loved you, Jack. You were his father. He wanted to be just like you."

"But he left the note for you."

28

THE NEXT MORNING Miles went to the principal's office to report to
Endicott. Don't push it, he wanted to say, Jack Mack is very close
to exploding.

Endicott's secretary waved him into the office and closed the
door behind him. The superintendent was there, and the vice-
principal, and two of the guidance people. Endicott stood behind
his desk running his hand through his hair. There was a sour smell
in the room.

"You're late," Endicott said. "Where were you? We're just winding up our strategy session on how to handle the announcement.
These two"—he indicated the guidance counselors—"say take it
head on, call it suicide, tell them it's time we all pulled together.
Howard and Alan"—he nodded toward the superintendent and the
vice-principal—"think we should make a less direct assault."

"Oblique," the superintendent said. "I think we should be
oblique."

The vice-principal nodded agreement.

Miles stood there, confused. Had he been summoned to this
meeting? And forgotten about it?

"Well?" Endicott said.

"The kids *know* it's suicide," Miles said.

Everyone turned to look at him.

"Everybody knows everything," Miles said.

The counselors nodded, and one of them said, "See?"

"Oblique," the superintendent said. "You agree, then, that since everybody knows everything to begin with, there's no point in putting . . . well . . . too fine a point on it. Just presume they all know it's suicide and go on from there. It's the *word* you can't use. That word will just get the others thinking about doing it. We'll have Cynthia Dodd in here again in no time."

"Cynthia Dodd is not the suicidal type," a counselor said.

"She just wants attention," the other counselor said.

"And needs attention," the first one said.

"Damage control," Endicott said. "Let's get back to the problem at hand. Miles here was a friend of the boy, so I'm told, and he's familiar with the boy's background, so I want to make sure we've got Miles' input here. We don't want things coming out later that are going to embarrass us and we don't want anything to look like a cover-up."

"Cover-up?" the superintendent said. "He killed himself at *home*. What cover-up?"

The vice-principal shook his head, no. No cover-up.

"There isn't any cover-up, that's the point," Endicott said. "But the school always gets the blame, you know that, and we want to make sure that when it appears in the *Globe* tonight, we don't have some half-assed investigative reporter saying the school was to blame and his counselors were out to lunch and the superintendent was away at too many conferences to be waging the war properly."

Miles saw once again that Endicott was not the fool he seemed to be. He was an expert at blackmail. And he was very dangerous.

"It's not the facts we've got to be afraid of; it's the way the facts are perceived," Endicott said.

They all agreed that this was true. They had all suffered from misperceptions about themselves and their work.

Nobody said anything for a moment, and then they all looked to the superintendent. "Howard?" Endicott said.

The superintendent was tall, and fit, and in his six-hundred-dollar suits from Saks he looked like an aging fashion model. They waited while he ruffled his silver hair and got ready to speak.

"This is your problem, Bill," the superintendent said. "It's your baby. The only thing is this: I don't want to be taken by surprise, so whatever you do, make sure you keep me informed." He tugged at his lapels, smoothing the suit jacket over his shoulders, a sure sign he was done.

"Got it," Endicott said. "That's right, Howard."

"Just keep me informed."

The vice-principal nodded his agreement.

"So," Endicott said, and he spoke into his little Panasonic so his secretary could type it: "Billy Mack, a senior, died at his home last night. His mother and father request your prayers for Billy. Billy was active in sports and planned to attend U. Mass. next year." He tapped the Off button. "Then I'll say something inspirational and we'll have the moment of silence. And you people"—guidance— "can take care of the hysterical ones and help them face up to suicide and so on and so forth. At the end I'll add a paragraph about behavior at the wake, attendance at the funeral, et cetera, et cetera. And that should take care of it. I thank you, gentlemen, for your help and your advice. The war room is closed."

As they all filed out, Endicott put his hand on Miles' arm and said softly, "I just wanted to make sure you were in on this, Miles. We don't want anything about the locker-room incident to surface now, of all times."

"Was I told to come to this meeting?" Miles said.

"It's sad about Billy," Endicott said.

"How did you know I'd be here?" Miles said.

"Oh, I knew you'd be here, Miles," Endicott said. "I know you."

In the corridors, girls were leaning against the lockers, sitting on the floor, hugging one another. They were sobbing, in an orgy of grief. It was luxurious. They loved it. Miles had seen this performance before and it was always the same. The girls sobbed and the boys moved silently up and down the hall, sulking, as if they were personally responsible for the death or as if they were offended that somebody else was getting all that attention just for being dead.

Years ago, the first time Miles saw it, he'd called it a carnival of mourning. Their grief had infuriated him because it seemed so fake and so easy. Using somebody else's tragedy to get off excess tension. Putting yourself in the center of a drama that wasn't even yours. Later, though, he came to see it as a kind of hopeful gesture. They sobbed and carried on because they wanted to be deeply feeling, deeply caring people. They wanted to take tragedy on themselves easily and naturally, the way their parents did. They were ready to suffer, too. It didn't matter who was dead, or if they liked him, or even if they knew him. One of theirs was dead and, by God, they were all set to mourn. The truth was that most of them were terrified at feeling nothing at all.

This morning, as he went through the corridor to the teachers' room, Miles noticed the gleaming hair of the girls and their swollen eyes and their mouths stretched horribly in grief. It would all be forgotten before the weekend was over, but it was very real to them right now, and as he passed, he put his hand on a shoulder or an arm, and said names as if they were a kind of blessing: Jennifer, Mark, David, Davey, Heather. They loved what they were doing and they loved Miles for giving his approval. At last he reached the safety of the teachers' room.

Kathy Dillard was sitting away from the table, looking out the window into the hard morning sun. Her face was puffed and red, and she had dark smudges under her eyes. She looked furious. Diane and Dietz were sitting at either end of the table, Diane collating book orders with packing slips and Dietz staring at a newspaper spread open before him. Coogan was mopping up coffee he had just spilled on the counter top.

"Miles," they said, looking up as he came in, except for Kathy who continued to stare out the window.

"Just the death notice," Dietz said. "There's no details at all."

"Thank God," Diane said.

The toilet flushed and Jeff Douglas came out. "There's no toilet paper, Kathy," he said. "Be warned." Kathy didn't seem to hear him. "What I can't figure out," Jeff said, "is why a kid kills himself. I can see why somebody like Cynthia Dodd would want to—or maybe even *should*, with a mother like that—but what can be so bad for any kid that he figures it's better to just end it all? I mean, why not rob a bank, have a good time, and *then* end it all. It doesn't make sense." He got some coffee. "My personal theory is that it's not the kids at all, it's the parents. This kid's father was a cop, right? That tells you a whole lot, right there. Cops' kids are always royally fucked. The biggest druggies, the biggest drunks, the biggest assholes in the school are always cops' kids."

Miles went into the toilet where he wouldn't have to hear any more of this. But he could hear, and he listened, as Jeff speculated on what Billy did, and why he did it, and whether he put the gun into his mouth or just under his chin, and finally Miles flushed the toilet three times in a row and couldn't hear him anymore. When he came out, Jeff was silent and Dietz was saying, "With cops, it's usually the booze that gets them. They drink themselves to death."

Kathy rounded on him. "Would you mind? Please? Just for today could we be spared the speech on booze. There are people suffering here. There are people in pain. God damn you, Dietz." She closed her eyes, unable to look at him any longer.

"Sorry," Dietz said. And then, "Hey!"

"What?" she said.

"I said I'm sorry. Look at me."

"What?" she said, looking.

"Okay?"

She got up and went over to Miles and whispered, "Coach is drinking again. I don't know what to do."

Miles put his hand on her shoulder, a reassurance.

"Could you help?" She was whispering still. "Please."

"What, pray, is this supposed to be?" Jeff said. "A play by Pinter? 'Sorry, hey, what, sorry, okay,' and little whispers going on between you two, and nobody looking at anybody. What am I, the odd man out?"

No one said anything.

"Look, the kid killed himself. I didn't do it."

They looked up at him, together, as if it were planned, and he was indeed the odd man out. Nobody made any move to include him, not even Diane. They remained silent.

"What? I've got syph? I've got AIDS?"

"You've got a cruel tongue," Coogan said.

"You people," Jeff said with contempt. "You wonderful people." And he left the room.

The wake that afternoon was at Hogan's Funeral Parlors. Outside in the parking lot, girls clung to one another, crying, while the boys stood together in small groups, smoking or complaining. It was getting cold, but not cold enough for them to go inside yet, and so they were hanging around in case something might happen out here. Nothing much had happened yet. Some teachers had arrived early, to make a quick visit and get away before the traffic got heavy. Flower trucks came and went. And other trucks. But nothing interesting. Still, you could never tell.

Miles parked his car and sat in it, watching from a distance, getting ready to face Jack and Eileen Mack and their raw grief. He tried to think how they must feel, but he could think of nothing. He looked at the traffic going by and the kids in the parking lot. The relatives were arriving. Every few minutes another big car drove up and another small, intense Mack got out, sometimes alone, sometimes accompanied by a wife. Jack Mack, Miles figured, must be the youngest of several brothers. They looked like businessmen who had just heard bad news—things might get better or worse, but right now they had to get through this difficult part and they were going to grit their teeth and do it.

Miles watched them get out of their cars and go inside. He had to face these people. What would they think—any of them—if they knew that an hour before his death, Billy had stood crushing his body against Miles in a frenzy of longing?

Miles got out of the car and went up the stairs to the funeral parlor. It was hot in the foyer, and as he paused to sign the register, he could see there was another wake off to the left, with a coffin somewhere out of sight and three very old women just inside the room, peeping out at the commotion across the corridor. Billy was in the large room to the right. A good hundred or more folding chairs had been set out, empty still, and a receiving line was gathered over against the wall. Eileen and Jack stood near the coffin, and the older Mack brothers trailed off, with their wives, toward a sort of conversational group at the end. Some teachers were shaking hands, offering their condolences, but mostly just family were gathered there.

Miles took a quick glance at the receiving line and went directly to the prie-dieu beside Billy's coffin, where he knelt to say a prayer and get his bearings. What surprised him most was how the family looked. He had spent more than an hour with the parents just last night, he had talked with them, and he remembered Eileen as a slack, middle-aged woman using prayer as an escape from reality and Jack as an aging, angry cop who felt tricked by life, and by what his wife had become, and by what his son had done to him. And yet here they were, looking like very different people. Eileen's hair was newly set, and Miles was surprised to see it was not a graying brown, but blond and stylish. She wore bright lipstick and a black dress with a neckline that showed a lot of shoulder. The dress was plain and very expensive. Jack Mack wore a dark suit, elegantly cut, that made him look like a banker. They were both small, a striking little couple bearing up handsomely beneath personal grief.

Miles knelt with his eyes closed, trying to pray for Billy, but unable to think of anything except the Macks. This new view of them was very disturbing. He couldn't make this family fit with what he knew about Billy, or with that first phone call from Billy's mother, or with what he had seen of the father on Back to School Night. Where was the prayer-crazed mother? The homophobic cop? These were just nice normal people who had suffered the loss of their son.

Someone tapped his shoulder and Miles looked up.

"Let me kneel down," Coach said. His face was beefy and red and his eyes were swollen nearly closed. He reeked of alcohol. Behind him were a great number of people from school, Endicott and the superintendent among them, and Miles thought he caught a glimpse of Kathy Dillard, looking stricken. He rose quickly and stepped out of the way. It was only then that he noticed the coffin was closed, and on the lid stood Billy Mack's graduation picture, a boy caught smiling, unawares.

Miles took Eileen's hand in his and said, "I'm sorry, Eileen. I'm very, very sorry." She leaned toward him and kissed his cheek and then smiled distantly at him. "Yes," she said. "Yes." He wondered for a second if she recognized him. He was still looking at her when he felt Jack Mack's hand around his own. "Thank you for coming," Jack said, and Miles looked at him but saw only Billy, that same disdainful curl of the lip and those hard eyes and the unconcealed hatred. Except Billy's look had been a mask. This was no mask. "I'm sorry," Miles said, and moved on to Jack Mack's brother and his wife—"Kevin Mack and my wife Trish. I'm an uncle. Computers"—and so on down the line.

There was a cry suddenly, a short strangled sound, and then Eileen Mack was at his side. Her eyes were wide and her composure had shattered completely. She looked terrified. "That man, that Coach," she said, whispering, hysterical. "He's the one to blame. Don't let him near me. Don't let him touch my son's body." Miles looked down the line to where Coach was standing, bewildered, until the vice-principal, pushed ahead by Endicott, said, "Come on, Coach, we'll just wait out here," and led him away. Eileen Mack pulled herself together again, for a moment, and took Miles' arm and led him back to the head of the line. Still holding on to Miles, she took her place and stared ahead, nodding at the appropriate times, as Endicott offered his condolences and said what a fine boy Billy was and how they would all keep him in their prayers. She waited Endicott out, but as he turned to repeat these things to Jack, she put her arm around Miles and began to cry softly against his chest. By the time the superintendent took her hand, she was crying openly, the tears coursing down her face. "No, no," she was saying. "It can't be. It couldn't be." Miles looked over her head at Jack Mack, who looked back and registered nothing. Miles said, "Jack?" but there was no response. Later he said, "Jack? I think Eileen could use your arm?" And still there was no response. He realized finally that Jack Mack was leaving him to his own devices—he had gotten himself into this position and now he was on his own.

For an hour or more they stood this way: Miles at the head of the receiving line, with Eileen Mack on his arm. Next to them, but apart, stood Jack Mack, composed and very cold. And then the family. They stood this way while the teachers and the staff filed by, and family and friends, and then the students, shy suddenly, saying they were sorry, and marveling at how old Miles was always at the center of things, good or bad. The seniors had voted only last week to dedicate their yearbook to Miles.

By nine o'clock on Wednesday, the hour of the funeral, the girls were beginning to look very tired and the energy had gone out of their mourning. They were cross, too, because to attend the funeral they had to have a special letter from home requesting they be excused from school. They had to take the note to the office, have it countersigned by the vice-principal, submit it to the secretary, and only then could they leave school. All their spontaneity was being drained away.

Nonetheless, St. Luke's was packed with students, and there was an honor guard of policemen, and everybody was relieved that it was going to be over soon. The choral group sang Catholic hymns before the funeral began and Fr. Goodman himself played the organ—he had attended Boston Conservatory and had played professionally before becoming a priest. Scores of candles burned before the statue of the Virgin. The main altar was banked with tier on tier of gladioli. And in the center aisle stood the six death candles that would flank the coffin; they were made from beeswax, deep yellow, and mounted on sconces of black and purple. They were immense and solemn, and they stood between the living and the dead.

The singing stopped and the organ stopped and for a long time there was only the sound of crying and the occasional cough. Finally there was no sound at all.

Then the doors of the church swung open, and Fr. Goodman at the organ laid into the deep and resonant chords of the *Dies Irae*, and slowly the coffin was borne down the center aisle, the pall-bearers at its side. Paul Ciampa led on the left and Cosmo Damiani on the right and the rest of the team brought up the rear. They all looked embarrassed except for Cosmo, who looked as if he might faint at any minute. He was gray and very thin and everybody was surprised to see him, because he was supposed to be in the hospital. A cold wind blew in through the open door, fluttering the candles and making the congregation shiver, until one of the ushers closed it and there was peace in the church again. Billy Mack's coffin was placed on its catafalque in the center aisle and the requiem mass began.

Everything went smoothly until the time for the homily. Nobody had expected a homily. What could you say, in public, about a seventeen year old who committed suicide? And why do it, knowing you would just get everybody more upset? But priests always thought they had something to say. Miles sat back in the pew and studied the toes of his shoes.

"This will be brief," the priest said. "We are here to commend to God the soul of Billy Mack, who has set out on his journey to God sooner than we would have him go. The manner of his death must make us all stop and think. Could we have done something to help? Could we have said something?"

He paused, too long, and when he began again, it was with a broken voice.

"Why he made the decision to end his life is something we can never know. But we do know that, whatever other reason there may have been, there was a yearning in Billy Mack that could not be satisfied by anything we were able to say or do. Many of you tried. Many of you wish you had tried harder. We do not know what drove him to it, but we know that God is wider than the human heart, and knows all things, and loves."

He seemed to be done, but he stood there, silent, and after a while he said, "Let us think of Billy Mack and let us give ourselves to life. The importance of living. The value of life itself." He leaned forward, straining, as if the words contained some secret meaning he could force out. "Only live," he said. "In the name of the Father and of the Son and of the Holy Spirit. Amen."

Billy was buried in Holy Name Cemetery and by noon everybody was back in school. The students had been caught up in the priest's homily. "But what was he saying?" somebody asked. Somebody answered, "It was the same thing as Miles was saying, 'Life is a banquet, and half the suckers out there are starving to death.'" They discussed this for quite a while. And Miles wondered, What *had* the priest been saying?

In the afternoon Miles was summoned to the principal's office. Endicott was standing with his back to the door, staring out the window. He turned and looked at Miles and then turned away.

"It went very well, don't you think so?"

"The funeral?"

"Everything."

"I suppose," Miles said.

"That priest who gave the sermon. Is he a fuzzy type? Big on personal relations, is he?"

"I don't know who he is," Miles said. "I don't usually go to mass."

"Really? I'd have thought you'd be right there in the front pew, sopping it all up." He noticed Miles flinch. "No offense," he said. "I wish that priest had used the occasion to talk about duty. You don't give yourself to life, you give yourself to duty. Those students could have used that message right now. They've got all that energy idling there now, and if they could just get into gear, they could get some real work done." He was still staring out the window.

"An automotive image," Miles said, and Endicott nodded.

"Well, it's an opportunity he missed. Too bad."

" 'Sopping it all up,' " Miles said, in Endicott's voice.

"That was quite a scene at the wake, with Mrs. Mack and you. I didn't know you were that close to the family."

"It was very difficult. Coach is dry again, by the way."

"Officer Mack didn't seem very happy, though."

"Officer Mack was burying his son. Maybe it didn't strike him as a very happy occasion."

Endicott turned and faced him finally. "That tongue of yours, Bannon. There's no need for sarcasm with me. As a matter of fact, I'm trying to help you. That's why I called you in."

"Sorry," Miles said.

"Officer Mack seemed preoccupied, I thought. I thought so at the wake and I thought so at the funeral today. Not just grief or shock. Something else."

"What are you getting at?" Miles asked.

Endicott looked at him hard for a moment, and then he pulled out his chair and sat down at his desk, all business.

"Immediately after the burial today, Officer Mack phoned me and said that he wants an interview. He didn't say he wants to talk. He wants an interview. And he doesn't want it today. Or tomorrow. He wants it on Monday."

"Yes?"

"It's not the incident in the locker room, obviously. That's a dead issue now. So what is it?"

"I have no idea."

"He said he wants to wait until Monday. He wants to make some kind of investigation first."

"Uh-huh."

"And I thought it must have something to do with you."

"Me? Why me?"

Endicott smiled at him. "Why not you?" he said. "You were the boy's friend."

29

THURSDAY WAS A TERRIBLE DAY. Nobody had recovered from the funeral yet, and the students were tired of crying and carrying on, and it seemed like nothing could happen to lift the gloom. But around lunchtime things brightened as snow began to fall. It was snowing hard, and sticking to the ground, and the word spread that it might snow all night and turn Friday into a snow day—no school—with a long weekend following, and then only a week and a half until Christmas. And that's what happened.

It was Friday night now and the plows had finally cleared the main streets so that Miles was able to drive to Diane's place for a glass of wine, and a chaw, and a chat. No talk about love or sex, no maundering about relationships, just a friendly visit: that was the understanding. Miles had agreed to it immediately, since he knew that once he got his foot in, so to speak, he'd be able to win her back.

"Miles," she said, sounding like any friend.

"Diane," he said.

She held the door open for him as he balanced on one foot, then on the other, to pull off his rubbers. He shook them at her. "Got a newspaper?" he said.

"Drop them on the carpet," she said. "The cold is coming in." She pushed him aside and closed the door behind him. "God, it's freezing out there."

"It's clear out there. It's clean."

"Keep it in mind," she said.

They talked about school for a little while, but Jeff Douglas' name came up, so Diane changed the topic, and then they talked about teaching composition, and about the new Woody Allen movie, and about stand-up comics. That led to politics and the next elections and the Democrats' inability to decide who they were and what they wanted to do. It was becoming a very pleasant evening.

They had a glass of wine. They munched at a little bowl of carrots and celery she had cut up bite-size. They chatted. It was very civilized.

"Do you suppose," Miles said, "that there are people all over Malburn doing exactly this?"

"Yes," she said.

"I like it," he said.

She smiled. It was very nice.

Diane was wearing jeans and a sweatshirt and woolen ski socks. Her hair was pulled back in a ponytail. With her granny glasses, she looked like a wise child. Miles shifted his weight in the big leather Eames chair. How long was it since they had made love?

"Diane," he said, with a new tone to his voice.

But Diane was having none of it. "What did you think of the homily?" she said. "At Billy Mack's funeral."

Miles returned his voice to a conversational tone. "I heard what he was saying, but I couldn't figure out what he was *trying* to say."

" 'Give yourself to life,' " she said, quoting. "To me, it had the ring of desperation. I think that priest is in trouble."

"The kids were fascinated. They thought he was telling them to live richly. Life is a banquet, et cetera."

"They'd love that," Diane said, laughing. "Anything that makes life easier."

Miles was offended. "I don't know," he said. "Does seeing life as a banquet make life easier? Or does it just emphasize the importance of not wasting it? Not letting it just go by untasted?"

"This is something *you* said in class. Right?"

"I did say it once, as a matter of fact. These kids don't see life as a series of opportunities, they see it as endless obligations. They see what their parents expect, and they see their own very very narrow set of expectations, and they don't ever get beyond those. They meet a girl in high school and they get married and have two point five children and save some money and buy a camper and resent the fact that life has given them so little. Life as a banquet is not the worst idea you could give them."

"No, of course not. And you're good at that. Opening new options for them."

"Life is too short to fuck it up completely. The way I have."

"Your life seems pretty good to me."

"I'm thirty-six. I'm in love. But nobody's in love with me."

"Have a chaw," she said, and held out the bowl of carrots and celery.

"We had something really good," he said.

"Don't start," she said.

"No, I won't. I won't. I just want to say one thing. And this is in the abstract, not the concrete. So it doesn't refer to us. Okay?"

"I'll bet," she said.

"No. Listen. There are *laws* to things, Diane. Cause and effect. Impulse and reaction. You know this better than I do because you've got a philosophical mind, and mine is only intuitive. But if you perform an action, it produces results. Right? You make a choice and that choice has consequences. Right?"

"Do you think I have a philosophical mind?"

"Listen. There are laws to things. Not just legal laws, but moral laws. The laws of human behavior."

"Perhaps I have a legal mind."

"You do. That's what I'm trying to tell you. There are laws to things and you're not obeying them. You set things in motion and you expect them to stop because *you* want to stop. But they can't stop. They have their own momentum."

"You weren't going to talk about us," she said.

"Just let me. Just let me," he said. "Never mind legal obligation or moral obligation, we're talking about laws of nature here. You call it a fling, but for other people it's falling in love." He paused, flushed and pleased at having gotten through it all. "I love you and you have a responsibility to that. *You* set it in motion."

"Very nice, Miles."

"Actions have consequences. There's something more than just legal responsibility or moral responsibility."

"Have a chaw, Miles," she said, handing him the bowl of snacks. "It *is* all over, you know."

"There's . . ."

"Poor little Milesy-poo," she said. "Nobody wuvs him."

He was just about to say, There's the responsibility of the human heart, but it would sound silly now, sentimental, and so he laughed and put his hands out and said, "Don't throw me out. Don't do it. Don't. I'll be good. Here, give me some of this fodder. Ummmm, good," and he began to pop the bits of carrot and celery into his mouth, desperate to be cute and winning. "Listen," he said. "Tell me. Why do you think that priest is in trouble?"

Diane thought for a minute, not about the priest but about whether she should let Miles stay or not. In the past weeks, with sex more or less behind them, she had begun to like him quite a lot as a friend. And he sometimes said some very smart things. A philosophic mind? A legal mind? She had a gift for logic, there was no doubt about that. And nobody appreciated it.

" 'Give yourself to life,' " Miles said.

"Father Ortega? He's desperate. He wants to pour out truth for you, some hard truth he thinks he knows, but he hasn't found any container for it. He's probably in love and badly conflicted."

"Do you know him?"

"Just his name, Ortega. He says the eight o'clock mass on Sundays. His homilies are always like that. Straining. He'll probably leave and get married and settle down."

They were silent for a while, and the Vivaldi on the CD player finally came to an end. "Some Miles Davis?" Miles said. "Miles *anybody?*" But Diane got up and put on Bach, played low.

"The calculus of the spheres," she said, as the music came up in the room.

"Who said that?"

"Everybody says that," she said.

"I went to mass all last week. I stopped, though. Why do you go?"

"Why did *you* go? Perhaps that's why I go."

"I was feeling good. I don't know. It had something to do with my mother."

"I go because I've always gone. It's a habit. It's a good habit."

"You're joking. You go out of *habit?* To mass?"

"Why do I go?" This was a good turn to the conversation. She had been right to let him stay. "Well, put in terms that would mean something to a psychiatrist, I suppose I go because of two reasons. One: by going, you acknowledge whatever gods there are. I suppose you could acknowledge them in the forest or at home, but I acknowledge them at church. And two: if you believe in a personal God—and I happen to—then, by going, you constantly leave yourself wide open to a divine communication."

"Wait," Miles said.

"Any moment can be ripe for revelation."

For some reason—he had no idea why—Miles felt like he had been struck in the face by an open hand. He began to blush.

"What?" she said. "Why are you blushing?"

"You're a believer," he said. "You believe it all."

She only looked at him.

He was embarrassed and confused, but he was aware that something he felt for her was falling away from him and being replaced by something else, something he didn't especially want. He had the crazy fantasy that someone inside him reached out and plucked that grain of belief from her and now it was his own: any moment can be ripe for revelation.

He left, and almost at once he forgot the strange and unnerving experience with Diane. He just wanted her to love him, he just wanted her to have sex with him, and never mind all that religious nonsense.

That night he lay awake, contemplating the responsibility of the human heart. You set things in motion. They have their own momentum.

He was thinking not of Diane but of Billy Mack.

30

MILES SPENT SATURDAY MORNING in bed reading *The Scarlet Letter*. It was snowing again, lightly, and the day was overcast, and it was a perfect time to think ahead to the rest of the school year. Choose books. Make plans. Long-range teaching preparation.

Miles had intended to teach *As I Lay Dying* this year, but his mother's death and now Billy Mack's death made him think *The Bridge of San Luis Rey* might be better. Or *The Red Badge of Courage*. Or even that marvelous old warhorse, *The Scarlet Letter*, which he hadn't taught in years. So he was reading it again.

He read slowly, meditatively, through the first five chapters, and decided yes, this was the book he'd teach. "She felt or fancied, then, that the scarlet letter had endowed her with a new sense. She shuddered to believe, yet could not help believing, that it gave her a sympathetic knowledge of the hidden sin in other hearts." It's what the kids feared most—being found out; having their hidden sins revealed. But "a sympathetic knowledge." His mind raced through the discussion opportunities in the word "sympathetic." The possibilities were endless. They'd love it. And for his advanced placement section, he could teach *San Luis Rey* as an extra. It would be a nice complement, with all that stuff about the economy of the great divine plan and readiness is all.

The snowy day and *The Scarlet Letter* put him in a mood to take stock of his life. It was not yet Christmas and already it had been an incredible year, a momentous year. He thought back to that first week of school, when he'd seen Paul Ciampa coming down the corridor and said to himself, If I'd had those shoulders, I could be Governor of Massachusetts today. It was a funny thing to remember, a funny thing to think in the first place. He didn't want to be Governor of Massachusetts. And he could see now—though it had worried him then—that he didn't really find those shoulders sexually attractive. Well, they were, they are, but not sexually attractive to him personally. They were just manly and solid and they made him wish he had been built like that as a teenager instead of being slope-shouldered and nerdy. Was he kidding himself? No. Maybe. So much had happened since that day.

Billy was raped that day and now he was dead. And Coach had gotten himself together, and fallen apart, and was together again . . . with Kathy Dillard, no less. And his mother, his funny old wonderful loving mother, had died. And he had slept with Robert. Was it so awful, what he had done? At this distance, with the shock gone and the sense of self-discovery long behind him, it didn't seem so bad. It was just something he had done, and now it was over. He had liked it in a way, though he had refused to let himself like it at the time. Which was crazy, because it was only sex, after all; it wasn't the end of the world. And then at once, only days after Robert and what had seemed the end of his world, there had been Diane, and real sex, and real abandonment, and discovering how to give pleasure. He was better at it now. Though it was still a stunt, still a performance. He knew that. He admitted it.

And Billy was dead. If he had held him close, pressed his own body against Billy's until they came and it was over, would Billy be alive today? Would that have been worse than what he'd done? In any case, he had failed Billy, as he had failed everybody who

ever loved him. His father, doddering into senility, unknown, un-
loved. His mother. Billy. And he had lost them all.

Back on that day when Billy was raped, he'd thought his mind
might fly out of his head, that he might come apart and everybody
would see exactly what he was. It hadn't happened the way he
feared. But it had happened. *He* saw what he was and he could
see now what he had come to. He was a man loaded with guilt,
legal and moral and psychological and intellectual and what else?
In small, subtle ways he had betrayed his friends. He had betrayed
his ideals. What ideals? Well, if he had any, he had betrayed them.
He was not, truly not, a very good person. Take Diane, for example.
He was not in love with Diane, he knew that now, but he wanted
her still. As power? As lust? As an opportunity to perform? Well,
he would let her be.

He would call Margaret. He still had Margaret. He would be good
to her. He would be generous. And besides, he could tell her about
what had happened between him and Billy that day up on the
rock, and then someone else would know. He could never tell Diane
about it. Any more than he could tell Margaret he'd gone to bed
with a man. Was this a case of dividing up the guilt to make it
livable? To keep any one person from knowing everything? To
keep himself from a final awareness of who he was and what he
had done? No, not that. He knew. He knew.

And he knew, too, that at least there was this consolation: having
lost his father and mother, having slept with a man and abandoned
a student to suicide, having given up on love, perhaps forever, he
had little left to lose. He had nothing left to lose. That was the
consolation—things could not get worse.

He went to the phone and dialed Margaret's number. She would
understand.

Margaret had refused to let Miles come for dinner, but she said he
could come by for a drink, and now she was ready for him. It was
eight o'clock. The snow had stopped and the plows had cleared the

streets and the sky was cold and clear. Tomorrow would be warm, the television said. Slush on Sunday. A mess on Monday. Still, it was nice to be inside on this wintry night.

She was missing an AA meeting on Miles' behalf. She was relieved to miss it, to tell the truth, because she did not want to see Dietz, and she did not want to hear about Coach, drunk or sober, and she did not want to sit and listen while a bunch of decent, honest, hardworking, salvation-minded alcoholics trotted out their personal lives as cautionary tales. Yes, AA worked. Yes, it was the only thing that worked. But no, she did not want to attend another meeting as long as she lived. It was better than being drunk, though, and so she'd do it, she'd attend and she'd listen and she'd tell her horror story too. Until she died, if she had to.

The six weeks since her collapse had taken her a great distance from the old Margaret. She knew that, though she herself could not see it or feel it. It seemed to her that she put on her public face in the morning and went off to a day's hard work, and she took off that face in the evening—except when she had an AA meeting—and got through the night in the usual ways: she read a book, she watched television, she drank tea. But the books she read were psychology books, where she searched out the nature of the abused wife, the professional victim, though she did not believe half of what she read. And the television she watched was what everybody watched, but she watched it with a different eye, and she concluded that many indeed have sickened for love, but few have died for it. And she drank tea and pondered and realized that—alone and out of love and out of patience with herself and with the world— nonetheless, it was good to be alive.

She was seeing Miles tonight to end it, finally. Love was like booze; if you just quit, cold turkey, you found it was a lot easier to get on with the business of living. She was no longer just another drunk clinging to sobriety; she was a responsible woman taking charge of her life. Miles must go.

He came in stamping his feet and flailing his arms in his huge down coat. He kissed her quickly. "Margaret," he said, "you look wonderful."

She was wearing a new maroon robe that billowed like a caftan and she had on stockings and heels. She intended to send him away, gently, and she wanted to look good while she did it.

"Your drink," she said, handing it to him and then taking his coat. "Come in by the fire." The little house had never looked cozier. It was an old house, a warm house, the very opposite of Diane's.

"Mmmm, nice," he said, and fell onto the couch, stretching out his legs in front of him. "I've been wanting to see you," he said.

"Me, too," she said. Before he finished his drink, she would be done with this.

Her tone caught his attention.

"I have a real problem with self-esteem, Miles. This little descent into hell that I've enjoyed for the past month and a half—two months really—has shown me a great deal about myself and about the abuse I took from Roofer and about the abuse I've inflicted on myself. All that abuse told me who I was."

"Margaret," he said.

"Listen to me. The abuse told me who I was. I was the one who deserved this. He'd apologize afterward, of course, and bring me presents, and say what a shit he was and how could I ever forgive him, and I forgave him because, in my sick mind, I thought it was right. He was doing what was right. And I deserved it."

She thought for a moment, and then she went on.

"I'm not one of those women who go on talk shows and revel in how they've been abused, savor it all over again in front of an audience. I've grown up at least that much. I never wanted it and I never should have allowed it."

"That's right. That's right," he said.

"And so I can't continue to allow it now."

"No," he said.

"I thought I was in love with you because, after Roofer, you supplied the abuse I needed. Mental. Psychological. But very real. And I don't need it anymore."

"Margaret, don't talk like that. What are you saying?"

"I'm saying I don't need it anymore. I'm free of that. Mind you, I've got nothing. Nothing at all. And I need a lot of things. But— and I want to say this nicely, Miles—one thing I don't need is you."

And Miles, to his own astonishment, put down his drink, said he was sorry, and left.

For a long time Margaret stared into the fire and watched her life in the flames. She loved him still, a little, of course. How could you not? He was a good man. And a needy one. And she dearly loved to be needed. But she couldn't and she wouldn't confuse that with real love. Not now. Not again. Not ever. It was going to be very lonely for her after this.

In a while she got up and made a cup of tea.

Miles drove home the long way so that he could pass Diane's house. He slowed down as it came into view, and for some reason he was not surprised to see a patch of light appear and disappear as the door opened and a man went in. Of course. Another fling. Or an old fling just checking in. Or maybe Endicott blackmailing her. Or Jeff Douglas about to kill her. Or maybe Billy Mack come back from the grave to tell her what he knew about Miles.

Suddenly his mouth tasted of burnt and rotting flesh. He felt bitter, murderous. Things *could* get worse. They always had. They always would.

Later, as he drove past the darkened church, he thought for just one second of his last conversation with Diane and the odd experience he'd had. He remembered she had said, "Any moment can be ripe for revelation." So he had something of hers after all. He would hold on to that.

31

MILES SAT IN CHURCH, alone, on Sunday afternoon. He'd been there for twenty-seven minutes and still nothing had happened. He wasn't expecting anything to happen, of course, but he couldn't help hoping something would. Like a miracle, for instance. Or a voice from heaven saying, I love you, Milo, even if the rest of them are all shits. Or even somebody coming in to look for a lost glove. It was very cold when you were just sitting in church. He had been here now for twenty-eight minutes. Maybe he was hoping Diane would come in and see him praying, and realize what a mistake she had made; then they'd go back to her place and fuck like rabbits and everything would be fine again. He thought about Diane for a while, and fucking, and then he prayed for faith. For hope. For that kernel of belief he had—or had not—plucked from Diane on Friday night. "Lord, I believe; help thou my unbelief." Twenty-nine minutes. He was going to give it a half-hour and call it a day. He closed his eyes to concentrate.

He felt less cold—maybe they'd turned on the heat in this place—and the pew seemed less hard, and he scrunched over against the side to get a little more comfortable. He was tired; he hadn't slept much lately. He felt like sleeping now. Last night he'd lain awake again, not with guilt feelings, real or imaginary, but with the feeling that Margaret had spoken God's own truth and he had heard it. There was no arguing with this. No defense was possible. He had abused Margaret as surely, as finally, as Roofer ever had. He had taken her goodness and generosity for granted. He had treated her love as a burden. He had used her. And he couldn't undo any of this. He would have to live through it, or beyond it. But it would always be there behind him: what he had done.

He would like to be held by somebody, and as he settled deeper into the pew and leaned farther over to the side, it was very much like being held. A strong arm behind his shoulder, a hand upon his heart, warm breath at his ear. It was very comforting, he was very comfortable. If he could stay this way, supported and comforted, for a while longer, a lot longer, maybe forever, then everything would be all right. He relaxed in his sleep and let himself be held.

"And this is only the beginning." He heard a voice say this, and he repeated the words, and they sounded very soothing.

Miles awoke thinking of Robert. He had been dreaming, he thought, but not about Robert. How awful to wake up thinking of him, and in church, too. He looked at his watch and saw that he had been asleep for nearly an hour. Ugliness, misery, and piss. A priest had thrown on the sanctuary lights and was busying himself about the altar now, getting ready for Benediction, or whatever they did on Sunday afternoons. A boy was lighting candles. Miles thought he'd just rest for a minute, and get his bearings, but some clown opened the church door and a blast of freezing wind came in.

Miles genuflected, blessed himself, and got out of there, quick.

Richy Polcari was spending the entire day with Robert and they were having a wonderful time. Robert and Richard. Richard and Robert. Richy liked to lie in bed and repeat their names over and over. He was doing this now, as he waited for Robert to come back from the shower.

Robert's favorite game was to have Richy come to his apartment and dress up in one of his suits, with a white shirt and tie and everything, and then wait in the living room until he was seated at his desk, poring over his papers. Sometimes Robert made him wait as long as five minutes, and Richy had discovered that the longer he waited, the more excited Robert got. When it was time, Richy would come in and stand next to Robert's desk, saying, "Haven't you finished writing that speech yet?" And Robert wouldn't say anything. "Haven't you?" Richy would say, and he'd lean against Robert, hard. "Well?" he'd say. And they'd keep this up until Robert couldn't stand it any longer. Then they'd go at it, crazy, right in their suits. Afterwards Robert would shower while Richy lay in bed, saying Richard and Robert, Robert and Richard, waiting for him to come back. They had great times.

Richy reached out and took a magazine from the top of the little bookcase beside the bed. *U.S. News and World Report*. Yuck. He reached for another. *The Guardian*, with little tiny print and crinkly paper. All the magazines were dull, so Richy pushed them aside and pulled out the big book at the bottom of the pile. It was the Malburn yearbook, last year's, and Robert had a bookmark sticking out. Richy flipped the book open at the marker—it was a parking ticket—and of course it opened right to his class picture. Section 3-C. Mr. Douglas was homeroom teacher. He was good-looking, but mean, and probably gay. Could that be? Well, he could be gay and not know it. Some people just didn't. He looked at the pictures of the other homeroom teachers: Miles in 3-A, with all that sexy hair; Ms. Novello in 3-B, she was cute; Mrs. Hendrix, who was old but nice, in 3-D. Miles had been mean to him too, but he hadn't really meant to be. He could tell.

Robert came into the bedroom wearing his robe. He was always shy after one of their big bouts of sex, and he was shy now, and smelled of Santos by Cartier which cost a hundred dollars a bottle. He lay down next to Richy, propping himself up on one elbow, and waited to hear what he'd say.

"Ticket," Richy said, waving the slip of yellow paper. "You forgot to pay it."

"Let me see it," Robert said, puzzled.

"It was in the yearbook, at my picture."

Robert looked at the ticket and at the yearbook and laughed softly.

"What's so funny?"

Robert began to laugh hard.

"Come on. What?"

"Oh, if you knew. If you only knew." He laughed again, and then got serious, and then he rolled over on his back and began to giggle uncontrollably.

Richy took the ticket from his hand and looked at it. "It isn't yours? What is it? 819EGZ? Who's that?"

"I won't tell you. I'll never tell you. You'd never believe it in a thousand million years."

"Orange Pinto. 819EGZ. I don't get it."

"You know him. You like him."

"Milo? Mr. Bannon? It's his ticket? But how come you've got it?"

"Think."

"You met him? To talk about me?"

"I picked him up."

"Come on."

"At the hospital. When the senator had his heart attack."

"I don't believe it."

"Really."

"Did he do it? Is he gay?"

"*I* did it. But he's gay all right. And bigger than a breadstick."

Richy didn't say anything for a while. He looked around the room, which seemed strange to him suddenly, as if he'd never really seen it before.

"What's the matter?"

"I just wish he hadn't, that's all. I wish *you* hadn't."

"It didn't mean anything, Richy. It was just for fun."

Richy didn't respond.

"It was just one of those nights. I needed to get it off."

"But in the hospital. God."

"It wasn't in the hospital. I only said that. It was in the Tom Cat."

"Miles wouldn't go there."

"He was there, I'm telling you. He was a little bit drunk."

"You're making this up."

"His mother had just died. He was flat out. He was a little drunk."

"I remember when his mother died and he was all broken up. He wasn't at the Tom Cat Lounge, ever. Why are you lying?"

"Look at the date."

Richy read the date on the ticket.

"I'm going home," he said.

"No," Robert said. He placed his hand on Richy's chest and looked into his eyes. This had all been in fun, he'd only wanted to make Richy a little jealous, and now it was completely out of control. "No," he said. "You're staying."

Richy pushed his hand aside and got up and got dressed.

"What're you doing? We were having a good time. If you're gonna be mad at somebody, be mad at Miles, not at me. All I did was give him what he wanted."

"I'm going home."

"Richy, I love you," Robert said. "You know that."

"I know it," Richy said, "but it's not the same now."

Endicott was sitting in his study having a drink with Jeff Douglas. Missy had just brought them a plate of crackers with some awful dietetic cheese—no salt, no fat, no taste—and she shot them the V for Victory sign as she left the room and closed the door behind her. They would need privacy, she knew. Her Willy was up to tricks.

"You'll regret that," Endicott said, as Jeff cut a piece of cheese and put it on a cracker. He waited until Jeff bit it into it, and made a face, and swallowed. "See?"

"What is it?" Jeff asked.

"It's B Soap. Are you old enough to remember B Soap? It was deep yellow, almost orange, and it cleaned your skin like lye. Took it right off, one layer at a time. B Soap. I don't know what the B stood for." He was feeling very good. "So tell me how things are going for you, Jeffy?"

Jeffy? Jeff Douglas sipped his drink and looked around the room. Lots of books on education, military tactics, the U.S. Army. No novels. No poetry. No history, even. Was Endicott the complete asshole he'd always presumed? It sure looked that way. And what, pray, was the purpose of this Sunday night drink?

"How's the tenure battle going?"

"Well, of course, you'd know more about that than I. Your excellent English Chairwoman, Ms. Waring, continues to want me out of Malburn High. She's showed me her written evaluations, and she's told me about the recommendations she's made to you and to the School Board. She's overlooked one thing, of course."

"Oh, yes?"

"Yes. That I'm the best teacher you've got."

Endicott smiled broadly and said, "Tell me about that."

Jeff counted off on his fingers. "One, I've got the best education. Andover, Harvard, and ten years at IBM. Two, I've got the best outside record. I've been yearbook advisor for two years, I've directed the school play with more success than anybody before. *Antigone*. Serious drama. None of that Kaufman and Hart crap. And in my free time I've written two novels, one of which is probably going to get taken any day now. And three—and it's a big three— I've got the best teaching record of anybody in the English Department. My kids *learn*. They learn how to think and how to discuss. They have opinions of their own which aren't just canned expressions of what the school wants them to think. They think for themselves, and I'm the reason that they do. Anybody will admit that. Anybody will swear to that."

"Good," Endicott said, nodding.

"I *am* good."

"Up to a point."

"Up to the point of my professional judgment?"

Endicott nodded again, judicious.

"Yes?" Well, he could play this game too. Just watch. "Diane always talks about my lack of professional judgment because she thinks those buzzwords are going to throw a scare into you and the School Board. But I've got a higher opinion of you than that. I think you can see through that. I think you know that anybody can sling language around to their advantage, and what really matters is what they accomplish. I think you know that I'm a good teacher. I'm just not in Diane's conservative mold."

"Traditional mold. Traditional, not conservative."

"What's the difference?"

"Traditional is a better defense. Conservative is a fighting word. Your teaching is not traditional, but it's solid. *That*'s what you mean."

So. Endicott was not a complete asshole after all.

"And you want to help me mount a defense?" Jeff said. "For tenure?"

"Well, I know that you don't get on with Diane Waring and I just want to make sure you get a fair shake. Is there some reason you don't get on with her? Is there a personal history I should know about?"

"I've got a wife and kids. I don't fuck around."

"Of course not. Of course not. I was thinking of Bannon. He seems to have it in for you. And I know he's close to Diane. You know that. And I wondered if he's prejudicing her against you? In tenure decisions, I try to weigh all the factors, even—and sometimes especially—the personal ones."

Jeff was lost. What did he want?

"Let me tell you what I want. This Officer Mack, whose boy just died, is making enquiries about Miles Bannon and of course I want to be of help. But my first job is to protect the school. So if there's something to know about Bannon, I want to know it first. Do you follow me?"

"No."

"If there was something too close between Miles and Billy Mack, and Officer Mack gets it in his head that Miles may in some way be connected with the boy's suicide, well, I want that information first."

"Miles is faggy, but I doubt he knows it. Is that what you're after?"

"I want Officer Mack quiet. And if that means throwing Miles to the wolves, so be it. By which I mean, if his friendship with the boy was inappropriate, then he probably should not be teaching here. Or anywhere. But this is not to prejudge him. I try always to be fair. I just want facts."

"And you want me to get them."

"Jeffy, get your act together. I called you here for a drink, and to find out how the tenure battle was going. I was just trying to help you think through your options—as Diane would say—and suggest how you can help your own case. I don't want anything from you. I only want to be of help."

Jeff thought for a moment, raised his glass to his lips, and found it was empty. "Allow me," Endicott said, and took the glass and poured him another drink.

Jeff ate a cracker with some of the ghastly cheese on it. B Soap must have been killer stuff.

Endicott was waiting, silent.

There was something homey and suffocating about this study. It was too warm. It smelled a little sour. He felt like he was being poisoned here. He was bigger than this. And better. He was a first-rate teacher, and a novelist, and a man. He'd get tenure fairly or not at all.

"I've got a suggestion," Jeff said. "Why don't you go fuck yourself?"

He made a great exit.

As soon as the AA meeting ended, Jim Dietz drove over to Margaret's house to make sure she was okay, since she'd missed two meetings in a row. Jim knew that there was an 80 percent chance of at least one relapse, and he was resigned to it, but he hated it just the same. And Margaret mattered especially to him, because he'd been the first one there after her suicide attempt, and because Bannon didn't seem to care about her the way he should, and because, frankly, he found her very attractive. In the past couple weeks he had entertained fantasies of their getting together, having a few laughs, maybe even a date. He could see them working together in AA, married even, helping people recover from addiction, doing good, constantly expanding the circle of people they had saved. A good life. And somebody to love.

He rang the doorbell and suddenly Margaret was there, smiling, looking beautiful in a maroon velvet gown. "Oh," she said, with only a trace of disappointment in her voice. "I thought it must be Miles." And though she continued to smile, she did not invite him in. He left almost at once, feeling foolish.

He drove to Coach's house, because Coach also had missed the last two meetings. What did these people think? That you checked in at the beginning of term and remained sober till Christmas? It didn't work that way. Sobriety was like money; you had to earn it. Coach was a pain in the ass, anyhow. He had straightened his life out at the beginning of the year and then he'd let Billy Mack's suicide drive him right back to the bottle. Well, it was a sign of how deeply Coach felt things, of course, and there was also the memory of Carol and the car crash. Guilt. But that was over and it was time for some rehabilitation here. And that meant AA and a religious dedication to the Program. What was the matter with these people?

Coach wasn't home. And he hadn't been at the meeting. So that meant he was in a bar somewhere or over at Kathy Dillard's house. Dietz decided he was not, even for Coach's sake, going to go look for him at Kathy Dillard's house. She used to be so good—everybody used to confide in her and listen to her advice and trust her—in the old days, when all she cared about was cars and toilet paper.

But now that she had Coach on the string, she was impossible. Short-tempered and intolerant and argumentative. And very imprudent. She didn't realize how dangerous it was to play around with alcoholics. Why did these non-alcoholics insist on meddling?

He drove to Arlington where Kathy Dillard lived and, sure enough, Coach's car was parked in her driveway. He stepped on the gas and drove right by. He decided to treat himself to a Big Mac and some coffee, and double fries, and when he was done, he sat back and thought about how people fucked up their lives. Why did they have to have booze? Coffee was enough. And a meaningful life.

He was driving back to Malburn by way of Kathy's street when it occurred to him that he might as well stop and say hello. He'd come all this way, after all. And Kathy was an old friend. Besides, you could never tell when somebody needed that extra show of concern that might make the difference and keep them dry, and let's face it, he could show Coach that concern better than Kathy could.

He lifted the brass knocker and let it fall. There was a long silence and then he lifted the knocker and let it fall again. At once Kathy opened the door a crack, looking fierce.

"What?" she said.

"I saw Coach's car in the driveway," Dietz said. "He wasn't at the meeting."

"So?"

"I was driving by, and I saw his car, and I thought I'd see how he's doing."

"You were just driving by? In Arlington?"

"We used to be friends, Kathy, you and I. What's the matter with you?"

"Come on in," she said, shaking her head, but standing aside from the door. "You're freezing the house out anyhow."

Dietz wiped his feet on the cocoa mat and then tiptoed through the foyer into the big living room. Coach was sitting on the sofa, his head in his hands, a beer in front of him on the coffee table. He didn't look up.

Dietz went over and sat next to him on the couch. He put one arm around his shoulders. "Hey, big guy," he said. "How ya doing?"

Coach shook his head and said nothing.

"It's gonna be all right," Dietz said. "This is all over now."

"Don't talk to him that way," Kathy said. She was standing at the door to the living room, as if she wanted no part of this scene. "That's condescending. It's insulting."

"Coach is sick. Coach has a disease."

"Coach is having a drink with me. A beer. One. What is so bad about that?"

"He can't stop at one. That's what's so bad about that."

"He can stop at three. He did last night. And he will tonight."

"I can't believe this. I can't believe what I'm hearing," Dietz said. "*You* know better than this." He nudged Coach. "Don't you! 'He can stop at three.' Of course he can stop at three. Or thirty-three. Or a hundred and thirty-three. But he has to admit he's powerless over it first. And he can't admit that with a glass of beer in his hand. You," and he pointed a shaky finger at Kathy, "you are a dangerous and destructive woman."

"Pish," she said.

Coach groaned and kept his head in his hands.

Dietz put his arm around Coach again. "You know where I am when you need me, Coach," he said. "And you'll be welcome. There's always a place for you in AA."

Dietz left, but he was so upset by the insanity of the scene that he knew if he did not keep driving, he would hit the nearest bar and have a drink. He drove to downtown Boston and from there onto the turnpike and, once on the turnpike, he just kept going across the entire state of Massachusetts and up through Lenox and across to upstate New York. He filled his car with gas then, and turned around, and drove home.

By the time he reached Malburn, Dietz had everything back in perspective. Coach was having a relapse. It happened. He was using Billy Mack's suicide as an excuse, of course, but that's how it always was. There was always an excuse. Coach would be all right. And so would Kathy. She wasn't deliberately keeping him drunk. It was ignorance on her part, and probably misguided love. That sort of thing happened. He'd never been in love, except with booze, and nobody had ever loved him, so he couldn't pass judgment. He wouldn't. He was nice and calm now and ready for bed. And to hell with everybody, drunk or sober.

He was ready to pull into his parking slot when he saw a car already there. It was Coach's car, and Coach was at the wheel, slumped over, unconscious. Dietz brought him around, dragged him out of his car, and with great effort got him into the elevator and up to his apartment. He made coffee and kept up a running stream of chatter. Jokes and toasts and stories. That's me, he said. And he felt only a little guilty at being terribly, terribly happy that everything had turned out so well.

Eileen had gone to bed and Jack Mack was killing time while he waited to go on duty. The house was cold and it felt big and empty, even the kitchen. Jack was sitting at the table, a beer in front of him, as he played with a book of matches. He lit one and held it out in front of him, straight up, and watched the little bulb of yellow flame burn orange, then red, and then turn yellow again as the flame descended the cardboard shaft and burnt out against his thumb and forefinger. He squeezed the match dead and dropped it into the big glass ashtray with the other dead matches. There were two packs there now, maybe more. And Jack Mack's thumb and forefinger were burnt black at the tip.

That ashtray had been on the kitchen table since Billy was a kid. He had always wanted to play with it, even when he was too small to hold it, but they held it for him, putting it up against a bulb so that the crystals sent a shower of light and color down on him.

Even as a baby, he liked anything pretty. Jack lit another match and watched it burn down to his thumb and fingertip.

"Shit," he said.

He tossed the book of matches into the ashtray and picked up the Sunday Sports as he heard Eileen coming down the stairs. He shook out the paper and then settled it on the table in front of him, so that it shielded the beer and the ashtray and made him look busy.

Eileen came into the kitchen wearing her blue bunny slippers and her old blue robe, her rosary clutched in one hand. He'd given her a new blue robe last Christmas, velour, and she'd worn it all year, but since Billy's death she'd gone back to this old thing that looked like it came out of a ragbag and made her look ragbaggy, too. Her hair was a rat's nest and her lips were moving as she said the prayers of the rosary. She could be your local crazy person, Jack thought.

"Can't sleep?" he said.

She looked at him as if she had just noticed he was there.

"Some tea," she said. "But without the caffeine." She ran water in the kettle and put it on the stove. She stood there staring at it.

"What are you doing?" he said.

She smiled to herself. "Staring," she said. She moved over to the sink and looked out into the driveway.

"Why don't you go to bed, Eileen? Why don't you try and get some rest?" He shifted in his chair. "You know?"

"I know. Oh, I know, all right. 'Why don't you try and get some rest, Eileen? Why don't you go to bed, Eileen?' " She turned from the window and faced him. "What you mean is, Why don't you get out of my sight, Eileen, why don't you go away, why don't you just die? Isn't that it? Isn't that what you mean? Then you'd never have to think of that boy again."

Jack shook his head and looked down at his newspaper.

"Don't you do that," she whispered, and in a second she was on him, her eyes wild, her face distorted. She snatched the newspaper from his hands and flung it to the floor. "Don't you do that to me. You did it to him all his life, turning away, making that face, letting him know what you thought of him." She pressed her fists hard against her chest and she seemed to crumble inside. "And then you said it to him. You told him he was a faggot, and he killed himself. Why? Why did you do it?" She began to cry, soundlessly.

"Go to bed, Eileen."

"He was all I had."

"Go to bed."

She turned to leave the kitchen, still clutching her rosary, when the kettle let out its high, shrill whistle. She moved the kettle from the stove to the cutting board where it hissed for a minute and then went silent. She stood, looking at it, for a long time. She stopped crying, wiped her nose with a tissue, and stared blankly out the dark window. Then she said, as if she had just noticed, "You're drinking. Before you go on duty?"

"I'm having a beer."

"Are you insane? Are you trying to destroy us all?"

"Shut it, Eileen. I've had enough of this."

"He's drinking. Mother of God."

"Shut it."

She lifted the kettle and poured the steaming water down the sink. She put the empty kettle back on its trivet. She wiped down the counter with a sponge. Then she shuffled across the kitchen floor in those awful bunny slippers, went through the living room, and started up the stairs. In a moment, though, she returned and stood in the doorway until Jack looked up at her.

"What?" he said. But he knew what she would say.

"If you try to make trouble for Miles Bannon, if you *keep* trying to make trouble for him, I'll leave you. And I'll tell why."

He looked straight ahead and said nothing. He took a sip of beer. He picked up a book of matches, tore one off, lit it, and watched it burn down to his thumb and fingertip. He pinched it dead and then Eileen left him and went upstairs to sleep.

Jack Mack was scared. He didn't know if Eileen was crazier with religion or without it. It was bad enough when she just prayed and pretended everything was fine, but this new kick of hers—blaming him for Billy's death—was more than he could take. And he didn't have to take it, goddamn it, it wasn't his fault.

It was Miles Bannon's fault. Miles had let the kid fall in love with him, he could have stopped it, he was a grown-up, for Christ's sake. He had probably encouraged it. Billy had been jogging with Bannon, Bannon himself had told him so, and for all anybody knew, they might have been jogging the day Billy killed himself. Something might have happened. Something might have been said. Miles Bannon probably knew plenty that he could tell.

One thing was sure: poor Billy had creamed himself just before he did it. Jack had found the body, and the note, and the crumpled jogging stuff beside the closet door. Just by chance, one of those wild chances that never occurs in real detective work, Jack had knelt on the far side of the body, and when he leaned over to support himself on the floor, he had placed his hand on the jogging shorts, still wet from Billy's run. And when he took his hand away, it carried the unmistakable smell of semen. He'd taken the shorts and the jockstrap and the shirt, and he'd hidden them in the cellar, behind the paint cans. He didn't know why. He just wanted nobody to know about this, ever.

But that was on Monday, and a week had gone by, and in that time he had become convinced that Miles Bannon knew something, Miles Bannon had probably played some part in it, Miles Bannon had taken his son from him.

He had an appointment tomorrow with that screwball principal. And he'd keep it, too, and to hell with Eileen. She'd never leave him. She wouldn't dare. He poured himself another beer. He had time for one more before he went on duty.

It was after midnight when Miles got into his car and drove to St. Luke's. He had the vague idea of stopping in to make a visit. He imagined a red sanctuary lamp glowing near the altar, a bank of lighted candles at the Virgin's shrine, the smell of incense lingering from the evening service. And darkness. And a feeling of being comforted. He'd say a little prayer, for faith and for forgiveness, and then he'd nip on home.

He went up the granite steps to the church and pulled on the huge wooden door. It was locked, of course. He looked at his watch, feeling foolish, and then he turned and started down the stairs. There was a noise behind him as the door was forced slowly open. Miles stopped and looked. He saw only two eyes and then a pointy little nose, and as the door was shoved farther open, he could make out the anxious face of the priest who had said the funeral mass for Billy Mack. Father Ortega. He looked very young up close.

"What's the matter?" the priest said. "What do you want?"

"I just wanted to make a visit," Miles said.

"Are you crazy? It's after midnight. Are you out of your mind?"

"I didn't know the church closed."

"Of course it closes. What did you think, it's a supermarket?"

"I'm sorry," Miles said.

"Where are you going?"

"Home."

"Are you all right? Are you going to be all right?"

"Yes."

"I can't do anything for you. I would if I could, but I can't."

"I'm fine," Miles said.

"I can't help it. I've got nothing left in me. I can't save people. I can't even save myself."

"Are *you* all right?" Miles asked.

"I just have to hang on," the priest said, "that's all any of us can do."

"And give yourself to life," Miles said, smiling, making contact.

"I can't," the priest said.

They stood on the church steps looking at each other.

"I can't," the priest said again. All this time, he'd been standing with one arm thrust between the door and the jamb, keeping the door open. Now he yanked it toward him and, in an instant, without another word, he disappeared inside.

Miles shivered in the cold air, wishing he had stayed at home. Was the whole world desperate?

32

AT MIDNIGHT MASS ON CHRISTMAS EVE, the pastor asked that they pray for the soul of Billy Mack and his bereaved family, for Fr. Ortega who was ill and on a leave of absence from his priestly duties, and for all those in the parish who were suffering loss and loneliness and despair. This was a time of joy, the pastor said, of new birth and new life and new beginnings. Let us start our lives anew. Let us rejoice and be glad.

Which Miles translated as: it's all ugliness, misery, and piss, so put a good face on it and cheer up. Certainly he'd had his own bellyful of loss and loneliness and despair just in his fling with Diane. Her fling rules admitted of friendship after the fact, and indeed she was willing to see him occasionally as a friend, but she kept a close eye on the line of friendship, and as soon as he crossed it, she threw him out. All his time away from her he spent plotting to be with her. And as soon as he was with her, he was miserable. He wanted more, he wanted her to see him as he was, and to want him. She didn't want him. It was as simple as that. What made it maddening was that he *did* want her. It wasn't love he felt; it wasn't obsession; it was something like greed, and it devoured him.

Christmas was not really a time of joy for Diane, either, since her life was in total disarray. Miles was continuing to be a pest, and she could tell that something was going on between Endicott and Jeff Douglas, and she felt an urgent need for a fling, but there was nobody she could rely on to observe her new fling laws, so her work life and her social life were hopeless. That wasn't what bothered her. Her spiritual life bothered her. It was not hopeless, she knew that, but it was utterly confused and confusing to her. For the first time in her remembrance, she went to mass and did not know what to offer, did not know what to ask. She had always felt called to some kind of secular sanctity, and she had thought that sanctity lay for her in the teaching vocation, but she had begun to doubt this. She had begun to know it was not so. Where, then, should she turn? What should she do? She prayed and opened her heart and the words of the Meditation Hymn spoke to her: "Yours is princely power in the day of your birth. The Lord said to my Lord, 'Sit at my right hand, till I make your enemies your footstool.' " She turned these words over and over in her mind and she was very unhappy at Christmas.

Margaret sat alone at midnight mass, listening for a word, a sign, some shred of comfort or of grace. And nothing happened. She went home and turned on the television and made cinnamon tea. She was watching some ghastly variety show, cheery and mindless, when it came to her that she should call up Miles and say, Happy Christmas. She dialed his number and let the phone ring and ring, but there was no answer. She hadn't wanted to do it, it was an act of pure giving on her part, and she was surprised to see how disappointed she was that Miles was not at home. Even now, at 2:00 a.m.

At 2:00 a.m. Miles was standing on the Macks' front porch, looking in their window at them sitting on either side of a Christmas tree. Eileen was wearing a pale blue robe and she sat with her face buried in her hands. Jack had a shirtbox balanced on his knees, and he leaned over it, like Eileen, with his face buried in his hands. No one said anything. If they were crying, Miles could not hear them. He placed the heavy basket of fruit outside their door and went down the path to his car.

He drove past Margaret's house where the lights were on, and past Diane's where there were lights on too, but he did not stop. He went home and got into bed and thought of his insane pursuit of Diane, and his rejection by Margaret, and his guilt over Billy Mack, and he found himself praying, "Let this be the end of it. Let this be the end."

Part IV

33

THE END, when it finally came, caught everyone by surprise.

It was the last day of January—a long, slow, cold month with too many snow holidays—and Endicott was absorbed in the problem of what to do if there was another blizzard. They could extend the school year by a day or they could petition the state to let them end the school year with 179 school days instead of the required 180. Technically, this was the superintendent's problem, but he left these little details to Endicott. And Endicott was happy to deal with them, because they kept him from thinking of the really unpleasant things, like Jeff Douglas' tenure or that Deirdre girl who was persecuting Kevin Foley. He knew Deirdre better than he wanted to, and he knew her famous tongue, and he had to laugh because often she was right. She was certainly right about Foley being an asshole. Still, Deirdre and the tenure problem and even the snow problem were minor skirmishes. He could handle them easily. No battle plans necessary. No heavy artillery. Which was all to the good, since problems on the home front had begun to heat up. Missy was restless again; she'd be leaving him soon, he could tell. He sat back in his big chair and looked out his office window. Missy was the one war he'd never been able to win.

At the end of January, Miles was teaching *The Scarlet Letter* with great success. For some reason, the kids liked the little love child, Pearl, whereas most years they hated her because she was dorky or just a symbol. This year they thought she was cool, they liked her wildness and her refusal to fit in. And most of all they liked that she was a child of sin—which, in itself, Miles found remarkable. This was the end of the millennium, the 1990s, when the idea of sin had long since been argued and bargained and psychoanalyzed out of existence, and so nobody believed in sin, let alone redemption. Nonetheless the discussions were lively, and Miles was able to push them far into that forbidden territory of private fears and beliefs. He made them raise and consider the difficult questions: who they were, what they wanted, what were their deepest values. "What is human compassion?" he asked them, "what is human cruelty?" Miles was lonely, with all the women in his life long gone, but still he was having a wonderful time. This is what teaching was all about.

At the end of January, Diane had just followed up on her revelation of Christmas Day by applying to Harvard Law, Boston College Law, and Suffolk Law. She had spent much of Christmas Eve and all of Christmas Day pondering the bizarre Meditation Hymn at midnight mass: "Sit at my right hand, till I make your enemies your footstool"—and that night as she lay in bed, it was as if she heard a voice crying in the wilderness, saying, "Be a lawyer, be a lawyer." It was a pretty funny revelation for Christmas, but it put her mind at ease, and she acted upon it at once. She began studying for the LSATs, which turned out to be a very interesting and demanding exam. She was up for it, and when she took them in January, she did very well. To celebrate, she went to a man's barber and had all her hair cut off. She sat in the chair and watched the chunks of auburn and gold and amber fall about her, and as they fell, she felt lighter, more free, set loose in the world of action and event. She would be a lawyer, and use her gifts in logic and in law to set the world straight. Miles had been right all along; she did have an essentially legal mind. By the end of January, Diane had written off Jeff Douglas as a bad memory. She wouldn't have him, even as an enemy, even as a footstool.

At the end of January, Coach was sober again and attending AA meetings almost daily. Kathy was happy. Dietz was happy. Richy Polcari, flirtatious one day and petulant the next, had taken to popping up everywhere in Miles' life and was making himself a major asshole. And Paul Ciampa, to nobody's surprise, accepted Harvard's offer of early admissions. In the teachers' room, Miles said, "If I'd had shoulders like that as a kid, I'd be Governor of Massachusetts today." Dietz laughed, and Coogan, and Diane smiled and shook her head, but Jeff Douglas raised his eyebrows and kept silent. Nobody mentioned that Cosmo Damiani had been hospitalized again, this time for nervous exhaustion.

At the end of January, Jack Mack had had enough. He was drinking before duty and even on duty, he was fighting constantly with Eileen, and he was haunted by the conviction that somehow, some way, this was all Miles Bannon's fault. And then one Sunday night, while Eileen was asleep and he was not on duty, Jack went down to the cellar and took Billy's running clothes from their hiding place behind the paint cans. He held them to his face, but they smelled only of dust and kerosene. He could feel the crusted spots, though, and they were semen. He was sure of that. He put the clothes in a little box and left it in the cellar—evidence. He went upstairs to Billy's room, unlocked the door, and for the first time since he'd found the body, he went inside. On the night it happened, he had scrubbed the blood from the linoleum floor, but in this half-light he could see streaks, smears of blood, the last living traces of his son. He sat at the desk where Billy had written his suicide note to Bannon. On Eileen's blue paper. He glanced at the wastebasket and saw the little mound of crumpled blue sheets. He fished one out and read it. He read the others. "Dear Miles," "Dear Miles, I'm sorry," "Dear Miles, You are the only one" . . . his heart began to beat faster and he could feel the alcohol rush to his brain. "You are the only one," it said. He smoothed the paper flat, and studied it. More evidence. He tipped the wastebasket upside down and went through the other stuff that fell out. No evidence. He opened the closet door and ran his hands over the top shelf. He pushed the shoes aside to see if there was anything on the floor. He went to the chest of drawers. Almost at once, in the back of the junk drawer at the bottom, he found a little tin box. Hedges, it said. English cigarettes. He opened it and inside found what he was looking for and half-hoping he would not find: four notes from Miles Bannon to his son. They were indiscreet, damning, incriminatory notes that sketched out the progress of his seduction of Billy. Billy had actually numbered them. 1. "Billy—Why don't you join me for a jog today? We can meet outside school or, if you prefer, at the entrance to Mitchell Park. I'll look for you.—Milo." 2. "Jog?" And at the bottom of the note, Billy had written, "He said he missed me." 3. "Jog? What the hell, let's do it!" 4. "Jog with me? Just so I won't be alone if I should drop dead again?" The four notes were folded into tiny squares, as if Billy hoped to make them too small for anybody to notice. He had saved them, numbered them, written on them. He had put them in this little tin cigarette box. He must have loved Miles Bannon and Miles Bannon must have known it and led him on. "What the hell, let's do it!" And look where it had got them.

Jack Mack sat for a long time looking at the sheets of blue note paper—"Dear Miles, You are the only one"—and at the four notes from Miles. This should convince Eileen. This should convince anyone. He decided to act.

On Monday, without an appointment, he arrived at the principal's office and demanded to speak with him. Endicott, sensing trouble, came out and shook his hand and escorted him into his office. Way back in December, at his son's funeral, Officer Mack had threatened to become a problem, but when he'd come in that Monday to pick up his son's books, he was just a broken man, no fight in him, no trouble brewing. But this was a different Officer

Mack, more like the tough redneck he had been in September, at the time of Billy's incident, when Endicott had persuaded him into silence. This Officer Mack was an explosion in the making.

"Please, please," Endicott said, gesturing toward a chair.

"I'm Jack Mack. Billy Mack was my son. And I want you to know I'm looking into this." He tossed a manila envelope onto the desk and stood there while Endicott took out eight duplicated sheets—Miles' notes to Billy and Billy's suicide notes to Miles—and read them, and read them again. "I've kept the originals," he said. "They're evidence."

Endicott, confused and alarmed, spread out the eight sheets of paper and continued to study them. Finally, he cleared his throat and said, "Well, it seems to me . . ." and he looked up to discover that Officer Mack had left and he was alone in the office and didn't have to pretend any longer. He had nothing to say after "It seems to me." It seemed to him that this was it; this was the explosion he'd been fearing since September.

For the rest of the week, Jack Mack was everywhere. At school, in the student parking lot, in the corridors, he was always hanging around, listening, collaring the odd kid. He showed up at McDonald's, at Burger King, at Domino's Pizza. He was at the Wednesday basketball game loitering around the edges of the court, and he was at Ciampa's house one night at dinner time, and at Hacker's, at Tuna's, and at Cosmo Damiani's. He was standing in the snow at Diane's door when she got home from school, and he showed up later at Dietz's apartment, and later still at Jeff Douglas'. He quizzed the secretaries. He reduced Coach to a sobbing wreck.

Sometimes he wore his uniform and sometimes he didn't. But always he asked questions about Miles and his relationship with students. How did they feel about him? Had they had him in class? For homeroom? Had they been in plays he directed? Did they talk to him after school? Late? Did he have close friends among the other students? Did they go jogging with him? No? Why not? Was it odd that all his student friends were boys? Good-looking boys? You hadn't noticed that? Wasn't there, in fact, a long history of Miles having favorites? Miles' boys? Name one girl he hangs around with, jogs with, drives home after play practice. Think about it.

By Monday the whole student body was talking about Miles. Billy Mack's father, who was a cop, was investigating Miles' connection with the suicide. It wasn't clear what the connection was, but it had something to do with their friendship. *That* came as a surprise to everybody, because nobody knew that Miles and Billy had been friends. Billy Mack's father actually thought they used to jog together, but that was silly because Miles always jogged alone, and on the back roads, so that nobody would whistle at him or say how skinny he was. Everybody knew that. Then Coach said he had seen Miles jogging with Billy Mack, but that didn't count, because these days Coach wasn't too clear on what he saw or what he imagined. But then Paul Ciampa said he had seen them jogging, so it must be true. And they must have been friends. It was too weird to think of Miles and Billy Mack being friends. Why were they jogging in secret? In Mitchell Park?

Well, of course, Miles had never married, and that was pretty strange. He was thirty-five or six, and good-looking, and very, very popular. Why wasn't he married? He had had a girlfriend for years, but they didn't look as if they did it together, and the rumor was that they had broken up right after his mother's death, which was probably about the same time he began jogging with Billy Mack. Was Billy Mack his girlfriend?

And it was true, of course, that Miles had always hung out with the boys. And he said really weird things to them, too. He told the Mouse, for instance, the first time he ever met him, that he was a many-splendored thing. "You're marvelous, Muldoon," he said. "You're a many-splendored thing." And in class once he said to Lombardi, "What kind of shit are you, Mr. Lombardi?" and Lombardi was too surprised to answer, so Miles had said, "You're basic bullshit, Mr. Lombardi," which was funny and typical of Miles, but not right for the classroom. But it was always the boys he said these things to, and it was sort of flirting, and he never said them to the girls. In homeroom, just this year, he said, "Life is a banquet, and half the suckers out there are starving to death." Which must mean *some*thing.

All the same, it was hard to think of Miles as gay. They couldn't imagine him doing it. And especially not to Billy Mack, who was gloomy all the time, and angry, and weird. Besides, everybody knew that Miles never put a hand on anybody, not even after the play opened when everybody was hugging and kissing. The most he ever did was a friendly punch on the arm. It was almost like he was afraid to touch you. He just never did it. You couldn't really imagine Miles having sex at all, because you'd imagine he'd be too embarrassed to take his pants off. For instance, he never used the shower room in the boys' locker room the way Coach did and Mr. Douglas and Mr. Foley and even the vice-principal. Everybody had seen them in the shower and knew how big their dicks were, and how small Mr. Foley's was—and none of them was as big as Hacker's or Cosmo's—but nobody had ever seen Miles in the shower, so that was in his favor, but maybe it wasn't.

Billy Mack's father was a cop, after all, and he was investigating Miles, and he said that he had notes from Miles to Billy, so it must be true, even though it sounded crazy. Then Michelle Stein said she had seen Miles drop a note on Billy's desk during study hall, so it was true. Everybody wondered what was in the notes. *They* had never received notes from teachers—just try to imagine it— except sometimes when a teacher said to see them after school, or tell your parents I gladly accept their invitation to dinner, or will you please give me a ride home, my car is shot. And a couple times Mr. Douglas had invited kids for a beer, but nobody was gonna tell about *that*, and Ms. Dillard was always giving kids a ride home whenever she got a new car, and Coach did too, and they all sent notes. But their notes were just harmless. Who knows what Miles had said in his notes?

There was a suicide note, too, that Billy left for Miles, and that was supposed to be the real proof.

Actually, when they thought about it, Miles *could* be gay. Not gay like Polecat—even Michael Jackson wasn't gay like Polecat—but just halfway out of the closet, or all the way out and keeping it quiet. Certainly he dressed better than the other teachers, and gays always liked clothes. And he pronounced every word when he talked. And somebody said that a teacher had said that Miles had said that if he had shoulders like Paul Ciampa, he'd be Governor of Massachusetts today. And it was true. He had definitely said it. Miles was a shoulder freak. And somebody else said that at the Back to School Night in October Miles had admitted he lacked self-discipline. And after that some man from the School Board had asked Miles, right in public, about homosexuality. So the School Board must know, too. The man had said he knew more than Miles thought he knew. And that *had* to mean something.

Besides, when you thought of some of the poems he taught, it all began to make sense. "What lips my lips have kissed, and where, and why, I have forgotten." And "Two roads diverged in a yellow wood." Sure. In Mitchell Park, with Billy Mack. Miles liked to read them the romantic stuff, with lots of kissing and bodies and that guy in *Of Mice and Men* who always wore a glove with Vaseline in it. Kink-eee. Aw-right!

Nobody believed that Miles had AIDS.

It was thrilling and it was shocking and it was certainly going to make the month of February go by a lot quicker. Even with winter break coming up on the 22nd, February was the worst month of all, with this goddamn snow and slush and freezing cold and no more snow holidays that anybody could see in the future.

A lot of kids felt bad that Miles was in trouble, but it served him right if he was guilty, and he probably was, so it served him right. Besides, everybody now began to remember that one time when Miles had been mean to them or sent them to the office or gave them a lousy grade. Miles wasn't all he was cracked up to be. He was probably just getting what he deserved.

Deep down, though, everybody knew it wasn't Miles that made Billy Mack commit suicide. It was Violation, that game, when the Roid Boys fucked him up the ass with a broomstick. That's when Billy dropped off the team and stopped talking to anybody and got really weird. But, officially, nobody was supposed to know about that, and nobody wanted to be the one to say it, so nobody did. It wasn't their business, and all your friends turned against you if you were a snitch, and the entire team was involved so it wasn't just the Roid Boys who would really get in trouble, and nobody knew *for sure* if it ever really happened. They knew it did. But they didn't have any proof. Besides.

In the teachers' room, people knew a lot less and talked about it not at all. Jeff Douglas stirred his coffee and said, "Interesting about Miles, isn't it? Billy Mack's father seems to be leaving no stone unturned." Dietz and Kathy and Coogan and Diane all turned to face him and the hostility in their looks shut him up at once. "Sorry," he said.

"No stone unturned is a cliché," Coogan said, and he was so pleased with himself that he reared back in his chair and overturned three coffee cups.

"Coogan!" they said. And, "For Christ's sake, Coogan," and "Grow up, you idiot."

Just then Miles opened the door and looked around experimentally.

"Miles!" they all said, with too much enthusiasm. Except for Jeff Douglas, who left the room, pausing at the door long enough to finger Miles' tie, and say, "*Love* your tie."

In the principal's office, Endicott was pacing up and down, repeating to himself, "What did Miles Bannon know and when did he know it?" He didn't for a second believe that Miles had anything to do with Billy Mack's suicide. That was just a crazy figment of Officer Mack's addled brain. Too much booze. Too much grief. Too much guilt? Had he abused the boy himself? You never knew about these things, especially with cops.

It was funny, it was ironic, that way back in September at the time of the incident, he himself had tried to blackmail Miles into silence by threatening to raise the question of sex: what was he doing down there in the locker room at the end of a long day? And Miles had practically leaped on him, taking the threat to its logical conclusion: "They'd think I was hanging around locker rooms to watch teenage boys undressing? Is that what you're saying?" At the time it seemed preposterous to both of them: peeking at teenage peckers.

But this was exactly the charge Office Mack was making. Molestation. Miles Bannon was fingering Billy Mack's little pecker, there was semen on his jock and shorts, and Billy killed himself because of it . . . according to Officer Mack. It was preposterous. There was semen on every teenager's jock and shorts. They had quarts of it. It spilled out of them night and day. So, they'd been jogging, Miles and Billy. So, Billy spilled a little come. So, Billy killed himself. That didn't say anything about Miles. Except the damned fool had written those notes. Had set himself up for this. Had always resisted good advice.

Miles would have to go. To be fair—and he always tried to be fair—it would be a blow to the school to lose both Jeff Douglas and Miles Bannon in the same year, but better to suffer this loss than to have the incident come out. Think of what a blow to the school *that* would be. He couldn't allow it. If Douglas hadn't been so high and mighty, he'd have gotten some information on Miles, saved his own ass, and—Endicott smiled at the thought—they could have gotten rid of Miles before there was all this fuss. And now look.

Endicott sighed, facing the inevitable. He'd kept the incident quiet for five full months, and before he'd let it blow now, he'd promise

Officer Mack to fire Miles. Admit to nothing, but fire him anyway. And meanwhile pressure Miles to quit. That's all Mack wanted, really. To crush Miles. Which wasn't altogether a bad idea.

He had to laugh. He was being blackmailed into doing it. He had no choice. He would bide his time, though. Officer Mack had as yet filed no official complaint. He might decide not to. He might drink himself crazy and get put away. Or have a car crash and die; cops were always having car crashes. Or he might realize what a damned fool he was and just stop.

So he could continue to hope while he waited to see what would happen. The big thing was to keep the incident quiet.

The end was in sight.

34

JEFF DOUGLAS WAS TIRED of being the best teacher in the school and not being appreciated for it. He was tired of taking shit from all those losers in the teachers' room. And he was tired of thinking about tenure. If he didn't get tenure at Malburn High, he would just quit and go back to IBM and make a fortune. IBM needed people like him, and they paid for them, and they'd take him back in a minute.

He'd left IBM and come to Malburn High—at half the salary—for one reason only. To teach. Teaching was his life, his vocation, his reason for getting up every morning. He loved it. He'd fought in Vietnam, and he had killed a man, and he'd had all the sex anybody could want, but there was no thrill like teaching. When it all clicked, and you asked the right questions, and you had them hooked and leaning forward, and you led them carefully, slowly, patiently up to that moment where they discovered something new and disturbing about themselves, or other people, or the world they were gonna inhabit for sixty or seventy years . . . God, there was nothing like it. It was selfless. It was pure giving.

It was even better than writing novels, because you were alone when the exciting things happened in novels, and then afterwards you lost all the joy in what you'd written by having to wait five years to get published. Or fifty years. Teaching was what he loved and what fulfilled him. And, by God, they were not going to take it away from him without a fight.

It was so unfair. It was Diane alone who stood between him and his job. Diane and that faggot Miles. Which was ironic, since Miles was just as imprudent in speech as he was, and just as reckless in his professional judgment, and still they all thought he was terrific. Even Diane, who ought to know better.

Miles was a pain in the ass. Even now, with the whole school talking about him, speculating openly on whether or not he was a fag, Miles showed up every morning in the teachers' room and drank his coffee and drooled all over Diane.

Was he slavering over her to prove he wasn't gay? Was he really in love with her? You couldn't tell with Miles. He wasn't much of an actor, but this was one hell of a performance, if it was a performance. The fling with Diane was over, kaput. Everybody knew that. And yet every morning, there was Milo, turning himself inside out in the hope that Diane would look up and notice him.

What bothered Jeff most was that Miles seemed unaware of what was going on around him in the teachers' room—the silence and then the forced conversation—and he didn't seem to know or care what was happening in the corridors . . . and, in the past couple weeks, things had gotten very rough indeed. Kids whistled at him. They giggled when he went by. They imitated his walk and added a little swish. Just yesterday Jeff had heard Lombardi say, "Cover your crotch, here comes Milo," and Miles must have heard it too, but he never let on. What was he made of? Why didn't he lash out and defend his manhood, feeble though it was?

Jeff's own theory was that Miles wasn't anything—straight or gay, bi or tri—he was just asexual. He had no sex at all. Miles was like a priest back in the days when priests wore black gowns and practiced celibacy. He was an absurdity.

Jeff thought about Miles all the time these days, and about Endicott. Why not dig up a little dirt on Miles and give Endicott what he wanted? One of those drama club kids would know things. Or Paul Ciampa, probably, since it seemed Miles went for the sports set, with shoulders. All the same, it was crazy to think that Miles had buggered little Billy Mack and that Billy had killed himself because of it. Endicott didn't believe it, Jeff felt certain. Endicott just wanted to use the accusation to get rid of Miles and get that insane cop off his back. Because Mack's father *was* insane, there was no doubt about that. Insane or a child molester himself. Endicott must be pretty desperate. On the other hand, if Miles had been stupid enough to screw some kid, or squeeze his schlong, or even pat a fanny once or twice, then he shouldn't be teaching . . . not at Malburn and not anywhere. Endicott was right about that. And what harm just to look into it, just ask a question here and there? After all, if Miles was clean, Jeff could say so, and Endicott would at least see that he was playing on the right team. And this was the moment to act, while Endicott still needed him and while there was still some chance of getting tenure.

But it was shitty to act as an informant.

Jeff decided to leave it to fate. If the opportunity to get some information offered itself, he'd accept. If not . . . well . . . if not, he'd have to see if he could nudge fate in the right direction.

Fate went into action in less than an hour. Jeff was prefecting the corridor during second lunch period when the football crowd started giving Polecat a hard time. It was nothing much at first, just the usual teasing and feeling his biceps and having fun. Hacker and Tuna and their crowd. It would be a while before they got around to slapping his books to the floor and goosing him when he tried to pick them up and God knows what they'd think of after that.

Jeff didn't feel like bothering with it, so he went into the men's room to make sure they weren't smoking grass or sniffing coke. The place was empty. He combed his hair and checked his teeth and wasted some time at the urinals, reading the graffiti. There was the old stuff—"Franco fucks dead niggers" and "Jennifer does it standing up"—but they'd already started in on Miles, which didn't surprise him. "Miles sucks" was there. Beneath that, somebody had written, "Miles sucks and swallows." And beneath that, "Miles sucks and swallows and comes back for more." Beneath that, somebody had written something that had been scribbled over and then crosshatched, and Jeff had to study it for a long time before he could figure it out. It said, "Miles sucks the life out of you," and for a second Jeff's breath caught in his throat. It was incredible. They'd kill you without a moment's thought if it was good for a laugh.

Meanwhile the noise level had increased in the corridor. There was loud laughter now, and shouts, and that high-pitched shriek that meant Polecat was in trouble, so Jeff got ready to charge out of the men's room and do battle.

Almost immediately, though, there was a silence. Jeff pushed the door open slowly so that it wouldn't squeak and he surveyed the scene. The corridor was full of kids, girls sitting on the floor whispering, boys standing around looking guilty or merely curious. Miles stood at parade rest in the middle of the whole crowd. Nobody made a sound. Miles had a fierce look trained on Hacker, and after a while he shifted that look from one to the other of the four guys—the Roids—who always traveled with Hacker, and he never blinked an eye or lost his control.

"What in hell do you think you're doing?" he said to Hacker, and it was clearly a rhetorical question. "Don't you think you've caused enough trouble in your career here? How *sick* are you?" He waited until that sunk in. One smart crack, one whistle, would have destroyed the performance, but nobody made a peep. Miles was in complete control. "Go to the office, Hacker, and wait for me there. And you, and you, and you. Now."

They paused for just a second, to show they didn't have to go if they didn't want to, and then they went, slouching along in silence at first, and then picking up bravado and mouthing off about Miles as they got out of sight. Miles turned and walked into study hall and Jeff heard him ask, "Who's supposed to be prefecting here?" and he heard somebody answer him, "Dietz. He's having a smoke."

Jeff stepped back into the men's room. Miles had done very well. He was a better actor than Jeff had thought, and braver too, but that wasn't going to help him now. Because, as Miles stood in the corridor, taking them all on, Jeff had found himself hoping someone would whistle and destroy Miles once and for all, and when they didn't, he realized in a flash that he would do it himself. Fate or no fate, he'd do it. He had made up his mind. He walked to the urinal and unzipped his pants and said, "Try this one, Miles," and he pissed against the porcelain with a vengeance.

He was washing his hands when Lombardi and a bunch of Basics came in, shouting and pushing. They fell silent as soon as they saw Jeff, and then Lombardi whispered something, and they all started laughing. Basics were always trouble.

"Mr. D, my main man," Lombardi said, and that just about killed them. They pounded one another and laughed like crazy.

"Don't give me that shit, Lombardi," Jeff said. "Save it for Milo." He pointed to the urinals. "And erase that graffiti, if you know what's good for you." He dried his hands, staring at the crowd of them while they stared back. How had Miles pulled it off? *"Capisce, paisan?"*

"Geez, why blame me?" Lombardi said. "I didn't do nothing."

"I didn't do *anything*," Jeff said.

"I didn't do anything either." Lombardi laughed like a lunatic. "Get it?"

Jeff shook his head and walked out just as the bell rang for next period. There were shouts behind him, and laughter, and he realized that if they ever made him teach Basics, he'd quit. Basics were hopeless. There should be internment camps for people like that. Huxley had the right idea.

The bell rang a second time.

Jeff yanked the men's-room door open, and shouted in, "Move

it, you dorks; the bell has rung," and he stood holding the door wide open as they straggled past him and drifted off to class. Naturally he had to wait for Lombardi—"I'm pissing, Mr. Douglas, gimme a break"—so he stepped into the corridor and took a drink from the fountain. He stood there, letting the water run, while he watched an interesting little scene between Miles and Polecat.

Miles was still red from his encounter with Hacker and his crowd, and Polecat was white, in shock from whatever they'd been doing to him, but he was fluttering around, trying to thank Miles for saving his skin, and it was clear that Miles wanted nothing to do with him. Polecat was determined, though, and he kept following Miles, saying something in that whiney, pesty voice of his. Miles turned his back on him, and Polecat said, "Miles," in a hurt voice that made Miles spin around and look at him, and then Polecat put his hand on Miles' arm, and Miles threw it off angrily. "Grow up, for Christ's sake," he said, "and these things won't happen to you." Polecat stopped and just stood there and Miles turned away. But he turned back and in a voice that was intimate, and gave it all away, he said, "Richy, you bring these things on yourself. Jesus!" He left to teach his next class.

Polecat stood where he was, holding back the tears, and then he crumpled and made straight for the men's room where Jeff Douglas was waiting for him, eager to be of help.

"Polcari," Jeff said. "You need a buddy."

Jeff put his arm around Polcari's shoulder, walked him down the stairs and out the front door of Malburn High, and drove him two blocks to Town Line Treats. Jeff had a free period and time to kill, and he'd decided to kill it with Polecat. They were getting comfy in a booth now, as they had their coffee and danish. Or rather, Jeff was having coffee and a danish. Polcari was having Darjeeling tea and a croissant. Which figured. But Jeff didn't mind. He was being very supportive.

"Enough about you," Jeff said. "Let me tell you about me," and he blushed as he said it because Polcari was so obviously thrilled. "I write novels, you know. I've written two of them, one was just an exercise to teach myself how to do it, but the other's going to be taken by a publisher very soon, I think. So I'm working on a new one that . . ."

"By who? Whom. Who's going to publish it?"

"Maybe Doubleday. Maybe Macmillan. They're not sure yet. Maybe one of the smaller presses, with class. North Point or Godine. Anyhow, I'm doing a new one now, set in a high school, like Malburn, and I'm trying to get a feel for some things I don't know a lot about. I think you could be a real help to me."

"Will I be in it?"

"Just listen to me first, all right? This book is about a high school where one of the teachers is gay"—he paused for a second to let that sink in—"and what I need is information, hard facts, names and places and streets, to give the book specific gravity. You know, to make it believable."

Polcari's enthusiasm faded a little.

"What do you think?" Jeff said.

"How come you're writing about gays?"

"It's a fact of life. With the percentages of gays to straights, there's bound to be a lot more gays in school than we think there are. And since you're gay, you know things that would be really useful for my book. You don't mind my saying you're gay, do you? I don't want to offend you."

"Are you? Gay?" Polcari asked.

"Good God, no!"

"Well, the book is about a gay teacher," Polcari said, "and I thought it might be about you."

"Oh, I see. No. No, it's not about me."

"I thought you might be gay." Polcari gave a little half smile, almost a smirk. "I thought you might be coming on to me."

Jeff stared into his coffee and said nothing. He could end this right now and tell Polcari to go fuck himself, but his professional judgment told him to hold on. How would it look if Polcari went to Endicott and said Mr. Douglas had taken him to Town Line during school hours and put the moves on him? This is probably how Miles got himself in deep shit. These kids were dangerous.

"Well?" Polcari said. He tipped his head, coyly.

"No, I'm not coming on to you. I thought you could help me."

"I was just kidding anyway," Polcari said.

"Have you ever made it with Miles Bannon?" He'd caught Polcari off guard and now he watched for the reaction.

Polcari blushed and pulled back and his expression closed in on itself, revealing nothing. But that in itself said plenty. Polcari knew something.

"Have you?"

"No."

"I saw you in the corridor with him, just before you came running to the men's room, and the two of you looked pretty . . . close."

"Maybe I have and maybe I haven't."

"You looked pretty intimate to me."

"Are you sure you're not gay?"

"I'm married. I've got two kids."

"How come you asked me out?"

"You were crying. You were upset. I thought the best thing was to get you out of that school for a little while. And I thought you were honest enough and mature enough to be willing to help me with my book. And not make this cup of coffee into more than it is."

"You're not my type anyway," Polcari said. "Just kidding."

"Let's get serious, Polcari. Okay? I want to know about your feelings. I want to know how you handle this stuff. Does that teasing get to you? From Hacker and that crowd?"

"I'm used to the teasing. It was Miles who hurt my feelings."

"Good old Miles."

"He wouldn't even let me thank him. He won't even be friends with me." Polcari thought for a minute. "And I know things, too. I could tell you things."

"I'm sure you could. Try me."

"Is your book about Miles?"

"I just need specifics."

"About what?"

"Well, about Miles, for instance, if you know any. About bars he might go to for pickups . . ."

"There are no gay bars in Malburn. You have to go downtown or out to Route One."

". . . or kids he's close to in school, or out of school, things like that."

"Like Billy Mack, you mean?" Polcari pulled a face.

"Well, yes, like Billy Mack."

"Miles wasn't close to Billy Mack. He never did anything with Billy Mack. He likes older men."

This was it. There was something to tell, and Polcari knew it, and Jeff knew that if he could come up with the right question, Polcari would spill it all.

As it happened, he didn't have to ask the question. Polcari told him everything he knew, with names and facts, with specific gravity.

"I know about Miles Bannon," he said. "I can tell you plenty about Miles Bannon." And he told Jeff how Robert, his lover, had picked Miles up at the Tom Cat Lounge and taken him home and slept with him. He told him about the parking ticket he found stuck in the pages of the yearbook, orange Pinto, 819EGZ, proof that he wasn't making this up. He told him—because he had begun to feel bad now—that Miles was a little drunk that night, and broken up too, because his mother had just died, and so he probably didn't really know what he was doing.

"On the day his mother died?"

"He was upset."

"I guess he was." Jeff was revolted. Miles was a pig, every gay he'd ever met was a pig, he wanted to get away from here.

"Miles is good. He's got good instincts."

Jeff had to laugh. Good instincts?

"He always tries to do the right thing."

"Sure, like porking your boyfriend on the night his mother dies?"

"I shouldn't have told you that. I thought you were interested in . . . I thought you cared about . . . I wish I hadn't told you that."

"Don't worry about it, Polcari. I just need facts for my book. Okay? So don't worry about it."

"I shouldn't have told you."

"What's the name of this bar again?" He took out a little notebook, and when Polcari told him, he wrote down Tom Cat Lounge. "And where exactly is it?" He wrote some more. "And what's the street like, I mean what stores are there, or businesses, and what are the people like?" He wrote and Polcari talked and in a while they both felt a lot better about what they were doing.

At the end of an hour Jeff had convinced himself he was taking notes for a novel and Polcari had convinced himself that he was helping out. Nonetheless, they drove back to school in silence and parted as quickly as they could.

Jeff went home that night uncertain what to do with the information he had. He could pass it on to Endicott as a trade for tenure. Or he could tell Diane what he knew and see if he could make a trade with her: if she'd withdraw her objections to his tenure, he'd promise not to reveal what he knew about her former boyfriend. Or he could shut up and lose tenure. He could say nothing, and simply leave Miles to the misery of living with himself.

God! In bed with Polcari's lover on the night his mother died! It was grotesque. Miles must be schizo, that was the only explanation. There was the good Miles, sauntering around the corridors, sending kids to the office, taking on the Roid Boys when they're having fun with Polcari: holier than God and righteous as hell. And there was the other Miles who sits by his mother's bedside for a month until she dies and then he takes off to a gay bar and goes to bed with Polcari's lover, of all people. Two separate Milos. And he could just imagine what the lover looked like. A geek. It was incomprehensible. He wasn't sure he believed any of it.

Really, when he thought about it, the only thing he had against

Miles was that he was smug and thought he was the best teacher in the school and that he was boinking Diane. And he was some kind of sexual maniac. And he had tenure, too, the shit.

He didn't care about Milo's private life. He didn't want to get involved in it in any way.

He decided to say nothing.

"Leave her to heaven," he said aloud as he got ready for bed, and his wife said, "Who?" and he said, "Miles." She thought how glad she'd be when he went back to IBM, and she rolled over and went to sleep.

The next morning he was later than usual, and when he got to the teachers' room, everybody was there, even the Mafia. They were all laughing at a joke that Dietz had just told. Jeff waited until the laughter subsided and then he said to Kathy, "What's this? What's the joke?" but she ignored him. "What's so funny?" he said to Coogan, and Coogan burst out laughing again, spraying coffee all over himself, so he said to Dietz, "Tell it again, Jim, I need a laugh." But Dietz turned ugly, the way he did sometimes, and said, "For Christ's sake, Jeff, give it a rest."

"Up thine," Jeff said. He turned to leave but he bumped into Miles, who stood there smiling like a goddamn Cheshire Cat.

"Here, have some coffee, Jeff," Miles said, reaching for a paper cup. "I'll pour you some."

"Get your fucking hands off me," Jeff said, and suddenly there was silence in the room. Everybody was looking at them—Jeff with his red face and Miles with one hand on the coffee machine and the other holding a paper cup.

Miles began to blush darkly.

"Christ," Jeff said. "This is *too* much."

He left the room and went down the corridor to the principal's office.

"I want to see Endicott," he said to the secretary. "I'm gonna get myself some tenure."

35

It was Valentine's Day and Miles was hanging on.

He went to mass in the morning, though he might as well not have bothered, since he faded out at the Introit and didn't come around again until after the Gospel, when he heard the priest asking everyone to pray for Fr. Ortega who had just left the priesthood to get married. It was the new fashion in the church not to cover up defections, and it certainly added drama to a morning's mass. Still, Miles wasn't surprised. Diane had said that the priest was a man in trouble and Miles' own encounter with him on the church steps made him seem like a man under torture. "I can't," Fr. Ortega had said, "I can't," and it was the cry of a man who couldn't go on.

Miles could go on, though. He knew that. Once, long ago, he'd thought the worst had happened. But he was discovering how much more could happen, and he was discovering that he could survive it all. They laughed at him. They made a fool of him. A kid had whistled at him in the corridor. Lombardi always made a show of covering his crotch whenever Miles went by. They wrote his name, and God knows what else, on the toilet walls. Worst of all, they whispered. It was the things he couldn't hear, the things he had to guess at, that bothered him most. He was friendless suddenly.

He was an object of ridicule and contempt, like Polcari, only worse, because Miles had once been the most popular teacher in school and now they thought he had molested one of his students, poor Billy Mack. He had always feared being laughed at, being exposed, and now it had happened. They knew his worst self. And it wasn't just the kids. The teachers' room was a trial all its own—whispers, then silence, then lively, forced conversation. And he could only guess what it was like around the dinner tables each night, for students and parents and School Board members. The speculation, the accusations.

They thought he was a child molester. They thought he had led Billy Mack up to that rock in the park to seduce him. How did they manage to make that fit with all the good things they knew about him? All those years of teaching? He would begin to feel indignant, outraged, and then he would remind himself that he was, in a way, guilty. Not of what they thought and said, but of other things, of everything. He survived the ridicule and the humiliation by an act of the will and by pretending he was not touched by it, he was above it.

Mass ended, and the last thing Miles remembered was the announcement about Fr. Ortega. He couldn't even remember going to communion, though he had. He had the taste of it in his mouth, bitter at first, then sweetish. He sat in the cold church, trying to think.

He couldn't think. One of the things he was most thankful for during these past weeks was his inability to think. Thought seemed reduced to simple apprehensions: morning, books, mass, school, homeroom. Until he got into class, of course, and then he was the old Miles, teaching *The Scarlet Letter*, urging them into discussions that brought Miles and Hester Prynne so close that even the students were embarrassed, but he never blushed or hesitated or held back. He had never taught better.

He was not trying to be brave or strong, like his mother when she was dying; he was trying to get through it, to hang on. It was a time for survival, not heroism. He thought sometimes of Diane's belief and wondered where she got it, where he could get it. He had given up thinking that any moment was ripe for revelation.

He left church and got into his car. It stalled. He let it rest, and then tried again, and again it stalled. He'd just paid nearly a thousand dollars for a valve and ring job, and a few incidental repairs, and the damned thing was still a mess. "God damn it," he said, and hammered the steering wheel with his fist. He tried again and the car started at once.

He drove to school, and skipped the teachers' room this morning, and went right to homeroom. Only a few kids were there, so he dropped his backpack on the desk and began chatting with them. "Valentine's Day," he said. "Did you send somebody a card, David? How about you, Heather?" Gradually, he coaxed them into conversation about boyfriends and girlfriends and the Valentine Day dance that was always such a drag and how corny valentines were, though it was clear that everybody had sent one, and how going steady wasn't what it used to be. By the time the bell rang for homeroom period, everybody was there and they were all chatting and having a good time and responding to Miles as if he were the old Miles, as if nothing had ever happened to Billy Mack.

"Time out," Miles said. "Let's settle down for the announcements."

He emptied his backpack on the desk, piling his books to the left and his papers to the right, and then he sat down and took his plan book out of the middle drawer. The plan book fell open to the right place, because somebody had stuck an envelope in it there, where he'd be sure to see it.

It was a square red envelope with his name typed across the center, a valentine probably. Without thinking, Miles picked it up and turned it over to see if there was a name or an address. The wall speaker crackled and Endicott's voice filled the room with the first of the announcements, but Miles could see they were all looking at him. He put the envelope down and began studying his plan book. "Open it," somebody said, and then somebody else said, "Milo's got a valentine," and a bunch of them said, "Open it, open it," and Miles had to quiet them down so they could hear the announcements. "Later," he said. But he was curious now, and he slid his finger under the sealed flap and slipped the valentine out. On the front was a picture of one of those little bears peeping out from behind a tree. He had a red heart thumping in the middle of his chest, and up at the top it said, "If you will be my valentine . . ." and, inside, it said, ". . . I'll let you suck my dick." The words were typed, of course, and a glossy color photo was pasted over the real card. The photo showed a huge erect penis and a mouth, wide-open, hovering over it.

Miles closed the card, and closed his eyes, and waited. He felt the blood rush to his head and a pounding start in his brain, and he thought, No, he must have imagined it. Nobody could do this. It was his own sick imagination. It was a fever. But then he opened his eyes, and he opened the card, and it was real. He slid the card back into the envelope, and then he tried to put the envelope into his inside jacket pocket, but the pocket wasn't big enough, and he forced the envelope, and it crumpled, but it wouldn't go in. He took it out again and slipped it into his top desk drawer, but he realized at once that he couldn't leave it there, and so he opened the drawer and put the envelope into his backpack, in the zipper slot inside. His hands were shaking and he couldn't pull the zipper closed.

Miles looked up then.

The notices had ended and the speaker had clicked off. They were waiting for the class bell. They were all looking at him.

He had got redder and redder as he tried to dispose of that card, and his head was pounding, and now as he looked at them, their faces a blur, he wanted to cry out, but no sound came. He felt scalded. He was just raw meat, exposed, and they knew—his whole world knew—that if you touched him, you would get blood on your hands.

He stood there, because he had no choice, and he let them look at him.

Miles was prefecting Detention and trying very hard to concentrate, but without much success. Tomorrow was his last class on *The Scarlet Letter* and he wanted to wind up in style, with a little lecture on the structure of the novel and a series of questions on justice and mercy that they should think about for the future and, more specifically, for the final exam.

Miles couldn't concentrate because of the deadly thoughts he was having about Polcari. He had been a pain in the ass for weeks now, popping up at the damnedest times with a big, knowing smile on his face, as if he and Miles were in league together, or as if they knew something that nobody else knew. It was an act of presumption and it annoyed the hell out of Miles. When Miles called him on it, and told him to smarten up, or just gave him a distant look that put him in his place, he'd sulk and pout and carry on as if he'd just been betrayed by his best friend. When Miles thought about it, he realized that this had been going on since the beginning of the year, but with a subtle difference now. At first Polcari had been trying to insinuate himself into Miles' life by flattery and by being a pitiful mess, but now he seemed to feel he'd been accepted, he belonged, he and Miles were buddies. It was incredible. It was very very annoying. And he had this way of looking—he was doing it now—as if he knew something that would surprise the pants off you if you ever found out. Miles knew at once what it was. Polcari was the one who put that card in his plan book. Polcari *knew*. But what?

Just thinking about it, Miles felt himself go red.

"What are you here for, Polcari?" Miles said.

"I cut gym. The usual." He gave Miles that smirky smile, but Miles refused to notice it.

"And you, Deirdre?"

"The usual."

326 \ John L'Heureux

"Which is?"

"I called the O an asshole." The O was Mr. O'Brien, who taught math and who claimed to have played minor league baseball, which is why he insisted students call him the O; it sounded to him like a baseball name.

"I see," Miles said.

"He can draw a perfect circle freehand, and I told him it's a good thing he can, because it's the only qualification he has for teaching algebra."

"And he didn't like that, I guess?"

"He sent me to the office."

"And you called him . . ."

"Asshole!" they all said together, Muldoon coming in a little late.

"And you, Muldoon? What're you here for?"

"I didn't do anything. I was just standing with Ginny, in the corridor, and Mr. Endicott came by and sent me to Detention."

"Standing? Not hugging?"

"We were hugging a little bit."

"This was during class, I presume?"

"Well, class had just begun. Maybe five minutes ago."

"Or ten?"

Muldoon grinned that wide mouse-grin.

"And why isn't Ginny in Detention?"

"She's got morning sickness. She has to go home right after school."

"I see. Well, Muldoon . . ."

"We're going to get married." Muldoon was beaming.

"Married?" Deirdre said. "You're only twelve years old."

"I'm sixteen," Muldoon said. "I'll be sixteen in May."

"The baby will be a retard," Deirdre said.

"No, it won't. We had ultrasound. It's a boy." He was very proud.

"And they think *I'm* screwed up," Deirdre said.

"You are," Polcari said. "You're both screwed up."

Deirdre looked at Polcari curiously. Miles, fearing what she might say, said, "Okay, everybody, let's just settle down and do some work. All right?"

At that moment Miles saw Diane at the door, waving him out to the corridor. As he got up and went to her, he heard Deirdre say, "Tell me something, Polecat. How did you get this way, anyhow?" Miles walked faster and pretended not to hear.

Diane was wearing red and, with her new short hair, she looked like a different person, younger and even more attractive.

"This will only take a minute," she said.

"I'll give you hours," Miles said. "I'll give you the rest of my life." He was trying very hard, but it fell flat, and he ended by shaking his head, no.

"Are you all right?" Diane said. "Are you okay?"

He thought for a second of telling her about the valentine, but he decided against it. "I'm hanging on," he said.

"This has got to stop," she said, "this business with Mack's father. I've called Tom McGrath and he'll see you tonight. He can't represent you in a trial because he's the school's lawyer, but he can give you advice and he can represent you—at least unofficially—to the police. He wants to talk with you first."

Miles began to panic. In court? In a trial? Did they all know something he didn't know?

"Represent me?"

"To the police," she said. "He'll make them call Mack off. This is harassment. It's persecution. He's lost his son, and everybody feels bad for him, but he can't be allowed to keep this up. He's destroying your reputation. He's destroying *you*."

"I got a card today," Miles said. "A valentine."

"I don't send valentines," she said. "Seven o'clock. At his house. I've got to go."

"You look beautiful," he said.

"It's the hair," she said. "Don't forget. At seven." And she was off down the corridor.

Miles watched her go, brisk, efficient, moving farther and farther out of his reach and out of his life. She was gone.

He realized it didn't matter. His love for her, if he had ever loved her, had disappeared some time ago. Even his lust for her had disappeared, that greed to possess her. She would go to law school, edit the *Law Review*, graduate at the top of her class, and clerk for a Supreme Court Judge. Or maybe she would pitch that kind of success to the winds and simply work in a storefront somewhere, in South Boston or South Philly, providing legal aid for people who couldn't afford to pay. Whatever she decided to do, she'd do it wholly and with style, taking on the Jeff Douglases and Endicotts and Miles Bannons and anybody else who wouldn't play by the rules, and of course she'd enjoy the odd fling in the meantime.

Was this just romance? A way of looking at his failure that made losing her seem glamorous? He had become such a liar. The truth was much more simple: he was relieved to see her go. She was too much for him. She was too rich in contradictions. She would be better as a memory.

He turned back to the classroom where Deirdre and Polcari and Muldoon were having a heated discussion about—he couldn't believe it—conformity.

"Go home, you guys," he said. "It's all over."

Instantly they stopped talking and packed up their books to leave. Deirdre was the first one out, and she said to Miles, "What assholes!" and was gone without even stopping to bang her locker. The other two followed, Muldoon looking crushed, Polcari looking triumphant.

"Happy Valentine's Day," Miles said, and he thought—but he was not certain—that Polcari blushed.

Greg McGrath was in Miles' advanced placement class, but he opened the door to Miles and led him into his father's office as if they'd never met. He wasn't especially shy. He was just taciturn and brilliant. He made Miles very nervous.

"So how're you doing?" Miles said.

"My father will be right here," Greg said. "That's the most comfortable chair." Miles glanced at it and then sat down in a straight-back chair near the desk. "Or that one," Greg said.

He stood there.

"What do you think?" Miles said.

"Of what?"

"Of me," Miles said, astonished he had asked such a question, and at a time like this.

"Oh, I *like* you," Greg said. And, as if that might be misunderstood, he added, "You're a very good teacher." He waited a moment and then he said, "I'll get my father."

Miles covered his face with his hands, and then he rubbed his eyes, and then he took his hands away and looked around the room. The walls were full of books and the huge desk took up one whole end of the room. The furniture was that reddish leather you saw in magazines.

"Good to see you again," Tom McGrath said, as he entered the room. He shook hands quickly, firmly, and then went around behind the desk, talking as he went. "I remember that class you taught on Back to School Night. Very impressive." He sat down and leaned across the desk, all business. "You understand, Mr. Bannon, that as attorney for Malburn High I cannot represent you in any trial, should this matter ever go to court." He went on for some time, covering himself legally. Then he sat back.

"Diane has told me everything, I presume, but I want to hear about it from you. I want to hear your side."

"It's good of you . . ."

"Yes," McGrath said. "Talk."

Miles told him everything.

"And that's everything?"

"Except that something did happen that day."

McGrath raised his eyebrows, nothing more, and Miles told him what happened that afternoon in Mitchell Park.

"This *is* what happened? No self-protective lies? He hung onto you, you pushed him away, he ejaculated. Period."

"Yes."

"You didn't hold him until he ejaculated? You didn't help it along?"

"No. I swear it."

"Just asking, Miles. I've got to know. So it was a crush, it got out of hand, you were—so to speak—an innocent bystander."

"Yes. So to speak."

"It never happened, then. You jogged, you parted, Billy went home. Period."

"But it *did* happen."

"It did happen if you're under oath. In the ordinary meaning of the words, it *never* happened."

"I see." But what he saw was more lies, years of lies.

"Now. You wrote him notes; explain that, please."

"I know, I know. It looks so incriminating, but it wasn't like that." Miles explained what it was like, why he wrote the notes, how he got himself into this situation.

"Dumb. Really dumb." McGrath thought for a while, made some notes, and then looked up. "So that's everything?"

"Everything."

"*Are* you homosexual?"

Miles hesitated for just a second. "No."

"Let me phrase it differently. Have you had homosexual relations? Even once?"

"Once."

"Tell me about it."

"This is worse than confession," Miles said.

"Yes, it is worse. I don't give absolution."

Miles told him about Robert.

"This is everything?"

"Everything."

"Anybody know this?"

"Nobody."

"And just this once?"

"Yes."

"These things tend to surface. In fact, you should count on it. And when they surface, they can be very damning."

"Yes."

McGrath thought a moment and then he looked up and said, "It was a fling."

Miles laughed, surprised.

"Lots of men have flings. Sometimes even with other men."

There was a moment of silence and Miles thought about asking him, and before he could make up his mind, he heard himself saying, "Have you? With a man?"

"Not with a man. Men don't interest me." He wrote something.

"With Diane?"

McGrath gave him a sharp look and then went back to his notes. After a moment he said, "I'm doing this for her, not for you."

Miles thought of saying thank you, but it didn't seem right somehow.

"She's very fond of you," McGrath said.

"We had a . . . for the lack of a better word, a fling."

"Of course." McGrath put his pen down and leaned back in his chair. "You're a Catholic. What do you make of her? All these flings she has, and yet she's very devout. She thinks she's a good Catholic. What do you make of that?"

"She's a believer," Miles said. He thought of the last long conversation they had had; any moment is ripe for revelation. "She just doesn't see any contradiction between loving God and making love to men."

McGrath laughed. "Like Mary Magdalen," he said.

"Like Mary Magdalen. That's good."

"But we presume Mary Magdalen gave up her profession after she met Jesus."

"Did she? Do we know that?" Miles had never thought of this, but as he said it, it sounded pretty good. Or daring, at least. "That's dumb too," he said. "And cheap."

McGrath was silent for a full minute. "She just about wrecked my life," he said. "I've never gotten over it." He was silent again. Finally he said, "You?"

"I got over it," Miles said.

"You're lucky."

"She sets things in motion and then they don't stop."

But McGrath didn't seem to hear him. He sat forward in his chair again, back to business. "So that's it? Nothing else? That's everything?"

"Everything."

"You can call me if you think of something else, anything, *anything* I should know. Meanwhile, I'll take care of it. I'll call the Chief, and have a little talk, and make sure that Officer Mack stops harassing you. This may go away if it's left alone. The less said the better."

"Yes."

He came from behind the desk and shook Miles' hand. "Don't let this get you down," he said, and putting his arm around Miles' shoulder, he walked him to the door.

Miles thanked him. "I'll give your best to Diane," he said.

"Oh, she's got my best," McGrath said, and he gave Miles a little smile. "She knows that."

Miles was home, drinking his second scotch, before he remembered the valentine. Which wasn't quite true. He had flashed on it while McGrath was talking about Diane, but he had pushed the thought aside, and afterwards, when McGrath asked if that was everything, he'd said yes, and meant it.

He should call now and tell him. But he'd want to see it, he'd want to keep it as evidence. McGrath was only a little older than Miles, but Miles knew that in most ways McGrath was old enough to be his father. He could see McGrath opening the valentine, reading it, looking at the picture without any expression, and then glancing up at Miles, and saying, "Anyone you know?"

Miles got his book bag and zipped open the inside pocket. He felt around but nothing was there. In a panic, he dumped out the books and papers. The bag was empty. The pocket was empty. He went through the papers. Perhaps he hadn't put it in the zipped pocket after all, perhaps he'd stuck it between some papers. It wasn't there. Nor between the pages of the books. He began to sweat. His mind raced ahead. Someone had taken it from his bag. Why not? They'd managed to get it into his desk in the first place. Or even worse, he'd lost it. And someone found it, a red square envelope, how could they miss it? With his name on the front of the envelope. And that photograph inside. He went through the papers again, then the books. He tried to go back to this morning in homeroom and that moment when he tried to put the envelope in his jacket pocket and it wouldn't fit. He'd reached for his book bag. He'd pulled it toward him and slipped it into . . . no, he'd unzipped the pocket, and then slipped it in.

Now, at his kitchen table, he reached for the book bag yet again, tipped it toward him, and saw there were two zippered pockets, one on each side. The red envelope was in the second one. He was trembling and sick from his stupidity. How could he have missed it? How could he have panicked so? He was out of control. The card had unhinged him. He slipped it out of the envelope now, and opened it. That huge erect penis. That open mouth. There was something almost clinical about it. It was not even sexy. It was just shocking. Just obscene.

He got a match and went to the sink and set the card on fire. He held it by one corner, pointing up, so that it burned right down to his fingertips before he let it go. The ashes fell into the sink and he washed them down the drain. Then he burned the envelope and washed those ashes down the drain as well.

He felt a sudden wave of relief come over him. He was free of this, at least. Nobody would ever know about the card.

But somebody had sent him the card. Somebody knew. Whoever it was could tell anyone, everyone. Perhaps they already had. Perhaps the truth was out.

He felt very much a child, at least in the business of truth.

36

BY THE END OF FEBRUARY the police department had agreed to investigate the allegations against Miles. No charge was brought and no arrest was made; it would be a simple investigation to get some hard facts and to put the boy's suicide to rest.

Officer Jack Mack alleged that Miles Bannon, a teacher for eleven years at Malburn High School, had seduced Billy Mack over a period of several months, culminating, on the day of Billy's suicide, in a sexual act which precipitated the boy's suicide. Officer Mack had collected all kinds of unofficial testimony that confirmed the possibility of a relationship of some kind—not necessarily sexual but certainly with sexual overtones—and, most important, he had notes from Bannon to the boy and a series of suicide notes from the boy to Bannon. Officer Mack had the jogging clothes the boy wore that day, with traces of semen on the jockstrap and the shorts, but of course that proved nothing. The piece of evidence that most excited Officer Mack was an unpaid parking ticket for Bannon's ancient Pinto, license number 819EGZ. The ticket was dated last September on the evening of Bannon's mother's death at New England Medical, according to Officer Mack, and it indicated that Bannon's car was parked at or near a hydrant, after midnight, in the Combat Zone. Parked very near, in fact, to the Tom Cat Lounge. On this same night he was alleged—no evidence provided—to have picked up and gone home with some man from the State House, thus confirming, for Officer Mack, the allegation that Miles Bannon was a practicing homosexual.

The evidence, if you could call it that, was patchy, speculative, and hopelessly circumstantial. All the information about Bannon's car and the ticket and the particular night was verifiably accurate, but it had purportedly been sent to Officer Mack in a badly typed, misspelled, anonymous letter, and there was some fear that Officer Mack may have composed the letter himself. Furthermore, homosexuality was not a crime in itself, and if Bannon had sex with somebody from the State House and they were two consenting adults, then that was their business. To prove Bannon had actually seduced the boy was going to require eyewitnesses or a confession by Bannon and, obviously, neither was likely to be forthcoming. The notes, once they were examined, proved almost nothing, except that (1) Bannon and the Mack kid had gone jogging together, and (2) Billy Mack's last thoughts were of Miles Bannon.

On the other hand, as Officer Mack rightly claimed, if this evidence had been brought to the Massachusetts Department of Social Services *before* the suicide, they would have been on Miles Bannon's neck so quick that he'd have had whiplash till the turn of the century. So there was sufficient reason to launch a simple investigation of the facts. An official notice to Bannon and to the principal. A few quiet interviews. A summary report. That's all it would take.

Besides, and off the record, they owed Jack Mack an investigation. He was a twenty-year veteran of the force, and his kid had just committed suicide, and he was in the process of drinking himself to death, or at least drinking himself into serious trouble while on duty. An official investigation would put a stop to Mack's private snooping that had brought McGrath down on their necks with his threat of a lawsuit for harassment. And maybe it would get Mack back into line before it was too late. Before he killed Miles Bannon. Or himself.

The investigation would be quick, efficient, satisfying. And when it was over, they could all forget about it and just get some sleep.

37

THE INVESTIGATION WAS LAUNCHED very quietly during the last week of February, when all the kids were out of school on midwinter break and when gossip could be kept to a minimum. Last September the chief of police had covered up some shit for Bill Endicott, an old Army buddy, and the last thing the chief wanted was for this Bannon investigation to hit the newspapers. He knew from experience that it was only one quick step for some smart-ass reporter to go from investigating Miles Bannon to investigating Billy Mack, and then the shit from last September would surface, and once it surfaced, it would sure as hell hit the fan.

The two policemen told Miles everything he needed to know about the investigation, and they did it nicely, with reassuring voices, with hands in their pockets, with an attitude that suggested they were really on his side. There were no charges, they said, just a routine investigation, and it would be over in no time. Was that all right? Miles nodded and listened and thought: here it is, the truth.

"Do you mind if we search the house?" the tall one said.

Miles laughed nervously; it was not a very funny joke.

"Do you? You don't have to agree to it without a search warrant, as you know, but we always ask first. For goodwill."

"You're serious? Of course. Of course. Do you want me to leave? What should I do?"

Miles went with them from room to room as they felt their way through closets and drawers, examining the contents, holding up his underwear and pajamas and his jogging clothes. They lifted the mattresses and examined his medicine chest and shuffled through his books and papers and paid and unpaid bills. They were emotionless, methodical. When they finished upstairs, they went down to his mother's bedroom and then to the bathroom she had used.

"What's this?" the short one said. It was a foot massager that had belonged to one of the Home Helps, but as the policeman held it up, Miles could see it looked like a penis, sort of, if you wanted to see it that way, and he could see they did. The policeman put it back under the sink where he had found it.

"Vaseline down here, too. A jar in the upstairs bathroom. Another in your bureau drawer. Three jars."

Miles said nothing. Who knows why there were three jars of Vaseline?

"These pills? And these? And these?"

Again Miles said nothing.

"Eleanor Bannon?" The policeman held the bottle to the light and read the label. "That's your mother?"

Miles nodded, angry, and said, "Take them, if you like, and test them. They're not amphetamines or uppers or downers or whatever kind of drug you think they are. They're pills she took while she could still swallow. For blood pressure. For pain. Who knows for what. She's dead, I'm relieved to say, and doesn't have to witness this."

"She died in September," the tall one said. "On a Wednesday. The twenty-ninth."

"Not the twenty-ninth," the short one said, and corrected him on the date.

"You're right," the other one said. "That's right."

Miles stood by, listening.

"Of Lou Gehrig's disease."

"New England Medical."

"On the fringes of the Combat Zone."

They looked at Miles.

"Right?" the tall one said.

"You haven't seen the attic," Miles said, and he felt very cold suddenly, and alone.

They followed him upstairs, and in the hallway outside the bathroom, he pulled down a hatchway with a rickety ladder attached. They gave him a look. While the tall one held the ladder, the short one climbed up and disappeared into the darkness above. They heard him coughing and they saw the beam from his flashlight searching out the corners. The tall one smiled. After a while his partner came down the ladder. His hands were filthy and his uniform was covered with dirt. A cobweb trailed from his shoulders. He began coughing again.

"There's asbestos up there," Miles said, "and fiberglass. We never use the attic."

"Shit," the policeman said, beating the dust from his clothes. The other one tried to hide his smile.

"You haven't seen the cellar," Miles said, and he led them downstairs and through the kitchen. He pointed to a door. "Down there," he said, and they both looked at him.

They opened the door and a blast of freezing air came into the room. "It's a tad chilly," Miles said. They went down a narrow flight of stairs to the cellar, with Miles following. His father's workbench was still there, with lots of rusting tools and odd bits of lumber and some old lawn chairs. When he first came home to stay, Miles had started to clean out the cellar, but almost at once his mother took a turn for the worse, and he'd just given up on it. There were stacks of magazines and boxes of old class notes and term papers just where he'd left them for the recycling people.

"Don't miss those," he said, pointing, and then he left the policemen to their work.

Miles went upstairs and put Streisand on the stereo, loud. After an hour or so, the two policemen reappeared, looking for him. He was in the living room, having a cup of tea and pretending to read a book of poems by Andrew Marvell.

"All done," they said. They looked frozen.

"What were you looking for?" Miles said. "What did you think you'd find?"

"We have to do this," the short one said. "It's nothing personal."

Miles laughed, a hard false laugh. "Nothing personal? Nothing *personal?* You go through my bureau drawers, you hold up my underwear to see if there are tell-tale stains, you ask about fucking Vaseline? And it's not personal?"

They stood there, polite.

"I'm sorry. I'm a little . . ." He knew they had the upper hand. "As a matter of fact, though, what could you expect to find that would make any difference one way or another?"

"Pornographic magazines," the short one said, "sexual toys, vibrators, dildoes, manacles, things that would indicate you might be into sexual practices that are unusual or suspect."

"Chains, clamps, poppers, all that equipment," the tall one said, "or nude photographs of boys, or videos of you doing it with a student, or two students, or three. Or with Billy Mack. Videos are very popular."

Miles was literally speechless. He could say nothing.

"Are you all right? Do you want some water?"

"He's got some tea. Drink some of that tea."

Miles sat down and took a sip of the tea. He was thinking of the valentine. If he had kept it to show McGrath, if he had kept it at all, it would prove to them he was guilty. He felt guilty. And dirty.

"I notice you don't have a VCR. That's very unusual."

"For sex offenders, you mean?" Miles said. "Or for just anybody?"

"It's an investigation, Mr. Bannon. We have to do this. But when we write our report, we'll attach a memo saying you let us do it without a search warrant. We'll be glad to do that for you."

"And we were very considerate," the other one said.

"Are you done now? Can you go?" Miles asked.

"We've only begun."

"We have to question you."

"We do it here, even though we could insist on questioning you down at the station."

"You're very lucky, Mr. Bannon."

"My God," Miles said.

The phone rang then, and it was Margaret, who had not called in months. He couldn't talk, but he would call her back, soon, all right? "You're the answer to my prayers," he said, and wished he hadn't. It sounded fruity.

"Are you ready, Mr. Bannon? Or would you like us to come back another time?"

Miles was ready. He would answer their questions, and he would give them the whole truth, up to a point.

Then he would call Margaret.

Margaret was feeling better than she had in years. In January, she'd had a relapse—two days on the bottle, but no pills this time—and after a week of depression, she had come back stronger than ever. She was attending AA meetings regularly, and she had asked Dietz to be her sponsor, and by now she was feeling so self-confident that she had decided to give Miles a call to ask how he was doing.

She knew from Dietz that Miles was under constant fire. Billy Mack's father was going around asking questions and creating gossip, and he had the whole school speculating on whether or not Miles was gay. Nobody had evidence but everybody had a theory. The crazier ones wondered aloud if maybe he really *did* have something to do with Billy's suicide. And the senior class had decided to dedicate the yearbook to Billy Mack instead of Miles. She could just imagine how Miles was taking all this.

She had thought for a long while before she telephoned him.

She was not going to risk her peace of mind, her new self, just to be kind to him. Or, worse, just to feel needed. Several days went by and she did not call.

Then one night, as she was leaving work, Mr. Collins asked her if she'd care for dinner. This was the third time he had asked. She wanted to go. She wanted him, in fact. She said yes. They lingered a long time over the meal, because they had everything in common, it seemed, including the fact that they were lonely and ready to fall in love. Afterwards, he drove her home and asked if he could come in. She said no. They sat in the car, talking, and then they sat there some more, not talking, and then she said yes. They went inside and made love, easily, naturally. Much later, after he left, Margaret went out to the kitchen and wrote her letter of resignation to Babcock & Collins.

The next day she called Miles.

It was safe to call Miles now that she was in love with Michael Collins. It was safe and it was easy. She could give, now, out of her abundance.

She would give Miles support, if he wanted it, and comfort. And acceptance, gay or straight, it didn't matter.

She would give him everything except her love.

"How long have you taught at Malburn High?" they began.

The two policemen had Officer Mack's notes to work from, and many years of experience in these matters, and their own healthy curiosity, of course.

After a long list of questions, they asked, "When did you first get to know Billy Mack?"

And, "When did you begin jogging with him? How often? Where?"

And, "Why did you invite him to accompany you when you jogged? Why him, rather than any others? Why alone? Why did you send him notes?"

And, "What did you mean by 'Let's do it!'?"

When Miles explained, they asked, "*Did* you do it? Have you ever had sex with a student? A girl? A boy? Did you ever just touch them, no harm intended? No?"

And, "If you were going to have sex with a student, which student would interest you particularly?"

When Miles was outraged by this question, the short one said, "Would it be someone like Paul Ciampa?" And the tall one said, "With those big shoulders?"

They watched as Miles shook his head and looked at them, silent, with hatred in his eyes.

"Do you have any coffee?" the short one asked. "I'd really like a cup of coffee. We can go on with the questions afterwards, if that's okay with you. Or we can stop now and come back later."

Miles made them coffee and they all went back into the living room.

"Tell us about the Tom Cat Lounge," the short one said.

"Or, if you prefer, we can question you," the tall one said. "Questioning takes longer, that's all."

"I've been to the Tom Cat Lounge once," Miles said. "I picked up a man—or, technically, I got picked up *by* a man—and I went home with him."

They were listening carefully.

"And we went to bed. We had sex."

"Would you care to say exactly what you did? You don't have to, but it could bear on the investigation."

"Mutual masturbation," Miles said. "And fellatio."

"Mutual also?"

"No. I was . . . the suck*ee*," Miles said.

They showed the trace of a smile.

"And that was all?"

"That was all." He was not blushing and he was not embarrassed and he did not know why.

"Have you been back to the Tom Cat Lounge?"

"Have you been back often?"

"How did you know about that, anyhow?" Miles said. "Do you have spies? Have you been following me for months?"

They ignored his questions.

"Have you continued your relations with this man?"

"Don't you know?" Miles said.

"No."

"But we can find out."

"Polcari?" Miles asked. "Is that where you get this stuff?"

"Pardon?" one of them said.

"He's on our list of students," the other said. "Richard Polcari—a.k.a. Polecat."

"Who made up the list?" Miles asked. "I'd be interested to know what names are on it. And where you got it."

"Can we return to this man at the Tom Cat Lounge? You say you went to bed with him once, you had sex of two different varieties, and you have not been back to see him. So how have you handled your sexual needs?"

"Handled?"

"No pun intended. Do you expect us to believe that you went to a notorious homosexual pickup bar, got laid—or at least had sex—and that was the end of it?"

"It was a fling," Miles said.

"A fling?"

"An experiment. I did it once. I didn't like it. Well, perhaps that's not true. I don't know if I liked it, but I do know that I decided that gay sex wasn't what I wanted in my life."

They were silent. It sounded very much like the truth and they didn't know how to follow it up.

"How did you feel about your mother's death?" the short one asked.

Miles looked at him and said nothing.

"When they called you at school to say she was going to live, you were annoyed, right? Why was that?"

"You went jogging right after the call. With Billy Mack?"

"Maybe you were lonely. You needed companionship. What do you think?"

Miles stared them down, silent.

They changed their tactics and went on to questions about the day that Billy killed himself. "What exactly happened that day? What kind of mood was he in? Depressed? Elated? Was he ever like that before?"

And, "You stopped to rest and see the view? What did you talk about? For how long?"

And, "Did you touch him?"

"No," Miles said, not even hesitating.

"No? Did he touch you?"

"No," Miles said.

They looked at him, and he looked back, and the silence seemed to go on and on. He waited them out. McGrath would have been proud of him.

"Nothing happened," Miles said. "We talked."

"You just talked, and then you jogged back to school together, and said goodbye."

"He jogged on ahead of me. He often did that."

"Why?"

"It was his way. He was shy. I suppose he didn't want kids to see him out jogging with a teacher."

"Why?"

"I *don't know.*"

"So he jogged ahead of you and went home and killed himself."

"I guess."

"He had semen on his jockstrap and shorts, you know."

"Well, it wasn't mine," Miles said.

They hadn't thought of that and they seemed surprised that Miles had. They exchanged a look. After a while the short one said, "Billy wrote a note to you just before he killed himself. He said . . ."

"I know. His father showed me it."

"No, he didn't show you this one. This was a draft that was found later. He did several drafts."

Miles said nothing.

"We have them all. Every draft."

"And?"

"This draft is incomplete. It says: 'Dear Miles, You are the only one . . .' That's all. It sounds romantic, doesn't it? I wonder what else he was going to write. 'You are the only one . . .' Well, I'm sure you can fill in the blanks, teaching poetry and everything."

Again Miles said nothing.

"What do you suppose he was going to say?"

"I suppose he was going to say that I'm the only one who ever listened to him."

They thought a minute.

"Sounds good to me," one said.

"Me too," the other said.

They stood up. "Do you have any idea why Billy killed himself?" the first one said. "What do *you* think?"

Miles tried to think why Billy killed himself. Because he was depressed. Because he was raped by the fucking football team and left lying on the locker-room floor in his own blood and shit. Because his father thought he was a fairy. Because his mother prayed he wouldn't be a fairy. Because he was in love with me and I didn't love him back. Because he was afraid of what he was. Because he couldn't go on.

"Well?" they said.

"I don't know," Miles said.

They put on their coats and prepared to leave, but at the door, the short one turned and said, "You went to the Tom Cat Lounge and got picked up on the night your mother died." He paused for effect. "Any comment about that?"

"I'm a weak man," Miles said. "And stupid. But I did not molest Billy Mack."

"We'll be back," the first one said.

Outside, the sky was overcast and it looked like it might snow. The two policemen stood on the front step, looking around, and then they walked to their car. They got in and sat there, silent. Then the tall one said, "What do you think?"

"There's nothing there," the short one said. "Jack Mack is losing it."

"He's lost it."

"And he's looking for someone to blame."

"He's found the right guy in Bannon. What a dumb shit."

"You think it'll stick?"

"Long enough to make him uncomfortable."

"Fellatio," the short one said, doing Miles' voice. "I was the suck*ee*."

They laughed and drove back to the station. It had been a shitty day.

The two policemen made their way down the official list of people to be interviewed. They had put together the list they got from Jack Mack, the complainant, and the list they got from Endicott, the principal, and then the chief of police went through and ticked off every fifth person, and that was the official list, allowing for exceptions. The exceptions, of course, were the teachers who were dying to be interviewed and who couldn't be refused. Nonetheless, the investigating officers were urged to keep the investigation small, tight, and brief.

From Endicott, the principal, they heard a great deal but learned very little. He praised Officer Mack, he praised his faculty, and he had unreserved praise for the superintendent, who, he said, had his finger on the pulse of the entire school, or should, since that was his job. And he praised Miles Bannon, too. But despite his efforts to be fair—and, he insisted, he tried always to be fair—the policemen concluded that Endicott had a private agendum, that it was somehow his intention to make Bannon look guilty. Of exactly what, they couldn't say.

From the teachers Endicott had named as Bannon's close acquaintances—James Dietz, Katherine Dillard, Jeffrey Douglas, Diane Waring—the investigators learned a great deal, much of it contradictory. They took notes and put off drawing conclusions.

James Dietz saw Miles Bannon as smart, slick, a subtle womanizer; everybody knew, he said, that Miles had two women on the string at once. One was an old girlfriend to whom he owed everything, a wonderful woman, too good for Miles. The other was a more recent acquisition from the English Department. Everybody loved Miles. It was one of those mysteries. And then he told them that he himself was in AA and, in case they weren't aware, Officer Mack had a serious drinking problem. Had they thought of intervention? Did they know the statistics on alcoholism among law enforcement officers? *He* did. He recited the statistics, impressively. Was anybody doing anything about it?

Katherine Dillard, whom Endicott had said was everybody's confidante, thought Bannon was a nice man, well intentioned, but basically selfish; she knew of a case where a friend of theirs—the Coach, actually—was really in need of Miles' support and understanding and he had done nothing at all to help. Nothing. Despite her specific request for help, though she rarely asked anything of anybody. And, for the record, Miles had never confided in her, that was for sure. But she doubted he was gay. He'd been going at it hot and heavy with a certain woman in the English Department— Diane Waring, as a matter of fact—and *that's* why he was unavailable to help his friends. She herself wasn't angry, though. She was just disappointed in him.

Jeffrey Douglas claimed to have nothing to say about Bannon, pro or con, though he did have strong reservations about Bannon's professional judgment. Indeed, Bannon's imprudence and his lack of professional judgment might explain why he found himself in this pickle. But Douglas was utterly indifferent to the man personally, he said. In fact, the senior class had voted last December to dedicate the yearbook to Bannon, and now they wanted to dedicate it to Billy Mack, but until they took an official vote and gave him the results in writing, Douglas intended to leave the dedication page as it was. And the yearbook, scandal or no, would be dedicated to Miles Bannon. That's how indifferent he was to the man. And as to Miles' being gay, he himself thought Miles was sexless, or asexual, a kind of eunuch. Certainly they would not find *him* calling Miles gay. Anyway, it was none of his business. When they asked him—it was routine; they always followed up leads—if he knew anything about an affair between Miles Bannon and Diane Waring, he said yes, it was probably so, but they should attribute the affair less to Miles' sexual prowess than to Diane's insatiability. They moved on eagerly to Diane Waring.

Diane Waring proved difficult in the extreme. She listened to their questions and answered none of them, confining herself to a little speech about Officer Mack's harassment of Miles, her own right to privacy, and the shocking lack of legal resources for innocent people who have been unjustly accused. Only this week she had been accepted to Harvard Law, she said, and she wanted them to know it was her firm intention to become a lawyer and fight people like you. She had short red hair and green eyes, and it was possible to believe she could drive a gay man straight, at least for the night.

The other teachers lined up evenly behind Miles Bannon. He was good in the classroom, hardworking, dedicated. He taught students how to think. He taught them to question authority. He taught them a moral sense, a standard of behavior, a code of values. He preached honor and integrity, charity and generosity, and he did it without embarrassment or apology, and the kids listened to him. He was wonderful. He was terrific. The less they knew him, the more lavish their praise. It was only his friends who did him in.

Teaching, the investigators concluded, was a strange profession. They were glad to move on to the list of students.

"I told them everything," Miles said. "The whole truth." And then he added, seriously, "Up to a point."

Margaret laughed.

And then Miles began what he had always considered the impossible task of telling Margaret about his secret life, his other self.

"With a *man?*" she said.

"I know," he said.

"Poor Miles. You should have told me." She could not look at him, and so she kissed him on the forehead, and drew him close to her, and held him tight.

He told her everything.

At the end, when she had heard about Robert and Billy Mack and the interrogation, she thought a while and, still holding him, she said, "I got drunk again. For two days. A complete and hopeless relapse. But I recovered."

"What are we doing? Sharing failures."

"Well," she said, her cheek resting against his shoulder, "maybe that's all we've got to share."

"Not love?" he said.

"No. Not that," she said.

He was silent.

He listened for what she might say next. Any moment can be ripe for revelation.

"Dignity," she said.

"What about it?" he said.

"It can get you through anything," she said.

The investigators had questioned only Paul Ciampa, Richard Polcari, and Deirdre Forster, when, as the chief of police had feared, a reporter got hold of the story beneath the story and the shit hit the fan.

It began slowly, with a sketchy little item on the first page of the second section of *The Malburn Times*. A teacher had been accused of a homosexual relationship with a student who had later committed suicide, it said. A known homosexual and an habitué of the Tom Cat Lounge, the teacher was said to have connections with the State House. An investigation of the matter was being conducted by two veteran officers of the Malburn police force. The chief of police had no comment at this time, but William Endicott, principal of Malburn High, was quoted saying that he had absolute confidence in his teachers and in the police force and he was assisting the investigators in every way possible.

On television that night there was mention of a suicide at Malburn High and of a high-level investigation that was under way. No further details were available.

The next day, reporters were at Endicott's door as he left for school and his "No comment at this time" did nothing to deter them. They followed him to his office, they badgered the secretaries, they interviewed the custodians and anyone else they could find in the building—two deliverymen, a plumber, and three department chairpersons catching up on the administrative work that was always backlogged at this time of year. The reporters found out that Billy Mack was the suicide, Miles was the suspect, and that they had gone jogging together. It wasn't much. Nonetheless, the second section that night carried a large headline: HOMOSEXUALITY AT MALBURN HIGH? And in smaller print, a subheadline said, *Popular Teacher Accused.* The few facts were augmented by interviews with people who knew Miles Bannon and thought the accusation unfounded. He was a wonderful man and a very popular teacher, they said. Miles Bannon himself was unavailable for comment.

Then a reporter from the *Boston Globe* got hold of a list of people who were interviewed by police and she began to do some interviews herself. She got some very short, sharp answers from faculty and several long, rambling speeches from Endicott, but school was back in session by this time and the reporter began to interview students, who were more talkative and better informed than faculty. She appeared one day in the corridors, looking very much like a student herself, and she asked them questions in a way that held their attention and made it easy for them to talk.

Miles was a great teacher, she learned, and for years he had been everybody's favorite, but since the news had come out that he'd been having an affair with Billy Mack—maybe it wasn't true, but you know, after all—well, everybody began to remember that he always wore nice clothes, and he talked funny and, even though he jogged, he wasn't really an athlete. He was very big on poetry, too, and the stuff he taught was like *Of Mice and Men*, which wasn't a poem, but a parent had complained about it, and the poems were love poems that were, you know, peculiar. Besides, he was thirty-five or thirty-six and he wasn't married. And, more than any other teacher, he was close to the kids, mostly the boys, and when he directed a play, he was alone with them in the school after everybody had left, and he drove them home, and he told them they were a thing of wonder and a many-splendored thing and stuff like that. And somebody said he was into big shoulders, he really liked them. And somebody else said he had been seen at a gay pickup place in Boston. Besides, Miles sent Billy notes. *Notes*, for crying out loud. One of the notes said, "Let's *do* it"—with the "do" underlined—and that was proof, practically.

So the story hit the *Globe*, and then the television, and for three days it was the hottest story in town. Miles Bannon, at the advice of his lawyer, did not comment and did not defend himself. He continued to teach his classes, though under the circumstances teaching was nearly impossible. The principal said he could not fire Bannon or even force him to take a leave of absence until formal charges had been brought. He had no further comment. Officer Mack had many comments and he repeated them again and again in interviews as he demanded that Miles Bannon be brought to justice. The newspapers said that Officer Mack was suffering from "strain" and "exhaustion," but the television cameras frankly revealed a man whose speech was muddled with drink. His wife stood behind him, twisting a rosary in her hand, saying nothing. By the end of the third day everything that could be said had been said many times.

On the fourth day Deirdre Forster was interviewed and said she didn't see why everybody was blaming Miles for Billy's suicide.

Why didn't they blame the guys on the football team who raped him. Why didn't anybody mention *that?*

"Raped him?" The reporter was doubtful.

"They shoved a broom up his you-know-what," Deirdre said. "They call it Violation." She explained, needlessly, "It's a game."

The reporter took notes—names and dates and accusations.

"Everybody knows about it," Deirdre said. "Just ask."

The scandal was out.

38

GIVEN THE NATURE OF THE SCANDAL, news coverage was sane and responsible, even if it was relentless. There were no sensational headlines—though LOCKER ROOM ORGY and HOMOSEXUAL HELL nearly made it into *The Malburn Times*—and all the news media concentrated on hard facts rather than on speculation, as they might well have, since there was so much of it. The names of minors were for the most part concealed, though Deirdre Forster featured prominently as the source of the initial revelation of the locker-room rape, as they had come to call it, and Billy Mack's suicide was played down as much as possible.

Newspapers and television became a kind of conscience for the town. How had it happened? How had it been concealed?

At first there was shock and outrage. How could this have happened here? Malburn was a small New England town, a bedroom community for Boston and the computer industry along Route 128. Working people lived here, ordinary people, people like us. This kind of thing didn't happen here. It happened in the inner city, in New York or Chicago, where kids took drugs and coke and where crime was a way of life. But not here. Not among our boys.

But it had happened here and no one had told. Five members

of the football team had raped Billy Mack with a broom handle. And, it was discovered, they had been sniffing coke and they had drunk some bourbon, and they were probably high and a little crazy. Then it was discovered that they took steroids. They were known as the Roid Boys. *That* was how it happened. Booze and steroids and a line of cocaine: they were out of their minds, they were not responsible, everybody knew that from watching "Sixty Minutes." But all the same, no one had told. How could you explain that an entire student body knew what had happened, and knew that Billy Mack had killed himself, and still nobody said anything? Not even when a popular teacher—Miles Bannon—was blamed for the suicide, did anyone step forward and tell about the rape. From September until March not a word was said. Was there no moral sense at all among these students? What had our high schools come to? Where were the teachers? Where were the parents?

Newspaper and television reporters had not let up for an instant, even by early April when the story was a month old. They interviewed everybody. They came up with every hidden thing.

They interviewed Cosmo Damiani at the mental hospital where he was recovering from a nervous breakdown. They suppressed his name, calling him only "the reluctant rapist," and they reported that he was sorry for his part in what had happened and that he prayed for Billy Mack every day. He had cried then, they said, and was unable to go on, though his parents finished the interview for him, saying that Cosmo's ambition was to complete high school and go on to college and study to be a doctor, so he could help humanity. The interviewer let it go at that, since the psychiatrist had told her that the shock treatments weren't working, and Cosmo's prognosis was at best pretty bleak.

The other four football players—names withheld—were steroid-free now and had sworn off drugs for good. They wanted to get back to the healthy life and go on to college. They blamed the steroids for what had happened. One minute they were normal guys celebrating a birthday and the next minute they were wild animals. The technical name for it was Roid Rage and it happened when you were juiced up, just like they said on "Sixty Minutes." Steroids had nearly ruined their lives, but they were starting over. They felt they were victims of a drug culture, and what their parents wanted to know was this: how could this have happened in a well-run high school? Where was the supervision? Where was the Coach?

The parents were not the first to ask about Coach. The School Board, the selectmen, the town council, and the mayor had asked the same question on the day the news first broke.

Where was the Coach?

The Coach, they all knew, was out drunk somewhere.

The newspapers reported this and the television showed it, live. Coach appeared on the evening news, sobbing into the microphone. "If I could only undo it all," he said, and added, confused, "If I could only have my Carol back." The woman by his side, Katherine Dillard, explained that Carol was Coach's wife and that she had been killed in a car crash. They brought the microphone back to Coach, who sobbed some more, saying, "I'm sorry, I'm sorry," as the tears poured down his face.

So it was useless to ask about the Coach. He was supposed to be responsible, but he was just a drunk.

"Who was responsible, then?" the School Board asked. And though they kept on asking where the chain of responsibility ended, they kept coming back to the principal of the school, William Endicott. What did he know? When did he know it?

The newspapers and television repeated these questions.

Someone had to take responsibility.

Meanwhile reporters continued to dig up news about Malburn High. A freshman girl was pregnant—Ginny Carty, name withheld—and getting married at age fourteen. This, however, was contradicted in the next day's paper; the girl was fifteen and she was not getting married because, though her mother was willing, the boy's mother was not. The girl's mother wanted everyone to know that she was proud that her daughter was taking responsibility for her actions by having the child. They did not believe in abortion. The girl's mother would raise the baby while the daughter finished school. The girl was going to be a doctor or a lawyer; she hadn't yet decided which. But she was already an ardent feminist.

The Malburn Times ran a long interview with Polcari—name withheld—about what it was like to be gay at Malburn High. He made Malburn sound like any other high school: a little teasing, a little horseplay, but all in good fun. It was one of the few reassuring things, the interviewer said, that she had heard about Malburn High. "Oh, it wasn't bad," he said. "And there were sympathetic faculty, like Miles Bannon, who wasn't really gay despite what you read in the papers. And there was another English teacher—Jeff Douglas, name withheld—a close friend, who sometimes took him out for tea and croissants." "And is he gay?" the interviewer asked. Polcari raised his eyebrows and said, "It wouldn't be discreet to say, since he's married and has children."

Over a month had passed since the scandal broke, and a committee had been formed to investigate athletes' use of drugs, with particular attention to the use of steroids. Another committee was formed to investigate sex, both heterosexuality and homosexuality, among both male and female students, and, if it existed, sex between students and teachers. And a third committee was formed to investigate moral values, with specific attention to why nobody had brought the locker-room rape to the attention of anybody in authority during all those long months. The forming of committees seemed to signal the approaching end of the matter, and since Coach had not been fired and Endicott had not resigned, there was a feeling of unresolved problems in the school, the School Board, the town.

Editorials appeared in the newspaper. Television anchormen offered think-pieces at the close of their shows. Sermons were preached in the many pulpits around Malburn. The editorials and think-pieces and sermons all took their starting point from the same question: who was to blame? The locker-room rape was passing from the news, they said, it was about to become a memory, but before it did, the question must be asked: who was to blame?

They answered the question. *We* were. By the example we give our children, by our lax moral principles, by our quest for the almighty dollar. By our use of cigarettes and alcohol, by our cutting corners in our work, by our cheating on our income taxes. By our movies, television, fast food. Advertisements. Pornography. Junk bonds. Arbitrage. Ours has become a culture without values or standards. Our children are our victims.

Billy Mack was a victim of mindless, drug-induced violence, but the five football players were victims as well. It is we who are to blame. Guilt, like charity, begins at home.

Deirdre Forster did not read editorials and she did not go to church, but she listened to the anchorman's think-piece about communal guilt, and she said to her mother, "That's a crock. Junk bonds didn't rape Billy Mack and neither did you or daddy. Those football players did it."

"Now, Deirdre," her mother said.

"Good girl," her father said.

Malburn High had been the right place for her, after all.

39

In early March, when the scandal was at its most sensational, attention focused mainly on the suicide of Billy Mack and on his rape by the five football players. In late March, attention shifted to Coach and especially to Endicott, and there was the feeling that somebody had to take responsibility, which meant that Coach would have to be fired and Endicott would have to resign. But the firing and the resignation hadn't yet been announced, and now it was April, and everybody was still waiting.

During all this time, Miles Bannon had receded into the background of the news. Officially, however, the investigation of Miles continued. Officially, the two policemen were still looking into Officer Mack's allegation that Miles Bannon had seduced his son and in some way had been responsible for the boy's suicide. Officially, they were still taking Jack Mack seriously.

In fact, however, the investigation had ceased at the moment the locker-room rape hit the newspaper. In fact, the police department was engaged in a mad scramble to cover up their original cover-up of the rape and to pretend that customary police procedures had been observed. In fact, Miles Bannon was less a concern to the police department than was their own Jack Mack, who was drinking on duty and giving stupid interviews and calling for justice. For the police department, Miles Bannon was a dead issue.

But for Miles himself, everything was just as it had been since January, when Jack Mack had started asking questions and the whole school had begun to wonder. There was always more: newspapers had called him a known homosexual and the kids repeated it constantly. They carved "Miles—69" on their desks and they inscribed it in the dirt on his car. They knew that he went to the Tom Cat Lounge, they knew he went there the night his mother died, they whispered "Tom Cat" behind him as he went down the corridors. They smiled at him in a certain way.

He got up in the morning—every day of January, February, March—and prayed to survive the day's insults and ridicule and contempt, and he endured it somehow, with kids looking at him funny, watching his crotch sometimes, flirting with him to catch him out. Nothing was beneath them. They would say anything, do anything, to expose him further, to see him raw.

He went on. He saw Margaret, and told her how it was, and he went on. And every new hurt was a surprise.

"Hello, you sweet thing," she said, as Miles came up the walk. "Come in, come in."

It was the second week of April, unseasonably warm, and Margaret was wearing a spring dress she had bought just for him, to cheer him up, to show she cared. She was in love with Michael Collins, and could not see him—would not let herself—and she pretended Miles was Michael.

"How's your new job?" Miles said, and listened for the answer.

"Wonderful," she said. "Here, I'll get your drink."

"But tell me," he said. "I want to know what you do, and who you work with—whom—and what they're like, and everything."

"Let's go into the living room," she said.

"Tell me," he said.

She told him. It seemed very odd to talk so much about herself, with Miles at any rate, and she realized she liked it. He finished his drink, and she got him another, and made herself another cup of tea. She was still talking about her job.

"Now you," she said. "More awful things? Or is it getting better?"

He thought a while, smiled, and said, "I can't go on. I say that all the time, and I pray for strength or faith or hope or something that will help me to go on, but more and more it seems to be true: I can't go on."

"But you do."

"Until now I have. But it's like being stripped and scalded and . . . it's not like anything I know. It's like walking around naked every moment of your life, in public, with everybody looking at you, sneering. No, it's worse than that."

"But you know who you are. That's how you go on."

He didn't know what she was talking about.

"It's a sense of dignity you have."

"Ha!" he said.

They talked for a long time, and he didn't understand a word of it, and then he went home.

Miles lay in bed thinking of Margaret and how strange she had become and how interesting. She was prettier than before, and she dressed better. She looked almost as if she were in love.

" 'You know who you are,' " she'd said. " 'That's how you go on.' " Which was funny, because of all the things he didn't know, the foremost was precisely that: who he was.

Billy Mack knew who *he* was, and so he killed himself. Maybe it was better not to know. Or maybe it was just better to kill yourself. Why not?

He got out of bed and went downstairs and poured himself a drink.

Drinking was one way to do it. Like Coach. Like Jack Mack.

Maybe he should just get in his car and drive to Boston to the Tom Cat Lounge and pick up some AIDSy looking guy and fuck himself into the kind of suicide everybody thought he'd earned.

And at once, just saying it, he realized that isn't who he was: for one thing, he didn't want to fuck a man, any man, and for another, it didn't matter what anybody thought. Not now.

If he could only hold on to this realization, he could get through anything they could hand out. Anything. He poured another drink, and concentrated, burning the words into his brain: that's not who I am, it doesn't matter what they think.

The next morning he was very hung over and he couldn't even recall why he stayed up so late . . . unless he'd been planning to join the crowd and drink himself to death.

40

It had rained all week. Today was the last day of April, and it was sunny and warm, and so the kids were impossible. They wanted to be outside playing baseball, or hanging around the mall, or making out with their boyfriend or girlfriend. Gina Lombardi was sent home from school for wearing a red foil earring that turned out to be a condom. Paul Ciampa was caught, for the first time ever, without his homework done. Cynthia Dodd, in a wild swing from her usual depression, was given Detention for singing in the women's room. Actually, she was standing on the toilet seat, with a marijuana cigarette in her hand, while she belted out "I feel good, the way I knew I would," à la James Brown, but she palmed the cigarette just in time, and got off easy. Cynthia was an extreme case, but spring fever had gotten into everybody, and all of Miles' classes were a mess. They talked and giggled and nobody paid attention. He himself couldn't wait for the day to end.

He prefected the cafeteria during the second lunch period, and for the first time since January, there had been no snide comments, no nasty jokes about him, at least none that he was aware of. He was feeling good, therefore, as he went upstairs to his American Lit. class and, when he heard the bedlam above him in the study hall, he stopped on the stairs and waited. He didn't want to have to yell at anybody and he figured he'd just give them time to quiet down on their own. But the noise kept up, and so he said to a kid who went past him on the stairs, "Tell them to cool it up there, will you?" The noise went right on and Miles faced the inevitable. Ugliness, misery, and piss.

At the top of the stairs, he stopped and looked at what was going on. They had cornered Polcari, and Hacker was holding him tight and steady while Tuna drew cat whiskers on his face with a felt marking pen.

"Don't wiggle," Hacker said as he tightened his hold on Polcari. "You trying to get me all excited?"

"Pretty pussy," Tuna said, "hold still," and he finished the last of the whiskers.

The football groupies cheered, but then it was all over, and they didn't know what to do. Hacker was still holding him, though, and he figured they might as well do something else to him as long as they had him here, so he said, "I think this pussy needs a pink belly. What do you think?"

"Pink pussy belly," Tuna said, and tickled Polcari under the chin.

Polcari said nothing and did nothing. He had stopped struggling. He was waiting for it to be over.

"Get his pants off," Hacker said.

"Don't," some girl said. "I'll tell on you, Hacker."

And somebody else said, "Cut the shit, you guys."

At once Miles broke through the ring of kids, his face white with anger. He grabbed Tuna by the shoulders and flung him hard, and since Tuna was bent over undoing Polcari's belt buckle, he was off balance and went sprawling full length on the floor. He banged his head, a dull thudding sound. Miles turned back to Hacker and Polcari, shoved Polcari to one side, and grabbed a fistful of Hacker's sweatshirt and twisted it. He rammed Hacker back against the wall, and leaned into him, with an awful look on his face. He kept staring into Hacker's eyes, silent, and then he said, very softly, "I promise you. You do that again, to *any*body, and I'll kill you." He ground his fist into Hacker's chest, pulled back, and punched him full force in the stomach. Hacker folded for a minute, half in surprise, half at the power of the blow.

Miles stood looking at him for a minute and then he said, "What scum you are," and he looked around at the little crowd, and added, "all of you."

As Miles turned and walked away, nobody said anything. They were embarrassed, ashamed. Some of them began to drift away to classes, and others got busy with their lockers or their books or a sudden need to use the john, but everyone backed off from the two Roid Boys, and even they could see that things were changing, that open season on Miles was coming to a close. They laughed, none-theless, and shouted "Motherfucker" at full voice until Dietz showed up, trailing cigarette smoke, and said, "Hacker, somebody keeps calling for you. Tell him to stop."

Miles got through his American Lit. class by refusing to think of what he had just done, but in study hall he had time to think, and he began to realize how completely he had given himself over to the enemy. Endicott would have him up on charges before the day was over. He had struck a student. Two students. He had used physical violence and he had uttered threats: wasn't this the defi-nition of assault and battery? Every time the door opened, Miles looked up, half expecting to see uniformed police ready to arrest him. How could he have done it? How could he have been so stupid?

He knew the answer, of course. It was rage and frustration. For months now he had been ridiculed, imitated, held up to scorn. His name was on every toilet wall in the school. Parents talked about him across the dinner table. Boys were warned to keep their dis-tance. No charges had been brought, it was all gossip and silly speculation, but to their minds he was guilty. And the result was this rage that had sprung out of him at the sight of Polcari being humiliated by those thugs. He hadn't done it for Polcari—he couldn't stand Polcari any more than they could—he had done it for himself. Spontaneously. Without a minute's thought for the legal consequences. And now they had him. He was done for.

Thinking of it made his heart race and the adrenalin pump through his body. He was ready to fight again. He would like to take them on, all of them, those ugly, vicious, mind-fucking bastards who picked on sissys like Polcari. Or like himself. Did they really think *they* were beyond the mindless fury of someone like themselves? If he knew one thing, he knew this: any of us can be broken in an instant.

He got up from his desk and stared out the window. The grass was beginning to turn green and there should be crocuses coming up before long. It was spring. Soon it would be summer. And he would be out of here on his ass, with a police record, with charges of assault and battery.

Miles gave the windowpane a sharp, quick punch. The glass shattered and spots of red began to appear on his knuckles, but he remained where he was, leaning on the windowsill, and nobody moved. When he turned around, he saw they were all looking up, expectant, and in a calm voice he said, "A little accident." He blotted his knuckles with a handkerchief. Some exchanged glances, but most of them, unaware of what had just happened, returned to whatever they'd been doing—reading or dozing or passing notes.

He strolled to the back of the room and leaned against the wall. Mark and Michelle had fought, and made up, and were fighting again, quietly. Jennifer was making mouths into her pocket mirror. Little Becky Hu was writing furiously in her notebook. Everything was the same as it had always been, except for Billy Mack.

If he could go back in time, Miles thought, would he still step away from the wall and drop that first note on Billy's desk? And would not doing it have made a difference? Or would Billy have killed himself in any case? Maybe certain things were fated from the beginning—falling in love, betrayal, death, despair—and nothing you could do would stop them. And you never knew until it was too late.

The bell rang, and as Miles returned to his desk, the kids went into action, banging their desktops, attacking the lockers, slamming their way through the last fifteen minutes of the school day. But they had lost their wild energy as, soundlessly, the news had gone around. Miles had decked Tuna. He had punched out Hacker. Something final was about to happen.

Miles went downstairs to his homeroom and sat staring at his desk while the vice-principal read the last notices of the day. The speaker clicked off, then on again, and this time it was not the vice-principal but Endicott himself.

"Will you see me in my office at the close of school, Mr. Bannon?" There was a crackling sound, as he rustled papers. "Thank you," he said.

The bell rang and within two minutes the room was empty.

Miles continued to sit at his desk.

He could, of course, resign. But what would that accomplish? He'd never get another teaching job, not now, with assault and battery on his record.

He shrugged and began putting his books and papers into his backpack. He zipped it up and was about to leave the classroom when he decided to check his plan book for tomorrow, just in case he was allowed to teach for one more day.

Inside the plan book he found a sheet of notebook paper on which someone had roughly drawn a cat's head with huge whiskers and beneath it they had printed, in capital letters, PUSSY. Miles sat down, exhausted suddenly. He wasn't angry or ashamed or even sad; he was exhausted.

The classroom door opened and there stood Polcari.

Miles looked at him. "What?" he said.

"Please let me talk to you," Polcari said. "Please!"

"So talk."

Polcari approached him tentatively, as if Miles might suddenly spring at him, and then he took a seat in the chair beside Miles' desk.

"I did it," Polcari said. "I'm the one."

Miles flipped the cat drawing at him.

"This?" he said.

"No. The Roids did that. Hacker. Or Tuna." And at once Polcari burst into tears. "I'm sorry," he said, sobbing. "Miles, I'm so sorry," and he went on crying.

Miles had not cried since before his mother died, and as he sat looking at this tall, skinny, hopelessly gay young man who was dissolving in his own tears, he thought how good it must feel, and how cleansing, to get it all out, to join the rest of humanity and weep over something you could never change. Like this skinny little fairy here and like all the whiners in all of history. The final breakdown of the self—tears.

"Miles," Polcari said, still crying.

"Forget it," Miles said. "It doesn't matter."

"You don't understand," Polcari said. And he explained what he had done. "See, my feelings were hurt when you wouldn't even let me thank you, and so when Mr. Douglas asked me about you, I told him."

"Told him?"

"About Robert and the Tom Cat Lounge and how he picked you up . . . and everything. Robert is my lover, so I knew about you, Miles. And I told Jeff. Then I felt bad I told him, so I tried to tell you I did it, but you didn't pay any attention to me, so I put that picture in your desk."

"The valentine."

"Yes. And then I felt bad I did it, so when the woman from the *Times* interviewed me, I pretended you weren't gay but Mr. Douglas was. To get even with him. For you."

"Richy. Good God. Don't you ever think of the consequences of what you say and do?"

"I know." He began to cry again, but only a little.

"You can't take words back. They do their damage and then you have to live with it."

"I know."

"You can wreck *lives* this way."

"I know." He added softly, as if he really didn't want Miles to hear him, "But you slept with Robert."

Miles was silent for a minute. "It's true," he said, "I did. And it can't be undone."

"That's why I said things."

"Yes."

"So it's not *all* my fault."

Miles shook his head. "No," he said. Miles wanted to strike him. Polcari had destroyed his life, had stripped him naked before the entire school, and Miles wanted to punch him once for each hour of misery he had caused. He wanted to stop him, forever, stop his crying and his tattling and his breath. Miles wanted him dead. He looked over at Polcari then, and the boy's face crumpled.

"It *is* my fault," Polcari said. "I'm sorry." He abandoned himself to tears, long silent sobs that shook his whole body. He did not cover his face, and the tears poured down, until he was too weak to go on. Then he stopped.

"It's all right," Miles said, and stood up. "Here." He tapped Polcari on the shoulder. "Stand up," he said. Polcari did, and Miles took him in his arms and held him. "It's all right," he said again. He held him close. "All right?" Polcari nodded. Miles patted him on the back a couple times and let him go. "Take care," Miles said softly, but Polcari did not return his look.

Someone cleared his throat, loudly, and Miles looked up to see Endicott at the door. Of course. It was inevitable.

"I'll be there in a moment," Miles said. He slung his bookbag over one shoulder, and looked at Polcari, and said again, "Take care," and then he followed Endicott out of the room.

Endicott closed his office door and took his seat behind the huge desk. He got up at once, went to the window, and lowered the blinds. The room darkened. "That's better," he said. "Sit down."

Miles sat, silently running through the latest charges. Assault and battery on two students. Hugging a third. No wonder Endicott lowered the blinds.

"Howard has given me some news," Endicott said. "The superintendent."

Miles waited.

"Officer Mack, it seems, has dropped his allegations against you . . ." Endicott shuffled papers, distracted, as if he were looking for something.

"Yes? But?"

"But not willingly. He didn't want to drop the charges—the allegations, rather—he was forced to. They're closing the investigation. Of you."

"But not of you? The incident?"

"Howard—the superintendent—asked me to tell you." He began looking through his papers again.

"Will I be hearing from them? Will I be . . . cleared?"

"What?" Endicott said. "No. You were never charged with anything, not officially. How can you be cleared?"

Miles savored the irony of that for a minute and then he said, "Thank you," but Endicott was very distracted and did not seem to hear him. Miles left the office.

And so he was free. There were no old charges and no new ones, despite his attack on Hacker and Tuna, despite his hugging Polcari while Endicott stood there watching. Something was up. Endicott must be in plenty of trouble if he'd passed up this opportunity to cause some.

Miles went out to his car and sat there for a minute wondering what to do. He should have a drink. He should celebrate with somebody. He should feel terrific.

He didn't feel terrific. There had been no charges, as Endicott said, so how could he be cleared? He would never be cleared.

They had merely investigated him. They had searched his bureau drawers and read his mail and asked his friends about him. They had revealed all the secrets of his life. They had published in newspapers the things he had whispered to Margaret in shame. They'd left him not a shred of decency to cover himself.

Suddenly it was a year ago, in May, a long hot night, and he had just helped his mother to the bathroom. She hobbled along on her walker while he hovered about, ready to catch her, and finally she reached the bed and settled herself on the edge of it. But she had wet her nightgown using the toilet and now it had to be changed. "Here, let me," he said, and tugged the nightgown from under her, leaving it loosely around her while he got out a fresh one. "Okay, here we go," he said, "just try to lift your arms a little," and he began to ease the nightgown up from her body. She realized suddenly that she was nude, in front of him. She looked down at her withered breasts and her shrunken belly and that secret patch of white hair, and she looked up at him, in awful shame, in resignation. She could not even lift her hands to cover her face. She let him change the nightgown and put her into bed, but she was different after that and she would never be the same again.

Miles sat in his car now, and he understood.

"Mother," he said. "I'm sorry."

He was free. He was home safe. And he was rapidly getting drunk. He called Margaret and said he needed her, he needed to see her and talk, could he come over? But she was on her way to an AA meeting.

He was desperate, he said.

"Do you want a word of advice?" she asked, and when he didn't answer, she gave it anyway. "Drinking isn't going to help," she said.

"I need you, Margaret."

"I have needs, too," she said. "Right now, they come first."

In a way, he liked her for it. She was tough. He could love such a woman.

He had another drink.

What was wrong? He was free, and safe, and if his life had been ruined, at least that part was over, and it was all up from here. So why this agonizing need? And why now? And what, dear God, *what* did he want?

Please help me, he prayed, and I'll do anything you want. Anything.

At once he checked the time. It was nine o'clock. If he drove fast, he could get into Arch Street before it closed—it must close sometime, everything did—and he could find that priest. The one that used *that* confessional, farthest back, on the left. He'd find him. He had that kind of luck tonight.

He brushed his teeth and gargled with Listerine and looked at himself in the mirror. Not too wonderful. He looked like a drunk who was determined to look sober. Nonetheless, he'd do it.

The car was a mess again. He got in and turned on the ignition, and the car jumped into life. But immediately it stalled. It had been doing this for the past month, and he should have taken it in, but who had time? Who could face it? He tried it again, and it stalled, and he tried it a third time. The car coughed a little, chugged, and finally started up. He floored it at once.

He drove through Cambridge and down through the center of Boston, where the traffic was still heavy, and then over to New England Medical. He thought of parking there, but it was too long a walk for a drunk, and he decided to take his chances on finding a place closer to Arch Street. He found one on Winter Street near the Combat Zone.

He tried the door at the Arch Street Shrine, but it was locked. Almost at once, however, it opened and a priest stepped out. Miles laughed with pleasure.

"This is always happening to me," he said. "The church is locked and then a priest comes out."

The priest had his back turned, locking the door from outside.

"I'm looking for a priest," Miles said. "He's the one who hears confessions in that last booth on the left. He's English, or maybe Irish."

The priest looked at him.

"I've got to talk to him. When my mother was dying, he was very helpful, and I need to talk with him now."

"We're closed," the priest said. "We'll be opening again at six tomorrow. You can come back then."

Miles heard something British in his voice. Could it be the same priest? Of course.

"Listen," he said. "I'm sure it's you. I've got to talk with you. Terrible things have happened. I've done things, but not what they think. I never seduced that boy. I let him fall in love with me, that was where I first went wrong. It was a sin of pride. And I used him, for my ego, I guess. I've used people. I . . ."

"You're drunk," the priest said. "If you want to go to confession, come back when you're not drunk."

"I'm not drunk. I'm just a mess."

"Come back tomorrow," the priest said. "Only stop drinking."

Miles leaned heavily against the door and watched the priest walk away. He needed another drink. He thought, for one insane minute, of going to the Tom Cat Lounge to get a drink. Not for anything kinky. Just a drink. They thought he went there all the time anyhow, so why not go? But no, he wouldn't. He wasn't like that.

He walked to his car and got in. He turned on the ignition, and the car started at once. Thank God for small favors. He checked the rear-view mirror, pressed his foot to the accelerator, and pulled out into the street. At once there was the crunch of metal on metal, a hard thud, and his car rocked back and forth, half in and half out of the parking place. "You dumb shit," somebody shouted, and Miles looked up into the face of a furious policeman. He had hit a police car.

"License and registration," the policeman said. Miles searched the glove compartment for the registration and finally came up with a familiar-looking envelope, but his fingers had turned thick and clumsy and he couldn't get it open. He gave it to the policeman. "And license," the policeman said. His partner said, "Get out of the car, please."

Miles handed over his license and got out of the car, determined to rise to the occasion.

"Walk along this line, please."

Miles walked it more or less successfully. "These shoes," he said, "they need new heels. My balance . . ."

"And this one, please, toe to toe. Look *up*."

"Will you recite the alphabet, please?"

"The alphabet? You're kidding."

"No, sir. We're not kidding. Recite it, please."

"A B C D E F G, H I J K L M N O . . ." Miles paused, gave a small choking laugh, and said, "For a second I forgot it."

"Let's get in the car."

"No, wait," Miles said. "Listen. A B C D E F G, H I J K L M N O . . ." He really couldn't believe this was happening.

"The next letter," the policeman said, "is P. As in please. Get in the car, please."

"Well," Miles said, aware that this was insane, "you've gotta admit that the Ps are hard."

"In the car."

"Do you read me my rights?" He couldn't seem to stop.

"You've got the right to shut up."

The other policeman mumbled something, which may have been his rights, but Miles had stopped listening because they opened the door of the patrol car and started to push him in. Two other men were already there, handcuffed, a skinny black man who looked only half-conscious and a huge biker with a blond crewcut. The biker spat out the open door. "Motherfucker," he said, and Miles could see that this was the real thing. He shut up at last.

At the police station they led him into a small room, brightly lit, and wrote down his answers to a long list of questions. Afterwards, he said to the policeman, "I'm really sorry about this."

"It happens," the policeman said.

"Could I have a glass of water?"

The policeman brought him a paper cup and waited while he drank from it. "You want some more?" he said, and Miles shook his head, but he realized suddenly how hostages came to love their captors. The policeman left the room and Miles could hear him outside, talking to somebody. "Bannon," he said. "In here."

There was a lot of yelling down the hall and then a crash and a scuffle and somebody hollering "Motherfucker," in rage at first, and then in pain. Then there was silence.

A fat man in a dirty yellow sweater came in and sat down at the table with Miles. "Bannon," he said. He put a black medical bag on the table and opened it and began to assemble his gear to extract blood.

"Are you a nurse?" Miles asked.

The man laughed and said, "Am I a nurse?" He found a vein in Miles' left arm and pushed the needle in. His fingernails were very dirty. "Blue blood," he said. "You must be fucking royalty." He wrote something on a label and stuck it on the vial. There was more yelling from down the corridor, then a harsh laugh. "Enjoy your stay, your majesty," he said, and left.

Miles had been sitting in the room for a long time when the policeman returned. "We're gonna move you," he said. "To Malburn. There's no more room here."

They put him in the back seat of the patrol car. "Wait here," one said, and the other one laughed. "Where's he gonna go?" he said.

They came back in a minute leading the biker, with a wispy-looking character following in the rear. The biker had a bruise on his forehead now and his hands were cuffed behind his back. One held his head down and the other pushed him into the car, but he fought them. "I can't sit with my hands like this," he said. "Then stand," the policeman said. They pushed the thin guy in next to him. "Act nice," he said.

As they drove slowly out of the police yard, the cop in the passenger seat slid open the plastic divider. "Next stop, Malburn," he said, and slammed the divider shut.

The biker looked at Miles. "You see this guy here? He was taking a piss and he reached over to the guy next to him and grabbed his dick. And you know what? It was a cop. No shit. He grabbed a cop's dick."

"I did not," the thin guy said.

"Don't tell fibs, Sally. I heard them charging you."

"That's not how it happened. He grabbed mine. And then he just *said* I grabbed his. It was false arrest. And it was entrapment besides."

"You're gonna do me next, Sally," the biker said to him. "Soon as we get in that cell." He nudged Miles and laughed, it was such a terrific joke. "Aren't you, Sally? Aren't you? Show us your mouth. Show us how you use your tongue."

He laughed hard, a crazy laugh, out of control. The thin guy began to laugh with him. Miles dropped his head on his chest and pretended to sleep.

It seemed a very long time before the ride was over.

At the Malburn station, the policewoman made a list of his valuables and confiscated them, along with his belt.

"Eighty dollars," she said. "You're in luck. You can make bail."

"Right now?" Miles said. "Let's do it."

She looked up at him and laughed.

"You got a long way to go yet," she said.

They led him into another room crammed with people. There was a large cell along one wall, with a bench where men were sitting, some of them drunk, some of them nodding off on drugs, and some just looking back at him curiously. "Over here," someone said, and pushed him through a group of men to where he would be fingerprinted. He let the policeman roll his fingers, one at a time, across the black ink pad and then roll them again on the official sheet. He wiped his fingers on the cloth they gave him. And then he took a card and held it at chest level as they photographed him front and left and right. "In here," they said, and he stepped through a doorway into a cement room, dank, windowless, and then he noticed a shower spigot at one end. "Strip, please," they said. He took off his jacket, looked around for somewhere to put it, and dropped it on the floor. He took off his tie and shirt, his undershirt, his pants, his underpants. One of them said, "Socks and shoes, too, please," and Miles looked up at him and saw that he was turned slightly, but deliberately, away. He was a witness only, not a voyeur. The technical nicety struck Miles as funny. He took off his shoes and socks and turned to face them. "Lift your testicles." He did. "Your arms." He did. "Turn around, please. Now bend over. Spread your legs. Now, with your hands, please spread your cheeks. More." Miles waited while they let him stand like that, and after a moment he dropped his hands, and stood straight and turned around to face them. "You can dress now." He threw his clothes on quickly, almost unaware of anger or shame. "Put him in the cage."

An older policeman came to get him. He looked at Miles closely and smirked. He led him to the other room, and as he unlocked the door of the holding cell, he said, "On Winter Street, huh, right near the Combat Zone? Back to the Tom Cat Lounge?" He pushed Miles in and closed the door behind him. As he locked it, he said, "Jack Mack was right about you," and he disappeared to wherever he'd come from.

Miles was behind bars in that long, narrow holding cell he had seen when they first brought him in to be fingerprinted. He looked down the row of men. The biker wasn't there, but the little fairy was. The room smelled stale, smoky, more like a locker room than a jail. Almost at once they called his name.

"Yuh," Miles said, trying to sound gruff.

"You want to make a call?" the policeman said. He was young and full of energy and looked like Paul Ciampa. "You've got bail."

"Yes," Miles said, "but I don't want to call anybody. I'll just pay."

The policeman came closer and explained how bail worked. "So you can call a friend," he concluded, "or a bondsman, but you've got to call somebody."

Miles thought of Margaret and Diane and Kathy Dillard, of Dietz and Coogan and Foley, and he looked at the card the policeman gave him with bondsmen's names on it: Godfather Bail Bonds, Bonita's Bail Bonds, Al Graf Bail Bonds—"The Bondsman with a Heart"—Ask for Millie Duckson.

"I'll stay," Miles said.

"It's your funeral," the policeman said. They called out the little fairy and took him away. They called out an old geezer, so drunk he had to be helped from the cage. And then the policeman came over to Miles and said quietly, "Look, mister, do yourself a favor. Make bail. Call somebody." But again Miles refused. The policeman looked at him a while and then shrugged. "Have it your way," he said.

"Bannon," they called, and now it was his turn.

The young policeman took him down a corridor, through a door, and down a flight of stairs barely wide enough for two. They turned, and continued down another flight of stairs, and then they entered a long corridor with empty cells on either side. They stopped at the third one on the right. With a lot of key rattling and clanging of metal, the policeman unlocked the door and slid it open. He said nothing. Miles stepped inside, and the policeman clanged the door shut and locked it. He retraced his steps down the corridor.

It was just like television. A wall of bars, two bunk beds, a sink and toilet side by side. The toilet had no seat, just the porcelain bowl, and it was right next to the bars where you could be seen from inside and outside the cell. A sort of picnic table with two attached benches was anchored to the concrete floor, for meals probably. And there was a tiny barred window, a foot high, two feet wide, up by the ceiling. What would happen in a fire?

There were two other men in the cell and Miles had seen them both upstairs. The old geezer lay sprawled on a bottom bunk, the little fairy huddled on the bed opposite, hugging his knees. Neither said anything.

Miles had a desperate need to pee. He glanced at the other two men and at the toilet and decided he would wait. But after a minute he could wait no longer. He stood in front of the toilet and unzipped his pants. He looked over at the little fairy who was leaning toward him, looking, waiting to check out the equipment. Miles turned around, slid his pants down to his knees, and hunched forward on the toilet, shielding himself. He closed his eyes and concentrated on peeing, and after a long while, it worked. He opened his eyes and began pulling up his pants, when he noticed the fairy had stopped hugging his knees and was standing by the bunk, smiling.

"Hi," he said. "I'm Harold."

Miles said hello.

"I'll do you, if you want," Harold said shyly. "I mean, if you want me to."

Miles shook his head. "No," he said.

The old geezer groaned, rolled to the edge of the bed, and threw up; a sour stench spread through the room. At the same time, there were footsteps in the corridor, and cursing, and the biker appeared with the young policeman walking behind him and another policeman at his side. The biker's hands were still cuffed behind his back. One held him while the other unlocked the door. They shoved him inside and locked the door again. The biker backed up to the bars and, from outside, they took off the handcuffs. At once the biker whirled on them and shook the bars, shouting "motherfuckers" and "bastards," and then he stopped and rubbed his wrists.

He looked at Miles and said, "I stabbed a guy."

Miles leaned against the wall next to the toilet and said nothing.

"What're you here for?" he said.

"Drunk driving."

"Chickenshit." The biker looked at Harold and said, "Well, look who's here. It's little Sally. I know what *you're* in for, Sally, you naughty girl. You been waiting for me? Huh?"

Harold got back onto his bunk and hugged himself.

The biker walked over to him, placed his forearms on the top bunk, and leaned forward so that his crotch was at Harold's face.

Harold skittered to the end of the bed, got off, and ran across to the bed where the drunk lay. He got up on the bed beside him.

The biker swiveled slowly around so that now his back rested against the top bunk. "You can run, Sally, but you can't hide," he said. He took a leisurely step toward Harold, and then another, and then he stepped in the pool of vomit. "Shit," he said. "You goddamn pig." He wiped the sole of his boot on the mattress. He took his time, wiping the sides, getting the instep nice and clean.

Harold huddled in the corner of the bunk, up by the old geezer's head.

The biker examined his boot from one angle and then another, and then he went back to the other bunk and sat down. He reached for a pillow, but there was none, so he took off his leather jacket, folded it neatly, and placed it behind him. He leaned back, his elbows braced on the bed and the jacket supporting him lightly, and he sighed. He stretched out his legs, and spread them.

"Okay, Sally," he said, "I'm ready."

Miles took a step away from the wall.

Harold worked his way down to the end of the old geezer's bed, got up, and stood by it.

Miles looked at him and shook his head, no. Harold shrugged.

"Get down on this, Sally, and open wide."

"Don't," Miles said.

"Don't get me mad," the biker said.

Harold moved across the room and started to kneel down in front of the biker, but Miles was there at once, pulling him up, saying to the biker, "Leave him alone. For Christ's sake."

"Leave *me* alone," Harold said, pushing Miles away. He gave him a look of real anger. "Mind your own business," he said, and added, "Grow up." He got to his knees and ran his hands up the inside of the biker's thighs. "Oh, look," he said. "Look at *this*."

Miles turned away quickly and moved to the front of the cell. He leaned his head against the bars and stared out into the empty corridor and tried to make himself deaf to the sounds behind him, but they went on and on. Miles' anger and revulsion were replaced by something else, sadness, and then by some other emotion he didn't understand. This went on for a long time.

The sounds had stopped, Harold had climbed into the upper bunk, the biker was asleep, and Miles was still standing with his eyes closed, his face against the bars, when the realization struck him, finally: I've been there too, he said to himself. This is who I am.

He heard the steps approaching, and he heard them stop outside his cell, but still he stood there with his eyes closed, knowing himself in this new way.

"This is what I wanted to see."

Miles opened his eyes and saw Jack Mack. His eyes were blood-shot, he looked exhausted, and it was clear he had been drinking. He was not in uniform.

"I wanted you in jail."

"Yes," Miles said.

"They made me withdraw my accusations."

"Yes."

"They put me on leave."

"Jack."

"Because I drink."

"I'm sorry," Miles said.

"I'm sorry," Jack said.

They were silent for a moment.

"He loved you, Billy did." Jack gripped the bars and leaned toward Miles. "Didn't he? Didn't he?"

"Yes."

"And you loved him?"

"I should have. I do."

"I did, too. I do."

Jack's face contorted as he fought back some emotion, and then he said, "He killed himself." He gripped the bars tighter, his hands trembling, and he touched his forehead to Miles'. "Why?" he whispered. "Why?" He began to shake, silently, as the tears came.

And Miles, crying too, said, "I know. I know." He was crying, at last, for Billy and for Jack Mack and for his mother and for Margaret and for himself, because we die, and we do not wish to die.

Through the bars, they clutched each other's shoulders, and they wept.

Miles sat at the picnic table, thinking, but trying not to think. This is who he was, the companion of queers and criminals. Harold. The biker. And Jack Mack, too. He could not hate them. *Mon semblable. Mon frère.* Humanity, up close, was not a pretty thing. Guilt was part of it. And he was part of it.

He lowered his head onto his folded arms and rested.

Was this a mood? Was this a way of feeling good about an awful situation? More self-flagellation?

Possibly. He was skilled at all these things.

Still, he was alive, and he was here, and he was part of it. He accepted it—all of it—without question.

He could not stop thinking.

Any moment is ripe for revelation.

He could not stop.

Dignity. It will get you through everything.

He woke during the night as Harold climbed down from the upper bunk to suck off the biker once again, but he was asleep even before the noise had stopped. The next sound he heard was the trustee's metal cart as he arrived with breakfast.

Miles raised his head and looked out through the bars. He rubbed his neck and rolled it around in a circle to get the kinks out. Then he rubbed his arms. They were all pins and needles.

Before the trustee could unload his cart, before the others had shifted from their beds, a policeman came rapidly down the corridor and said, "Bannon. Out." He hustled Miles from the cell and along the corridor and up the stairs. When they were alone in the interrogation room, he said, "You're out of here, Bannon. No charges. No nothing."

"How come?" Miles said. "They arrested me."

"Forget it," the policeman said. "It never happened."

"Except under oath. Right?"

"It never happened, period," the policeman said, and when they'd given Miles his money and his watch and his belt, the policeman tore up the record of the arrest, saying, "Chief's orders."

He led Miles to a metal door, pressed a buzzer, and they were outside in the parking lot.

"How come?" Miles said.

"It's Jack Mack," the policeman said. "He was killed in a crash last night. By a drunk driver."

Miles took a deep breath. Tears sprang to his eyes.

"The Chief wants it done with. Finished." The policeman opened the door and started back inside. "So you walk. And that's the way it is."

41

OFFICER MACK HAD A LARGE FUNERAL, with all the town brass in attendance. The priest gave a very nice sermon on the spiritual joy to be found in tragedy, and the chief of police and Mack's fellow policemen offered enthusiastic testimonials to his career as a law enforcement officer. He was killed in the line of duty—officially, at least—and so his widow got a good pension. His death marked the end of a very sad period for the town and for the school, the chief said.

Indeed, it seemed as if his death not only marked the end but actually brought it about. As if, after his death, it was somehow wrong to enquire if a crime had been committed, and by whom, and why. Thus Officer Mack's burial marked the end of the police investigation of Miles and the end of all the other school investigations as well: of the football players, of Coach, of Endicott, and, insofar as an investigation was appropriate, of the superintendent of the Malburn school system. Everybody wanted the nasty business of this school year to be over and done with. They wanted it put behind them.

And so now it was only a question of tying up the loose ends. For this reason, the School Board was meeting in executive session, closed to the public and with the records sealed. Endicott was there, and the superintendent, and four members of the board. Tom McGrath, as attorney for the school, was chairing the meeting. Jared Whiting, that fat, balding idiot, was doing his best to sabotage it. To everyone's surprise, however, the superintendent had it all nicely under control. They'd been in session for nearly two hours now and McGrath leaned back, comfortable, as he watched the super-intendent move to wind it all up.

"Okay, Bill," he said to Endicott, "it's down to push and shove. You're out, you know that, but how do we save your face? That's the only question."

They had already settled the question of Coach; he was fired. He might sue, of course, but he wouldn't. He was done for. And they had settled the question of the football players; though four of them would graduate without penalty, they would not be allowed to receive their diplomas on stage. The fifth, the Damiani kid, would be hospitalized indefinitely, so he wasn't their concern. And now, as the superintendent said, they had to settle the question of Endicott.

"I retire—that's agreed—but with four year's salary," Endicott said. "That will take me through to retirement at sixty-five."

Jared Whiting smacked his bald head in dismay. "You've got your Army retirement. You've got your school retirement to age sixty-one. What are you trying to do? Bleed us to death?" He tried to alert the others. "The ship is going down," he said. "We're all going with it."

"Legally, of course, you don't have a leg to stand on," McGrath said to Endicott. "We could fire you in an instant." They all turned to him; he was a lawyer, after all. "The Mack boy's brutal rape that you simply covered up. His subsequent suicide, clearly the conse-quence of what they'd done to him. Your failure to take action on Coach. Your devious mismanagement of the Bannon investiga-tion—you set him up, you knocked him down—you're lucky he doesn't sue you for professional misconduct or libel. And that's only for starters." He paused, and they all turned to Endicott, who said nothing. McGrath went on. "So you see, retirement is an easy way to go. I recommend it."

"One year's pay," Endicott said, "and I'll retire after graduation."

"I think that's reasonable," the superintendent said. "You've had a bad year, that's true, but I think that in light of your previous strong service to Malburn High, and with the submission of your resignation at once, we can manage a year's salary." He turned to Mrs. Lash, who was business manager for the school system. "Don't you think so, Mrs. L?"

"No way," she said. "Are you out of your tree? This is a *town* budget. How do you think we'd get away with requesting a bribe of fifty thousand dollars? We can't do it. Period. No way, Jose." Mrs. Lash was a CPA and an investment counselor with a keen ear for the way young people expressed themselves.

The superintendent gave her a warm smile, a long look. "Mrs. L," he said. "I bet you could come up with something."

"Howie," she said, "you'll be the death of me. All right, we could ask for ten thousand. How about that? Ten thousand?"

"A full year's salary," Endicott said.

"We could fire you," Jared Whiting said, rubbing his bald head.

"Take the ten," the superintendent said.

"Ten," Endicott said. "But I get to give the graduation speech."

They looked at one another, the superintendent nodded his agreement, and McGrath said, "Done."

Everybody shook Endicott's hand. He looked very pleased. The difficult part was over and only the mopping up was left to do. But nobody really wanted to do it.

McGrath eased them into it. "Now there's only the minor business of Miles Bannon. We owe him some kind of apology, I think," McGrath said, "since he took the larger part of public blame while the rape incident was being covered up. He was martyred, really. His reputation was attacked, his moral character impugned . . ."

Endicott couldn't stand it. "But he was *seen* at that Tom Cat place," he said. "Besides, he was never *officially* charged with anything."

". . . and generally he was held to be guilty until proven otherwise. How do you repay a man for being held up to public ridicule? Is an apology enough?"

They argued that for a while, and then agreed to give Miles a merit raise of five hundred dollars, to be added annually to his salary.

They had done their work well. They were feeling generous and satisfied. They wanted to go home.

"Is that it, then?" McGrath said. "Can we adjourn?"

"One last bit of business," the superintendent said, and he leafed through a file of papers. "A tenure appeal by this Jeff Douglas. What's the trouble with Douglas, anyway?"

"Get to know your faculty," Endicott said, but he was practically out of office, so they all just ignored him.

"There's a note here dated May 7—that's yesterday—saying he's sold a novel to North Point Press." The superintendent looked at them in turn. "Is that good?"

"That's very good," McGrath said.

"They're with it," Mrs. Lash said. "North Point is the cutting edge."

"Well, he's got a good tenure review from you, Bill," the superintendent said. "Your kind of guy, I guess. But there's some awful bad reviews from Diane Waring, his chairperson. No professional judgment, she says. Imprudent. Indecent and abusive language. It says here that he gave a student the Bible to use as a basement pass. What does that mean?"

"Talk about indecent," Jared Whiting said. "That's who ought to be investigated, that Diane Waring. I've heard things. I've heard plenty."

"Oh?" McGrath said.

"She goes to church and all, but I've heard she has these flings. I've heard, in fact, that . . ."

"You hear a lot of things," McGrath said, "and so do I, of course, but rumor is only rumor and can usually be discounted."

"Bull pucky," Jared Whiting said. "It's more than rumor, let me tell *you*." And then he told them many things and some, though he didn't know it, were actually true.

The meeting got completely out of hand, however, with rumor and innuendo and gossip all becoming fact, and McGrath trying to contain the subject and control the discussion, and Mrs. Lash gasping and saying, "What the hey!" until in the end McGrath persuaded them that the discussion was pointless since they couldn't fire Diane without taking her to court. They thought about that, but he assured them they would never win, that they were stuck. So, as a sop to the departing Endicott, they agreed to give Jeff Douglas tenure and to tell Diane she was going to have to put up with him. That way they could at least make her life miserable.

"She's leaving Malburn anyway," McGrath said, now that he had beaten them down to sheer pettiness. "She's going to Harvard Law."

"Nevertheless," Jared Whiting said, feeling he had made a point.

"To summarize," McGrath said, "for the record. The boys graduate, but not on stage. Coach is fired. Bill here retires after graduation with a ten-thousand-dollar severance."

"*And* I speak at graduation," Endicott said.

"*And* he speaks at graduation," McGrath said. "Miles Bannon gets a merit raise. Jeff Douglas is awarded tenure. Diane Waring would be stuck with him, except she'll be at Harvard Law. Is that it? I think that's it."

"What about Howard," Endicott said. "He gets off scot free? Where was he when the . . . incident occurred?"

"Yes," McGrath said, "that's right." He assumed a tired voice: "The board officially requests that the superintendent spend less time at conferences and more time in the Malburn school system."

"You bet," the superintendent said.

"Meeting adjourned," McGrath said. "That's a splendid-looking suit, Howie. You certainly can wear them."

The superintendent stood to his considerable height, pushed back his shock of silver hair, and smoothed his lapels. "Saks," he said, with his fashion-model smile. "The one in Chestnut Hill. It's all in the tailoring."

42

It was the middle of May and Miles had not yet adjusted to the fact that it was, indeed, all over. The investigation, the harassment, the sneers in the classroom, the snickers in the corridor, the jokes, the whispers, the crazy speculation: it was all over. Even the graffiti in the men's room were gone.

Nobody cared that he'd been tossed in the slammer. Nobody cared that he'd pushed Tuna and struck Hacker—or, as it was said, that he flattened Tuna and kicked the shit out of Hacker. Nobody cared that he had once gone to the Tom Cat Lounge and for a few months had been known as a queer and a pervert. Everybody was a little embarrassed, it was true, but nobody cared very much.

Miles cared, though, and Margaret cared.

Margaret cared a lot, it turned out. Miles had thought for a while that she didn't care at all, that she had her needs, as she said, and those needs came before everything else, including him. But that wasn't quite the case. Her needs were survival and what she called dignity, and they were large enough to include him, or so she said. He was needed, too. Well, it was a nice thought.

She was generous, and open, and she had been through so much.

He knew, because she had told him, holding nothing back, or almost nothing. And for once he had stepped outside himself and listened.

He had discovered, listening, that she had a great sense of humor. She was very witty, very sharp. How had he missed that? He had discovered, too, that what he'd thought was an iron core beneath that calm exterior was not the core at all. She was determined—a day at a time, she said—not to fall again, since she'd hit bottom more than once and didn't like it there. But that iron determination had a core of its own, a touching vulnerability that lay at the heart of her being, and he found it very attractive, very moving. It made him want to hold her, protect her. It made him want to give himself to her.

This was the beginning, he feared, of a kind of love he hadn't known existed. He feared it because it would cost him everything and, of course, he wanted it for the same reason.

Still, he was not about to risk loving anybody. Not old Miles. Not yet.

It was the end of May and school was nearly over for the year. Miles and Margaret had celebrated their survival with a dinner at Chez Minou and now they were dawdling over coffee.

"That was nice," he said. He raised his coffee cup to her. "We're nice."

Margaret smiled at him. He *was* very nice, really, and he'd been through so much. She knew, because he had told her everything; as always, she had listened. She listened differently now that she needed nothing from him, and hearing him in this way, she saw a different Miles, more honest, more generous, more . . . what? There was just more to him, somehow.

Could she ever love him? She didn't know.

They sat there, looking at each other, thinking their very different thoughts about love. The waiter left the bill and Miles paid it, and still they stayed on, as if they were waiting for something they knew would happen.

And then it did. Mr. Collins came in with his wife, and Mr. Babcock and his wife, and they paused at the table to say hello. Miles stood up. The hostess waited while they went through awkward introductions and handshakes and necessary smiles, and then she led them to a table in the corner. As they sat down, Michael Collins cast one look back at Margaret, and she looked at him, and Miles knew.

"So that's the competition," he said.

Margaret looked at Miles, and for a moment she hated him and loved him.

It was the middle of June, the day before graduation, and they were watching *The Barber of Seville* on television. Miles hated opera, but he was watching it so he could be with Margaret, and he was careful not to make fun of the way the singers looked or how preposterous the story was or what a truly ludicrous form of entertainment opera had become. It was embalmed. It was mummified. It combined music and dance and drama in all the wrong proportions. It took suspension of disbelief to the extreme—to the suspension of good sense and common sense and any sense at all. It was high seriousness lavished on a joke: the rickety plots, the melodramatic action, the stereotypical characters. How could anyone take this seriously? He hated it.

"What a glorious voice," Margaret said. She meant Pavarotti.

"It is," Miles said. "It's glorious."

"Are you enjoying this?"

"It's fun. It's very good."

"You hate it." She laughed.

Miles laughed, guilty.

"I'll make tea," she said. She clicked off the television and they went into the kitchen and she put the kettle on. "Cookies?" she said. "This is what we've come to in our old age, cookies and tea during intermission."

"What kind of cookies?"

"Chocolate chip. And there are a few gingersnaps left, from Belgium."

"Not homemade?"

"Learn to bake, sweetie pie."

She went into the pantry for a minute and came out with two packages of cookies. She put them on the table and went back and stood at the door. She looked preoccupied.

"What?" Miles said. "What is it?"

"I've been thinking about opera," she said, "and, you know, I think that in a way you're right. Who cares about all that recitative? It's pointless. And silly."

"Exactly," Miles said, but not wanting to go too far, he added, "the arias are nice, though."

"What they ought to do is have more concert renditions of opera. You know? Just get all those big fat people up on stage and let them sing their hearts out."

Miles laughed.

"What?" she said.

" 'Get those big fat people up on stage.' I could just see them."

"Let them sing. That's what they're good at. They can't act, most of them, and they're either too old or too fat or too vain to look the part they're playing, so let them do what they can do."

" 'Those big fat people.' "

"Well, they are," she said. She took a deep breath, and before his eyes she puffed out her chest enormously and made her waist disappear and added three chins, transforming herself into a fat middle-aged opera star, dizzy with self-love. "Figaro, Figaro, Fi-i-i-garo," she sang, and her face was strained in concentration.

Miles laughed, and she laughed, and Miles jumped up from the table and came and put his arms around her. "Wonderful Margaret, funny Margaret," he said, and hugged her, and laughed.

"The tea," she said.

He laughed some more, and that night as he lay in bed about to fall asleep, he thought of her transforming herself into this ridiculous creature, just to please him, to make him laugh, and he laughed again, from his heart. Spontaneously, as if she were there beside him, he reached out to touch her.

"Margaret," he whispered to the empty room. "Margaret."

43

FROM HIS CLASSROOM WINDOW Miles could look down on the football field where the huge platform had been erected for the graduation ceremonies. For two days now the custodians had been assembling the platform and anchoring it into place, and since early this morning the graduation committee had been decorating it, with crepe paper around the railings and with heavy drapes around the sides— in school colors, blue and white—and with the state flag and the U.S. flag and school banners on the platform itself. Decorations were the same every year, but this year there were new flags, and the day was bright and sunny, and Miles was up for it. The yearbook was dedicated to him, and as the senior class' favorite teacher, he would sit on the platform and assist in the graduation ceremony. That is, he would read out the names of the graduates and Endicott would hand over the diplomas. Miles did not have to make a speech. Since early this morning, however, he'd been suffering a terrible temptation. Here at graduation was his opportunity to denounce them all—Endicott, Douglas, Polcari, Jack Mack, the entire police department—with their investigators and their strip searchers and their amused maliciousness. He had rejected the temptation at once; it was an evil idea and it would produce only evil. Moreover it was melodramatic. And silly. In real life, people didn't do such things. Why didn't they, he wondered?

Miles was up here in his classroom waiting for the procession to begin. Endicott and the superintendent and the minister who would give the invocation always brought up the rear of the procession, and this year Miles would be walking with them, but rather than hang around the gym with all those kids waiting for the signal to start, he was waiting alone up here where he belonged. From here he'd be able to see the class marshal lead the procession out from the gym, and then he'd go downstairs and hook up with the others and still be in plenty of time.

From up here Miles could just barely make out the faculty section of the bleachers, so he couldn't be sure who was there. He saw a red dress—it looked like a warning flag from here—and he knew that must be Diane. In the past months she had streaked her short hair blond and had taken to wearing red, and it would be like her to show up for graduation dressed like this. Her new public personality was scary. Where once she had spoken softly in the corridors and whispered to her faculty, "These are your options," now she barked at anybody, anywhere, and she laid down the law to her department, and when she said, "These are your options," she added, "take it or leave it." He couldn't imagine making love to her now. He couldn't imagine her having flings.

Out on the field, everybody in the bleachers turned to look up the hill to the school. Miles waited at the window, and in a moment he saw the class marshal move into view, and then the band started to play "Pomp and Circumstance," and he saw the first crowd of seniors start down toward the field. Paul Ciampa was up near the front, looking handsome, manly. Miles thought, if he were to be born again, he'd like to come back as Paul Ciampa, and then he smiled, because he could see that nothing ever really changes.

He left the window and took the stairs, two at a time, down to the gym where he'd tag onto the end of the line. He got there in less than a minute and waited out in the corridor. Behind him, the men's-room door opened and out came Muldoon. His eyes were red and puffy and he looked like a very sad mouse. He'd just been crying and when Miles said, "What's the matter, Patrick? Are you okay?" Muldoon burst into tears again, and it was almost a minute before Miles could understand that he was crying because Doggina had died this morning. "Doggina?" Miles said, and then remembered the Italian dog, but at that moment he saw the last of the seniors leave the gym in procession, and he clapped Muldoon on the shoulder and said, "Buck up, Muldoon. You're going to be a father in July." "August," Muldoon said, crying some more, but Miles didn't hear him because he was dashing across the gym to join the procession, in the company of the superintendent and the minister and the principal of Malburn High, Captain William Endicott, U.S. Army, Retired.

The senior boys wore dark blue gowns and the girls wore white. Seated in the bleachers, costumed for this rite of passage, they looked mature and responsible and good. They were attractive young people about to go off to college or out into the world. They looked ready for whatever they might meet. This was the theme, at any rate, of the minister's invocation.

Endicott was next, and he used the occasion to review his accomplishments in office. He talked at some length about the expanded modern language lab—which, in fact, he had opposed—and how it prepared students for the new internationalism of the present day. He moved on to talk about the television news that was piped into classrooms twice daily, with only a few minutes of advertisements, and how he had arranged it at minimal cost, only pennies a day, really. But when he started in on faculty retreats and the Malburn High family, Miles tuned him out and spent the next ten minutes studying the faculty.

A family indeed. Coogan was there, and Kevin Foley, and Dietz—skinny and furious—sat between them. Dietz was angry at the world these days, but particularly at Miles for taking Margaret away from him and at Kathy Dillard for taking Coach. Coach was living at her house, and she was taking care of him, she said. But she and Dietz had had a terrible scene in the teachers' room last week when he accused her of encouraging Coach's drinking and she had rounded on him and said, "He's fine with me. He never drinks too much when I drink with him. And he *needs* to drink. He's had a lot of tragedy in his life." Dietz lost it then, and called her a co-alcoholic, and she'd run out of the room and hadn't been back since. But she was here now, sitting off to the side, alone, her chin propped on her fist. She looked angry and sad and—could it be?—a little drunk. Miles turned away from her and let his gaze rest on Diane Waring in her aggressive red dress and, next to her, Jeff Douglas in a navy blazer and a crimson tie. They looked like a couple, Miles thought, and for a second that impression was heightened as they leaned together and laughed and Diane touched Jeff's arm. Could it be? Was it a fling?

Miles looked away from them to the group of graduating seniors in their blue and white gowns. He looked just in time to see Ben Nardone pass the blue and white balloon to his girlfriend, who passed it on to Polcari, of all people, and Polcari popped it into the air so that somebody could bat it, and they did, and then it was a free-for-all. It happened every year—somebody sneaked in a balloon and blew it up during Endicott's speech and then all the seniors batted it around until it exploded. Everybody except Endicott expected it. This time the balloon lasted only a minute or two. It was a pleasant relief for everybody.

Miles tuned back in to Endicott's speech just in time for his peroration.

"And so I leave you for new tasks, new challenges," he said, "as I begin my new job as president of the Advisory Committee on Secondary Education. It is a job my entire life had prepared me for. It is a job that my time as principal of Malburn High will enrich beyond telling."

He was winding up, finally.

"In the United States Army, where I was proud to serve for twenty years, we were men of discipline and willpower. There is no life that discipline will not improve. No problem that willpower will not solve. You'll discover this to be true on your journey through life. Remember it. Remember you heard it here.''

Endicott sat down and everyone applauded. His wife had left him again. Miles knew it. They all knew it. Why begrudge him a little applause.

The superintendent, gorgeous in a dove gray suit, moved to the microphone to begin awarding prizes. He beamed down at the crowd and they beamed back at him, and it was clear to everyone that he was a wonderful superintendent of schools. "Friends," he said, his rich voice caressing the word. "We now proceed to the awarding of prizes. It gives me enormous pleasure . . .'' but Miles did not hear what gave the superintendent enormous pleasure because he knew he was up next, conferring the diplomas, and he was remembering the lines he had composed this morning while shaving.

"Generation of vipers,'' he would begin, quoting Scripture, and then he would denounce the hypocrisy and malice of all those people who had humiliated him and tried to destroy him. He couldn't remember now those wonderful, satisfying lines he had recited, but he could remember the emotion he'd felt: a fierce exultation in destroying his enemies. He hadn't cared what would happen afterwards; he merely saw himself doing it, denouncing them, and the bitter satisfaction he felt was enough for him. They could fire him. They could jail him. It didn't matter. That had been this morning, when, for one awful minute, he had given himself to the idea of vengeance.

Now, with the superintendent's smooth voice in the background and with Endicott somewhere behind him, Miles toyed with the idea once again. Vengeance is mine, saith the Lord. But he looked out at the students' families, and at the faculty, and at the seniors as they leaned forward to see who was getting the awards, and he remembered his night in jail, and reminded himself that he was one with them. The same guilty clay. The same frail hopes. He thought of Billy Mack.

"Billy Mack," the superintendent said, and Miles looked up sharply, listening. "The Thomas Jefferson Prize is awarded annually to a senior boy in recognition of his good character, high moral values, and fine sportsmanship, apart from any consideration of academic performance. I am pleased to say, however, that Billy Mack's academic record was a fine one, and I know we will all remember him with affection and admiration. The Thomas Jefferson Medal will be accepted by his mother."

Looking more frail than ever despite a new permanent and a new blond rinse, Eileen Mack made her way across the grass and up the steep steps to the platform. The superintendent handed her a little white box and leaned forward to kiss her on the cheek, but she pulled away from him and merely shook his hand. She turned to leave, and as she crossed to the stairs, she veered toward Miles and, leaning over him, she whispered, "You've killed both of them now. I hope you're happy." And then she went down the stairs and took her seat.

"Finally," the superintendent said, "the good citizenship award. This is given annually to a senior boy or girl who has shown outstanding traits of leadership, responsibility, and initiative throughout his or her four years at Malburn High. It is the single most prestigious award given to a graduating senior and it is with great pride that I announce this year's winner: Ms. Deirdre Forster."

There were gasps, because everybody had been expecting Paul Ciampa, but surprise gave way to laughter and then to wild applause. Deirdre Forster! She came up to get her medal and the laughter and applause continued, but Miles was unaware of anything except Eileen Mack's whispered words. "You've killed both of them now. I hope you're happy."

The applause ended finally, and the superintendent sat down, and Endicott took over and announced the conferring of diplomas, but Miles still sat there, stupefied. Everyone was looking at him. He looked up, blindly.

Endicott tapped the microphone and glared, saying, "We'll try again. And now for the conferring of diplomas. Mr. Bannon will call out the names." He stepped back, and waved Miles forward, and this time Miles responded.

He got up slowly, as if he were confused, and at that moment there was a loud, long whistle. It was not quite a wolf whistle, but it was meant to be, and the audience knew it. There was an awful silence, and then nervous laughter, and then silence once again.

Miles approached the table heaped with diplomas and stood before the microphone, looking out at the audience. Only minutes before, he had intended to say nothing. Then Eileen Mack had accused him—perhaps justly—of having killed her son and husband, and he'd been stricken into silence. Stricken, silent, he listened to that long cruel whistle, and it brought back all those months of whistles and graffiti and sneers and quick glances and gross, humiliating gestures.

Miles stood before them, at the microphone, and found his mind had cleared, and his vision cleared, and what had seemed the perfect opportunity for vengeance now seemed something else. He must confess. He must explain to them. He didn't want to do it, but he had no control left.

"This past year," he began, "a young boy committed suicide because terrible things had happened to him and because some simple, good things had not. I am guilty," he said, wishing he had not said it, wishing he could stop.

He paused because there was a hiss from the audience, and with his new and awful vision, Miles saw at once that it was Hacker. Everyone froze. Miles wished that he could stop talking, leave the microphone and go sit down, but he was sick, possessed, and he went on.

"I am guilty, and so are some of you. We are a godless and a hypocritical generation."

There was another hiss, louder, and it was picked up by others in the audience.

"If we have no room for God," Miles said, "at least let us make room for human dignity . . . since out of that can grow compassion and forgiveness and a kind of truth."

But at "human dignity," there were more hisses, and Deirdre began to chant, "Mi-*lo!* Mi-*lo!* Mi-*lo!*" and the chant was picked up by other students, and soon nobody could hear a word Miles said. He went on for a minute nonetheless, until the babble of sound made it impossible for him to speak. Standing there silent amid the hissing and applause and laughter, Miles realized how preposterous the whole scene was. And that realization restored his sense of irony and brought him back to his old self.

The chant went on.

Miles looked around him at Endicott and the superintendent and the minister. He took in their horrified looks, and he began to laugh.

At his laughter, the chant faded away into cheers and applause, though by this time it was not at all clear what or whom anybody was applauding. Endicott, seeing the time was right for taking charge, jumped up and took the microphone, saying, "And *now* . . ." but he was drowned out by laughter because he sounded so much like the MC on a quiz show. He went right on. "And *now* we'll have the conferring of diplomas."

The graduation marshals began to move into position.

"Marshal!" Endicott shouted, hurrying them up.

Miles began to call names and hand out the diplomas.

Once again he felt stripped and foolish, known by anyone who cared to look. He had tried to confess, and he'd been greeted with a whistle and hisses and applause. They didn't want this ugly revelation. They wanted to see him in their own way, not naked and ashamed. Nonetheless, he had confessed. Nonetheless, he had tried.

He watched as, innocent and honest and casually cruel, the students passed before him and shook his hand and, smiling, moved beyond him, one by one, into their good, untroubled world.

As they went slowly by him, Miles began to feel relieved of his awful secret burden and elated to be free of it. By the end he was feeling something very like joy.

After the ceremony, when he had greeted parents and congratulated students and exchanged compliments and thanks, Miles got into his battered old Pinto and drove to Margaret's house, still trying to grasp what had happened on that platform.

At its simplest, he had confessed and they had hissed and applauded. Something else had happened, too. It was as if, in some nightmare, he was waiting outside an emergency room for word of life or death, and finally the doctor came out and said, "He'll live," and then, walking away, the doctor had turned and laughed and said, "The patient, by the way, is you."

Miles saw himself once more before that crowd, confessing, and once more he felt ashamed, ridiculous, a fool. But now, as he pulled up in front of Margaret's house, he felt stirring in him feelings he had only sensed before: acceptance, a flickering hope, and peace.

He got out of the car and slammed the door and, at the same instant, the front fender fell off. As if he were some demented priest, Miles looked at it, gave it a quick blessing, and turned smartly up the walk to where Margaret was waiting for him.